THE ARIZONAN

THE ARIZONAN

JAY LUCAS

SAGEBRUSH
Large Print Westerns

First published in Great Britain by ISIS Publishing Ltd.
First published in the United States by Green Circle

Published in Large Print 2008 by ISIS Publishing Ltd.,
7 Centremead, Osney Mead, Oxford OX2 0ES
United Kingdom
by arrangement with
Golden West Literary Agency

34746576 S

British Library Cataloguing in Publication Data
Lucas, Jay, b. 1894
    The Arizonan. – Large print ed. –
    (Sagebrush western series)
    1. Western stories
    2. Large type books
    I. Title
    813.5'2 [F]

ISBN 978–0–7531–8013–6 (hb)

Printed and bound in Great Britain by
T. J. International Ltd., Padstow, Cornwall

CONTENTS

CHAPTER ONE

A Coward's Shot

There were four in the room — old Newt Davis, his wife, their daughter, and Bob Edwards — but not one of them suspected the tragedy that was to strike among them within moments. It makes one wonder if there can be such a thing as premonition, in which so many believe; has not Shakespeare himself assured us that coming events cast their shadows before?

They were in the shabby old living room of the Bar Diamond, and upon them had fallen that peaceful silence that can come only to old friends, to those who have known each other so long and so intimately as to feel no slightest need for conversation. Each sat with drowsy thoughts, pleasantly conscious that the others were near. On the rough sandstone slab of the hearth, old Tab lay curled, dreaming whatever pampered, ancient old cats dream.

In the broad fireplace the cedar logs popped and crackled as only cedar does, sending little tongues of flame licking up toward the wide blackness of the chimney. From the wood-box close by an odor as of many pencil shavings stole out to fill the room; it mingled with stray wisps of smoke to form a drowsy incense. A coal-oil lamp threw its soft light on the group.

Bob Edwards lounged comfortably in a rawhide-bottomed chair. He slowly puffed his hand-rolled brown cigarette, and his eyes strayed contentedly over the peaceful scene. He was aware of a tranquil feeling such as he had never known elsewhere; he felt vaguely surprised that in twenty-four hours he had fitted back into the Bar Diamond as though he had never left there. Fine people, he thought, the Davises — the salt of the earth.

In his heart, he longed to take the job as range boss that old Newt had offered him — had indeed spent most of the day coaxing him to take. But no, he couldn't do it; it would not be fair to himself or to his future. He had been saving money; he was ready to start his own little brand.

He thought with relief that he had seen the last of the big "company" ranch down South; he had never liked it. At least all that he had liked about it was the fat pay check that he had drawn during the latter part of his stay there — he had worked up to become range foreman.

Well, that good job had let him save enough to start a little outfit of his own. Still plenty of room in Arizona, hardly any fences except horse pastures. Not, of course, what it was when Newt had come driving his cattle from Tom Green County, Texas; but, on the other hand, the Apaches could not take one's whole herd in a night, and perhaps a scalp or two to boot.

Strange, the thought, that such a gentle little man as Newt had made a success of it in those days; one could not imagine him fighting Apaches. But fought them he had, and so well that his Bar Diamond had grown to be one of the most important brands in northern Arizona, Newt one of the important men.

There he sat, small, wrinkled, kindly-faced, shabby — so shabby that a stranger might have guessed that there wasn't two dollars between him and starvation. Still, that was but typical of the old-timers' hatred of ostentation.

Bob's eyes went slowly to Mrs. Davis. She was even smaller than her husband — a neat, gray-haired little woman bent over her knitting, peering through thick, old-fashioned glasses. She seemed to feel his gaze on her; she raised her head to smile gently back at him. She had always been far more the mother to him than the boss's wife.

Bob was troubled: If old Newt wanted him as range boss, was it his duty to stay, after all the Davises had done for him? Certainly not, he told himself; old Newt could find another man as good or better. But —

One might have ventured a guess at what that "but" meant if one saw how his eyes rested on Stella, daughter of the ranch. This although Bob himself could not guess, had not yet even reached the stage of trying to guess.

Something had happened to Stella while he was gone. He had left her a long-legged, somewhat scrawny adolescent whose whole life seemed devoted to inventing methods of getting herself killed in some particularly disagreeable way — why, her father's cowboys had grown wrinkled from devising plans to keep her off horses that they themselves would prefer to see the other fellow ride. "Wild as a jack rabbit," they called her; some of them had grinned and said that she looked about as ungainly.

And there she was now, a poised, grown-up young lady with dignity. Bob could not get over her having dignity; it was such a shock. She sat looking into the smoldering fire as though dreaming, seeing things that were not there. Bob surveyed her covertly. Big, clear black eyes; they had acquired a trick of meeting yours very squarely, but with a faint hint of reserve. Mouth not too small, and very well shaped; it smiled at one with a range-born friendliness just tinged with reticence. Bob remembered it as usually twisted out of shape making grotesque faces at somebody — generally at him.

And where the deuce had all her odd, tomboy angles gone to? Slender though she was, she seemed to be all long, smooth curves from head to foot. Queer about girls!

Her eyes raised suddenly and met his. As suddenly, they dropped back to the fireplace; a faint pink showed on her cheeks. Bob reddened, thinking that his clumsy stare had embarrassed her. It did not occur to him that he, too, had changed a good deal in five years, that another than he was puzzled regarding a half stranger, half chum who sat across the wide hearth.

Yes, Bob Edwards had changed; the responsibility of running a large outfit had given a new set to his face, had steadied his slow drawl. Having to dominate a large crew of "hard-boiled" cowboys, most of them older than himself, had brought an almost grim twist to the corners of his mouth.

He settled luxuriously in his chair; he was glad to be through with that. Worse than the cowboys had been the "mud gang" in charge of ground work — corrals, the few fences, dams, and such. This mud gang, gathered as it was from the riffraff of mining camps, railroad-construction crews, from goodness knew where, had been the bane of his life. It should have been none of his concern, but the job had been shoved off on him after the wild crew had nearly killed their own foreman.

Yes, Bob had handled them; he had solved their problem by thrashing one of their huskiest once a week or so. Not a very gentlemanly way of doing things, and hardly according to the cowboys' usual code — but it worked. Brave indeed would have been the man who dared say a word against "Big Bob" Edwards in front of that mud gang; he could and did lick the biggest of them, and therefore he was their hero.

All this, of course, Stella did not know; she just wondered what had become of the somewhat gawky young cowboy who had ridden away five years before.

Old Newt spoke suddenly:

"Bob, you shore are an Arizona cowboy!"

The little grim twist left the corners of Bob's mouth. His tanned face lit up in a quick grin — a very likable grin. He slowly took the brown cigarette from his mouth.

"Well, what would you expect me to look like? There must," he added, "be hundreds an' hundreds of us."

Newt shook his head.

"No. I mean yo're sorter —" He scratched his gray head, looking for the word. "— sorter — uh — typical — That's it, typical! — o' the best of 'em. You can always be depended on to do the right thing, far as human nacher will let you."

"Why, I got principles an' try to stick to 'em, if that's what you mean — we all do."

Newt looked at him fondly with his faded old eyes; he nodded slowly, twice.

"Yo're an Arizonan — typical Arizonan."

There was another silence. Old Newt was shuffling through some dog-eared scraps of paper — old envelopes, leaves from a dingy tally book, even a corner or two of newspaper. His brow wrinkled as he tried to work out the intricate puzzle of his own special brand of book-keeping. Presently he looked up again. He spoke in a slow, gentle drawl:

"Bob, how much you got saved?"

Bob did not resent the question. He was proud of his accomplishment; cowboys' wages were pretty low, and even the foreman of a big "company" outfit got none too much pay.

"Twenty-five hundred. I figure that should give me a pretty nice start — maybe I can borrow a little more at the bank."

Mrs. Davis looked up from her knitting, beaming on him.

"Why, Bob! However did you save all that much?"

"Oh, tradin' horses a little; bought a lot or two in town and sold at a good profit — different things."

Old Newt nodded approvingly.

"B'iled down, you got a good business head under yore hat. Bob, you'll be a big cattleman yet."

He jabbed a stubby forefinger at the soiled papers.

"Bob, as near as I can figger, I got around a thousand in cash at the bank. I'll lend you that to help you get started."

Bob gasped. The pure kindliness of it touched him.

"Why, Newt, I couldn't — I mean, I'd be glad to pay you good interest."

A little flush stole up the old man's withered cheeks. He started to speak hurriedly, checked himself. At last he drawled with gentle sarcasm:

"Son, I'm a cattleman, not a money-lender. There'll be no interest."

Bob twisted uncomfortably in his chair. He should have known better — should have known the code. He would be very glad to have the extra money, but he could not take it without interest; that would smack almost of charity. But then old Newt had always been like a father to him so —

"We-ell, we'll talk it over in the morning."

Old Newt stood up and stretched.

"'Bout time we were goin' to bed; I got lots to do tomorrow. Wonder if it's still cloudin' up; we shore do need a rain."

He crossed to the door, opened it, and stood an instant framed against the brilliant moonlight — a bent, kindly little figure. He stepped outside, closing the door after him.

Those in the room heard the crash of a rifle from a short distance off. They started. Bob spoke:

"One of the fool cowboys shooting at a coyote from the bunk house."

He went to the door, trying not to appear nervous; there was nothing to be nervous about. Mother and daughter, staring after him uncertainly, not yet fearing, heard his gasp of horror.

"Bob! What —"

Mrs. Davis's knitting tumbled unheeded from her lap as she rushed to the door, her withered face suddenly white. She saw Bob Edwards come leaping back into the lamplight, saw him slam the door behind him. She saw in his arms a limp figure, a gray head hanging back queerly. Something dark and wet spattered on the floor.

Stella screamed. For an instant Mrs. Davis stood with both clenched hands to her face, and then she was running forward; she was a woman of the frontier, accustomed to doing things, instead of fainting as might one reared to gentler surroundings.

"The — the lounge, Bob!"

Bob hurriedly, gently, laid the still figure on its back. Now mother and daughter were kneeling beside it, quickly cutting the shirt from the bloodstained chest; Stella, too, was of the frontier breed, although a generation younger.

Bob stood towering over them — six feet two of strength. His face was ashy white, the white of a wild, overpowering anger; his eyes blazed like coals of fire. He whirled; two leaps took him across the room; he grabbed up a carbine from the corner, threw the breech open to see that it was loaded. He ran to the door; he was twisting the knob when Mrs. Davis's voice came to him, a voice strangely calm for such a time:

"Bob, help us! You can't find him."

She was right. He dropped the gun and ran back to the lounge. As he leaned over it, the tired, sun-bleached eyes opened. Old Newt's lips trembled futilely a moment, and then he spoke; they had to lean close to hear his words.

"They — they got me!"

Bob laid a hand gently on the old man's forehead.

"Now — now, Newt, you'll be all right." He did not believe it, nor did the man to whom he spoke.

"Bob, the — the women — they can't — Bob, stay an' hold — an' hold the range — for 'em. Stay — hold the range! Bob —" His voice trailed off; his eyes closed.

Even while stooping to listen, the gray-haired little woman had not wasted a moment. Now the old man's chest was bare, displaying the tiny, dark hole. She motioned to Bob, who gently rolled the limp figure over, exposing the jagged wound where the bullet had passed out.

A soft-nosed bullet! Bob Edwards shook as though with the ague, but he managed to help with the dressing, marveling always at the steady hands of mother and daughter. And always his eyes kept straying to the carbine on the floor. A hail came from outside:

"Hey, what was that shootin'?"

"Here, quick, Red! The old man is shot."

The door flew open. A wiry, red-haired cowboy stood gasping in unbelief. Bob whirled to him.

"Quick! Saddle up an' go for a doctor. Kill your horse — but don't let him drop till you get there."

The door slammed; footsteps went racing off, spurs clanking. Presently there came the clatter of a madly running horse; the sound dwindled and died away in the moonlit night. Now other men were coming. The door was flung open among shouts of consternation, exclamations of uncontrolled fury; that women might hear some of the words was forgotten. Bob turned on the incoming crowd.

"Stay out! You can do no good."

"Is — is he hurt bad?"

"Yes."

The door closed gently, but the vague shuffling told of men huddled close outside. From the hills came the wild, weird howl of a coyote; it sounded very like a death wail. The old woman whispered:

"Is — is he —"

Bob threw a towel across the bloodstained chest and pressed his ear close.

"He's alive, but —"

"Hot water, Stell — quick!"

The girl ran to the stove — later there would be time for tears.

Working like a swift, silent automaton, she boiled towels, dried them so quickly that they scorched. She forced her mother — old-fashioned, reluctant, bewildered — to help her remove the first hasty bandages, to assist her in swabbing the wounds with fresh antiseptic, in redressing them. Bob stood there awkwardly, afraid of getting in the way; he knew this to be a task that could be better done by the gentle hands of women.

They finished the dressing, pulled the blankets up over the still, gray figure. The old woman sat helplessly beside the lounge, her eyes never leaving that pallid face. She had aged years in these few terrible minutes. This was Newton Davis, the dashing young cowboy she had married; the man beside whom she had struggled and suffered on their first shabby little ranch back in Texas; the man whose covered wagon she herself had driven to the new Arizona Territory, braving hostile Apaches. And at last, the man with whom she had been placidly enjoying her quiet, prosperous autumn of life.

There he lay. Her Newt.

Stella went to a chair by the fireplace. She tottered a little now; two silent tears trickled down her cheeks; her shoulders were beginning to rise and fall. A hand touched her arm.

"Oh, Bob, it's — What'll we *do?*"

The years rolled back. He was once more the big young cowboy comforting the little girl who was hurt.

"There now, Stell! Red will get the doctor here soon."

"But —"

"I know, Stell. I'll stay an' look after things — he wanted me to."

Her hands went up and seized his, tightly. Of course there was nothing Bob could do, nothing anybody could do; her senses told her that. But a faint shade of

11

peace stole over her; Bob could always find something to do; with him to take charge, that paralyzing blow did not seem so utterly crushing.

The terrible night passed. Still a faint, tremulous gasping came from the pallid lips of the old man. With the gray of dawn came a staggering rush of horses drawing up at the door.

The doctor came hurrying in, the inevitable little black bag in his hand; he walked stiffly after the long ride. Bob had not seen him before; he was that young Doctor Varney who had just come to Danvers. He looked cold, and hard, and unfeeling; his quick voice was nonchalant — this was but another case to him.

"Boil some water."

Stella spoke: "I have some boiling."

"How long has it boiled?"

"Two hours. We were expecting you."

He glanced at her in cold surprise — surprise that a ranch girl should know enough to have sterilized water ready. Without another word, he jerked the covers back and began quickly, roughly, to strip off the bandages. While his long white fingers worked dexterously, he spoke without turning his head:

"Get a wagon with gentle horses. Pile in two or three mattresses."

A little wail came from the old woman: "Oh, he can't be moved!"

Bob spoke, eagerly: "Has he a chance?"

"None here. Perhaps one in a million at a good hospital."

12

Still over his shoulder, he spoke again: "Can you afford to send him to Doctor Barnes in San Francisco?" The rough furniture did not hint of the prosperity of the ranch.

"Yes."

"If we can get him there alive we —"

A moment of silence while the doctor worked. He seemed almost terribly competent. Bob's unfavorable opinion of him began to change; he now felt almost glad that it was not kindly, pottering old Doctor Jones, who never seemed quite certain what to do. This younger man neither hesitated nor stopped to think. Bob spoke:

"It's San Francisco, then. I'll get the wagon ready."

He went to the door and gave an order to one of the men outside. Soon the wagon came rumbling up, pulled by a team of sleepy brown horses. Mrs. Davis turned distractedly to Bob.

"I'm going with him!"

The doctor, now washing his hands methodically, sniffed at her over his shoulder.

"I'd advise you to stay at home; relatives are the worst thing in the world around a sick man."

Bob spoke gently:

"Better let her go."

A shrug. Doctor Varney turned to Bob.

"I'll ride with him to the railroad."

"Can you go with him to San Francisco? We can pay the bill."

Drying his hands on a towel, the doctor gave Bob a sarcastic glance.

"The kind of doctor I am doesn't ask about a fee until he's through with a case. Get a wide board for a stretcher."

Bob did not take offense at the sarcasm; instead, there was respect in his face as he turned away to fulfil the order. Perhaps Doctor Varney was short of civility, but he seemed to make up for that in competence.

Gently though they moved the old man, they could not avoid a slight twist of the shattered chest. The pain aroused old Newt. His eyes opened slowly; they strayed around, perplexed; he did not remember what had happened to him, could not understand what was going on.

Slowly, it came back to him. His glance strayed to his wife, to his daughter, and finally rested on Bob. Bob guessed that he had something to say, and bent over him. A faint whisper came:

"Bob — hold — the — range!"

The eyes closed again. Doctor Varney was stuffing pillows and folded blankets at both sides of the old man until it was impossible for him to roll in the slightest when the wagon swayed.

At last the wagon crept off, the young doctor squatted by his patient's head. Pete Hudkins drove, and beside him on the seat was gray-haired little Mrs. Davis, her black bonnet nodding as they bumped over the stones.

From the doorway, Bob and Stella saw the wagon climb the ridge and disappear around a bend in the road. Then Stella turned. Groping with one hand, she crossed toward her bedroom. Bob took a step after her, stopped. He saw her door open, close again behind her. He heard the squeak of the springs as she threw herself across the bed. He swallowed a groan that came to his throat.

And then, with white, set face, he turned and left the house to walk to the corrals, where the cowboys had gathered in a knot. He was now in charge of the ranch.

CHAPTER
TWO

The Nester

Bob, with his long stride — not the clumsy gait of so many cowboys — walked up to the men. He knew most of them from five years before; the Bar Diamond held its riders a long time. There was "Shorty" Jones, who had been with the Rafter H when Bob left, and two or three others who had been years in the neighborhood, riding for different outfits.

He expected a slight coolness; he had thought that some of those old hands who had stayed with Newt would be expecting the good position as range boss. But he was mistaken; his announcement that he was in charge brought only friendly congratulation. He was still one of the crowd; and also his status had never been just that of another cowboy — he had been almost like a son to the Old Man.

It is an unwritten law on a cow outfit that no matter what happens, the work must go on. Bob noticed that the horses had not been wrangled; work seemed to have been forgotten in the excitement. He refrained from criticizing, casually suggesting that a couple of the men do what should have been done long before. As they rode away, he turned to the others.

16

"Now, I want to know who might have done that shooting. Has the outfit been having any trouble lately?"

There was a slow shaking of heads; everyone seemed as puzzled as Bob himself. Shorty Jones answered:

"No more than the usual trouble any outfit has in these parts. Some rustlin', of course — nesters doin' most of it."

"Newt told me last night about having some trouble with sheepmen. Are they worse than they used to be?"

"Sheep!" someone grunted.

"We-ell" — Shorty rolled a cigarette — "it sort of keeps pilin' up. The sheep range is bein' et barer an' barer all the time in this drought. Nearly out of water on the sheep range — the dang things keep gettin' ga'nter all the time, an' they try to crowd 'em in on cattle range."

"Who's sheep, mostly?" asked Bob.

"Butch Johnson's — he's the ringleader, an' Jeff Morehouse is backin' him pretty strong. They been gettin' pretty *bravo* lately; claim this is all free range an' they have as much right on it as anyone else."

"Oh, sure! Ruin their own range with their blattin' woollies tearing up the grass roots, an' then want to do the whole country the same way. That's sheepmen every time! Any trouble with the other cow outfits around here?"

"Nary bit — gettin' along with 'em fine as silk; the row with the sheepmen is makin' 'em stick together."

"The nesters — are they very bad?"

"Not too bad — for nesters. Only a feller called Al Boyd. He's a tough egg."

"Well, when the horses come in, get saddled up."

Bob turned away. It struck him that he should try to find the spot from which the bullet had been fired, that he should look around there.

He remembered the low stone walls of an old Indian ruin at the summit of a ridge opposite the house, and he figured that it would have been a likely place of concealment for whoever had fired the shot; it faced the moonlit door. He started toward it. Not, of course, that he expected to find anything that would be of much help to him.

Even before he came to the ruin, he found tracks of a horse which had left there in a fast lope. Brand-new shoes on the horse; the tracks were very clear-cut. Probably, he guessed, those shoes had been put on for the occasion and would immediately be removed, changed slightly in shape, and refitted. That would absolutely prevent any positive identification of the prints.

Unskilled though Bob was in tracking, one thing was very obvious to him; this was no cow pony; the hoofs were too large and clumsy. "Nester" came to him immediately; the nesters rode all kinds of horses. Or, of course, it might be a sheep-outfit horse; the few horses the sheepmen owned were as badly assorted as the nesters'.

He followed the tracks away from the ruin, in the direction in which the horse had been traveling. For a

18

moment his eye lighted up. Was the horse slightly lame? That would make it much easier to find him.

No, not that — but there was something wrong with the tracks just the same. He followed them almost a hundred yards, sometimes bending over them, again standing off at a distance to see them as a whole. Not lame; but the horse seemed to have a clumsy trick of slapping down his left hind hoof when he loped. Certainly a mount unsuited to cow work, and no doubt seldom if ever used for it.

He turned back toward the ruin. He had found out nothing but what he had felt satisfied of already; that the shooting had not been done by a cowboy — a cowboy would scorn a big, heavy plug like that. Anyway, Newt and the surrounding cattlemen had always been on the most cordial terms.

At the ruin, a little yellow glint between two of the fallen stones caught his eye. He picked up an empty .44-40 cartridge. That was of as little help as the horse tracks; that caliber gun was very common.

He examined the shell carefully; there were two little scratches, about a quarter of an inch apart, received from the edge of the chamber. This, too, helped little; not one carbine in a hundred was as smooth on the inside as it should be — cowboys and sheep-herders alike were notoriously careless in cleaning their rifles.

And then he dived upon something else. Now, *that* was more like it! Part of a block of fusee matches, glued together at the rear ends. One seldom saw fusees any more; sulphur matches had almost replaced them. The fusees had the advantage of lighting in a howling wind, but their choking, malodorous fumes more than counter-balanced this. Once in a while one would see a prospector or some other old-timer who stuck to them.

Now, if he could just find out who used fusees around here — and that should not be difficult — the search would be narrowed down a good deal. Probably most of the users might be eliminated instantly, either because they could not have been there the night before, or for lack of any possible motive. Bob, feeling much more satisfied, placed the fusees carefully in his pocket.

He began to hunt around for footprints. Of course, the bushwhacker would try not to leave any, but that would be somewhat difficult, at night. There was where he had stood; he had likely rested the carbine on the top of the old wall when he fired. The ground underneath was bare and sandy, but it had been carefully brushed over with a handful of weeds to remove any tracks. The fellow was clever enough.

Bob pottered about in the ruin, but found nothing else. He went outside and began to circle the fallen stones. The fellow had been careful to step from one of those stones to another; one could not tell which way he had gone out. Pretty slim chance of finding tracks.

Thinking hard, it came to Bob that his best bet was to find where the horse had been tied; the man might have left footprints as he mounted. Of course, he might have been clever enough to shuffle his horse back and forth across them, but the chances were that he'd have been in too much of a hurry — too scared after what he'd done.

It was easy to find where the horse had stood, tied to a limb of a big cedar. And there was a footprint! — left as the man swung into the saddle; the rest had been rubbed out. A single boot print, but clear as it could be. A huge boot, almost twice as large as Bob's own. Low, run-over heels.

This track, again, seemed to bring it down to a nester. Sheepmen hardly ever wore boots, but nesters did quite often; they liked to ape cattlemen, much as they might damn them. A nester who used fusee matches and had extraordinarily large feet. Well, that had narrowed things down a great deal.

Bob hurried back to the corrals, where the men had saddled their horses and were waiting for him. He hid his eagerness to question them; one never knew who might be mixed up in this sort of thing. He spoke casually:

"Well, you boys know better than I do what's to be done. Just go ahead today; I have some things to look after."

Shorty spoke: "We was figgerin' on shovin' the cattle out o' the breaks today; the water's about gone there. An' Bear Canyon dam is pretty near dry; someone had better go there to pull bog."

"Shorty's shore good at pullin' bog," hinted "Red" Selby. Pulling bog is a task that every cowboy hates.

Shorty snorted indignantly, but said nothing; few tried to argue with the quick-witted Red.

Bob casually pulled out his tobacco and papers.

"Smoke, Shorty?"

"Uh-huh."

21

Shorty rolled a cigarette. He was reaching to his shirt pocket for a match when he noticed that Bob was proffering something.

"Well — fusees!" he said. "Thanks, Bob, but I'd rather die a nacheral death than be choked by them things."

"Say," interjected Red Selby interestedly, "I ain't seen any o' them things in years; I thought they didn't make 'em any more."

"You have, too!" Shorty corrected. "Al Boyd uses 'em most of the time when he's ridin' — too clumsy to keep a match lighted on a horse."

"Boyd — I don't seem to remember the name," mused Bob.

"You ought to; I'm pretty sure he moved in before you left here. He's a nester over near Bald Mountain — a sorter giant."

"Oh, a big fellow?" Bob had to struggle hard to hide his excitement.

"Big! Must be near seven feet tall, an' built like a grizzly bear."

"What's he like — just one more big-footed nester, I suppose?"

Red broke in:

"Bob, if you saw him comin' up the draw, you'd swear they was two battleships sorter misplaced. We caught him rustlin' a few days ago, but, for some reason we couldn't figger out, old Newt wouldn't prosecute — wouldn't do a thing about it."

Bob felt like whooping. Here it had all worked itself out, without his having to say a thing that might bring suspicion. Not, of course, that he suspected any of those boys of knowing anything about the shooting, but he didn't want any stories to get around until he himself was ready to spread them.

Shorty came back to something of more interest to him than casual remarks about a nester:

"Say, Bob, who's goin' to pull bog?"

Bob wanted to be diplomatic on his first morning as range boss.

"Why, I'd suggest that it might be the last man to pass between those big cedars at the end of the flat."

It took a second or so to reach them, and then there was a mad rush for horses. They tore away from the corrals like so many wild Comanches. Slender, wiry Red Selby took the lead by a length, waving back tauntingly at the others. Bob did not wait to see who won or lost; he did not care. He quickly saddled a horse and turned away from the ranch.

An hour or so later he came upon a youngster of perhaps twelve, riding a scrubby pony whose tail was full of sand burrs and witch locks. He hailed him:

"Say, sonny; I'm lookin' for Al Boyd's place. Can you tell me where it is?"

"Dad's place? I reckon I can."

The boy was regarding Bob with open dislike and suspicion. Bob waited, but had to ask again:

"Well, where is it?"

"Acrost that ridge. But he's busy an' won't see you."

Bob grinned. "I just want to drop in and get acquainted; I'm the new range boss on the Bar

23

Diamond. I was coming over last night — real late — but I didn't have time."

The boy gathered up his reins. He seemed to regard Bar Diamond cowboys and rattlesnakes as very much on the same social footing. Bob was beginning to feel disappointed; it looked as though he would get no answer to his carefully hidden leading question. But as the boy turned off with a sniff, he spoke:

"Dad is often out late nights — besides, he wouldn't want to see you nohow." He rode off aggressively.

"Thanks, kid!" shouted Bob after him.

The youngster little suspected what he was being thanked for.

A few minutes later, Bob rode up to the house. After the fashion of the country, he halloed loudly before coming too close — this was all the more advisable in dealing with a man of Boyd's reputation. While waiting, he glanced around in some surprise.

Why, this place was not at all like most nesters' homes; it was neat, and freshly painted, with a patch of flower garden in the yard — Bob well knew the work that little garden must have cost in this dry time. Evidently Boyd was not lazy, whatever his faults.

The door opened. Framed in the doorway appeared a huge figure of a man. But in spite of his great bulk, of his heavy blond beard, he looked almost handsome. He reminded Bob of a picture he had seen once — a bearded viking, or something of the sort. But this fellow would pick the viking up and break him between his hands. Bob felt something like awe in looking at the giant figure.

Too, he seemed to be fairly young, in spite of the beard — hardly middle-aged. And, in spite of his bulk, he looked as wiry as a cat. Bob had never seen such a man before. After a surly glance at Bob, the man turned to speak to someone within.

Bob gasped. Through the doorway he had caught a glimpse of a woman's face. Why, she was a beauty, in every sense of the word! She was small, dainty, golden-haired, with extremely regular features. A feeling of amazement came to Bob, surprise that such a woman as that should have married this big, surly nester, surprise that she could be old enough to be the mother of the boy he had seen. What a strange pair this was!

Boyd turned back aggressively.

"Somethin' you wanted?"

Bob swung from his horse and went toward the man. He tried to make his tone friendly, or at least entirely civil:

"This Mr. Boyd? I'm Bob Edwards, the new range foreman of the Bar Diamond. I just thought I'd pay a friendly call while I was riding over this way — sort of to get acquainted."

"I don't get friendly with cowboys — I know all about you already, if you're one o' the Bar Diamond gang."

He had said it in a truculent growl. Bob Edwards looked at him calmly.

"Smoke? No? Got a match on you? I happened to run out."

25

Bob took the reluctantly proffered block of fusees; they exactly matched those in his pocket. Casually, he glanced at the other's boots. Yes, they were fully big enough to have made the track of the night before — and it was doubtful if another man in all Arizona possessed as large ones. Bob decided that there was no use in trying to be courteous to this fellow. He spoke plainly, but not insultingly:

"Well, just what do you know about me — as a Bar Diamond cowboy?"

The nester showed white, even teeth.

"I know that you're a low-down rustler, tryin' to ruin honest men that's workin' to make a livin' in this God-forsaken, burned-up country."

"You're kinda blunt-spoken, I notice," remarked Bob placidly. "Now, me, I like this country fine. I suppose, now, you yourself didn't ever happen to steal a calf, sort of by accident?"

"I shore did! An' I'm goin' to steal more of 'em. I'm not the kind to set down like a lamb an' let you an' yore gang steal me blind. There's yore answer, cowboy!" The white teeth flashed again.

Bob was trying to decide whether this man was mad or just possessed more pure "cussedness" than the rest of his kind. He rather inclined to the former theory; those blazing, flashing eyes of a peculiarly dark blue did not look just right. But sane or not sane, all this shouting, all this calling him a rustler, was getting under Bob's skin.

"Boyd, let me give you a little plain talking to — some fellows may be afraid to, but I'm not. You know

26

very well that a jury would never convict you of rustlin', because some clever lawyer would see to it that there were nesters on the jury."

"I got a right to trial by my peers."

"Shore! And a horse thief should have a jury of horse thieves to try him? Well, what I'm getting around to is that us cattlemen — the law being what it is — sometimes have to look out for our own interests. Got all that?"

"Threatenin' me, are you?" roared the nester, his face quivering with rage. Evidently, as Bob had suggested, he was not used to such blunt talk as this; his size cowed most people.

"Heck, no!" Bob laughed unpleasantly. "I wouldn't think of doing anything like that. Just hinting that you'd do well to take a long circle around the next Bar Diamond long-ear you see."

By this time the nester's face was flushed almost purple above his dense beard. Bob was keeping a hawklike watch on the big right hand. He was ready to shoot a revolver out of it if necessary; he rather figured that such a lesson was just what this nester needed.

This very concentration trapped Bob; it was the nester's left hand that came whipping up, from behind the door jamb. In it was a carbine which had been left standing there already cocked — of course Boyd had peered from the window before opening the door. Wild triumph showed in his glaring blue eyes.

"*Now*, cowboy, what you got to say!"

"Repeatin' what I said before."

27

Bob stared coolly into the muzzle of the gun; if he was going to be shot, whimpering would not help a bit, would only give the nester satisfaction.

"I got my wife to witness that I shot you in self-defense — that you rode up to the door an' threatened me, like cowboys always does little ranchers like me."

Bob, the picture of indifference, began coolly to roll a fresh cigarette.

"Well, whang away, and have it over."

The great finger began to press the trigger; the nester's eyes glared as he might glare at a mad dog. For a moment eyes met eyes. Presently the expression in the nester's began to change. The gun came down; the butt grounded with a crack beside the huge boots. To Bob's amazement, the big, thick-lipped mouth opened and a huge, throaty laugh rumbled forth.

Bob spoke, almost humorously; it was easier to speak that way now that the gun was not pointed in his face:

"Boyd, you're throwin' away a fine chance if you don't shoot."

"Can't do it, cowboy! You got too much nerve."

There was frank admiration in the tone — admiration that had come in spite of all the nester could do to fight it off.

"Well," remarked Bob, "I reckon I'll be goin'. Come over an' see us some time."

He turned coolly on his heel, mounted, and rode away, leaving the other man staring after him, still holding the carbine by the muzzle.

Once out of sight over the hill, Bob jerked his silk kerchief from his neck and mopped his face shakily. There was sweat on his forehead, although the day was not warm. He knew that he must be slightly pale. That was the closest call of his life, and now that it was over he had time to be scared stiff. He felt immensely thankful that he had stood up to it as he had, and so left a good impression on Boyd; it might keep him from further rustling.

Well, he had found out all that he wanted to know. Everything pointed to Al Boyd as the bushwhacker of the night before — even the bore of the carbine, whose muzzle Bob had been given far more opportunity to examine than he relished.

Should he swear out a warrant immediately? He could see to it that the jury had no nesters on it; Bob understood enough of the law to know that he could get a change of venue to another county, where the case would be tried on its merits, without any partisan feelings.

Suddenly Bob, to his surprise, found that he was actually feeling sorry for the big nester. The poor fool, like all nesters, fancied himself persecuted by the wealthy cattlemen, when the simple fact was that his herd of scrubby cattle was too small to afford him a reasonable living. Why, when Bob had worked for the Bar Diamond before, he had carried many a quarter of beef, even many a sack of flour, to the family of some starving nester for whom kindly old Newt had felt sorry.

Persecution! But could you tell the nesters that nobody wanted to bother them — even if they did bite the hand that fed them? It seemed a law of nature that all nesters should be fractious, dissatisfied, cantankerous, and always blaming someone else for the fruits of their own shiftlessness.

Shiftless? Well, that word could hardly be applied to Al; that neat place showed unremitting toil. Yes, there was something about Boyd's terrible forcefulness that appealed to Bob, himself primarily a fighter in spite of his easy-going way. Boyd, poor fool, had thought himself justified in firing that shot; perhaps had even considered it his simple duty to his family. Bob wondered for a moment if there couldn't have been something other than range enmity behind it, but he dismissed the thought. What other dealings could Al have had with old Newt?

Bob remembered that glimpse of the pretty, gold-framed face of Mrs. Boyd. Looked like a fine little woman. Sure would be tough on her if Al were hanged, or sent to jail for life. Or — perhaps she'd be better off rid of a brute who must make life miserable for her. Strange family, indeed!

Bob came back to realities. Newt had been shot — bushwhacked. He was practically sure to die. As the man in charge of the outfit, the man who had to settle Newt's affairs for his wife and daughter, it was up to Bob to see that Boyd got his deserts. If the law failed to avenge the kindly little man, well — Bob's jaw set grimly. He was an Arizona cowboy, with the Arizona cowboy's code a part of his very bones.

Bob did not go directly back to the ranch; he had nothing to do there. He let his horse wander almost aimlessly on a loose rein. As he rode, he was taking note of the condition of the cattle, of what he guessed to be the percentage of calves — light, because of poor feed — of the grass.

He found a seven-month-old slick-ear, and roped and branded it. He turned across to a little water hole he knew, to see how high it stood, how many head were watering there. All these were things of great interest to any cowboy, but of special importance to the range boss responsible for the condition of the stock.

It was close to sunset when he came within sight of the ranch. All the men seemed to be back already; he guessed that they had done a scant day's ride after all the excitement. Then he noticed an unusual bustle around the place. The remuda was being driven hastily in, as though new mounts were to be caught. Why? There was no night work to be done.

He hurried down, and toward the house. Stella met him. Her eyes were very red, her face drawn. He went toward her and leaped from his saddle.

"Matter, Stell?"

He held his breath, waiting for the answer he feared.

"He — he's dying. They got him no farther than town. He sent — sent word for all of us to see him before —"

"Oh, you poor kid!"

Big Bob Edwards himself felt like crying. He did not know whether he felt more sorry for the gentle, harmless old man or for the daughter. And then he thought of the poor, gray-haired little woman, Mrs.

Davis. Yes, on her the blow would be hardest; it was the end of her life, so far as life meant anything to her.

"Bob, hurry! He may be —" Stella was dabbing at her eyes with a small handkerchief.

Bob ran to the corral and roped a fresh horse. He turned to a man who was saddling quickly.

"Who brought word?"

"That feller."

The man to whom he had spoken pointed to an honest-looking, red-faced little cowboy whom Bob had never seen before.

"Who sent you out with the word?" he asked.

"I reckon it was the doctor; I was a stranger in town an' didn't know nobody." He added: "Too doggone bad; they say old Newt was as square as they make 'em."

Everybody was mounting hastily. Someone was leading Stella's horse toward the house; she was hurrying to meet it. A sudden thought came to Bob; he turned.

"Everybody leaving?" he asked.

"Shore! The old man said he wanted to see all of us boys before he died. He would!"

This from a heavy-set, wild-looking cowboy. He had spoken with a queer, choking note in his voice. Now he turned to swear viciously at his horse to cover his feelings.

Bob shook his head. "It don't look right to me — to leave the place. Not with nesters an' sheepmen kicking up."

"Well, I ain't stayin', for one!"

The wild-looking cowboy stuck out his chin aggressively. Too aggressively — he was scared of

32

appearing a sissy. Bob had a sudden inspiration; he turned to the stranger.

"Pardner, could you stay an' keep an eye on things till we get back? I'll pay you well."

"Shore I'll stay — an' you won't pay me a cent either. I'm only too glad to do a thing like that for accommodation." He looked concerned; he saw the grief of the others.

"Who are you ridin' for?" asked Bob. He liked the looks and manner of this young fellow.

"Ridin' chuck line over six months now; they're firin' cowboys instead o' hirin' 'em in this drought. I forget what three squares a day look like."

The young stranger tried to grin; he only succeeded in looking worried.

"Well, pardner," said Bob, "you got a job now as long as you want it. Just keep an eye on things till we get back. Drop over to the cook shack an' rustle you up something to eat; the cook's coming with us."

The little crowd was already stringing out from the ranch, grouped dismally around Stella, whose bay swung off in a quick trot. Bob loped until he caught up, and silently they drew out of sight of the ranch, a cloud of dust hanging in the dry air behind them.

Never once did it occur to Bob, to anybody, that the message might be a ruse. They had no suspicion that the shooting of old Newt was but the first move of a grim plot that was closing in on them. Not even to the honest little cowboy who had been made a dupe did this occur.

CHAPTER
THREE

The Stranger's Death

The moon hung brilliant in a cloudless sky, so bright that but a few stars showed as pale specks. The crags stood out in bold relief, the buttes. It was as bright as day, with a strange, metallic brightness, but there were no half lights; the shadows were so black that they might have been gaping holes reaching through the earth.

The riders pressed on, knee to knee. Bob and Stella rode in the lead now, rode in silence. From the men behind came an occasional murmur; no one raised his voice. The odor of sweating horses was strong, the tang of sweat-drenched leather. Hoofs clicked on the stones; a horse blew its nose.

Bob glanced up; for a moment or two his eyes rested on a faint star. It did not shimmer; that meant that it was past midnight. From under his hat brim, he stole a glance at the girl beside him. Her face seemed as white as the moon itself, but her head was high, her lips set.

They reached the top of a high ridge. Below them three or four lights shone faintly; at this hour the little town of Danvers was almost in darkness. Bob opened his mouth to speak but changed his mind; in silence the band swung rapidly down the ridge. They passed the first house, a crude, unpainted shack. A piece of broken, rotten board sidewalk showed on their left; they were in Danvers. Bob spoke, his voice low:

"Where should we go? Have they — built any hospital since I was here?"

Stella answered.

"No."

"Then — the doctor's house."

"Yes."

Stella touched her horse's neck with a rein, and swung into a side street, Bob close beside her. Once more Stella turned a corner. She pointed with her quirt:

"That house — the white one on the corner."

Bob was surprised; the house was in darkness. Then his head sank on his chest as he realized the significance of it. Old Newt was dead; he needed no more light, no more care.

Vividly before Bob's eyes came a picture of the gentle, kindly little cattleman; it was as though old Newt Davis stood before him, tiny, wrinkled; the bleached, sun-paled blue eyes seemed to twinkle at him with gentle kindliness. Something clogged Bob's throat; he could not swallow it. Never again would he see in the flesh this little man who had been almost a father to him — more than a father.

Bob heard a choking little groan beside him. He spoke, his own voice unsteady, his face drawn:

"Now, Stell!"

He swung slowly from his horse and dropped his reins. He and Stella went slowly, slowly up the graveled walk, their heads bowed. Behind them, some of the cowboys remained in their saddles; some dismounted; none spoke. Bob knocked at the door, paused, knocked again. He heard a faint noise within; the yellow gleam of a kerosene lamp came through a window and shone on a stunted rosebush.

While they waited, Bob thought bitterly that it was not fitting for the body of old Newt to be left thus in darkness on his last night above the ground. Then his usual fairness spoke; a doctor could not waste time on the dead; he had to rest himself that he might minister to the living. But why did not Mrs. Davis —

In the middle of his thought, Bob heard the shuffle of slippered feet. The door opened; a tall young woman looked at him inquiringly. She was handsome, but cold — a fitting wife for Doctor Varney. She looked annoyed at being disturbed thus during the night — looked, rather, as though she were withholding her annoyance until she found out the gravity of the mission. Bob spoke:

"I'm Bob Edwards; this is Miss Davis."

"Yes?"

Bob stared. She did not even invite them in.

"But — uh —" He stopped, began again: "Where is — uh — Newt Davis?" He felt that he should say, "Newt Davis's body," but he could not.

The woman brushed back a wisp of hair that had fallen across her face.

"Why, he left on the evening train for San Francisco. Doctor Varney and Mrs. Davis went with him."

Bob gasped. He felt Stella's shoulder press closer to his arm as though for sympathy, for protection; a mystery was beginning to dawn slowly upon them. Again Bob spoke, his voice hesitant:

"How was he — last you heard?"

"Doctor Varney said he was showing a slight improvement, but that he had very little chance of recovering."

Now Stella was crying quietly. Bob, without knowing it, reached up a hand and gently took her arm. He turned again to the woman:

"A man came dashing out to the ranch this evening; he said that Doctor Varney had sent him. He brought word that Newt was dying here and wanted to see all of us before he died."

Now the woman looked astonished.

"But that's impossible! It's — there's some mistake."

Bob stared at her helplessly; it was one of the few times in his life that he felt completely at a loss, baffled.

"But — What should we do?"

Mrs. Varney thought quickly; she seemed to have all her husband's deadly competence.

"I'd suggest that you have the station agent wire the train."

He turned away, slowly. He glanced back to see Mrs. Varney cross the little porch — her face looked softer now — and gently place an arm across Stella's trembling shoulders. He heard her speak, heard Stella's sobbing answer.

"Won't you come in and lie down, dear? This is too much for you."

"No — th-thanks. I'm — I'm going with them to find out."

"Perhaps that's better" — soothingly. "Then come back here — you must!" She patted Stella's shoulder as the poor girl turned away.

"What did she say?" whispered a cowboy.

"Huh?" Bob spoke confusedly. "I don't know — I mean I'll find out."

The cowboy stared at him. Bob gently helped Stella into her saddle and then swung quickly to his own. They went clattering down the street, the cowboys behind them. A freight train had just left the station and was puffing heavily through a little pass a half mile off.

Bob strode hurriedly across the platform, into the waiting room, and toward an open window. He felt Stella beside him, felt the trembling of her shoulder. There came the clack of telegraph keys. A thin man wearing an eye shade glanced up at them absently and went on pounding the key. A white, hand-rolled cigarette hung from a corner of his mouth. They waited.

The message finished, the man stood up and came toward them. He gave Stella a friendly, respectful nod.

"What can I do for you, Miss Davis?"

Bob spoke:

"Can I send a wire to — uh — to a passenger on a train — the train that left for San Francisco this evening?"

"Sure." The man glanced at the clock. "Mojave Springs'll catch it if I get it out right away."

Bob took the pad and pencil thrust toward him. He was beginning to compose the message when he heard the man's voice again.

"Somethin' for you, Miss Davis — just came in a few minutes ago."

Holding his breath, Bob watched Stella snatch the yellow sheet and glance through it hastily. She dropped it and turned away, her handkerchief raising to her eyes. Numbly, Bob picked up the sheet. He had to force himself to read:

PATIENTS CONDITION STILL UNCHANGED STOP
SHOULD REACH SAN FRANCISCO SAFELY

VARNEY

Now it was Bob who dropped the telegram. The window seemed to swim before his eyes. He spoke, his voice hollow:

"When — when was that message sent?"

The man glanced at the yellow sheet, at the clock.

"About twenty-seven minutes ago."

They walked dazedly from the waiting room. The cowboys were grouped outside the door, their anxious eyes all turned on Bob. He spoke to them:

"He's all right — on his way to San Francisco."

Stares. An incredulous gasp. Red Selby began to speak:

"I don't like the looks —"

Hurriedly, Bob broke in on him:

"So everything is all right; he's still got a chance. We'd better take Stella back to Mrs. Varney's for the night, and then all go to the hotel."

Red caught Bob's warning glance; in it he saw the same uneasiness that he himself felt. He understood. Another was going to speak, but Red nudged him and jerked his head meaningly toward Stella. Red gave a deep sigh of relief, partly pretended, partly real.

"Well, I don't know where the mistake came up, but it shore feels good to know that the Old Man's still alive an' has a fightin' chance. That's all old Newt ever asked for — a fightin' chance."

Shorty Jones spoke. He was a better actor than Red Selby; anyone would have thought his relief genuine.

"Well, I can sleep now — I'm dog-tired. Let's be goin'!"

Stella noticed nothing wrong in the men's manner; she herself was too tired; she had been through too much that day, and she had had no sleep the night before. They mounted, presently to stop again before the Varney house.

Again Bob walked with Stella to the door. This time it opened before he knocked. Now Mrs. Varney was fully dressed, her hair neat. She invited Bob in for tea, but he declined. Absently, it ran through his mind that she was very Eastern, a newcomer in Arizona; to invite the foreman in and ignore the other cowboys was unpardonable. The tea, too — a Westerner would have offered coffee.

She led Stella to a lounge. Bob caught her eye meaningly, and quite casually she followed him outside.

On the porch, he leaned toward her and whispered quickly:

"Get her to bed as soon as you can; don't let her get to thinking. There's something wrong somewhere."

"What?"

"If I only knew!" Bob's whisper was a groan.

"I understand. I'll give her something harmless to make her sleep."

"Thanks!"

The woman's eyes rested questioningly on him a moment. Then she smiled understandingly. With the smile, all the formality dropped from her; in an instant, she had become friendly, warm, likable. She reached up and gave Bob's arm a little squeeze.

"I'll take good care of her for you; I used to be a nurse."

Bob felt his face burning as he turned away. What a foolish mistake she had made, to think that he and Stella — But he was very glad that Stella was there; he did not want her to go back to the ranch with them — not just then.

Gravely, the little knot of cowboys rode down the street. They turned a corner as though going toward the hotel. Only when they were halfway there, well out of sight and hearing of the Varney house, did Shorty speak:

"Well?"

"Well," Bob answered uneasily, "the sooner we get back home the better. The more I think of it, the more it looks to me like a trick to get us all away from there."

"But why?" asked Red.

"Maybe," blurted someone, "we'll find the place burned to the ground when we get back?"

They were now circling quietly through the streets to reach the road home. Bob thought a moment, and shook his head.

"I don't think so. That would only stir up a lot of sympathy for the outfit, and wouldn't do enough damage to hurt us a lot — the buildings are all 'dobe."

"Then — what?"

Bob rode a long distance in silence. He was thinking so hard that it almost made him feel sick — to no purpose. He turned back to his men.

"Let's lope 'em up, boys!" He had no answer.

The tired horses struck a heavy lope. The moon sank behind a jagged divide, and the close-packed little band of weary men rode on through the darkness.

It was after sunrise when they swung around the bend and came in sight of the ranch. The Bar Diamond lay peacefully below them. Cattle wandered sleepily back and forth, or crowded around the water troughs. The trumpeting of a bull came to them. A horse or two grazed close to the wrangle-trap fence. They rode in a slow trot now; any faster gait would kill the tired horses. The men, two nights without sleep, looked somewhat drawn and hollow-eyed, but not nearly so much so as might others in their place — the open-range cowboy becomes accustomed to eating when he can, sleeping when he can.

From far off, they could see that the cook-shack door was open. Then they saw something like a shadow lying before it — but there was nothing to cast a shadow. The dark thing took form as they came closer; all eyes were fixed on it; they did not glance at each other. Presently their horses were ranged around it.

Bob's lips were tight drawn as he read the marks on the ground. The cowboy had dropped, had twisted around painfully, had crawled about six feet back toward the open door. Even the least feeling of the men shuddered at the gruesome signs, things not to be described.

Bob dismounted quietly and stooped over the cold body. He searched the pockets and drew forth a dog-eared letter. He opened it and read it; he had to find out something about this poor fellow. He turned to the men; his voice was low, trembled:

"His name is Jack Daly. He was supporting his mother — in Prescott."

That was all he could gather from the letter; and that was why this cowboy had seemed so worried about being out of work.

A bitter oath came from the lips of one of the men. Bob thrust the letter in his pocket.

"The outfit will look after her."

He sighed. He spoke again:

"Someone should go for the sheriff. We're all dog-tired. Reckon I can stand it, if someone will wrangle me a fresh horse."

Red Selby came forward; his face matched his hair in color. "Bob — uh — I lay down under a cedar yesterday, meanin' only to rest a minute, but I — uh — I fell asleep. I'll go."

43

Red's tone, his face, admitted that the nap had been deliberate. Bob did not care; he nodded dully.

"Good thing you did. Go ahead."

He turned to the others.

"Look around, you boys, and see if you can find anything else wrong; I'm going up to the house. No, leave him there; throw a tarp over him. The sheriff will want to see him; I suppose he'll bring the coroner."

He went up to the house and pushed the door open. Wild disorder was everywhere. Things were upset, drawers pulled out and their contents scattered all over the floor; it gave the room a strange, unfamiliar look.

He went to old Newt's bedroom; his eyes immediately swept to the corner usually occupied by a cheap, old-fashioned safe. The safe was still there, but it lay on its back, its light door twisted and ajar. A crowbar lay beside the safe, a heavy pickax on the old man's bed.

Papers were strewn around. Bob peered into the safe. Not having known what was in it, he could not tell what was missing.

Presently he went back to the living room. He could not understand this. Old Newt had never kept more than a very few dollars in the house; he had always done business by check. Nor were there any ornaments or other things of value; like most Westerners, the family cared nothing for what they called "knick-knacks". The table cutlery and such things were hardly better than might be found in the homes of many laborers.

His eyes went to the mantelpiece, where he remembered having seen Newt's gold watch. It was gone. Other things would be gone, too — things that Bob would not miss. There could not have been very much in the safe — perhaps fifty dollars. The entire haul was not likely to amount to more than a hundred dollars' worth.

Who would murder a man for a hundred dollars? More likely a nester than a sheepman; nesters were habitually in dire poverty, and that would look like a lot of money to one.

How about the rest of the house? Bob crossed through the litter to Stella's room. The same disorder; everything on the dressing table upset. He walked around the bed. As he was setting his foot down at the end of a step, he quickly raised it again — so quickly that he almost fell.

There beneath him, in a little patch of spilled talcum powder, was a single immense boot print.

He stood looking at it dully. Dully, he realized that he was back just where he had been the morning before. He tried to think, but he found that he could not; his head was too thick — he was too tired, had gone too long without rest. There came a clank of spurs as a cowboy crossed the porch. He went to meet him.

"Sam, tell all the boys to go to the bunk house and take a sleep; we can't do any good draggin' around this way."

He threw himself wearily, fully dressed, on the lounge. If he could sleep, it would clear his head.

That big boot print —

CHAPTER
FOUR

Sheep!

At one o'clock in the afternoon the sheriff and a deputy arrived. With them were the coroner and a coroner's jury of six men — men picked because their curiosity and liking for the gruesome overcame their aversion to a long ride.

The inquest was no more fruitful than are most inquests. The tarp which had been thrown over the body was removed; the six men stood around gravely, and presently announced that Jack Daly had been murdered. Some of the cowboys outside the group sniffed; they could not understand why such nonsense was necessary. The body was loaded into a wagon, and one of the jurymen drove away slowly, his horse tied behind. The rest of the jury waited to ride back with the sheriff.

Then came an investigation of the robbery. Sheriff Ben Wilson, an old friend of Bob's, was a quiet man approaching middle age. As a sheriff he was competent — in spite of his hesitating manner, he did not fear the devil himself — but he had no more detective training than had Bob. Bob had scant faith in Wilson's ability in such a case as this; his puzzled face was not reassuring.

At last the little band mounted and turned back toward town. One man seemed to be remaining. Bob turned to him.

"Hello, Clay. Sorry I didn't get a chance to speak to you sooner."

They shook hands. Clay Bozart was an old friend of Bob's, now owner of the V4, just beyond the Bar Diamond.

"Howdy, Bob. Glad to hear you're runnin' this outfit now; you'll make a good neighbor."

"You on the jury?"

"Yeah; Wilson asked me to, seein' as this is on my way home — haven't been home in a week."

"Drinkin' again?"

Clay Bozart reddened slightly, and his eyes fell. Bob placed his hand on Clay's shoulder; in spite of this young fellow's weaknesses, Bob had always liked him.

"Clay, you'd better cut it out, now that your father is dead and you're running the outfit. I'd sure hate to see you neglect things till you go broke."

Coming as it did from an old friend beside whom he had ridden many a long day, Clay did not resent this.

"Bob — uh — this is my first real drunk in six months. I — uh — I'm sort of improvin'.."

"Good!" Bob slapped Clay's shoulder. "Besides, with the sheep outfits and the nesters kickin' up like they are, us cattlemen will have to hang together and watch what we do."

"I know more about that than you do."

"What do you mean?"

Clay removed his Stetson and held the crown toward Bob. Bob whistled.

"Whew-w — looks like a bullet had clipped a piece out of it! When did that happen, and where?"

"Last week, over near Al Boyd's place. Some sheep-herder took a crack at me off a ridge."

Sheep-herder? Bob thought of the big boot prints.

"Clay, don't you think it might have been Boyd?" he asked.

"Gosh, no! We're pretty good friends. Oh, of course he cusses me a bit, like he cusses all cattlemen, but he don't mean nothin' by it. He's all right — jest windy."

"Don't be too sure. Better watch your step over round his place."

"Huh — Al Boyd!" Clay shrugged off the warning.

Bob felt uneasy. Somehow, he had a feeling that this somewhat wild, good-natured young cattleman might be the next victim. But there never had been any use in talking to Clay. Bob scanned the weakly handsome face, the trim but undeveloped figure. Clay would go his own way; he would always be his own worst enemy. Worst of all, thought Bob, Clay would be sure to let the V4 run down, to lose it sooner or later and find himself broke.

Clay was rolling a cigarette. He seemed to be hesitating. At last he spoke:

"Bob, one o' my men come to town last night. He told me that while he was ridin' around he saw sheep in Long Valley."

"What! On our range!"

"Uh-huh. I — I don't like messin' into another outfit's affairs, but if I —"

"Another outfit's! If we try to handle 'em separate, they'll lick us one at a time; they're well organized. Whose sheep, do you know?"

"I — uh — I think it's Butch Johnson's."

Two or three cowboys were standing eying Bob as though waiting for something. He turned to them and spoke quietly:

"Tell all the boys to saddle their best horses. I'd better go talk things over with Butch."

The men's eyes met; for an instant a slight, sarcastic grin seemed to pass between them. Talking things over with the sheepmen might not turn out to be nearly so peaceful a matter as Bob's words seemed to make it. They turned away. One of them called:

"Catch up the horses, boys; we're goin' to 'talk things over' with the sheep-herders."

From under his hat brim, Bob watched the movements of his men. To the last one, they were hurrying as he had never seen them hurry before. Good! They were loyal to the outfit; they felt the cowboy's usual contempt and dislike for sheep-herders. Clay Bozart spoke hesitantly:

"Reckon I'd better go with you, Bob, don't you think? Like you say, it's all our fight."

Bob thought quickly. If Clay went with him, Clay, as the owner of a large outfit, would be expected to take the lead in any argument with the sheepmen. Bob did not want that; Clay was too weak to hold his own against such as Butch Johnson. On the other hand,

Clay's cowboys would prove invaluable if it came to open fight later on; therefore Bob did not want to offend him. He spoke easily, casually:

"Clay, I think there's enough of us to handle the thing all right. You might be doing better to go back to the V4 and let your men know what's up — have 'em prepared in case we need 'em later on. Thanks a lot, just the same."

Young Bozart looked relieved, though he tried to hide it. Bob hurried to the corral, which was almost hidden in a cloud of mounting dust as the men roped horses. He beckoned to one of them.

"Shorty, you'd better stay here and keep an eye on things."

"Why pick on me, Bob?"

"Someone has to stay and look after the place."

Shorty was stubborn.

"If there's a fight, I'm goin' to be in it. I'm not goin' to sit here takin' it easy."

"The last fellow left lookin' after the ranch," remarked Bob dryly, "didn't find it so easy. You have to stay, Shorty — unless you're afraid."

That settled it. Although Shorty only sniffed half angrily, he drew himself astride the corral and glumly watched the others saddle and ride away. Clay went with them; it would be little out of his way to go with them four or five miles and then turn off toward the V4. Shorty was left alone.

Bob heard the sheep long before he saw them — a vague, murmuring sound ahead. Presently, from the shoulder of a hill, he could see them spread out below

50

— about two thousand head. The men had stopped their horses to survey things before riding down. Red Selby spoke, drawling sarcastically:

"Shore must be valuable sheep!"

"Why?" asked Bob.

Red waved a hand.

"Look at all the herders it takes to look after 'em."

Another nodded toward the sheep.

"Never saw a sheep-herder use a big tent like that before."

"Butch Johnson," guessed Bob. "Reckon he's camping with the band himself — in case of anything coming up. Well, let's go on down."

They came to the first herder, a Basque. Bob guessed him to be a caporal; the common herders were generally Mexicans.

"What," asked Bob sternly, "are those sheep doing on cattle range?"

"*No sabe.*"

Bob sniffed; any caporal would know at least some English. He tried in his broken Spanish:

"*Porqué las ovejas aquí?*"

"*No sabe. Parlez vous Français?*"

Bob swore under his breath. The fellow was actually making fun of him, meanwhile staring him brazenly in the eye; from Roman days to our own, the Basque has always been a ready fighter and a good one. A cowboy spoke, softly fingering his rope:

"If we'd drag him a few feet an' sorter shake his wits up, he might know somethin'."

That the Basque understood every word of it could be told from his bold, level glance at the speaker. But it made him think slightly better of things; he pointed toward the large tent, a grin on his face.

"The boss — ask him, *señor*."

Bob turned away, his men close behind him, and rode toward the tent. On the way, he nearly rode over a man stretched on his back on the hillside, under a convenient bush. The man sat up, a grin on his face, a cigarette dangling lazily from one corner of his mouth.

"Hello, Bob. Didn't know you was back in this country."

Bob looked down at him coldly.

"Hello, Blackie. What are you doing here? Quit punchin' cows?"

"Uh-huh — too much hard work in it, an' too little money. Take a *pasear* around the band, Bob; you'll be surprised at all the boys got to lookin' at things like I do."

"This *does* look easier!" Bob glanced at the two six-shooters on the man's hips.

"Uh-huh — tell the cook to wake me up when chuck's ready."

"Blackie" Dobbs lay back again, his hands clasped behind his head, a little curl of smoke mounting from his thin lips. His manner was hardly short of insulting; he had no fear of Bob's shooting without more reason than this.

"Butch Johnson in the tent?"

"Uh-huh."

Bob caught uneasy glances among his men. This thing seemed to have been all prepared for them; they seemed to have been expected; perhaps a scout had ridden in to announce their coming. Bob saw two or three men lounging toward the tent — Americans; they looked like ex-cowboys. He caught sight of several others sprawled around the hillside close at hand; all, apparently, merely enjoying a life of ease, like Blackie Dobbs.

Bob spurred his horse around the bush, peering into it. He saw what he expected; a patch of blue steel showing through the leaves — the barrel of a carbine.

"Well, boys" — he tried to make his voice sound casual — "let's ride down an' see Butch."

The man on the ground grinned up at him.

"Shore — he'll be glad to see you."

Bob rode toward the tent. He glanced hastily at his men. Their faces looked blank, worried; they had not expected to ride into the middle of a little army. Bob thought of turning back, of going home and returning when he was better prepared. No; he could talk to Butch anyway, try to reason with him.

Almost to the tent, another thought came to him. What if Butch had decided to force a battle on the spot, while he had the upper hand? By this time Bob heartily wished himself ten miles away, with time to think. But now it was too late to retreat; a thickset, square-jawed man, not unhandsome, was already pushing the tent flap aside and coming out to meet him.

"Howdy, Butch."

"Hello, Bob. Git down an' wait for chuck; it won't be long now."

Butch spoke politely, as though he had mistaken this for a friendly visit. Bob answered just as politely:

"Thanks, Butch; we dropped over to talk business — 'turkey' for dinner, sort of."

"Wild turkey?" Johnson lighted a cigar.

"I never waste time on wild talk, Butch." Bob carried on the little joke.

"Cigar, Bob?"

"No, thanks. Didn't your caporal or someone make a mistake? Long Valley here is Bar Diamond cattle range."

"It is?" Johnson looked astonished at the information.

"Uh-huh — cattle range to Torres Canyon."

"Well, that's too bad. I'll have the men drive 'em off."

He turned as though to call to the caporal. Then, apparently on second thought, he faced Bob again, apologetically.

"Bob, I have to think of the other sheepmen's interests as well as my own. Course, Bob, you can show patent papers on this land here. Got 'em with you?"

He was, like his caporal, making fun of Bob, but in a slyer way. Bob kept his temper; he would do well to keep his temper, for he was practically trapped. Men were coming dawdling up on all sides, all of whom carried rifles or carbines as well as the usual six-shooters. Bob's little band was completely surrounded, and still there were a few men lying among

54

the rocks and bushes on the hillside. Bob's mounting uneasiness made it easy for him to keep anger out of his voice.

"Butch, how much privately owned, patented land is there in Arizona?"

Butch blew a puff of cigar smoke in the air, considering. "Well, offhand, I'd say a lot less than one per cent — outside of railroad land. The rest is public land, open to anyone that wants to use it."

"But divided up by a sort of understanding. Getting down to cases, I can feel some sympathy for a nester that has nothing and wants a homestead and a few cows. You have about as big a range as ours; don't you think you'd better keep to it?"

"Bob," Butch Johnson turned a friendly eye toward the man above him on the horse, "there's no money in cattle, an' a dang sight less in punchin' cattle — even for a foreman. How about takin' a bossin' job with me? I'll double whatever wages you're gettin' now."

"Sheep!"

Bob's disgusted glance at the flock from the corner of his eye was answer enough. Johnson flushed.

"Think you're too good to herd sheep?"

"I sure do! Going to get those woollies off our range?" For the first time Bob's voice showed temper. He felt that he had been doubly insulted; asked to become a sheep-herder, and asked to betray his outfit.

"Those 'woollies' stay on *my* range."

"Your range?"

"Uh-huh, I've taken it over. I've as good a right to it as anyone else."

"Let's be going, boys."

The sheepman made a signal with his hand. The circle of carbines swung negligently in toward the trapped cowboys, although the muzzles were not yet raised. Johnson dropped his mask of politeness; he grinned gloatingly up at Bob.

"You came here lookin' for trouble. You're goin' to find it! Think I'm fool enough to let you go for more help an' come back again?"

Bob dropped his reins on the saddle horn and began to roll a cigarette. He gave the sheepman a glance of cool contempt, and lighted the cigarette.

"Well?"

Johnson nodded approvingly.

"What I always heard about you is right; you sure got nerve. You're jest what I need, an' what I'm willin' to pay for. What's the Bar Diamond payin' you?"

"None of your business, Butch; anyway, I don't know."

"If that ain't like a cowboy — don't know!" Butch grinned.

"Sure is! — we think of things besides money. I wouldn't work for the likes of you for five hundred a month."

Butch reddened and swore. With a hasty movement, he turned and signed to his gunmen. The encircling carbines and rifles whipped up. Around the cowboys ran a little ripple of sharp, metallic clicks as the guns were cocked.

"Going — going to shoot us down in cold blood?" asked Bob in unbelief. He had a queer feeling in the back of his neck, as though his hair were trying to stand on end.

"Jest that. After this one lesson, the cattlemen will shore leave us alone." And he meant it; a ghastly lesson for the rest.

To Bob's dazed mind came a picture of Clay Bozart. Yes, the weak Clay's range would be seized next, and the owner would not dare to fight back. Then the little outfits; if their owners fought, they could be easily overcome. Bob turned slowly and faced the man.

"The butcher always!"

Johnson snarled. He had begun life cutting meat in a butcher shop; next he had bought a tiny, run-down cow outfit, from which he had furnished an amazing amount of beef to a railroad-construction crew, and later to the neighboring towns. In spite of one three-months' jail sentence for possessing cow hides with the brands cut out, and another case or two which good lawyers had got him out of — there had been some talk of bribed jurors — he had done well. He had ended in sheep, as more profitable, although more of a gamble, than cattle. He did not like to be reminded of his humble beginnings, now that he was a man of wealth and smoked high-priced cigars. Probably he would have given half his holdings to be rid of the nickname he hated. He whirled to his cutthroats.

"Cut loose on 'em, boys! Don't let a one of 'em git away!"

Bob's breath was coming rapidly. He wondered if he would hear the crash of the guns — or not. His eyes traveled wildly to the top of the ridge; if he only could get up there!

And suddenly his arm swept over his head in a signal. At the top of his voice, he yelled:

"*Down!*"

The sheepman's eyes darted up the ridge, following Bob's. He was just in time to see two men sink quickly behind a boulder. He shouted quickly to his men.

"Hold on, boys!"

Bob sneered down on him.

"Did you think," he asked with sarcasm, "that I'd be fool enough to poke my neck into a trap without leaving a way out? Tell those rats of yours to clear out of here!"

Johnson's face was red, even to his thick neck. Now it was his breath, not Bob's, that was coming rapidly. He spat an oath.

"If you're riddled, they won't do you no good."

"I know it," said Bob calmly. "Nor you either. If anyone shot from the ridge, who'd be the first to drop?"

Of course there was only one answer to that — Butch Johnson himself. The sheepman stood blustering inarticulately, his lips trembling with futile rage; he seemed to have but set a trap within a larger trap. Bob turned away contemptuously. He spoke to his men:

"Let's get out of here!"

Johnson hesitated. He glanced an instant at Bob, but immediately his eyes strayed nervously back to the ridge. He turned as though to enter his tent, where he would be out of sight.

"I wouldn't!" taunted Bob. "You mightn't get through the flap — pretty thin walls, anyway. Thirty men shooting down —"

"Let 'em go!" The sheepman flapped a hand toward his men, his face twisted with fury.

"Well, *adios*, Butch! I'll be seein' you!"

The circle separated, leaving a wide lane. Through it Bob rode calmly, followed by his men. Once more he waved toward the ridge top and shouted:

"Stay down, boys!"

Fifty yards clear of the circle, Red Selby rode up to him.

"Who — who's up there?" he whispered in amazement.

Bob turned toward him a face on which the sweat was beginning to appear; his own eyes looked almost as astonished as Red's.

"Wish I knew!" he whispered back. "Must be a couple of Butch's men that wandered up. I tried to shout like Butch."

"Good Lord!" gasped Red.

As they neared the ridgetop, the two men stood up to greet them — a shiftless-looking pair, seemingly more stupid than evil. One of them grinned knowingly at Bob.

"You an' Butch fixed it up like he wanted? You went to work for him?"

Bob answered coolly:

"Me and Butch talked things over; we know where we stand now. What are you two doing away up here?"

59

"Why, we thought we saw a deer crossin' the ridge, an' we figgered we might get a shot at it; we're sick o' mutton."

"I don't blame you for wanting something fit to eat, but you shouldn't have got so far away. Don't let it happen again." He looked at them severely, reprimandingly. "Better go down and see Butch; he has something to say to you."

He turned away, his face stern. The two looked shame-faced. As Bob crossed the top of the ridge, his last glimpse was of them strolling casually down toward the camp, their carbines trailing beside their thighs.

An old saying crossed Bob's mind: "Too many cooks spoil the broth." Too many cooks had surely spoiled Butch's — too many undisciplined men whom he could not watch. Bob gave himself no credit at all for the sudden wild inspiration that had come to him at sight of the two — the sudden wild gamble, rather, that was his last hope in desperation.

But the wide, respectful eyes of his men, turning toward him often, said that there might be another way of looking at the thing: Bob had bluffed on a pair of deuces — the other man's deuces, at that — and had forced his opponent to let him retire with half the stakes. Retire, to hold a stronger hand next time. That morning, the cowboys had been reasonably loyal to their range boss; now they were wholly loyal to Bob Edwards — to Big Bob Edwards, personally. If any of them had been given to abstractions, he might have said that Bob had already won a large and valuable stack of blues — that he had strengthened himself greatly for the next deal.

They went trotting down the ridge, safe from carbine fire from behind. A sharp-featured, sun-dried young fellow gulped a long breath; it seemed to him the first full breath he had dared to take in hours.

"*Whew-w-w!*"

"And," said Red suddenly, "jest think *what* Butch will have to say to them two when he finds out it was them!"

He threw back his head and laughed, a laugh broken by a shrill, wild yell that floated mockingly back over his shoulder and toward the sheep camp.

"Aw, shut up!" said Bob disgustedly, mopping his face. He spurred his horse and struck a fast lope. Perhaps in a month or two he could laugh at this — but not now.

CHAPTER
FIVE

More Mysteries

There were four or five days of comparative quiet. In this short time Bob found himself famous. Stories of him buzzed through northern Arizona — Homeric stories. There were so many versions of what had happened at the sheep camp that even the witnesses were beginning to wonder if their memories were not playing them tricks. He had planned it all with superhuman cleverness; he had carried it through with a cold-blooded, diabolical nerve that made "Billy the Kid" and his kind seem cowardly pikers. Just why he had not shot everyone in the sheep camp did not seem quite clear — unless he had just wanted to play with them.

All this sudden reputation made Bob feel so foolish that he could hardly look one in the eye. As far as he could see, all he had done was to walk blindly into a trap and escape from it by a sheer stroke of luck, but with little grace. He longed to collar every hero-worshiper and tell him the truth, but he realized that the current stories would help him in the coming fight.

There he was, between the horns of a dilemma; his natural unassuming honesty prompted him to tell the truth; policy advised him to help the stories along. The result was that he had little to say on any subject; he became almost taciturn. And of course everyone agreed that all those nerveless, iron fellows were thus modest and unassuming — until you stirred them up; and then . . . One could hardly blame a young man of Bob's quiet disposition for feeling disgusted.

Even the men who had been with him were inclined to join in the hero worship — all but the incorrigible Red Selby. Red, forming a nickname from a predecessor's, had once soberly addressed him as "Bobby the Bad". Only once! Red received a glare that sent him mumbling off, wondering if there wasn't, after all, something to that talk.

Bob, of course, had all his life heard long tales of stockmen's wars — had indeed heard minute accounts of most of them from men who had been participants. Even if he had not, common sense would have told him what to do; hire all comers at high wages, paying little attention to their ability as riders or ropers. He wired to every livery stable in northern Arizona that all who came would go on his payroll. Men came swarming like flies.

He departed from tradition in one respect; he deliberately offered slightly less than he knew Butch Johnson to be paying. The result was that the real "toughs" went to Johnson; those who came to the Bar Diamond had at least some conscientious scruples.

He got a wild-enough crew at that; there were a good many who seemed to be in it more for the love of a fight, of excitement, than for the money. Still, most of them seemed to come because they had been long out of a job and no other offered; the drought had hit their business hard. Some of these last did not seem overly enthusiastic about the thing, but Bob did not worry about them; he knew that they, with his old hands, would form the backbone of the outfit once they had time to work up partisan spirit, to get the feeling that they were really Bar Diamond cowboys.

Then, there was a surprising number who had quit their jobs on neighboring cow outfits to hire out to Bob. Some of these came for excitement, for the extra pay, because of their hatred of sheep and sheepmen, or for various reasons known only to themselves.

Why a great many others — steady men who had stuck on one ranch for years — had come, Bob could not figure out, until a few cautious questions elicited broad hints that they had come on their bosses' suggestions. The surrounding outfits did not want to get mixed up in the affair if they could help it, but they would give Bob all the undercover support they could.

Stella was back at the ranch, with a woman from town to keep her company and act partly as housekeeper. Bob had been so rushed that he had found little time to talk to her; it seemed to him that he was always trying to do six things at once and making a botch of all of them. A week or so after the affair at the sheep camp, he was talking to a neighboring cattleman who had dropped by, when he saw her beckon to him from the porch. He excused himself and went to her. He followed her into the living room.

"Sit down, Bob."

She motioned to a chair. She seemed worried, abstracted.

"How is he?" asked Bob quickly. He thought she was anxious about her father. They kept a relay of cowboys riding between the ranch and town to bring the twice-daily telegrams.

She handed him the latest yellow sheet. He read quickly:

BARNES OPERATION SUCCESSFUL STOP NOT OUT OF DANGER BUT DOING WELL STOP STRONG HOPE FOR RECOVERY

VARNEY

"Great!" Bob sprang to his feet, his eyes dancing.

Stella spoke quietly: "He's not out of danger yet."

"The heck he isn't! Varney don't know all the fight is in that easy-going little devil! *I* say it'll be no time till he's back here at the ranch, hoppin' around lively as a chipmunk."

She bent her head and sat looking into the cold fireplace. She spoke; her voice was low and very troubled:

"Will he have any ranch to come back to?"

"Huh?" Bob stared at her. "Isn't the outfit in fine shape? Oh, you mean the sheepmen. I don't think you need worry about that."

"I *don't* mean the sheepmen. The outfit is broke."

"Broke! You're — Why, Newt never owed anyone a cent! He had the strongest business of its size in Arizona!"

65

Now she raised her head to look at him. She seemed pale and drawn, but something indefinable reminded Bob of an expression he had seen on old Newt's face more than once — a set, dogged look that held more fight than any amount of bluster.

"Bob, I've just run onto the biggest mystery of all. We're broke — might as well sell the outfit and see if we have anything left."

Bob's lean brown face was usually handsome in a rugged way. It did not look so handsome now: his lower jaw was thrust out too grimly; there was a bleak look in his eyes, and his mouth widened, thinned, hung down at the corners, until it reminded one of some grizzled old Indian chief. Through his mind flashed the huge expense of paying and feeding all those men who kept drifting in. He had thought of it before without worrying very much; once a half-formed plan had come to him, to be immediately thrust away as unnecessary. Now he sprang to his feet.

"Wait here, Stell. I want to see old Simpson before he gets away."

He hurried out, hatless. He saw the cattleman to whom he had been talking just turning up the road on his horse. He gave a shrill, cowboy yell, and when Brad Simpson looked around, he beckoned with his whole arm. Brad came riding back, and at Bob's invitation dismounted and seated himself on the edge of the porch.

Bob sat down beside him, slowly and painstakingly rolling a brown cigarette. He knew very well that what one had to say did not always count so much as how one said it, and he was thinking hard to find the best manner of approach.

At last he got the cigarette lighted. He turned, and for a moment surveyed the cattleman in silence. Brad Simpson was medium-sized, gaunt, hard, with a thin, hooked nose and grizzled gray hair; very obviously a man who would form his own opinions and stick to them, right or wrong, like a bulldog. He had the name of being "close", too. He looked it. Bob's hope of getting anything out of him was none too strong.

"Well, Brad" — Bob knew that, with Brad, he had better come straight to the point and not waste words — "I've found out that the Bar Diamond has bit off a pretty big mouthful to chew. Just where do the rest of you cattlemen stand about helping us?"

Brad's face did not change, but it was quite a while before he spoke. He always thought before he spoke.

"Three of my men have quit me an' gone to work for you; they'll all fight. I don't want my outfit mixed up in no wars."

"I know you don't. But if we get licked, your place is right in line for the next raid; it would make fine sheep range."

"Well?"

"Well?" Bob echoed.

Old Brad stood up and shook his worn chaps straight.

"Three or four more o' my men are actin' restlesslike. I'll fire 'em when I get home, an' they may drift over this way. I think that'll be all you can expect of me."

Bob motioned to where the old man had been sitting

"Sit down, Brad. I'll throw my cards on the table."

"That's good. I figgered you had somethin' you was holdin' back." He sat down again.

Bob hated to say it, but he blurted:

"Brad, this outfit isn't in as good shape as people think; it can't stand all this expense." He waved to the men loafing around.

"Well?" Brad's lips were tightening.

"If we lose, you'll have the expense of trying to fight the sheepmen all by yourself — and danged little chance of winning. Then, to put it blunt, if this outfit goes broke, so does yours."

Old Brad hooked a boot heel on the edge of the porch. He wrapped his arms around his knee and sat gazing straight ahead, apparently absently, as though he had already forgotten what Bob had said last. Thus they sat in silence a very long time. At last Brad turned, to remark casually:

"Bob, I couldn't give you a check — nothin' with my name on it. Meet me in town tomorrow, an' I'll have somethin' in cash for you. Will that help?"

"*Will* it!"

"No — let it go a day or two; meet me Wednesday. I want to see some of the other cattlemen first." His lips tightened harshly. "I'll see to it that they all throw in as much as I do, accordin' to the number of cattle they have."

Bob felt like whooping. If old Brad couldn't jar money out of the neighboring cattlemen, nobody could; certainly he would do much better than Bob himself —

Bob would ask diffidently; old Brad would scold and demand. Yes, and receive.

"Say, Brad, you don't know how you —"

"Pfhut!" The old man made a snorting sound and started toward his horse. He turned back suddenly.

"You'd better drop over an' see Clay Bozart. I don't want no dealin's with that young pup."

"Clay isn't so bad."

"Huh! We'll see! We'll see how he antes up. I hate to watch a good outfit goin' to rack an' ruin."

Brad jerked his cinch tighter, climbed into his saddle, and rode away. Bob looked after him with a friendly eye. He guessed that about half of Brad's contribution would be meant for his share of the expenses, and the other half as a gift for his old friend Newt Davis, and Newt's daughter Stella, who had somehow managed to get the outfit in trouble. But Brad wouldn't admit this to anyone. Furthermore — Bob grinned to himself — having given a substantial amount, he would insist that other cattlemen with equal range give equal sums. And when old Brad insisted . . .

Suddenly his unfinished interview with Stella came back to Bob. What the heck *had* happened to the outfit anyway? What was the mystery she spoke of? He leaped to his feet and hurried into the living room.

He found Stella seated where he had left her, still staring into the fireplace as though she had not moved. He sat down in the chair he had occupied before.

"Well," he announced, "I've fixed it so's the other outfits will stand their share of the fight — money, I mean. You don't have to worry about that."

She nodded half-hearted thanks; it did not seem to interest her very much.

"What is it, Stella?" he demanded. "What came up, anyway?"

She faced him; she tried to keep her tone cool and businesslike:

"I was looking through Dad's papers today, and I found this in an old envelope."

She handed him a thumbed, creased sheet of paper, apparently several years old. He took it and spread it out on his knees. He began to read, his eyes widening in astonishment.

"Huh? *What?* Your father's note — for fifty thousand dollars!"

She nodded without speaking. He read again, gasped.

"Given to old John Bozart — Clay's father — before he died!" Bob could not believe it.

"And due three months ago."

"But," he blurted, "maybe it was paid — or this wouldn't be here."

She shook her head.

"Notice up in the corner; it's marked, 'Copy.'"

"Didn't you know anything about it — or your mother?"

Again she shook her head.

"No. We thought the outfit was in the clear."

"But what did he borrow it for? Where did it go?"

"That's it! Not into the outfit."

"Could old John —"

Bob bit the words off just in time. He had been about to ask if old John could have "had something on" her father. Well that he didn't — if he ever wanted to speak to the daughter again.

Bob thought back quickly, trying to recall Newt's manner toward John Bozart; it had always been cold and formal, as though he disliked the man, but always somewhat more than civil. At the time, Bob had taken it to be an effort to get along amicably with a neighboring cattleman whom he did not altogether like. It seemed to him now that there had been something peculiar in the mutual attitude of the two men. Stella's voice broke in on his thoughts.

"So now you know why the outfit's broke; of course it can't meet that note."

"Well" — Bob did not mean it for a platitude — "there's worse things than being broke." He was thinking of Newt.

"I know it; that's why I can stand it as well as I do. Dad's recovering. But" — her voice quivered — "what'll he do if he gets back and finds the outfit gone?"

Bob tried to make his voice sound mildly playful.

"Well, his daughter might marry some cowpuncher that can hold a steady job — or maybe get a little outfit of his own — an' take care of the old man."

Of course it was a wholly hypothetical case, dealing with an entirely imaginary cowboy to appear in the future. Nevertheless a little pink crept up under Bob's eyes; he became aware of the pink, and a second or two later his face and neck were flaming crimson. He added hastily, floundering:

"If she wasn't too good to marry a common cowpuncher!"

A trace of color returned to her face. She met his eye squarely.

"Her father was a cowpuncher, and she wouldn't marry anyone *but* a cowpuncher. But she wouldn't saddle her father and mother on a cowpuncher that couldn't afford to keep them — and she wouldn't leave them."

Something about how she said it made Bob feel like shouting, "Great girl!" But, of course, that wasn't the thing to say. What was?

Stella's voice came level, unhurried; it never occurred to Bob that she was deliberately and quickly changing the subject.

"But the outfit isn't lost yet. Do you think it has *any* chance?"

"Well, you saw what I got into the other day, and got out of. We might have some more luck."

Her head came up suddenly; she gave him a strange, speculative stare as though she had never seen him before and were sizing him up.

"We might, at that! When I was a little girl, I always believed Big Bob Edwards could do *anything*. Maybe I was right and — Excuse me, Bob; I must run back to the kitchen and see if Mrs. Doheney is getting dinner."

She walked calmly, with dignity, from the room. Bob stood staring after her, scratching the back of his neck. He felt that something had happened, or was going to happen — or something. Presently he picked up his hat and left the room.

That morning he had thought of himself as being as busy as six men; now it came to him that he had to do the work of seven — one of them a wealthy banker. Oh, well, he'd do the best he could, and if he lost the fight . . . He nodded vehemently several times.

Red Selby happened to be passing. Bob whirled suddenly on him.

"Listen here! Why aren't you down at the bunk house polishin' up your guns? We got to hold this range for the old man, *sabe*?"

Red stared. Bob was glaring at him fiercely.

"Good *night!*" murmured Red, as he walked off shaking his head. Those stories about Bob were true, after all; he was just as "hard" as everyone said he was.

But it never occurred to Bob that Stella was lying across her bed crying. Men don't understand girls — the girls see to that.

CHAPTER
SIX

Butch's Gunmen

Next day Bob rode over to see Clay Bozart. Although it was not more than ten miles to the Bozart headquarters, the country between was so rough that it took nearly two hours to get there. Bob had the copy of the mortgage in his pocket; he and Stella had not decided whether he was to mention it to Clay or not; she had left that up to him, to depend on circumstances.

Of course the logical thing was to telegraph old Newt to ask about it, but to upset him thus in his critical condition was clearly out of the question. Bob especially was averse to it; he had an uneasy suspicion that he could not drive away, a fear that behind that mortgage lay something that Newt would not want to be known. He cursed himself for suspecting that the kindly little man could ever in his life have done anything that could not bear the light of day — but how else could one explain it?

He had ridden less than five miles, trying to find an answer to the riddle, when a hoarse shout from a ridge made him look up quickly. He saw a man coming thundering toward him on a large, clumsy horse. The man shouted again — not the shrill yell of a cowboy, but a harsh, angry bellow. The man was shaking his fist.

Al Boyd, the nester! Bob suddenly realized that he was passing within a mile of Al's place. *Now what was the matter?*

Al came plunging up and nearly crashed into Bob before he could stop his own ungraceful mount. His face was almost purple. He sat shaking his fist almost under Bob's nose; he seemed too angry to speak.

"Good morning," said Bob gently, politely. It was about the most insulting thing he could say under the circumstances, but this fist-shaking business got under his skin.

"You — you —" At last Boyd found his voice; it was thick and inarticulate with rage. "Turn around an' ride back here with me; I got somethin' to show you, Mr. Cowboy."

"Sorry, Al, but I have something to do this morning besides ride around with nesters."

"I tell you you're comin' — or I'll know why!"

"What is it? How far?"

"Jest over the ridge. Come on!"

It struck Bob that there must be something indeed that Boyd thought of interest to him. He hesitated a second, and turned. Until they were halfway up the ridge, Boyd's horse was kept to its fast run. Bob, on a swift, wiry sorrel, easily kept alongside in a lope. Soon Boyd's horse was winded and had to be drawn down to a walk.

So they passed through the cedars, slowly, neither speaking. Bob looked thoughtful, grim. He was

75

remembering something that had made little impression on him at first: when Al came charging down the ridge, his hulking mount had slapped its left hind hoof down at every leap, in a peculiarly clumsy manner. Bob remembered the tracks at the ruin from which the ambusher had fired on Newt; this horse had had the same trick. He wished he had thought to examine Al Boyd's tracks back there. Suddenly Al's voice broke in on him again:

"Rope that calf!"

Bob looked ahead. In a little clearing stood a cow and her six-month-old calf.

"Rope her yourself, Al; she's too scrubby to be a Bar Diamond." Bob wasn't taking orders from the nester — and he had something else, too, on his mind.

With a snarl, Al unstrapped his thick maguey rope. He put the spurs to his horse and struck out after the calf. The cow and calf were gentle — they had probably been reared around the house — and so did not dash away in the swift run of true range stock. The nester threw a huge, wide loop, and missed.

Bob, following after, was not watching the man; his head was bent, studying the horse tracks. Bob was not an expert tracker as are desert cowboys; but as far as he could see, those hoofprints beside him were just like those he had found at the ruin; certainly the horse did slap its left hind foot in just the same manner.

Bob's face was hard as he looked up. He saw the nester make a second great loop, throw, and miss. With a third, it was the same. Bob was sick of the farce. He took his long, slender rawhide reata from his saddle horn, sent his wiry sorrel shooting ahead like a bolt, and presently a tiny loop was snapping deftly over the calf's head. There came a thud, a little spurt of dust.

Then Al was off his horse and racing with his pegging string in his hand to tie the calf's feet. As Bob rode up, coiling his reata, the nester took hold of a leg and quickly flopped the calf to the other side.

"Look at that!" he bellowed, pointing.

Bob blinked as though his face had been slapped. He dismounted, and stood staring down at the calf. There was no doubt of it; a black, fresh Bar Diamond brand stood out clearly on its side. The mother was in Boyd's AB iron; indeed, Bob hardly needed to see a brand to know that such poor stock did not belong to his outfit.

"*Now*, what you got to say?" demanded Boyd savagely.

Bob did not answer. He turned and began to break dry limbs from the nearest cedar. He built a little fire and, while it was mounting, went to his saddle and drew his short running iron from its scabbard. He waited in brooding silence while it heated, and then, still without a word, vented the brand.

A possible explanation came to him. He pulled a tally book and a stubby pencil from his chaps pocket, and very carefully wrote a description of the calf, turning it over to see both sides. Al Boyd, in his triumph, could not be silent any longer.

"Drawin' a picter of it?" he asked gloatingly.

Bob snapped the book shut and thrust it back into his pocket.

"Sort of. All my men are going to have a good description of this calf — just in case any more might turn up vented from our brand to yours."

It would be just like a dumb nester to try such a game as that — have Bob vent one calf, and then rebrand a few more that looked like this one. A real cattleman wouldn't even think of such a childish trick.

"What — what you hintin' at, cowpuncher?"

"I'm hinting," remarked Bob coolly, "that you'd do well to keep a civil tongue in your head, if you know what's good for you."

They were facing each other, close. The nester did not dare risk gun play with Bob; he had sense enough to know that he would have no chance whatever. But there were other ways besides shooting. Suddenly his fist darted up from near his hip. One blow would crush this cowboy's head — Al knew his own terrible strength.

There came a sharp crack. Al found himself stretched on the ground. He knew his strength, but there were several things he didn't know: that a huge, muscle-bound man cannot box; that speed more than mere weight determines the force of a blow, as it does of a bullet; that starting a punch from the hip is mighty bad judgment. Nor had he suspected Bob's talent as a fist fighter; Bob had reached the age where he never talked of his fights and would rather forget them.

The big nester sat up. His mouth was wide open; it gave him a rather silly look. If he felt anger, it was drowned in utter amazement; it had never occurred to him that anyone could knock *him* down.

"You — you —"

"Knocked you down, Al. How did you like it?"

Still Al sat gasping. Bob gave him a glance of contempt, swung on his heel, mounted, and rode slowly off. Slowly, because he was debating with himself whether or not he should go back and take Boyd to town to the sheriff, charging him with the shooting of Newt and Jack Daly.

No; the evidence, plain enough though it was to Bob himself, might not make much impression on a jury. Bob could not carry horse tracks to town to show in court; even if he did, probably half the jurymen could not tell a horse track from a mule track. Fusees? They, too, would mean little after a clever lawyer got through explaining them. Forty-four-forty shell? No, it wouldn't do. He'd find more evidence later on, and if he didn't — well, he wouldn't let Boyd get away with it, law or no law.

Following an abandoned road — a shorter and better one had been built to the Bozart ranch — he came upon a deserted homestead, the house and corrals weathered and going to ruin. Someone was camping there; he saw horses in the corral. Probably some of Bozart's men; both his and the Bar Diamond cowboys stayed there on occasion when working cattle in the neighborhood. Bob shouted, but no one answered, so he rode on without stopping.

When he reached the V4, he found Clay pottering about, mending the door of the saddle house. It annoyed him to see Clay wasting his time thus instead of being out looking after his cattle; the boss was doing the work of a boy who could be hired for ten dollars a month, and doing it badly at that.

Clay was by now all over his spree. His skin seemed clearer than when Bob had seen him last, and he had a livelier air. He waved a hand; he seemed delighted to see Bob.

"Why, hello, stranger; long time no see you here."

"Howdy, Clay. Just thought I'd drop over."

"Glad you did, Bob; glad you did. Light an' set down."

Bob dismounted, and they seated themselves in the wide opening of the saddle-house door. Bob reached for his tobacco, but Clay hurriedly pulled his out and offered it; he seemed bent on doing his visitor every possible honor. They rolled cigarettes, and Clay lighted both, shielding the match with his hand.

"Well, Bob, what's the good word?"

In the cattle country, as among Indians, it is regarded as a breach of etiquette to bring up business immediately upon one's arrival; a certain amount of small talk should be indulged in first.

"Say," asked Bob indifferently, "is that some of your men camped at that old place this side of Al Boyd's?"

"Uh-huh. I got three o' my boys over there — to see if they can't steal a few head off the Bar Diamond."

Bob grinned. "I can't remember us asking you to vent any brands lately."

"We're too slick!" assured Clay.

"You beat me, then," remarked Bob glumly. "I had to vent one on the way over here."

"Huh?" Clay glanced at him, saw that he meant it. "Ours? Some mistake one o' yore men made?" he asked.

"No — Al's."

Bob told him the whole story. Clay shook his head.

"Bob, I think you got it wrong. Al don't know as much about cattle as us that was raised in the business, but he has better sense than to try anything as raw as that. I figure it must be that some o' yore men made a mistake an' misbranded it."

"Don't sound likely to me."

"You know how cowboys are. One gets as much fun out of range-brandin' a big calf as a dude hunter does out of findin' a deer. Lots of cowboys that are honest every other way don't spend much time lookin' around for the mother when they find a big slick-ear."

"Well, it *could* have happened that way, I reckon; but I wouldn't put that trick past Boyd."

"Oh, he ain't so bad. I was ridin' over near his place a couple o' days ago an' met him. What do you suppose? Danged if he didn't ask me in for dinner. A real feed, too, he gave me."

"He did!"

"Uh-huh." Clay looked ahead unseeingly, licking his lips. "Say," he murmured, "that's a slick-lookin' piece o' calico he has. Wonder how she come to take up with him?"

Bob caught more in Clay's words than appeared on the surface. He turned, to growl half angrily:

"Clay, I'd advise you to have some sense an' keep your eyes off married women."

"I didn't mean nothin'!" hastened Clay. "But that little blonde is a lot too good for the likes of him. Smart as a whip, too."

"Listen here, you poor fool!" Bob took the liberty of long acquaintance. "There's plenty of girls in Danvers. Leave Mrs. Boyd alone, or Al will plug you so fast you won't know what happened; that feller's dangerous."

"Bunk!"

"I know town fellers do that sort of thing — bothering respectable women and girls — but a cowboy's supposed to have more principle; we're not town fellers."

From Bob's tone, he seemed to regard all "town fellers" as too low to be classed as human beings. Certainly the cowboys' peculiarly strict code of honor was something foreign to a large number of the somewhat ratty young men who infested the cow towns. Clay, on his many drinking bouts, had associated too much with men of the latter kind.

"Aw, Bob" — Clay looked disgusted — "you're makin' a mountain out of a gopher hill. I didn't mean it that way. Can't I say a woman is good-lookin'?"

Bob did not know whether to believe Clay or not. He could hardly realize that he himself, like most cowboys, was inclined to be a little too "techy", as he'd have called it, in protecting the character of a woman. He changed the subject, by telling Clay fully of his conversation with old Brad Simpson, of their plan to collect money to carry on the battle against the sheepmen.

"So," he concluded, Mrs. Boyd forgotten by this time, "if you could — uh — I mean, yore outfit is bigger than old Brad's. That is —" He stopped, floundering. It was a lucky thing indeed that Brad had taken upon himself the job of collecting the contributions; Bob was proving a ghastly failure at it.

Presently Clay spoke:

"Bob, this outfit is in worse shape than yores — what with the drought an' the low price o' beef. I shore do want to do my part, but I ain't got the money right now. Maybe next week — in a few days."

Bob knew Clay's failings well enough to know that his "few days" meant never; Clay would mean well, but he could not raise the money, would not get around to it. He was about to ask if the other could not, then, supply a few men, when Clay spoke again.

"Bob, there's somethin' else I wanted to see you about. I — should have seen to it sooner, but I didn't want to bother old Newt — an' then he got shot, an' — an' I didn't want to bother Stella right away." Clay's face was red.

"You mean this?"

Bob drew the copy of the mortgage from his pocket.

"That's it! You — come over to do somethin' about it?"

"I come over to tell you we can't meet the note."

"That's — that's tough!"

Clay looked supremely uncomfortable. Bob felt almost sorry for him; he could understand how he must feel. Probably broke himself, in danger of losing his outfit, and so compelled to foreclose a mortgage on a neighbor. Yes, Clay must be about broke. He mismanaged his outfit in every way imaginable; he hardly pretended to look after it.

"What did old Newt get the money for, do you know?"

"I ain't got an idea. But it was takin' so much out of this outfit that got it into the shape it's in. Don't blame me, Bob, for lettin' the place run down; it was that way when my old man died — that fifty thousand."

That, to Bob, was another way of looking at it; perhaps there was some truth in what Clay said. But the place certainly had not improved under Clay's management.

"Well," asked Bob, "how much more time can you give us?"

"I — I'm sorry —"

Bob's heart sank. No time given.

"Ten days?" he asked, half-heartedly; ten days would do him no good.

"I — I reckon." Clay shifted his feet uncomfortably; the slight postponement seemed to be forced out of him because he was too weak to resist. "Bob — I — I —"

"I know!" sighed Bob. "I don't blame you, Clay; it's your money, an' you've let it go more than three months now."

There was silence for a moment, both men too embarrassed to speak. Bob broke the silence, speaking half to himself:

"I'll try the banks; I might be able to borrow the fifty thousand — have them take over the note."

84

Of course he knew it would be a waste of time to try. With drought, and with the price cattle brought, he would be laughed at for asking half the sum. But Clay looked up eagerly, hopefully.

"Think you can raise it, Bob?"

"Well, I might raise some of it. How much would you need to run you a while, till things get straightened out on the Bar Diamond — I mean till we see how old Newt comes out?"

"Why, a couple thousand would settle up some of the most pressin' things. If you can get me that, I can give you a month, anyway, before I'll want any more. You know I won't crowd you 'less I have to."

Bob had a plan now: He could draw two thousand of his own savings if absolutely necessary, and give it to Clay. He had every confidence that Newt would straighten the matter out when he came home, and repay his loan. If Newt died — well, he could have Clay guarantee to pay back the two thousand if he had to take over the Bar Diamond.

Either way, there was no risk in it, and he figured he owed more than that slight accommodation to the outfit that had reared him. He had had a small account all his life at the Danvers bank, and he had kept on sending his money there while down south; there had been no bank near him there. He had worked hard for this money, gone without many things he would have liked; very naturally he was reluctant to part with it. He'd put Clay off as long as he could, but he'd have the money if Clay found himself too hard-pressed.

"Well, I should be able to raise that much. Give me a little time, will you?"

"Heck, yes! Every minute I can without losin' this outfit. I don't want to —" Clay shook his head gloomily and did not finish.

"Sell us out. I know. And shore thanks for the extra time; it's white of you, Clay."

"Aw —"

Clay turned on his heel and went off hurriedly; he didn't want to listen to thanks. Bob nodded after him. He was perhaps Clay's last friend, the last one who would say a good word for him. Not that he could feel toward Clay the respect that must go with full friendship — the young fellow had too many faults, too many weaknesses, for that — but he did feel sympathy toward him. If Clay had been born short of willpower and other desirable things, that was his misfortune, not his fault; but he had his good points, too — pretty darned good ones, when one knew him well. Bob nodded again, swung on his horse, and rode off.

The second day after that, Bob rode to Danvers, alone, to meet old Brad Simpson. He had considered taking two or three men with him, because of the amount of cash he would be bringing back, but he had decided that that would be a totally unnecessary precaution — nobody would know about it; the cattlemen contributing would be the very last to want it to get out that they were supporting the fight.

He had hardly tied his horse and stepped up on the board sidewalk when the swinging doors of a saloon burst open almost in his face. Boyd, the giant nester, stood there looking at him. Al's face was slightly flushed; evidently he had been drinking.

"Hyar you, Bob! Saw you through the window." The liquor had brought out a strong Kentucky accent which Bob had not noticed before.

Bob's heart sank. The last thing he wanted was a fight now. His eyes flashed over the nester, and he could not help seeing that Boyd, dressed up for town, made a striking figure. His great body was covered by a long black coat of a style somewhat out of date but quite imposing. Black trousers, with the boot tops inside. Low stiff collar with a black string tie; black, wide-brimmed hat. Everything was scrupulously clean; his wife's doings, thought Bob.

The nester came forward; he could walk straight. Bob was almost panic-stricken; he did not know what to do. And then a great paw crashed down on his shoulder.

"Bob, you're all right!"

The truth dawned slowly on Bob: Al was in the best of humor toward him. Liquor often completely reverses a man's disposition; it seemed to have made Al the soul of geniality, without an enemy in the world.

"Come on in, Bob, an' have a drink on me."

Bob was only too glad to comply, for the sake of the peace. They entered the saloon. The nester spoke to the bartender in the voice of a foghorn.

"Give Bob a drink — best in the house!"

He turned to the little crowd with a grand wave of his hand.

"Look at him — at Bob! That's the feller knocked me down. Knocked *me* down!"

He seemed to be taking great pride in showing an eighth wonder of the world. To Bob flashed back the strange liking for this man that had come to him after their first meeting. Anyone who could take a licking in this spirit, drunk or sober, could not be very bad.

"Heck, Al," murmured Bob diffidently, "that was only a sort of accident; you'd knock my head off next time."

"I might, at that. But you're too good a man to fight me — so am I."

A pretty mixed statement, but Bob understood what he meant.

"Well," the bartender drawled, wiping a glass, "I hope neither of you cute little tricks get drunk enough to take a paste at the wall; I don't want this joint tumblin' around my ears."

The nester roared hugely, as though this were some splendid joke which only he and Bob could understand. Bob finished his drink.

"How about another?" he asked.

"Got plenty now, Bob. What'll the little woman say if I go home showin' signs?"

"Would she raise Cain?" Bob grinned slightly at thought of the tiny woman scolding this giant.

"Huh! She ain't that kind. Bob — listen — she's the finest little woman — Well, I ain't the kind of man to have his wife an' fambly see him showin' signs. This'll be wore off before I get home. I bought her some blue ribbon."

"Al," Bob spoke seriously, "do you know, I come to figger you're a pretty darned good feller, after all."

"I am; so are you." No argument there. "Well, I got to be a-gittin' back to the little woman. So long, Bob."

Bob watched the huge back go through the swinging doors. And that was the man who had shot Newt! Who, wondered Bob, was good, and who was bad?

Kentucky — that explained it; a Kentucky mountaineer and feudist, taught since childhood that it was a point of honor to bushwhack and kill the enemy of his family. And Al had thought gentle little Newt his enemy! Bob sighed as he pushed through the doors; he could wish it had been someone else besides Al Boyd.

And then it came to Bob that Boyd, sober, would as likely as not take a shot at him himself the first chance he got — or might even make a chance. Bob shook his head; things were getting too involved for him.

Now to see about getting that two thousand dollars. Bob knew that technically he could not demand money from a savings account without ninety days' notice to the bank. This rule was not usually enforced unless the sum happened to be very large, but Bob judged it wise not to let the matter go until Clay forced his demand; something *might* come up.

The cashier had to whisper to the manager, and there was a slight trace of annoyance toward Bob, but the money was produced, in large bills.

"Maybe you'd better put the balance in a checking account. I might need some of it."

"It's better. We don't like to have to break a savings account without notice," said the cashier.

Bob waited while the man opened the new account. He would have liked to have put the two thousand in it, too, but after his sudden demand he thought he'd wait until next time he came to town — unless Clay needed it sooner. He thanked the cashier for overlooking the bank's rule, shoved the new check book into his pocket, and went out to the sidewalk. Here he paused to look up and down the street.

He saw a horse he recognized as Brad Simpson's tied outside another saloon — the Blue Front. Brad would be there; he had undoubtedly left the horse directly outside as a sign. Bob went down the sidewalk and entered. Three or four men were lounged against the bar; Brad was seated by himself at a table back in a corner. Bob strolled casually back to him. Brad was standing up as though to leave, thrusting an envelope into his pocket.

"Hello, Brad."

"Howdy, Bob."

They shook hands. Bob felt something bulky, crisp, left in his hand; the others in the saloon could not see this, for Bob's back was to them.

"Drink, Brad?"

"No, thanks. Jest dropped in here to write a letter. How's things out yore way?"

"Pretty good. Shore wish it would rain; the country's burnin' up."

"Uh-huh." Brad moved toward the street door; apparently it was but the most casual of meetings.

Bob, of course, could not leave immediately after Brad. He strolled to the bar and ordered a drink.

Absently, his fingers buttoned the flap of his right chaps pocket; there was something very valuable there now.

One foot on the rail, he chatted casually with the bartender. Old Man Dukes had pneumonia now and wasn't expected to live. The Rafter H had shipped the day before. Had Bob heard that Lem Shultz had broke the faro bank at the Spreadeagle? But the darned fool had lost most of it back next night; he'd be in the hole again inside of a week.

Presently Bob finished his drink and hitched his chaps straight, preparing to leave. The doors swung open, and a thickset, square-jawed man stood glancing into the bar-room. Butch Johnson!

He saw Bob at the bar. He spoke to someone behind him and entered. Four others followed, one of them Blackie Dobbs. For an instant the eyes of each flicked toward Bob, and then they seemed studiously to avoid seeing him. They strolled down the room slowly, spurs clinking. They separated, two of them going beyond Bob, three remaining between him and the door. All went to the bar and calmly ordered drinks.

The three or four others in the room hastily emptied their glasses and hurried out, wiping their mouths with the backs of their hands. Immediately they had left, Bob cursed himself for the mistake he had made; he should have gone with them, or forced a showdown while there were neutral witnesses. In the first place, he shouldn't have let the sheepmen get on both sides of him; now, whatever way he turned, he would have men at his back.

Five witnesses to say that he had started the trouble. The bartender's word could not do much against the five — even if he would tell the truth, which was unlikely; he'd be afraid.

Bob started casually to step away from the bar. He didn't think they'd let him, but they did. He had hardly moved when he saw two men sliding down to close in behind him. That wouldn't do! He backed hastily to where he had been, and the two slid away. Butch spoke; his eyes were hard.

"Bob, I been thinkin' over some things you said to me the other day, an' I'm inclined to take 'em personal."

"I meant it that way, Butch." Coolly.

He might as well say that as anything else. He wondered if his gun was loose in the holster; he dared not precipitate things by touching it to find out. He wished wildly that he had two guns; he had never carried more than one. Now Butch stepped out from the bar and stood facing him; there were two men on each side. Bob rolled and lighted a cigarette.

"Well, Butch, it looks like you got me, don't it?"

CHAPTER
SEVEN

Robbed

Bob appeared calm, almost unconcerned. He coolly flicked the ashes from his brown cigarette. Inwardly, he was in pretty much of a panic, but he couldn't let that show on his face; at least he would not give the sheepmen the satisfaction of knowing they had him scared. Butch spoke:

"Goin' to apologize, Bob?"

It ran through Bob's mind that an apology would be easy to give and would mean little, especially since he had nothing in particular to apologize for. But of course it would do no good; those men were there to kill him on one pretext or another. So why apologize?

Bob pursed his lips and blew a little cloud of smoke into the air. It seemed the coolest thing in the world. He turned his head slowly a trifle, his eyes a trifle more, to give Butch an almost amused glance.

"Me! Apologize to a sheepherder!"

Bob felt hugely proud of himself; he had not thought it was in him to carry it through thus. But cool though he appeared, his mind seemed to be straying disconnectedly. He remembered having heard that a man facing death in the jaws of a lion felt no fear.

Perhaps he was in the same condition — sort of numbed. Well, so long as the sheepmen didn't see him show scare, it was all right. Butch spat an admiring oath.

"Bob, you got *nerve!*"

"Uh-huh — some."

"Say, let's talk it over again — about you goin' to work for me. Honest, I need yore kind bad; you'd be surprised at what I'm willin' to pay you."

"I'd be more surprised, Butch, to find myself workin' for a sheep outfit."

Bob's cigarette had gone out; he found himself lighting it, then slowly waving the match out and dropping it. The red-faced sheepman spat out one of the vilest words in his large vocabulary. He wheeled suddenly toward his men, his mouth opening to give an order.

But the swing doors moved, and three more men entered the room. The first was medium-sized, nearing middle age, with a thoughtful, almost timid look on his face. Sheriff Ben Wilson! There, thought Bob, was a man who had *real* nerve, and didn't have to force himself to act coolly. The two following him? Deputies, probably.

The three entered with that peculiar, slow, rolling walk often found in men who have spent their lives in the saddle — not unlike the swaying gait of sailors ashore. That their coming was wholly fortuitous was clear from Wilson's surprised glance at seeing Bob with sheepmen — a glance he quickly hid. He came toward the bar.

"Drinks, everyone?"

Bob answered quietly: "Thanks, Sheriff, but I'd rather not if you don't mind; just had one. I was just leaving."

Without hurrying, without looking back, he went toward the door. He heard a shuffle of someone starting to follow him, but the sheriff spoke again:

"Jest a minnit, Butch. I want to see you about somethin'; heard you was in here."

Bob could not guess from the calm drawl whether Wilson really did want to see Butch or had grown suspicious of what might be going on. Anyway, nobody followed him out.

He hurried around the corner to the livery stable. He had meant to saddle quickly and get out of town, but by the time he reached the dilapidated old building, his knees felt slightly queer; he was glad that there was no one there to see him.

He sat down on a bale of hay, and cursed himself for every kind of coward he had ever heard of. It never occurred to him that it is but human nature to feel more scared after a danger has passed than while it is present. Whew-w! Hope he didn't get into *that* kind of jam again!

A half hour later he had almost regained his composure. He heard the hollow clatter of a horse coming up the wooden driveway from the street. He looked up to see Brad Simpson swinging from his saddle. The old man's face was a mask of fierce, grim joy.

"Well, Bob, I heard about it!"

" 'Bout what?"

"The doin's in the Blue Front — the bartender told all of us. Young feller, you got the nerve of a frozen rattlesnake."

"Oh, shore!" groaned Bob disgustedly. Soon he added: "I won't lie about it, Brad; I was scared stiff — shivering inside all the time."

Old Brad grinned sarcastically.

"Well, how did you expect to feel — like doin' a jig-dance? Nerve ain't not bein' scared — it's kickin' scare in the seat o' the pants an' standin' there. Like you did."

"I haven't got nerve," insisted Bob stubbornly.

"Well," compromised Brad dryly, "you'll do till someone comes around that has. How long'll that money I gave you last?"

Bob shook his head gloomily.

"Not long. Over fifty men now, and more piling in every day. I'm paying 'em eighty-five a month, and feeding 'em; you see how it mounts up."

Brad sighed.

"Yore old hands — they only gettin' regular wages?"

"Getting the same as the rest — I haven't told 'em yet. I'm going to play fair with them."

Brad gasped.

"You're an ijit! Old hands should fight without any extra."

"They would — but I won't let 'em." Bob's chin was beginning to jut out as it did when he was stubborn.

Brad shook his head and groaned.

"You're a *fine* business man!"

Bob changed the subject:

"How much more can you raise?"

"*I* dunno." The gloomy tone said, "What's the use, anyway?"

"Well, do your dangdest."

Bob stood up and went to the box stall for his horse. Brad immediately replaced him on the bale of hay, where he sat staring glumly at the floor. Bob had saddled and was leading his horse out when the old man raised his head for the first time.

"Bob, how — uh — how many old hands have you?"

"Eleven."

"You was payin' 'em — how much?"

"Forty."

"Forty times eleven . . ." His voice trailed bitterly away.

"Danged old skinflint!" muttered Bob under his breath as he left the livery barn.

He had a few purchases to make before going home. The news of the affair in the Blue Front must have spread all over town, added to wild yarns of his doings at the sheep camp. In the stores the customers stepped back respectfully and the clerks came hurrying to wait on him. When he bought a dozen sacks of tobacco and a few tablets of papers, the clerk made more fuss over it than if he had sold half the stock for cash. His manner seemed to waver between servility and the familiarity of old pals; Bob could not recall having ever seen him before. People he could not remember went out of their way to say "Hello, Bob!" deferentially.

Bob wondered what sort of story the bartender was telling anyway. Of course, as the only neutral eye-witness, he would make the best of it; he would be all puffed up over his temporary importance, and besides it would bring lots of business.

As Bob left the store, he almost ran into a little group coming down the sidewalk. There was a pool-hall loafer, a cowboy, and between them they dragged a man whose toes scraped the ground and whose head rolled queerly. Bob sniffed with disgust. Some fool dead drunk! The loafer was grinning broadly at what he thought a very funny situation; the cowboy was red of face and muttered feeling things under his breath.

Clay Bozart! With a shock of surprise Bob recognized the drunken man; he grunted disgustedly. Clay did not recognize him. The V4 owner was too far gone; his eyes were rolled back in his head.

The loafer grinned a cheerful "Howdy, Bob!" that went unanswered. The cowboy's red face turned even deeper red; he glanced away in order not to meet Bob's eye, although — or perhaps because — they were old friends. This young man, "Slim" Blake, had worked with Bob on the Bar Diamond years before; a fairly good hand with horses and cattle, and a cheerful, willing fellow whom everyone liked.

Bob walked dejectedly down the street; he hated to see Clay in that condition. He entered another store, and when he came out again, he found Slim waiting for him on the sidewalk.

"Bob, need another cowhand?" Slim's face had a dogged, disgusted look.

"Matter, Slim?"

"Huh! When I have to drag the boss down the street, dead drunk, an' throw him in a box stall — well, I'm through!"

"Heck, Slim, Clay has his good points." Bob had to force himself to say it.

"I know it; he's the best-hearted feller I ever worked for — shore fine to us boys. But enough is enough, Bob; I'd rather have to work harder for some other outfit an' keep a little self-respect, sort of."

Bob had been vaguely considering a certain plan, but he had not been able to think of a man who could help him carry it through. How about Slim?

"Slim, I'll pay you eighty-five a month to go to work for Butch Johnson. Likely he'll give you as much more."

"Huh?" The cowboy stared; he did not get the point.

"Then you might meet me once in a while and let me know what's going on — how many men he has, and what he's paying 'em, and anything else you can find out."

"Spyin'?" Slim seemed torn between the temptation of the huge double wages and a dislike for anything underhand.

"Well, sort of. But I know very well Butch has men spying on us; it would be only giving ourselves an even break."

"Dang it, Bob — I — uh — I don't know what to say."

"Don't want to see the sheepmen win, do you?"

"Sheep!" Disgust at the word crossed Slim's face. "Well, Bob, I reckon anything you do to sheepmen is fair enough — only too danged good for 'em. All right, I'll hire out to a sheep outfit."

His face looked as though someone were holding a rotten egg under his nose. Bob had to struggle hard to keep from grinning.

"Fine, Slim! Let's not be seen together. You can get word to me if anything comes up."

"Wisht I could get my back wages now," grumbled the cowboy, "but it'll be tomorrow mornin' anyway before Clay can set up an' make out my time. Dang the fool! He's a pretty good kid most ways."

He started toward his horse, but turned back.

"Say, I saw Al Boyd doin' a lot o' talkin' with Butch in the saloon. Better keep an eye on that nester."

"I will; don't worry!"

"Better; he's *bad*."

He mounted and rode away. Bob paused to roll a cigarette, and presently he too was trotting out of town.

He felt very important and slightly awe-stricken at having so much cash on him. Lucky thing that nobody knew that he was carrying all this; it would be easy for some hold-up man to take a shot at him out of the cedars.

He rolled the two little bundles into one, which he tied securely with a leather thong fished from a pocket. Then he had the valuable package buttoned safely in his chaps. Yes, he'd drop back to town in a day or two and put the two thousand in his checking account.

The roll he'd got from Brad — it would last no time, with the big gang he'd have to pay and feed. Wouldn't be so bad if it were only money. How many poor cowboys would lie dead out in the cedars before this thing was over? Would it be another Tonto Basin war? Looked as though it might.

He was riding through a little gulch half a mile from the edge of town, the road following a wash. His horse raised its head and pricked its ears forward. Bob glanced toward where the horse was looking. He had a brief flash of a crouching man half concealed in the bushes, of a carbine pointed at him.

He knew no more.

His first consciousness was a feeling of dull, dismal pain in his head. Slowly it came to him that he was lying somewhere, that his shoulders were lower than the rest of his body.

Presently he managed to open his eyes, but he could see nothing except a blur. There seemed to be something filling his eyes, he passed a shaky hand across them. Huh! His hand was wet, smeary.

He tried to rise, but only slipped farther down the hill. Another effort; this time he sat up. He found that he had rolled halfway down the fill at the lower side of the narrow road. He tried to remember whether Conejo had bucked him off or had fallen with him — couldn't have bucked; he hadn't bucked in nearly two years, and never very hard. But what had made the darned animal fall?

Bob tried to stand; he staggered and sat down again, heavily. Wow, but he'd taken a tumble! Dang a horse that will fall while traveling in a slow trot! Most old, stove-up horses did it sometimes, but Conejo was young and active, and freshly shod with his hoofs pared short. Like most cowboys, Bob dreaded a fall with a slowly traveling horse. It comes unexpected, when one is relaxed; it is nearly sure to catch one.

Well, he could stand up at last — sure wobbly!

He climbed painfully up the bank and into the road. There stood Conejo fifty yards off, with hanging reins. The saddle? A trace of mild panic came to Bob; a fall like that could tear up an eighty-dollar saddle, might even break the tree. Bob could walk pretty well by this time, although his knees felt shaky. He hurried to the horse and began an inspection of his riding gear.

Why, there wasn't a mark on the saddle! His rope hung in neat coils, and the saddle strings hadn't even got crossed over the top. What the — !

His head was clearing by this time. He suddenly remembered the precious little package he had been carrying. His hand fell to his right chaps pocket. He found it — empty.

Only then he remembered the carbine muzzle pointing at him from the bushes beside the road. Could it be — ? He inspected the saddle more closely, examined Conejo for skinned knees. No, the horse had not fallen. He felt the wound above his right ear.

There was one quick way to settle the thing: he went to where he had noticed his hat lying by the roadside, picked it up. That settled it; a sharp stone couldn't tear through a good Stetson in that manner.

Numbly, without the least hope of success, he climbed down the bank, searching every inch of the way. Of course he didn't find that little bundle. He scrambled back up to the road.

Where was it he had caught that glimpse of the man? Was it behind that algerita bush? He went up there. Behind the bush, the signs were plain, although brushed over very carefully.

And there lay an empty .44-40 cartridge. Bob picked it up and smelled it. It had a strong tang of burned powder; it had been fired very recently. He thrust it into his pocket.

He pottered around, mooned around; between his aching head and the loss of the money, he felt gloomy indeed. By rights there should be a huge boot track here; there always was. But search as he might, he could not find it this time; he could find nothing but the shell.

The man must have left his horse up on the ridge and picked his way here on stones, so as not to leave tracks. And those he had been forced to make behind the algerita bush he had carefully obliterated. After doing that, he had rushed down, quickly snatched the money from Bob's pocket, and disappeared, stealing back up to his horse. Of course he had taken Bob for dead, with all that blood over his face and head and shoulders; pretty mess he must have looked!

Bob sat down on a boulder and thought. Not a bit of use in telling Sheriff Wilson; no use in letting anyone know that he had suffered this loss. Who had done it? He had not been able to recognize the man.

Boyd? The nester had left town not so very long before him. Al had been half drunk — or was he just pretending to be? Why had he been so unexpectedly friendly with Bob — and before witnesses? Looked very much like a clever scheme to throw suspicion away from him.

Of course it might have been done by Butch and his four men — or one or two of the most trusted. Butch had tried to kill him once that day; and besides, his taking the money would prove a severe blow to the Bar Diamond. Yes, Butch would do it, gladly.

But how had he — or anyone else — found out that Bob was carrying the money? Nobody would know of his meeting with Brad but the two of them and Stella. Nobody at all knew of his own two thousand — unless he had been spied on through the bank window.

He returned to the road. He knew it was futile, but he searched once more in the place where he had lain. He saw a little pool of water in the rocks of the wash; he went to it and washed his face and head thoroughly. He wet his neckerchief and removed all he could of the blood on his shirt. His hat? That was ruined; he'd have to get another.

The cattlemen's money as well as his own, gone — money badly needed. Well, as he'd lost it, there was but one thing he could do — pay it back. Things might go bust without it. He groaned.

Five years of saving and scrimping and planning, raising enough to buy a little outfit. And there it went.

With it, too, went all his dreams of his own brand. It might be ten years before he could save that much again; good jobs like his last did not hang on bushes. Why the devil had he ever got mixed up in a sheep war anyway — even Newt's?

He swung dejectedly into his saddle and retraced the short distance to town. By the back way, he entered old Doctor Jones's unobserved. The pottering old man dressed his head without asking any questions. Of course he knew that there was a cattle-sheep war on; anyway, he had lived long enough in Arizona not to show curiosity about such things. He even sent out for a new hat and shirt for Bob.

Quite presentable now, but with the edge of the white bandages showing under his hat, Bob rode down to the false-fronted business section of town and entered the bank. At a desk, he slowly wrote a check for five hundred. He had not counted what Brad gave him, but he could put his balance back when he found out how much it was. Could not have been much under five hundred.

Every letter and figure he wrote seemed to pain him; each stroke of the scratchy pen represented days of toil and hardship and saving and planning. At last he shoved the little slip through the window. The cashier glanced curiously at the bandages peeping from under his hat. To his question, Bob answered shortly:

"Horse fell on me — just cut up a little."

For the first time the cashier looked at the check; his hand was absently reaching toward a little pile of bills at his left. He turned to Bob quickly, surprised at this second demand.

"You — you want cash?"

"Uh-huh."

Bob watched the bills being counted out to him; he thrust them carefully in his pocket.

"You've a lot of money to be carrying on you, Bob," remarked the cashier.

"Think so?" asked Bob with feeling.

He returned to the street and mounted. This time he was not going to be such a fool; he'd wind around among the cedars until he got back to the ranch. He rode out a side street and over a hill, far from any road. When he got home, he'd put the money in the safe.

Heck! He'd forgotten that someone had torn the safe up; he must still be pretty groggy. Awful wallop he'd got; Doctor Jones had said that just a hairbreadth farther in and he'd have been done for. Sheep wars — bah!

CHAPTER
EIGHT

Boss's Orders

This time Bob arrived home without incident. He found a little delegation awaiting him. He had barely unsaddled his horse when it approached. At the head, evidently the spokesman, was "Whitey" Wheeler.

This Whitey was perhaps the only man on the Bar Diamond at first sight of whom one would be inclined to think "gunman". He was sallow, cold-eyed, with a thin mouth. He always spoke in a dry drawl, almost too low to be heard — a voice strangely devoid of the slightest expression, as though he were absently talking to himself. Most of his type had gone to the sheepmen for the higher wages offered; indeed, Bob thought it more than curious that Whitey had chosen the cattle outfit, so curious as to be suspicious.

"Howdy, Bob," drawled Whitey in his weak, dry voice. He spoke looking fixedly into the air to the right of Bob's ear; he had never been known to look directly at one to whom he was talking.

"Hello. What's the trouble?" Bob did not sound at all cordial.

"Uh — us boys heard some stories that the Bar Diamond was — uh — in bad shape."

"Financially?" Casually though Bob spoke, he was wondering where *that* story had got started.

"Uh-huh."

"Well, what about it?"

"Why — uh — we figger, if you don't mind, we'd like to get paid by the week."

"You would, eh? Have you been here a whole week, Whitey?"

"Uh-huh — week yesterday."

Bob had a hard time to keep from saying something sarcastic, but little though he liked some of those men, he had to get along with them, had to keep them in the best possible humor. He nodded solemnly.

"Well, that's queer. I'd just figured out that you boys might like a weekly pay day, although it's not usual on a cow outfit. In fact I've just been in to the bank to get the money. Let's call the rest of the boys."

He drew a roll of bills from his pocket, and out of the corner of his eye watched with satisfaction the look of surprise that came to the faces of the little group. He stripped off a bank note casually.

"Sorry I haven't anything smaller than twenties, Whitey; I won't be able to give you the exact amount. Of course," he added pleasantly, "if you boys want me to, I can send to town for change. It's your money, and you're entitled to it whenever you want it."

Whitey spoke hastily; he seemed almost ashamed.

"No, Bob; this is fine. Thanks a lot." He pocketed the bill quickly.

Another came forward; a fat, lazy-looking young fellow with a blank red face.

"Say, Bob, could I get a little extra — sort of advance?"

Bob could not let this thing go too far — and "Tub" Grimes would have little influence with the rest of the men. Bob turned directly facing him and gave him a long, cold look.

"If you boys don't trust the outfit for more than a week's wages, do you expect me to be so soft as to give you advances?"

"I — uh — I was only askin'."

Tub quickly took the bill Bob thrust toward him and backed into the little crowd that was now gathering. Bob grinned at some of the others, as if between him and them there was a joke on Tub Grimes.

As paymaster, Bob did a roaring business for a few minutes, but the rush fell off sooner than he had expected. He entered the last man's name and the amount in the back of his tally book, and turned.

"How about you, Sam? Don't you want your pay?"

"Aw, Bob, I'm afraid I'd lose it. Can't we settle up when I'm quittin', or when I need somethin'?"

That was the usual cowboy way of doing business with the boss; Sam had come from the little Triangle H a few miles to the south. Most of the men felt the same way; they'd worry more about the money in their own pockets than in care of the outfit.

"Suit yourself. Of course I'll take care of it for you, Sam, if you want me to. Don't be afraid to let me know any time you want it."

Bob coolly rolled up the remaining bills and thrust them in his pocket, as though handling so much money was but another little job he had to do almost daily. He nodded cheerfully at the now respectful men and turned toward the ranch house.

But when his back was to them, his face became hard. Why had Whitey talked the others into that demand? It looked very much as though Whitey had known that Bob was to be robbed on the way home, as though he had tried to embarrass him, and so perhaps get some of the men to quit.

Bob would have liked to conceal his misadventure from Stella, but as that was out of the question, he thought that the sooner he had it over the better. He knocked on the living-room door, and entered, removing his hat.

At sight of the bandages, Stella sprang to her feet, her hands going to her throat, her eyes widening in alarm.

"Oh, Bob — what — what — ?"

Her voice was panic-stricken. It surprised Bob that she should show all this emotion over the sight of a cowboy's bandaged head.

"Now, Stell, it's nothing to get scared about. Some darn fool took a shot at me just outside town, an' that's all."

"All!"

"Sure. It did knock me out of the saddle, but you see I'm none the worse for it."

She stared at him a moment and then sat down. Bob, with elaborate carelessness, threw himself into a chair and stretched his long legs out in front.

"Well, I met Brad. Got a nice little roll from him."

She nodded absently. She seemed far more interested in Bob's wounded head, on which her eyes were still fixed, than in the money. She was a trifle pale.

"Lucky I got it. Some of the new hands were demanding weekly pay. I gave it to them so quick it made their heads spin."

He said nothing about the loss of the money; he did not mention that it was his own savings he was paying out. No need in letting Stella know that he had been knocked out for so long, that he had come so near being killed. Later on, if the outfit got back on its feet, he could settle that matter.

Why didn't Stella say something? There she sat, staring at his bandages but probably not seeing them — thinking.

"Well," he asked, "what do we do next?"

She did not hesitate; her tone was very low but firm: "We quit."

"Huh?" he gasped.

"Bob, if we went through with this thing, how many men would be killed before it was over? Is it worth it?"

"Why — maybe not many."

Bob's tone did not sound very convincing; in fact he could not keep the scared look from his own face. This was just what he had been struggling to keep out of his mind all the time. She spoke again:

"I don't want to see any of the boys killed. Has it occurred to you that you, being foreman, are pretty nearly certain to be shot before it's over?" He did not catch the little tremble in her voice.

111

"Oh, heck!" He spoke with conviction this time — oneself is never going to get killed; it's always the other fellow. "I can take care of myself; I'm not worrying."

"No? Didn't take very good care of yourself today, did you? All that saved you was somebody making a bad shot — a shot maybe half an inch out."

"Yes, but that won't happen again. I was careless."

"It *will* happen again — no matter how careful you are. I mean it would, only that we're through. You may pay off all the new men."

There was no mistaking the determination in her tone. Those were orders to the foreman.

"But — good gosh!" Bob threw out his hands in despair. "We *can't* quit now!"

"We have quit. Anyway, Bob, even if we did win the fight, what could we do? Sell the outfit next day to raise that fifty thousand dollars. Why get a lot of the boys killed, then, when we can't hold the place anyway?"

That was sound logic; it was another thing that Bob had been fighting to keep out of his mind. To continue the war under the circumstances seemed sheer craziness; there was no way of holding the range.

The thought recalled to Bob old Newt's last words to him: "Bob — hold — the — range!" A pretty job he'd given him — after he himself had sunk it in debt so much that, war or no war, it was already as good as lost. Now that Newt seemed due to recover, Bob could bring himself to curse him heartily.

"We-ell, Stell, it's quitting I don't like. If we hang on a few more days, maybe something will turn up."

She sighed, almost sarcastically.

"Something turn up! If you'd read Dickens, you'd see how foolish that sounds."

Bob flared mildly; he was angry with her for wanting to give up so soon.

"I *have* read Dickens's stories — some of 'em. Just because I'm a cowboy, you don't want to think I don't know anything."

"I didn't mean it that way, Bob. I mean — well, that we're through. So the sooner you pay the men off the better."

She stood up to leave the room. Bob, in a panic, leaped to his feet and followed her to the door of her bedroom.

"But, Stell, we *can't* just quit like that!"

"What can we do?"

She turned to him almost fiercely. He could not help seeing that her eyes were filled with tears; he guessed that she wanted to hurry from the room before she began to cry. After all, she had been born and reared on this ranch; it was her home. To leave it — and to leave it penniless — would be a terrible blow.

"Why, Stell, I — Give me until tomorrow anyway. Maybe I can figure out a way that won't call for fighting; there must be *something!*"

"It's no use!"

She was turning away again, but he seized her arm in desperation.

"Just one more day, Stell!"

"A-all right."

She broke away from him, and the bedroom door slammed in his face. She had given in, not because he had convinced her, but because she didn't want him to see her cry. Behind the door, her teeth sank into her handkerchief; she *must* not let him hear her cry. Oh, why had all this come up! The old Bar Diamond — her home!

That was easily the hardest evening of Bob Edwards's life. Around the men, he had to appear calm, confident, entirely self-reliant; he could not, or would not, disappear until bedtime. But he could hardly bring himself to look them in the eyes; he had a sneaking feeling that tomorrow he would be paying all of them off.

Quitting, without having done a thing! To continue the farce seemed more than foolish. To give up without a struggle of some sort — the thought sickened him.

His bandaged head brought politely solicitous inquiries — which he knew in most cases to conceal more curiosity than concern. His brief, almost uncivil "Trouble with a fellow" soon halted the questions.

He went to his room and lighted the coal-oil lamp. As foreman, he had the privilege of this little room to himself — a mere cubby-hole boarded off from the main bunk house. He had always regarded this privacy as a doubtful advantage; a cowboy loves to see a big floor strewn with tarp-covered beds, likes the sociability of it. Tonight he was thankful for this crude, unpainted little retreat.

He had about given up hope of a plan. He had picked up a magazine and was trying to read when the door from the main room opened. Red Selby came in and seated himself nonchalantly on the floor — another peculiarity of the cowboy is that he is inclined to look upon a chair as an uncomfortable thing to be reserved for use in the presence of "company".

"What's the matter, Bob?" he asked. "Yore face looks so long you remind me of the old gray mule we wrangle on sometimes."

Red was the one man on the outfit to whom Bob could confide his troubles. He was glad that Red had come in.

"What's not the matter!" he groaned dismally.

"Well, spill it to yore Uncle George. Yore girl go back on you?"

"A girl went back on me all right — but she's not my girl, an' I wouldn't want her on a bet."

"Sounds like you have it bad." Red Selby wagged his head.

"Listen, Red. She's the craziest — why, she's the —"

Bob choked on his words. Red nodded sympathetically.

"I know. I was that way about a little Mexican girl once, when I was younger an' didn't have the sense I have now."

"Red," asked Bob, "do you want to get thrown through the window on your ear?"

"You wouldn't, Bob. You're too much bigger than I am; it ain't chival'ous."

Bob looked down at him disgustedly from his seat on the bunk.

"If you want to use long words, better buy a dictionary. Let me tell you about how danged crazy girls can get to be."

He told everything. Red listened attentively, often nodded sympathetically.

"Well, Bob, it does look like we're blowed up high enough to ketch stars in our hair. Dang her anyway! If ol' Newt was here, he'd fight to the last ditch — easy-goin' as he looks."

"Well, what do we do?" demanded Bob.

"Quit. We can drift up into Nevada an' get a job. I always wanted to see that country anyway."

"I'm not quittin'!"

"No! Bob, don't you know when you're licked?"

"Danged if I do! Not this time anyway. Newt told me to hold this range for him, and held it's going to be, till he gets home anyway. If he lives, of course."

Red sighed.

"Reckon I don't get to see Nevada after all. Well, Bob, if you're gettin' into anything dangerous, let me know an' I'll go along to pertect you. Besides, a feller like you needs somebody with some sense along, to tell him what to do."

Red stood up, yawned, gave Bob a pitying glance, and returned to the main room. Bob grinned affectionately after him. That last had been Red's way of saying that he'd stick with his pardner through thick and thin, no matter what came up. Good old Red!

Bob sat gloomily staring at the floor. The fact that quitting, after he had made such a promising start, was boss's orders would make no difference to anybody. No, they'd say Bob Edwards had quit — had run away from it. That was why he couldn't do it; he couldn't let

116

himself get the name of being a quitter. Not to speak of not being able to go back on old Newt.

Fifty thousand dollars — a sight of money! What had the old man done with it? Bob wondered why he had not known always that there was something queer about Newt Davis. Dang him! Still Bob could not go back on him; the old man had done too much for him in his life.

He turned to condemning Stella, and all her sex from Eve onward. Just like a fool girl! Why, even a fortune teller couldn't guess what a danged girl might do next — always the wrong thing.

Well, he'd show her! He'd hold the range for her whether she wanted it or not!

All of which meditation led to only one definite fact: Girls were the ruination of the world, especially to that part of it inhabited by cowboys.

CHAPTER
NINE

Pingüe

Bob woke up long before daylight next morning. He lay staring at the gray square of his little window. What was that he had been dreaming about?

Oh, yes! Of a very shabby covered wagon crawling along the road, pulled by crowbait horses — "poor whites" of the lowest class moving they knew not where, nor cared. He, in rags, was driving, and Stella, none too well washed, was beside him on the seat. Back under the tattered canvas sat old Newt, grumbling to himself as some old men do, and Mrs. Davis. Mrs. Davis was holding a very young baby in her arms.

Dreams were queer things — an old woman like that with a baby. But of course the baby must be her grandchild.

The obvious meaning of this came to Bob. He sat up in bed with an angry grunt, and felt in the dim light for his boots. That crazy girl! He got one boot on, and found himself sitting with the other in his hand, scratching the back of his neck. Now, if —

What was he doing, putting on his boots before his trousers? One would think he was a center-fire, ashamed to show his boot tops! He yanked the boot off. What ailed him, anyway?

He got all his clothes on right this time, and stole from the house; he did not want to wake the other men. He went to the corral, saddled, and rode aimlessly away from the ranch.

An hour or so later found him but a mile from the Bar Diamond. He stopped on a hilltop to watch the changing colors of the eastern sky. Rose, pink, purple, swinging and melting into each other. He'd seen this all his life, but never was it twice the same — and never did it fail to give him that feeling of awe. And always this breathless stillness in the Arizona dawn — one felt that one could hear a pin drop a mile away.

The colors faded, the sun rose. Bob, jogging back toward the ranch for breakfast, happened to notice some little pin-points of dull green ahead of him and to one side. Loco weed? No, not the right blue-green shade; one could tell loco as far as one saw it.

What else could be green in this drought? Curiosity made him rein across to examine the weed more closely. He dismounted and plucked a stem. He had a vague feeling that he had heard its name — something that sheep thrived on.

Sure encouraging! Get this stuff all over the range and the cavalry could not keep the sheepmen off. What was this called, anyway? He could not remember. He swung back into his saddle and turned away.

Pingüe! The word leaped suddenly into his mind after he had almost given up thinking about it. Instantly he remembered what he had heard of it; it had slipped from his mind for a time because the weed was of little interest to cowboys.

Sheep thrive on it? Why, it was their most deadly poison. A band driven on it inadvertently might have a thousand head poisoned within an hour; it had not the slow, cumulative action of loco, although it appeared and was eaten under much the same conditions — drought conditions, with no other green feed.

It came to him that if this stuff was really thriving, the sheep war might solve itself. He had a little figuring to do, of course; let's see — But he'd better hurry back or he'd be late for breakfast.

Having eaten hastily, he hurried to the ranch house. There was nobody in the living room, so he helped himself to a volume of the battered encyclopedia; he remembered when old Newt had bought it second-hand at an auction. He found a chair and spread the book on his knees.

Here it was:

Actinea Richardsoni . . . Asterlike form . . . long, narrow, dark leaves; six to twelve stems from six inches to a foot tall . . . more or less green the year through . . . poisonous to sheep —

There was a long, technical account of just what it did to a sheep's insides, but Bob was not interested in that; he could not understand it anyway without using the dictionary.

Well, he hadn't found out anything new. Still, his face did not look so long now; he was, in fact, beginning to look almost hopeful. Perhaps the pingüe would do him no good, but it at least was a straw to grasp at. Bob was one of those fortunate ones who would clutch the straw and persuade himself that it was a large and buoyant log. Yes, and swim out, grinning, with the straw in his hand.

Oh, well! He had at least found the Latin name of the stuff. Only trouble was that nobody around here spoke Latin.

"What are you doing, Bob?"

He looked up to see Stella in the doorway. He grinned.

"Readin' Dickens, ma'am," he answered politely.

"Oh, Bob, don't be silly!"

"Heck, I didn't mean it that way!"

Something about her face made Bob feel contrite for his flippancy; there was a washed-out look to her eyes, as if she'd spent part of the night crying. She came into the room; she walked slowly, like an old woman.

"Bob, when are you going to pay the men off?"

"Tomorrow. You gave me another day." He looked at her as though accusing her for trying to go back on her word. She stood there silent. No use in arguing with Bob; and she *had* given her promise.

"Stell, know anything about pingüe?"

"Do I what? What's pingway?"

Stella looked as though she suspected him of more untimely flippancy.

"It's — a weed. Excuse me, Stell; I have some business over on the sheep range."

"Sheep range! Are you crazy, Bob?"

121

He went to the door. He was thinking so hard that he spoke absently:

"It's not me — Uh — I mean — I guess so."

"Bob! You'll get killed over there!"

There was panic in her voice. She rushed after him and seized his arm. "Bob! I won't let you go!"

He turned sternly.

"See here, Stell! You've butted in and about ruined everything already. You gave me one more day to find some plan, an' I'm doing as I please that day."

"But, Bob —Well, will you take somebody with you? Don't go there alone!"

"Sure — I'll take Red, if you want me to." He compromised to that extent.

He went hurrying down the steps with spurs clanking. He turned once to call back, " 'Bye, Stell!" Stella's eyes followed the tall, clean-cut figure to the corrals. She saw him speak to Red, who was just mounting. Then, his long reata on his arm, he entered the corral to catch a fresh horse.

Range-bred that she was, she could never tire of watching the smooth, unerring ease of Bob's roping. His riding was much the same. There, she thought, was a *cowboy* — and when Stella thought that, it meant that no more could she say.

She saw him lead Flight out and saddle him — a horse to match the man. Solid blood-bay but for a tiny white star in the middle of his forehead. Every muscle standing out, but not angular — just like his master, she thought; it was Bob's private horse.

And she wished Bob would stay away from the sheep range; she knew something was going to happen.

Riding along side by side, Bob and Red fell to talking of Flight. This horse was somewhat of a mystery on the outfit. When Bob had left there five years before, the bay had been so young that it was impossible to say just how he'd turn out. Prophecies of experts were favorable, but they all far undershot the mark. Flight had become a wonder; he was now the fastest thing in that part of the country at least. He was as gentle as a kitten. And he was almost pampered and spoiled to death by Bob.

The strange thing was that the best horsemen would have called him thoroughbred at a glance, and insisted further upon it after having examined him. This although Bob had picked him up a tiny, half-starved dogie colt whose mother had probably been killed by mountain lions, and had reared him on a bottle.

There was a possibility that his mother was some highly bred mare that had wandered far from home. Or of course it might be that he was some sort of throw-back to the fine Arab stock whose blood was so strong in the wild horses of that part of Arizona — years before, a wealthy stockman had by his will freed his herd of imported Arabs, and they had taken joyously to the wild bands, leaving many descendants.

"Bob," Red said, "why don't you take him to Phoenix or Los Angeles an' race him? You'd clean up some money."

"Because, Red, I got better sense."

Red was shocked, indignant.

"You — you mean to say —"

"Uh-huh. I'd get him beaten, running on a smooth race course, or anything that way. Out here, I'd put a little bet on him against any of 'em."

Red looked disgusted.

"Just like you — don't know what you got. I know more than you about hot-bloods, an' I'd put my money on Flight running on any course. I mean in any race more than a quarter mile."

"We-ll, I'll try him in a small race some day. Better keep your eyes open for pingüe, Red; we're on the sheep range now."

Red glanced around, sniffed.

"Sheep range! I thought it was Sarah's Desert. Pingüe! Why, there ain't even a cactus growin' here; the woollies have swallered 'em or tromped 'em down."

"That's it." Bob looked gloomy. "Not a scrap of feed — they have to either run 'em on our cattle range or see 'em all die."

"Serve 'em right if they did die on 'em, for overgrazin' that way. Sheep should all be dead anyway."

They rode for an hour, two hours. They saw a few tiny patches of stunted pingüe, no more. As Red dispiritedly remarked, there "wasn't enough of it to give a jack rabbit a stomach ache". Red was sunk in the depths of dejection.

Not so Bob. The pingüe had given his thoughts a certain trend. What if the stuff did fail to show up here? He had another plan working in his head, still far too unformed to be discussed with Red — a bare, hazy outline of a plan. He had some hard thinking to do, but he felt certain that a true plan of action would come out of those jumbled ideas.

They were following an old trail on the summit of a ridge. They swung through a patch of cedars, and almost bumped into two men who sat their horses as though waiting for them. Bob brought Flight to a sudden stop; he barely kept his hand from dropping to his gun.

"Uh — hello, Jeff."

"Why, howdy, Bob. How are you?"

"Just great!"

Bob spoke sarcastically; he thoroughly disliked this fat, oily little sheep owner, Jeff Morehouse. Red seemed to feel even more strongly on the subject; he smothered a snort and rode a short distance ahead to wait for Bob.

There was a moment of silence, while Bob and Jeff eyed each other. Morehouse had the next sheep range beyond Johnson's. The mere fact of his being here on Butch's range showed that he was helping Butch in the war. Financially, of course — Jeff would not risk his own precious hide.

With Jeff Morehouse was an ugly, scar-faced Basque. Why hadn't they taken a shot at him and Red before he saw them? Bob could guess the answer easily: Jeff had about half the nerve of a rabbit. What he might pay someone else to do was something else again. The fat sheepman looked very uncomfortable.

"Uh — sure glad to see you, Bob."

Bob was calmly rolling a cigarette. He gave Jeff a sarcastic, amused glance.

"I just know you are, Jeff!"

"I — uh — Bob, I was just goin' over to see Butch about some sheep I'm tryin' to sell him. Strictly business, you understand."

"Uh-huh. Oh, shore!"

Bob did not pretend to believe it, but he answered with a reasonable amount of politeness. If Jeff didn't want to start a row, he wouldn't. But hanged if he'd pretend to be friendly, or to believe anything Morehouse said.

"Bob" — Jeff was trying his hardest not to appear uncomfortable — "I hear you an' Butch have some trouble? That right?"

Scared to admit that he'd visit Butch if he really knew of it.

"What!" Bob looked astonished. "Me an' Butch have trouble! Why, I visited him at his camp a few days ago, and only yesterday the two of us stood side by side at the Blue Front bar. Well, well — what stories do get around!" He shook his head.

The sweat was beginning to appear on Morehouse's oily face; he seemed almost on the verge of a breakdown of some sort. This polite, ice-cold humor of Bob's was shaking any slight courage he might possess. Bob felt a wild desire to lean forward suddenly and yell "Boo!" just to see what would happen.

"Well, Jeff, I'll be driftin' along if you don't mind. Give my regards to my pal Butch."

He was turning away, but Morehouse stopped him.

"Ho — hold on, Bob; I wanted to see you about something."

Bob swung his horse back. "What?"

He thought the other would have been only too glad to see him go. What was it, anyway?

"Why — uh — uh — why, I was wonderin' where I could buy a couple o' good, gentle saddle horses. Has the Bar Diamond got any to sell?"

"Sure. We have several that we'd let go; easy-gaited as you'd find. Of course they *might* buck a little a cold morning. But you wouldn't mind that, would you?"

"I reckon not. What you askin' for 'em?"

Bob could hardly keep from grinning. He would give a good deal to see this fat little sheepman on a bucking horse. But his mind was working fast. What did Morehouse really want with him? Why had he called him back?

There was something in the wind. Bob had noticed the hesitation while Morehouse was thinking up that story about wanting to buy horses. Final evidence was that the fellow would pretend that he'd even consider a horse that by the wildest chance might buck. Morehouse had something up his short sleeve. All this had taken only a moment to figure out. Bob answered the question:

"Why, we can't talk prices until you see 'em; drop over some day."

Once more he was turning off. This time it was the Basque who intercepted him. He spoke for the first time:

"Got makeens?"

"What's that? Makings? Sure."

Bob deliberately but none too obviously swung Flight so that his left side was toward the Basque; that

127

would leave his right hand free and out of reach of the other. With his left, he passed across tobacco and papers.

Very slowly and carefully the man rolled a cigarette. He returned the tobacco, and began a long search through his pockets. Not finding what he wanted, he spoke again:

"Got match?"

"Uh-huh."

Bob eyed him narrowly as he handed two or three matches across. By this time there could be no doubt whatever that there was some trick somewhere. He could not guess what it was, but the mere fact that they wanted to hold him here talking showed that he'd better be getting a long way from here. He turned easily to Jeff:

"Which way you going? Oh, yes — to see Butch. Well, go ahead; I'll stop here a few minutes to rest my horse."

He wanted them to get going first; he had decided not to turn his back to them. He glanced casually to see Red puffing a cigarette fifty feet off, and very openly watching the scene. Red had been wise to get back there as a sort of lookout. Jeff cleared his throat slowly, nervously.

"Why, Bob, I reckon I'll do the same; we're in no hurry."

"Don't let me delay you, Jeff!"

Bob's eyes met the sheepman's. Now they were as cold as ice; there could be no mistaking his meaning.

128

"Uh — uh — well, I'll be over to see about the horses."

He and the Basque turned away. Bob watched them until they were out of pistol range. Still, he did not believe they had meant to shoot; their fine chance had been before he saw them. Then what had they been up to?

Red was waiting, a look of disgust on his face.

"Bob," he demanded, "what made you waste yore time talkin' to that kind o' tripe?"

"Well, I couldn't very well ride by without saying 'Howdy.'"

"Couldn't you? I did." Red sniffed.

"But," asked Bob, "can you guess what he was up to anyway? Why was he trying to hold me there talking?"

"Jest because you're pals. Let's go; the air is kinda bad around where he's been. I think a lot more o' Butch; anyway, Butch has sand enough to come out in the open with what he wants to do."

Red was turning his horse.

"Hold on, Red — not that way. Let's back-track 'em a way and see if we can find out anything."

Back-tracking in that dry, sandy ground was very simple. They trotted silently along for perhaps two hundred yards, keeping their eyes on the ground. Suddenly Red exclaimed:

"What the —"

He was about to stop his horse, but Bob broke in quickly:

"Keep on — keep on! Act as if you hadn't seen anything."

They kept on following the old trail as if they had seen nothing. Red spoke nervously:

"What's it about? Three horses — an' one of 'em cut straight down the ridge in a dead run."

"Easy! He had two fellers with him, and he sent one of them flying to Butch's camp for men."

"Then let's get out of here, for gosh sake, before we meet 'em!"

"I've a notion it's too late; they may be all around us right now. The ground was all scuffed up back there where the two had been standing their horses a long time, waiting for us."

Red shook his head.

"Looks tough. I'd a feelin' all the time that Old Man Selby's handsome son Red would get killed if he stuck around that fool Bob Edwards."

Bob glanced about, as though casually. He could see no sign of men. The same glance had showed him that this ridge commanded the country for two or three miles around — Jeff might have been watching them for nearly an hour from up here, as they rode around below.

"Say!" Red spoke quickly without turning his head. "I got a glimpse of a man on horseback down there to our right, in the cedars."

"That means there's more."

"What do we do?"

"Keep right along till we come to the next little patch of trees ahead of us; it's the end of a line running up from the draw below. Then, once we get out of sight in the cedars, let's turn and ride down like the Comanches were after us."

"Pretty thin line of cedars runnin' up! They'd see us before we went far."

"Can't help that. It'll give us a few yards' start."

"What if they're waitin' for us ahead in them trees?"

"Can't be helped."

Red sighed.

"Wisht I'd lived a better life! All my sins is comin' stompedin' before me like a herd o' spotted burros. Is that a sign o' somethin'?"

"Oh, shut up!" growled Bob, uneasily.

They were entering the cedars now, they were halfway through them. Bob was relieved to find nobody there. He suddenly whirled Flight.

"Let's go!"

Side by side he and Red went plunging down the side of the ridge, twisting back and forth to take advantage of the scant cover. Flight could have gone much faster, but Bob held him back, waiting for Red on the slower horse.

They had better luck than they expected; they got more than a third of the way down before a shot rang out, a yell.

"All right, Red — turn him loose!"

"Man ahead!"

"Swing right!"

It forced them from the cover to the bare side of the ridge. Now guns were popping in several places below. A hasty guess made it six men down there. Bob glanced back over his shoulder.

"Three following us!" he shouted.

"I — this fool horse will fall with me!"

"Got to risk it! Look out! Somebody ahead! Cut back to the left a little — got to go between 'em."

Now bullets were flying around, but most of them far wide of the mark. The men on both sides below were closing in, trying to intercept them. A sudden cry from Red:

"They got my horse! He's goin' down!"

"Hold him up! Hold him up! Keep him going till we hit the cedars."

"No use, Bob — Flight can't get away rode double. Go ahead; I'll be all right."

Bob dodged quickly as a bullet hissed close to his head. Then it came to him that it was foolish to dodge after it had passed. Red was right; Flight could not carry both away. But one thing left:

"Keep him on his feet till we hit the cedars, then hide. I'll lead 'em off."

The line of dark trees was now but a few feet ahead. Bob plunged into it with a breath of relief. He glanced over his shoulder to see Red's horse leap wildly, spasmodically, between two trees and suddenly collapse; he saw Red throw himself sidewise so that the falling horse could not roll on him.

Men coming, coming crashing on both sides; in a moment more they'd have discovered Red. Bob threw back his head and let out an ear-splitting yell of defiance. Purposely, he dashed against the dead branches of a fallen cedar, went crashing through the brittle limbs noisily.

132

"Come on, sheep-herders; get me!"

They were coming crashing after him. Had they found Red?

"Hurry up, you sheep-herders! *Ye-e-ee!*"

He raced over the low ridge beyond the draw; the ground under him was level now, the cedars thinner. Flight was outdistancing the others. That would not do; they might go back. Bob tightened his rein, tightened it still more.

Now the pursuers were catching up rapidly. Just as they had expected, it seemed that Bob's horse was not fitted for a long run, was tiring. They had him! Yells rang out behind. Soon they would be able to see him, they would be within range.

Bob's mind raced through his smattering of Spanish. Suddenly what he wanted came to him. He yelled again, and finished with a shout:

"*Viva la vaca!*"

Pretty good war cry at that, he thought: "Long live the cow!" Again he shouted it. They were gaining too much; he let Flight out a trifle.

The trees had been growing more and more scattering. Presently he saw ahead a big, sandy flat; he remembered having noticed it from the ridge. Now he carefully judged the distance his pursuers were behind. He wanted them to come from the trees just too far back for pistol range.

He swept out onto the flat. His left hand was pumping steadily back and forth, firm on the rein, keeping a smooth pull on the bit. He glanced back. Here they came, just breaking from the cedars — and

133

there was Butch himself in the lead. Again Bob threw back his head.

"*Viva la vaca!*"

All the way to the middle of the flat, a mile across, it seemed a neck-and-neck race. Exultant shouts were ringing out behind. A thoroughbred could not stand that pace any longer on such rough ground; soon they would catch up. They had him! Run down like a coyote on a flat, to be surrounded and killed! Then they would have the cattle range with little further resistance.

Here they were, in the middle of the flat. Now they were gaining rapidly. Hadn't they known it! A shot or two rang out behind; they were getting within range.

There was a sort of grim grin on Bob's face. He turned once more to call his war cry.

"*Viva la vaca!*"

He had been riding like any cowboy, with his boots thrust to the heels in the big stirrups. Now he slipped his feet back until his weight came nearer his toes; there might be a shade less jar on the horse that way. He stood up, leaned forward, all his weight off the saddle. He shouted back over his shoulder:

"Come on, sheep-herders!"

And lower: "Go it, Flight!"

All at once Flight seemed to lengthen out like a stretching cat; his belly sank until one might wonder where he found room for his flying, slender legs. From the sun-baked ground under Bob came a rattle like a long roll beaten by an expert drummer — faster, faster! — but never a hundredth of a beat out of time.

134

The wind whistled by Bob's ears. Under him the saddle rose and fell with gentle, rapid palpitations; still he did not touch the seat. He wanted to look back, but he dared not; that slight twisting of his body would throw the horse ever so little off balance, cause a slight break in the perfect rhythm of the hoofs.

At last his soothing call:

"E-easy, boy! Ho-old up there!"

The dull-green wall of cedars was but a few yards ahead. Bob's hand tightened on the rein. The blood bay swerved wildly from side to side, pushed on the bit, shook his head. He was running, and he did not want to stop; only too rarely Bob gave him his head this way, let him do what he loved to do.

Now Bob had him stopped, facing back. Far off, almost back to the middle of the flat, a group of chagrined men came thudding heavily on panting, wallowing steeds. Flight reared high in the air, still excited by his run. While he was up, Bob contemptuously waved a hand in farewell. Then he turned and trotted calmly, insultingly, into the cedars. Sheep-herder horses try to catch Flight!

He kept straight on, until he found a stony wash, and up this he turned. He did not think they'd try to follow him, after he had made fools of them that way. That was the reason he had done it, to discourage them completely. He tried to persuade himself that he had not wanted to show off his pet horse. Flight was almost the sole thing of which Bob was inclined to boast; he had to watch what he said about him.

135

Presently he left the wash; it was swinging left too much. He circled just inside the edge of the cedars, where he would be out of sight. Once he went cautiously to the edge to peer forth. Butch and his crowd had turned off north in a slow walk; they were neither following him nor going back to where he had left Red. Of course they would have taken it for granted that Red had merely got separated from Bob and had gone home another way.

At first after his race Flight had been taking in huge, smooth lungfuls of air; his sides were not quivering as another horse's might have been. Already his breathing was back to normal. Some horse!

Bob struck a fast trot. He was worried about Red — there had been many shots fired just after he had left him. Could it be that they had got him? Bob was not superstitious, but he wished that Red had not been joking about death just a few minutes before they parted.

Soon he was close to where he had seen him last. He shouted, cautiously, not too loud. No answer. Panic came over him. Good old Red; what if —

Having ridden up at a new angle, he missed the place slightly; he had to turn back. There, ahead — the dead horse. But no sign of Red. His heart in his mouth, Bob dashed up. He saw a figure lying with its head against the dead horse.

"Red!"

"Huh!"

Red sat up with a jerk, rubbing his eyes. Bob glared down on him.

"Red, you fool, if that's another of your jokes — pretending to be asleep —"

The cowboy stood up, stretched, yawned again. He spoke in a tone that was almost a whine:

"Dang it, Bob, ain't a pore cowboy got a hard-enough life under a foreman like you, without gettin' bawled out for takin' a nap when he gits a chance? You're gettin' so danged cranky lately!"

"You fool! Me ride up here and see you stretched out like that!"

The sleepy look left Red's face. He spoke suddenly:

"Gosh, Bob — I — I hadn't thought of you feelin' that way about it! Aw, gosh — get down an' kick the pants off me for a brother to the wrangle mule."

"Here, get up behind me."

Red looked gloomy now.

"I should have to walk home, Bob."

He took his saddle from the dead horse, and with it he swung up behind on the bay. They struck out toward the Bar Diamond, slowly, not to strain Flight with his heavy burden. They could not go the shortest way, for they did not wish to cross any open ground. Red was silent until they had almost got back to the cattle range, then he spoke:

"Well, we didn't see any pingüe, did we?"

Bob spoke over his shoulder:

"I'm sort of glad we didn't. I have a plan coming without it, if I could get the danged thing straight."

"An' yore bright notion about pingüe only got us in trouble, an' got my horse killed."

Bob shook his head.

"No; without the pingüe, I'd never have thought of the other plan. I've a feeling that running onto that stuff this morning was the turning point, sort of, in this mess the outfit's in."

"Well, what's the plan, anyway?"

"Why — it's — uh — not exactly a plan yet. I'll tell you after I get it straight in my own head."

A little farther on, within sight of the Bar Diamond range, Bob spoke: "Red, what do you see in this little valley we're just leaving?"

"Huh?" Red stared around. "Nothin', only bare ground with no feed."

"Look again. This is different from any valley within a hundred miles of here."

A long pause. Bob could feel Red twisting behind him to see all sides without dropping his saddle.

"Danged if I see anything different in it from any other place — only less feed."

"Well, I'd have seen no more when I left here five years ago; managing a big outfit teaches a fellow a lot. Then, I could see nothing but brands and long-ears —"

"Thanks for the lekcher," interrupted Red, "but I'm anxious to know what's so queer about this valley before we leave it."

"Best site for a dam in this part of the country. Just build it in that little rocky break and you'd have a lake nearly a mile long."

Red, behind, was squirming again, looking back.

"Jumpin' jack rabbits, but you're right! There'd be water enough for half the sheep in the country — an' Johnson so short of water, too."

Bob nodded.

"It's just what I wanted to find out — what sort of stockman Butch is. He's the rottenest in Arizona, not to see this."

"Well, what of it?"

"A whole lot! Here we are — Bar Diamond range. Better drop your saddle and come back after it with an extra horse, or bareback, some time. Flight's getting too much strain for one day anyway."

CHAPTER
TEN

One Birthday!

They got to the Bar Diamond almost an hour before sunset. At the corral, where Bob unsaddled, he found Shorty and three more of the old hands squatted on their heels, talking; the old hands generally kept a lordly aloofness from the extra men. They glanced inquiringly at the baked sweat on Flight's coat; they guessed that something worth hearing had happened if Bob had run his pet that much.

Red told them; it was too good to keep. They howled with mirth; the idea of sheep-herder horses trying to catch Flight! As Bob left them, they were hurrying away, separating, to spread the story — with, of course, suitable embellishments according to their imaginations. As Bob went up the steps of the ranch house, he heard behind him a yell and a high-pitched shout:

"*Viva la vaca!*"

He knocked at the door, then pushed it open to inquire loudly:

"Anybody home?"

Mrs. Doheney came from the kitchen with some of her eternal sewing in her hand. She was a widow, a

140

shade over forty, and undeniably pretty in spite of a double chin and a plumper figure than was fashionable.

"Stella home?" he asked.

"She's not back yet, Bob; she went out riding a couple of hours ago."

She glanced toward the mantelpiece as though looking for something.

"Oh, there it is. She didn't give it to you this morning."

"What?"

To Mrs. Doheney's clear blue eyes came the knowing look of one who holds a secret but will not tell. She went to the mantelpiece and came back with a carefully wrapped package in her hand. Bob took it, mystified. He saw writing on the paper: "To Bob Edwards from the Bar Diamond — Happy Birthday!"

"Well, for goodness sake!" he gasped. "I'd forgotten about it myself." He was twenty-seven today.

He was turning away when he saw the disappointed look on Mrs. Doheney's face. She wanted to see him open this, to see his surprise. He went back, laid the package on the table, and drew his knife to cut the string. He unwrapped the paper, and stared in astonishment at the fine pair of binoculars in a case of the best English pigskin.

Even to Bob, the maker's name on the binoculars was known — the world's best. There was no name on the case, but a cowboy does not need a name to judge leather; after twenty years of the hardest use, this pigskin would but have taken on a richer, deeper look.

It was typical of Bob's calling that he laid down the glasses almost unexamined and passed his fingers in awe over their case, sniffed it, and held it at arm's length to gaze wonderingly at it. Of course the woman could not see in mere leather the beauty that he did. She spoke almost impatiently.

"Look through the glasses."

Reluctantly he laid down the fine case and picked up the binoculars. He had used glasses before, but never this kind; she had to explain to him the individual eye adjustment as Stella had shown it to her. At last he got them focused properly. Standing in the doorway, he peered through them a moment, then lowered them in astonishment to look with his naked eyes.

"Why — why I can read the brand on that cow like I had her tied down on the floor here! Wonder where in heck Stella got 'em?"

"Wrote Doctor Varney to send the best he could find in San Francisco."

Bob had a queer feeling. And here he'd been calling Stella names to himself, calling her a fool!

"She wants you to understand," assured Mrs. Doheney, "that they're a present from the outfit, not from her." The plump little woman looked very prim as she said it, but there was a knowing look in her blue eyes.

Bob could understand — or thought he could. While there might be some truth in his theory that no one knew what a girl would do next, to anyone who had known Bob a month he was an open book; his straightforward manner left no room for doubt; he

142

would do this, and he would not do that. In spite of all his striving and danger, working here while Newt was gone, he would not take a cent of pay for helping his friends; that was an easy guess for anyone. Therefore those glasses which he could not refuse. *And* the case.

These were Bob's conclusions, and he was right — well, partly right.

"Now that other package; that came in your mail."

Bob did not notice that Mrs. Doheney's tones had grown slightly frigid. She kept away from the second package as though it were hot; she allowed Bob to pick it up himself. It was smaller than the first; it seemed to be a little cardboard box wrapped in paper. There was no sender's name.

"Who the heck is this from?" he wondered aloud. "Nice writing."

"Yes — a *girl's* writing."

Her blue eyes had a cold, hostile look, and her lips pursed accusingly after the last word. She spoke again, with elaborate unconcern:

"It was just after this case came that Stella went out riding."

Bob did not see any connection. Puzzled, he drew his knife again to cut the string.

"Reckon, I'd better open it."

"It *might* be a good idea." With her short nose in the air, Mrs. Doheney flounced out of the room.

Bob stared after her. Why, she acted as if she were mad at him for something!

Bob cut the string and unwrapped the paper. As he had thought, there was a little cardboard box. Gingerly, he lifted the lid.

And then his jaw fell, his eyes opened. In the little box lay a thick roll of bills tied with a leather thong. It was the money of which he had been robbed. He knew without counting it that it was all there.

He slumped into a chair, not knowing whether his relief or his amazement was the greater; in fact he did not know whether he could stand up again or not, such was his surprise. Of all the totally inexplicable mysteries that had come up within the last few days, this was by far the most amazing to him. His arms hung down beside his chair. He would hardly have been surprised if a purple rattlesnake had come up through the solid boards of the floor and spoken to him in English. Anything might happen on this blamed outfit!

From what Mrs. Doheney had said, he judged that this package had been a surprise to Stella — so she hadn't got hold of the money in any way and mailed it to him secretly to save his feelings. He compared the handwriting on the two wrappers. Stella's he knew well — somewhat scratchy and boyish. This other was elegant, flowing, with beautiful curves, and written in ink of another shade than Stella's.

Bob groaned. He would almost rather not have got this money back than to be confronted with this fresh mystery to puzzle his worried head. A woman? Who?

Finally, after a last headshake, he stood up to go. From the doorway, he saw a small delegation of cowboys — some of the old hands — coming toward the house, solemnly headed by Red Selby. Now what was up?

They trooped across the porch and stopped facing him.

"*Viva la vaca!*" snapped Red. He brought his right hand up in a smart salute which consisted of closing his fist and jabbing his outstuck thumb in his right eye.

Bob did not know whether he wanted to swear or to laugh. Some more of Red's clowning.

"Well?" Bob asked, trying not to sound irritated.

"Bob, Stella sort of mentioned to us that this was yore birthday, an' we thought we should do somethin' about it besides puttin' the chaps to you later on — an onforchunate duty forced on us by the pervailin' custom of rimmy cow outfits."

Red cleared his throat, and continued:

"Bob, after us boys talked it over, we figured you're a pretty good sort o' plug, takin' you on the run, in spite o' you sometimes usin' such immodest words as 'isn't' instead o' good, plain 'ain't'. Also you have been accused of puttin' g's at the end o' words like 'ropin'' — a heenyous offense for a feller that can ride an' rope like you do."

Once more he cleared his throat. There was a distant look in his eyes as he tried to remember his studied speech. Then his eyes brightened; it had come back to him.

"Bob" — he held forth a paper-wrapped bundle — "us fellers, on behalf o' the other fellers, take a helluva lot of pleasure in presentin' you with this small token of

145

our affetchun an' — uh — esteem. We hope you will understand the speerit in which it was given."

Bob gingerly took the package and unwrapped it. There was nothing but a large, neat bouquet of freshly picked purple flowers. They were very pretty flowers and carefully arranged.

They were flowers of the loco plant.

Bob looked at them as though touched by the cowboys' kindness; he had been prepared for something of this sort since Red's speech began. He held the loco blooms to his nose and sniffed as though the faint odor pleased him. All the time, he was hastily concocting an answer.

"Boys" — he turned to them gravely — "I'm touched to the heart with this unexpected — uh — gift. Believe me, I'll keep them in water till they die, an' then press some of the flowers in a book like a schoolma'am. The pressed remains I shall keep as long as I live; an' never can I gaze on them flowers without bein' forcibly reminded o' the kind cowpunchers who gave them to me."

Someone in the back of the little group said, "Ouch!" and ducked his head; the others looked somewhat blank and taken aback; the joke had sort of gone off at the wrong end. Red had a dazed, glassy look in his eye; he was trying frantically to think of something that would save his face and reputation; he didn't seem to be having much luck.

But Bob took no chances. He gave them a last pleasant nod and a, "Thanks, boys," and stepped back into the house, closing the door after him.

146

He escaped quickly by the kitchen door, saddled a fresh horse, and struck out over the hill in a lope. Supper or no supper, he wasn't coming back until all the boys were in bed, and then he'd sneak into his own little room. Perhaps he should slip his blankets out and spend the night under a cedar. What Red had said about "pervailin' custom" was all too true; the cowboy whose birthday unfortunately became known must expect to have the chaps put to him with thoroughness worthy of a better cause; that he happened to be the foreman would make it all the worse for him.

Riding through the darkness, Bob cursed and grinned alternately. No one of his age and size could look forward with equanimity to the prospect of being stretched face down over a barrel, a dozen willing men holding his legs and arms, while one of the heftiest swung a pair of heavy cowhide chaps heartily and brought them down with resounding crashes against the part of his anatomy which was uppermost. If he got cranky about it, so much the worse for him, both then and later; he would acquire the name of being a hopeless grouch.

True, the Bar Diamond had the fairest custom he had ever heard of; if a man refused to reveal his birthday, it was the rule to appoint one for him, and to see that it was always remembered. Still this didn't offer much consolation to Bob just now.

Darn fools! Wouldn't he look nice stretched over a barrel, with all that big crowd of men yelling around him, and those chaps whipping down steadily!

147

An hour or so after dark it began to get chilly. Bob made a little fire in a draw where the light could not be seen from the ranch. He had chosen a thick patch of cedars, so he was sheltered from the light wind. He stretched out and tried to sleep; he did succeed in dozing more than once. He was reviewing the day.

Had anyone before ever had such a birthday! It had begun with a wild-goose chase hunting pingüe, and ended with a little fortune in bills sent to him unregistered by an unknown and mysterious woman. At least he thought it had ended.

Darn those fool boys! It wouldn't be so bad except that he'd likely have to ride all the next day.

About ten o'clock he was shivering in spite of his fire, one side cold, the other roasting; he had no coat with him. He decided to steal back to the hill above the house and see if things looked as though the boys had gone to bed. He caught his horse where it had grazed off a few yards with its reins trailing.

From the top of the hill, he stared. There were lights in every window — ranch house, bunk house, cook shack, and all. Men were hurrying around with lanterns. What the heck? There couldn't be all that excitement over looking for him to put the chaps to him.

He went loping down the hill, his heart beating faster and faster as he rode. He leaped from his saddle and ran across the porch. The door was flung open, and Red, racing out, crashed into him. Red's face was scared, white.

"What's the matter?" gasped Bob.

148

"Uh — uh — Stella's gone! Here's a note came back tied to her saddle horn."

Bob grabbed it and dashed in to the light, his heart in his throat. His hand trembled so that he could hardly read the soiled paper. It was a hastily penciled scrawl:

Fire all yur men an yoll get Stella back. Ef you dont —

That was all. Bob shivered more at the long, badly-drawn line than he did at the words.

CHAPTER
ELEVEN

Swift Eagle

Panic swept over Bob, but he fought it down. Everybody else on the ranch was panic-stricken; he had to keep his head. He tried to think quickly, but to think here was impossible; men were crowding into the room until it was packed, and they all seemed to be shouting at once — suggestions, plans, theories.

Bob tried to get details from somebody, but as soon as one began to talk rationally, five or six more interrupted with different stories. Bob shrugged with despair, nodded to Red, who seemed cooler than the rest, and pushed his way through the excited crowd. On the porch, someone seized his arm, spluttering advice to get bloodhounds immediately. He shook him loose angrily.

"Leave me alone! Get back in the house!"

With Red Selby beside him, he escaped into the darkness. They hurried down to the corrals, around them, and there, hidden from the others, they squatted on their heels with their backs to the logs.

"Well, what *did* happen?" asked Bob.

"You know about as much as anyone else. Her horse came wanderin' in, with its bridle an' that note tied to the saddle horn."

"When?"

"It was just gettin' what you could call dark. We thought it was a loose horse — I mean we didn't know it was saddled — at first."

"Which way did it come?"

"Along that cow trail at the foot of the ridge."

"What has anybody done, so far?"

"Why — nothin'. What was there to do?"

Bob swore. He turned to remark bitterly that but for Red's crazy jokes he himself would have been there, but he stopped himself. Of course Red had not known what was going to happen. And if he had been there what could he have done?

"Well," he asked, "have you thought of anything we can do?"

"Why we can think of nothin' only sendin' somewhere for bloodhounds to trail 'em."

"Where could we get bloodhounds, for goodness' sake?" snorted Bob.

"Why — uh — there should be some somewhere."

"Should! If you'd followed hounds as much as I have, you'd know how little they can do on a cold trail in this dry country — especially in this drought. By the time we got 'em here, they wouldn't know there was any trail."

"We-ell, what else is there to do?"

"Sit down an' smoke a cigarette like you've been doing!" Bob's tone was bitterly sarcastic — too much so.

"Clever, ain't you, Bob?" Red's voice quavered with anger at the slur. "Think I'll sit down an' smoke a cigarette an' let you or anybody else talk to me that way?"

He was ready to fight on the instant. Bob caught his breath; he was in the wrong, and he knew it.

"Red, I apologize. That crack was uncalled for. I — I'm pretty upset, I reckon."

"Then don't cuss other people for bein' the same," spat Red. "Nobody's afraid of you, Bob."

"Heck, Red, I apologize. What more can I do? For goodness' sake, don't let's start a fight — now."

"I don't start fights — I finish 'em."

Bob felt like striking him; with his superior size and strength, he knew that he could whip him almost with one hand. But he also knew that Red was in the right. He had known Red's temper; he should have been more careful of what he said.

"Red — uh — the trouble is that we're both badly upset, to act like a pair of fool kids this way."

A stony silence for a moment.

"Well, Bob, what do we do — that's sensible?"

That was better!

They sat a few moments silent in the darkness, both thinking hard. Red passed over the "makings", to roll cigarettes. Bob did not know whether this was done absently, in sarcasm, or in dry humor, and he did not dare ask. He spoke:

"Bloodhounds seem to be all I can think of, too. But where could we get any in time?"

"They likely have some at the penitentiary — but it would take more than a day to get them, even if we wired."

Another silence. Suddenly Bob spoke.

"Say, how about Indian trackers? Are they as good as people say they are? You were raised on the reservation, I heard; you should know something about 'em."

"Yeah; my dad had a tradin' post in the Navajo country. Bob, I don't like to talk about some trackin' I've seen 'em do; everyone would think I was a liar. You've seen desert cowboys that had to be able to track cattle to hold their jobs; Nevada boys is the best at it. Well, after seein' a ten-year-old Navajo trailin' a rabbit through the rocks, you'd say them Nevada boys couldn't be depended on to follow a wagon road without gettin' lost."

"Say, maybe we got an idea! How long would it take to get a good Navajo here? The ones living near the railroad are pretty useless."

"That's it!" The eagerness had gone suddenly from Red's voice. "Course," he added, "it don't make any difference to 'em if the trail is dry, so long as it hasn't blowed or rained on it too much."

"Tell you what: let's ride to town as quick as we can, an' wire somebody in Flagstaff to look around for one; if we could get one there, he'd be able to come down by train in no time. Then there's Winslow an' Holbrook, there'd be sure to be some of 'em from 'way back in tradin' at one of 'em. Let's go!"

They hurried quickly around the corral and took their ropes from their saddles, which rested against the bottom log. They entered the corral, and stooped low to see the outlines of the horses. Red found that in the darkness he had caught the wrong one — one too young and soft for a hard ride. Muttering irately, he liberated it and caught another. They saddled quickly, and Bob took time to lope up to the house and leave word that he was going to town; he did not pause to say what his plans were, but it would look queer if he simply disappeared.

They had chosen strong mounts, and they pushed them mercilessly. In record time, they were stopping the sweat-lathered horses at the railroad station in Danvers. They rushed into the waiting room and to the window. The same slim man with the hand-rolled white cigarette was in the office; he was lounging back reading a magazine, but when he heard the running feet, he hurried to the window.

"When," asked Bob quickly, "is the next train leavin' Holbrook for here?"

"One just left; it'll be several hours till the next."

Bob groaned. Holbrook was out. So was Winslow, for no one would have time to search the streets and the outskirts of town before the train passed. Flagstaff still remained; but it was a pretty good chance at that.

"Here, gimme a telegraph blank."

The man shoved a pad and pencil across, and Bob wrote quickly. He glanced up once to ask:

"What do you call that train?"

"Number 7."

Bob finished the message and pushed it hastily across the counter. The operator glanced at it:

154

SHERIFF
FLAGSTAFF
 RUSH RUSH SEND GOOD NAVAJO TRACKER
ON NUMBER SEVEN IF CAN FIND WIRE ANSWER
COLLECT

R EDWARDS

"Get that out quick!"

The man ran across to his desk and threw himself
into the chair. Bob shouted to him:

"Who's sheriff now?"

"Donnevan." Red answered before the operator
could.

"Wait!" called Bob. "Sign it 'Bob Edwards'; I know
him."

He watched the man's white, thin hand fluttering
dizzily above the key. That anyone could read such a
crackling buzz seemed a marvel to him. He turned to
Red.

"Well, we have an hour to wait. What do we do?"

"Why," drawled Red judiciously, "we might set down
an' smoke cigarettes." Now there was a faint twinkle in
his eyes; quickly though he could flare up, he never held
grudges.

"Aw, lay off!" groaned Bob, flinging himself on a
wooden bench.

Having sent Bob's message, the man waited to
receive another or two — routine railroad business.
Then he strolled from the office and sat down with
them; this night shift was a tedious job.

"Somethin' wrong?" he asked concernedly.

155

Bob told him what had happened. The operator looked almost as shocked and indignant as the cowboys had been; everybody liked Stella; this outrage would drive the countryside wild.

Soon Bob became restless, uneasy; here was this man sitting talking with them instead of listening for an answer. Of course it was too early for it yet, but Bob hoped he'd go back to his desk soon. Should he nudge Red and walk outside for a while?

"Yes, sir," the man continued, "whether they hurt her or not, whoever done it is takin' a fine chance o' bein' strung up to the nearest cottonwood limb. It's the dirtiest sh —"

In the middle of the word, he turned and darted into the office. Through what to Bob was a meaningless clatter of keys, the Danvers call had come as clear as a bugle note to the operator. Bob hoped he would remain there until his message from Flagstaff came in. Donnevan would have to rush around to find anyone before the train passed. Shouldn't be much more than an hour until he heard something.

"Here we are!"

The man had come running back through the door with a slip in his hand. Bob grabbed it eagerly. Quick work on Donnevan's part — he thought thankfully.

BOB EDWARDS
DANVERS
    WIRE GUARANTEE FIFTY DOLLARS FINE STOP SWIFT EAGLE IN JAIL STABBING HOPI
                             DONNEVAN

156

"Wire the guarantee!" ordered Bob quickly.

The man hurried back to his desk. Bob sighed with relief. This was the best piece of luck he'd had in a long time, the sheriff having a Navajo in jail waiting to be sent for. Of course it remained to be seen how good a tracker he was; there are Navajos and Navajos. Presently Bob turned to Red.

"While we're waiting, let's go up to the livery stable an' try to rent three more horses. We'll want one for the Indian, and ours are dead beat."

Red shook his head. "After Lew sees the shape ours are in, he won't rent us any."

"Then we'll buy 'em. Come on. We can borrow another saddle."

They stopped at Ben Wilson's house on the way. The sheriff, sleepy-looking and unexcited as usual, drawled something about "dropping out to look into it".

They did not have to buy horses. When Lew Brewer heard of the abduction, he profanely stated that he would not rent any to them — he would lend them, free. If they were injured by the ride, the Bar Diamond could settle for the damage any way it wanted to, if it wanted to. Also, Lew had some good strong ropes that he would gladly lend to anyone who wanted to make the right use of them, when the abductors were found. And furthermore, he'd take a sulphurous pleasure in pulling on the loose end. Why, the blinkety-blank dash — dash —

Although cowboys are none too reserved in their language, most of them looked askance at Lew for his habitual profanity. This time Bob could not find a thing wrong with it; he considered Lew very restrained, under the circumstances, his brimstone-reeking words very much to the point. Red murmured approvingly:

"*That's* what I wanted to say all night, but I didn't know how."

They left Lew choking in a cloud of his own vituperation, and returned to the telegraph office. During the long wait, they asked a dozen times if the train was on time; it always was.

There was strong gray daylight when at last they heard a distant whistle. The rails began to click and hum. Then around the curve the train came, puffing. It sailed grandly into the station and came to a noisy stop. The two men glanced eagerly back and forth along the line of cars.

Suddenly Bob's heart sank. A withered old Indian was feebly scrambling from a coach. He was dressed in patched overalls and worn shoes, and the greasy remains of a Stetson hat covered his long gray hair, which was tied in a knot behind his head. Bob went toward him with dragging feet.

"You Swift Eagle?" he asked.

The old man peered at him; he was nearly blind. He spoke, in broken English:

"Huh? Me Whiskey Jim. Gimme dime."

He looked his name. Bob groaned hopelessly. Perhaps in his far-distant youth this man had been Swift Eagle; now "Blind Snail" would have fitted him better. If Donnevan had been standing there, Bob might have murdered him. Was this a joke, or just plain stupidity?

Bob heard an exclamation from Red, and turned. He started; his eyes lighted up. From the other end of the coach a copper-skinned youth had come on silent, moccasined feet. He stood there now, his face as blankly expressionless as though he were thinking of something a hundred miles off. Bob spoke quickly:

"You're Swift Eagle?"

The youth made a slow gesture, bringing his right index finger up to his chest.

"Swif' E'l."

The sounds could not be represented by English spelling, but there was no mistaking what he meant.

"You speak English?"

The youth stared blankly. He did not even know the meaning of those three words; he knew only that English for his name. He must have come from very far back in the huge reservation, from back in the wild, broken country almost unknown to white men. Bob Edwards felt like whooping; had Donnevan been here now, Bob would have cheerfully given him his saddle, and perhaps two or three horses to boot.

Bob examined Swift Eagle as though he were something he was buying for a high price. Hardly more than eighteen, if that. Rather undersized — many Navajos are fairly tall — but with the slim, wiry grace of his people. Long, thin face; high cheek bones; thin, aquiline nose — handsome beggar; must make the young squaws' hearts flutter, with his lordly, disdainful air.

A dandy, too. He wore a purple plush garment, something between a shirt and a coat, which hung far below his waist; it was richly ornamented with beads. Plush trousers; beaded moccasins; very heavy belt of turquoise-set silver plaques around his waist — but practically every Navajo had one of those. Bracelets; more turquoise and silver. And long hair — all too often the younger Navajos had shorn heads — held in place by a crimson silk handkerchief twisted around his forehead. Many of the older men dressed thus, but a youngster who followed those old fashions must surely be from far back.

"Where you come from?" asked Bob.

Again an expressionless stare. Bob turned to Red.

"You were raised on the reservation; you should know their lingo."

"Too hard; I never could pick up much of it."

"Why?" asked Bob. "Boys along the border talk Mexican just as well as they do English."

Red sniffed.

"That's different — easy. They say a Navajo has twelve hundred and seventy-two different ways of saying horse, and as many more for every other word. I don't know whether that's right or not, but I do know they use a different word for the same thing every time you hear 'em say it, accordin' to what they mean about it."

"Well, you must know some; try him."

Red faced the Indian hesitatingly, and spoke. Swift Eagle grunted a curt monosyllable, and then, seeming to think better of it, rattled off something swiftly. Again Red spoke to him, and this time the Navajo answered more slowly. Red turned.

160

"Far as I can make out, he says he comes from the country beyond the Jil-at-sitl. They're a sorter bronco tribe up somewhere toward the Natural Bridge; wild as jack rabbits."

"Ask him if he can track."

Again Red tried his halting Navajo. Young Swift Eagle heard him, gave him a supercilious look down his thin nose, and turned his back without answering. Bob might have felt much the same if some Eastern "dude" had asked him if he'd ever been on a horse — but Bob could not have answered so well.

"He says he can — some," stated Red, gravely.

"Well, let's be going."

Bob turned toward the horses. He was going to tell the Indian which to ride, but evidently that information was unnecessary. Without the least change of expression, Swift Eagle swung calmly into Bob's own saddle, which was on the best horse. He mounted from the off side, Indian style; it took the horse so much by surprise that it had not time to buck before the youth was seated on its back; then the animal gave a vague crow hop, but philosophically dropped the matter at that.

"Hey," said Bob, "that's my mount. Here's yours."

The Navajo didn't even glance at him; he turned silently away. Red again translated:

"He say him wantum that horse — an' we're only danged, bleached-out white men anyway, so that's that."

Bob's face held an expression something between anger and a grin. He did all that was left him to do; he

161

swung into the borrowed saddle and, with Red beside him, loped to catch up. He signed to the Navajo youth to ride faster.

Swift Eagle wasn't ready to ride faster. From inside his velvet shirt he produced a pipe, which he held toward Bob, showing that it was empty. Bob, with an impatient grunt, passed him his sack of tobacco. The Navajo filled the bowl, and then signed for a match. Why use his own match when there were white men around?

The pipe going properly, Bob held out his hand for his tobacco. Swift Eagle politely overlooked such ill manners and thrust the sack somewhere inside his shirt. Then he swung his quirt across the horse's flank and struck out in a fast lope. Bob snorted: "Of all the impudence —"

"No," sighed Red, "jest Navajo. They're all that way when you get back a ways; know too much about the cavalry to fight the white men, but they class us several degrees below hop-toads."

"Well, if he can track, I'll let him get away with it; if he can't, I'm goin' to work him over so's his old mammy wouldn't know him before I let him get away."

"Better leave him alone; remember he was locked up for knifin' a Hopi." Red shook his head. "Navvies are the most low-down, treacherous, two-faced Injuns in the world — when they're dealin' with white men or other Indians. They hate the Hopis, an' the Hopis is just as good as we are — jest as civilized, in their own way; *fine* Injuns."

"The Navajos must sure hate whites!"

"They don't; they think we're too low-down to be hated."

"The big-headed fool!" Bob glared at the Indian's back.

CHAPTER
TWELVE

The Long Knife

They got to the ranch to find not over a dozen men on the place; the rest were scouring the range, trying to find trace of the missing girl. It seemed that the extra men were almost as furious as the old hands; indeed, this outrage seemed to have instantly wiped out the distinction between old hands and extras.

Bob had hardly arrived when he noticed the sheriff with a little group gathered around him; there seemed to be some excitement. Bob hurried over.

"What's up? When did you get here?"

"Got here before daylight. We picked up the tracks all right; followed 'em over nearly to Al Boyd's place, but lost 'em."

"Al Boyd's!" Al seemed to be mixed up in everything.

"Uh-huh. They got her as she was ridin' through a patch of cedars. She seemed to have put up quite a scrap. We found these on the ground."

He handed Bob a small white handkerchief with the initial S on a corner, and a man's spur. Bob held the latter in his hand, looking at it closely. It was of a common type, so common that it would be hard to remember it even if one had seen it before. A broken spur leather explained its loss; probably the rowel had hung on a stone or root in the struggle, and it was not noticed in the excitement and semidarkness.

"Look on the shank," drawled Wilson.

Bob turned the spur over. There, crudely engraved, evidently with a small cold chisel, were the initials *AAB*.

"Huh!" Bob turned quickly. "What's Boyd's middle name?"

The sheriff answered:

"Can't say, but he signs his name Albert A. Boyd."

Somebody spat an oath.

"Let's go over there an' string him up."

"I wouldn't!" murmured Wilson regretfully. "I don't want no trouble with you boys. I got somethin' private to say to Bob."

The little knot of men drew away at the hint, but they stayed together; they were whispering angrily. Wilson spoke quickly:

"Bob, I'd better get over there an' pick him up right away, before there's any trouble. I'll have to hire a lot o' special deppities to hold him."

"But — but if he's got Stella, taking him away might cause trouble for her."

"I thought o' that. But what can I do? I can't let the boys lynch him, an' they'll do it sure as shootin' if he's left at home."

"Why — I reckon you're right. But I don't like it a bit."

The sheriff shrugged, and motioned to his two men, who stood by themselves a little way off. The three swung into their saddles and trotted into the cedars. They were hardly out of sight when the little knot of cowboys broke toward the corral where their horses were. Bob intercepted them.

"Hold on, boys! Those three will fight; you can't get Al without killin' 'em, an' killin' a sheriff's serious business."

They hesitated; they had not thought of that. Bob continued quickly:

"Better wait till we can get the whole crowd together; then we can take him out of jail; there'll be so many of us, with people we pick up in town, that Wilson won't do anything."

There was a little argument — not much. Bob's plan seemed sensible. The cowboys turned and went slowly toward the bunk house.

"Why didn't you let 'em do it?" growled Red.

"Because that might be the end of her — somebody might want to get even," Bob told him.

"Good Lord! I hadn't thought of that."

All this time the Indian had sat his horse almost without moving; of course he did not have the slightest notion of what it was all about. Bob beckoned to him.

"Let's go get fresh horses. Come on, Red."

"Huh! Ain't you goin' to take all the other boys that's here?"

"No. I don't want to make a racket going through the country; that would scare 'em off before we got within

166

a mile of 'em. They might take her with 'em, or they might —"

He did not finish. Red gasped. The seriousness of this thing impressed itself on him more and more. They quickly caught fresh horses, and motioned to the Indian to change his saddle to one of them. He did so, and mounted, to sit gazing expressionlessly at the horizon.

"Statue — heap big little chief!" Red sniffed.

"Well, we'll soon see what he can do — if anything. Come on, Eagle."

At first it was merely a matter of tracking the horses whose riders had been following the trail; this was almost as easy as following a road. The Navajo hardly glanced at where he was going; he left this part to his two companions. Then they came to a wide, stony wash. The ground on both sides was cut up by many hoofs; this was where the sheriff and his men had lost the trail and circled a long time seeking it. Bob waved a hand.

"All right, Eagle; let's see what you can do."

The Navajo rode down the wash in a slow walk. He sat hunched over in his saddle as though half asleep. Bob wondered why he did not dismount to examine the stones. He went almost a quarter of a mile, the two white men following eagerly, and then he turned and loped back. By this time Bob was beginning to lose confidence in him; he seemed too casual about the thing, did not seem to care a hang whether he found the trail or not. And here it was already well along in the afternoon.

Then up the wash, in a slow walk again. Before he had gone a hundred yards, he suddenly reined his horse over near one bank. He pointed to the stones, and grunted something that Bob of course could not understand.

"What is it?"

Bob swung from his saddle; Red, too. They stared at the ground stone by stone. The Indian gave an impatient, almost angry grunt and slipped down beside them. When he pointed this time, his finger was within an inch of a pebble. Bob picked it up. Now he saw a faint gray stripe on it.

"Bunk!" he snorted disgustedly. "A horseshoe wouldn't leave that kind of mark; it would leave a white scratch."

Red translated with difficulty. The Indian youth gave both a glance of utter contempt. He picked up a forefoot of his horse, seized the shoe in two fingers, and made a motion as though jerking it off.

"Whew-w-w!" whistled Bob; he understood the pantomime.

The Navajo held out his hand for the stone. Bob gave it to him; he drew it hard across the side of the hoof and handed it back.

"Yes, sir!" gasped Red. "Jest the same color. But how the jumpin' jack rabbits did he spot it from 'way out in the middle o' the wash?"

Bob was humble enough by now as far as Swift Eagle was concerned. This was the trail of the abductors; of course the sheriff and his men had ridden shod horses, and loose, barefooted horses would not keep to those stones. Bob shook his head.

"They say an Indian has eyes 'way better than a white man's — must have."

Swift Eagle had mounted again; they were following him up the wash.

"No," Red disagreed, "doctors say they ain't. It's only that they learn to use 'em this way; they don't overlook nothin'."

"I don't believe it; they *must* see better."

"We-ell, I've heard pretty smart old Injuns claim that white men have eyes a few thousand times better than theirs; that's the only thing about whites they respect."

"Why should they say that?" asked Bob, unbelieving.

"Because a white man can take a piece o' paper with nothin' on it only a lot o' little dirty smudges, and see words on it; no Navvy tracker ever had good enough sight to do that. I've seen 'em starin' an' starin' at a paper, for hours at a time, but not a danged word would it say to them; they can't understand it."

The wash ran at right angles to the first part of the trail. The Indian followed it up for over a mile, and then turned into a narrow side wash. For all this time the trail had kept to the stones, winding from side to side to avoid sandy patches. Soon it left the smaller wash to cross a rocky mesa; here there was some earth to show hoof-prints. The Navajo slipped from his saddle to zigzag afoot, bent over. Presently he pointed to a fairly clear print — pointed with a trace of triumph on his copper face.

"What's he sayin'?" asked Bob.

169

"One horse bein' led."

"Think he's right?" asked Bob uneasily.

"Huh!"

Crossing the mesa, the Indian did not hurry; he again filled his pipe with Bob's tobacco, kept the sack, and borrowed a match, although he had pocketed nearly a box of them at the ranch that morning. This time Bob only grinned good-humoredly; he had put two extra sacks in his chaps pocket, and a plentiful supply of matches.

They followed down the side of the mesa and came to a level spot where there were few stones, the ground soft and thickly covered with cedar humus. Swift Eagle, ahead, swung his horse from side to side; something like a very faint grin came to his face; there seemed to be a slight twinkle in his eyes as he looked at the two white men. He pointed.

"What is it?" Red was circling.

"See!" Bob waved his hand, embracing the scattered tracks. "They opened out, and sort of wandered around crisscrossin' over each other. Anybody seeing the tracks — barefooted — would think it was loose horses."

"Pretty clever!" exclaimed Red admiringly.

"Uh-huh — sure. But I don't think it'll do 'em much good. Here, Eagle; have another sack of tobacco."

The Navajo youth took it gravely, but this time his eyes met Bob's as though he might have said thanks if he knew how. Although he understood no English, he could not help seeing that those white men were marveling at his skill. Nobody is so fond of showing off

170

as a young Indian buck — and where could he find a more impressed audience than this?

There was something almost friendly in his attitude as he took the trail again. For one thing he went much faster; before, he had taken very little interest in the thing; helping white men was but a shade better than being in the white man's jail.

Pretty soon they came to where the abductors had begun to grow careless, figuring, no doubt, that they had gone so far as to be safe. There were many places now where the two cowboys could follow the tracks easily. The speed of the pursuers increased.

"How many horses," asked Red, "did you make out back there?"

"Three. Better ask the Eagle about it; he'll likely tell you what color they were an' what the brand is." Bob was reaching the stage where he could joke, things were going so well.

It took Red a long time to get this said; he had to drop his reins on the saddle horn and use both hands. At last he fell back beside Bob; they kept behind out of the Indian's way most of the time.

"He says three here, but five where he found the trail first; two kept on up the main wash."

"Could we — No, we're right; he said back there that one horse was led."

They had gone perhaps five miles more when Bob gave a sudden exclamation: "Say! We've been so busy watching for tracks that we didn't notice how late it was getting. Only couple hours till dark."

Red looked up blankly; he, too, had not noticed the passing of time.

"Can you hurry him up a little?" asked Bob uneasily.

Red loped up beside the Indian, presently to fall back again.

"He says it is better not to go too fast and lose the trail."

"But — dang it! — looks like we're headed for Zorro Mountain. It'll be dark before we get there, an' then we can't keep on. Tell him he *as* to hurry."

Once more Red went forward to talk to the Navajo. He had not said a dozen words before Swift Eagle suddenly stopped his horse and turned to face them. Bob hurried up.

"What's the trouble?"

Red swore feelingly.

"He says if we don't stay back out of the way an' stop botherin' him, he'll go home."

"Tell him like fun he will. He'll go back to jail."

Red translated.

The young Indian never turned a hair, but from somewhere a long, wicked-looking knife with a home-made handle appeared. He toyed with it meaningly, twirling it in his delicate fingers. Few white women have hands as soft and well formed as an Indian buck's, or as small; it takes a hundred generations of lordly idleness to breed such hands. Swift Eagle had not troubled to speak, but Red translated dejectedly:

"He says he can throw that into one of our gizzards before we can get a gun halfway out."

"There's two of us!" reminded Bob furiously.

172

"He says he don't give a Hopi hoot — an' that's the poorest kind of hoot there is. He's not goin' back to jail."

"All right." Bob gave in bitterly; there was nothing else left. "Tell him to do what he wants to."

Red spoke in halting Navajo. The knife disappeared, but the Indian came riding back to them. Impudently, he held out his pipe, showing the bowl empty. Bob would have liked to strangle him then and there; he had to keep his lips shut tight to keep from saying something the meaning of which Swift Eagle might guess from his tone. Furiously, he handed over his last sack of tobacco.

The Navajo did not bother to fill his pipe; he thrust both pipe and tobacco inside his velvet shirt, gave Bob a look of withering contempt, and turned his back.

Now, instead of going faster, he went more slowly than before. Bob was boiling; never in his life had he so longed to send his fist crashing into another man's insolent face. Only a cub, too — what must an older Navajo be like!

Dark it almost was when they entered the rugged foothills of Zorro Mountain. The Indian went more and more slowly as the light failed. He swung from his saddle, and threw the reins to Bob to lead the horse; he might have been throwing a bone to a mangy dog. Bob gritted his teeth, but took the reins. Oh, but what wouldn't happen to this fellow tomorrow!

At last Swift Eagle stopped. For a quarter mile he had been barely poking along, bent over so as to be almost going on all fours. Turning his back to the white men, he seated himself on a boulder and drew out his pipe. There they could stay for the night, to be ready to take the trail at dawn. To a Navajo this sleeping on the bare ground meant no hardship in the least, but Bob and Red stared at each other blankly; the nights were cold, the ground hard, and they had nothing to eat.

"*That's* why he was so slow!" groaned Red. "Wanted to keep us out here all night to get even with us for somethin' or other. My opinion of Navajos is —"

Red gave his opinion, fluently, monotonously, and feelingly — Lew Brewer could have done very little better. Bob was too bitter, too angry, to join him in it. He dared not speak at all; if he did, he would lose his temper and strike the Indian. And Swift Eagle was their only hope; without him they could not expect to find the place where Stella was concealed, although it could not be far off now.

His pipe finished, the Navajo threw himself carelessly on a sandy spot. Within a minute he was asleep, one forearm for a pillow, his knees doubled up, relaxed as a kitten. The white men tried to follow his example, but with no success; they could not even force themselves to doze, although they pretended to each other that they could.

Two hours or so passed. The air was getting chilly. Red sat up with a groan.

"What's the use! Let's set up an' shiver ourselves warm."

Bob joined him. He felt that his teeth would soon be chattering. Why had he not brought a coat? He wished he had even a slicker. Slicker! It had been many months since one needed that around here.

"Look at him! Look at him!" growled Red savagely under his breath.

Still the Indian slept like a child. In the bright starlight, they could see his lips partly open, his white teeth flashing in a gentle smile. What was he dreaming of? Of that unknown country of canyons and buttes that was his home? Of some pretty, dark-eyed little squaw who waited there for him? Presently Bob stood up and began to flap his arms, trying to get his blood circulating enough to warm him. Immediately a quick rattle of words came from where the Indian was; he was sitting up.

"He says" — Red spoke hesitantly; he feared that Bob had had about all he could stand — "he says for us to stop makin' all that noise an' let him sleep. He says we should go away down the wash so's not to disturb him."

"That's enough! Here's where I land on him!"

"Don't, Bob!"

Red leaped and seized his arm, held him back. Hot-headed though Red himself was, he had learned to treat Navajos with a sort of bitter, furious patience.

"I tell you —"

"Listen, you idjit! How'll we find her without him?"

That sobered Bob. With a groan he threw himself on the ground. He had to stand for it. But wait — just wait! — till tomorrow, after she was found.

Bob lay watching Red sitting miserably on a rock, outlined against the starlit sky. He would be silent, but

175

he would not leave there. Presently he saw another figure in outline. Swift Eagle had stood up. Bob saw him poised, with head thrown far back, motionless. There came a quick, whispered word in Navajo. Bob scrambled to his feet and hurried to him.

"What is it?"

Still with his head thrown back, the Indian sniffed the air. Bob sniffed, too; he could smell nothing. Swift Eagle made a beckoning motion and started silently up the little canyon. The other two hurried after him, afoot; it seemed that he did not want the horses along. He stopped, and whispered some words to Red.

"He says to get our spurs an' chaps off — they make too much noise — an' our hats."

"Why the hats?"

"I dunno — reckon he thinks they show up too plain against the sky." Red was kicking off his chaps, removing his spurs.

They had not gone ten yards when another order came.

"He says to take off our boots! He says we make more noise than a house falling down."

"Tell him to go to the devil!"

Bob suspected that Red's words were a polite explanation of the fact that white men's feet were too soft to allow them to walk barefooted; it sounded like something that way. With a shrug, the Indian started on again. He made no more noise than a shadow. The other two felt painfully conscious, that, try as they might, their high-heeled boots clattered like mules going over a wooden bridge.

176

"What did he hear?" asked Red presently.

"Why, he smelled —"

Bob broke off, sniffing the air.

"There you are!" he whispered. "Wood smoke."

Soon they rounded a bend in the canyon. The Indian had stopped. Pausing beside him, they followed his eyes to where he was looking. A hundred yards off, a little square of yellowish red seemed to appear and vanish, to flicker queerly. For a moment they could not guess what it might be.

"A window!" whispered Red. "There's no light in the house, only an open fire burnin'. Say — what do we do?"

He was intently excited. So, for that matter, was Bob; it seemed that they had come upon the end of the trail.

"Let's sneak up to the window an' look in," suggested Bob.

"Let young Snow-in-the-ears do it; Navvies is good at sneakin'. He can come back an' report to us."

"Might be better. Does he know what to look for — that it's a girl?"

"I'll tell him."

It took Red a long time to get it straight; his command of Navajo was about exhausted. At last Swift Eagle grunted that he understood. He signed to the white men to wait where they were, and disappeared in the darkness.

Bob anticipated at least an hour of standing there shivering. Once he thought he saw something darken the lower part of the window, but he was not sure. He wished that he could stamp his feet to warm them, but he dared not.

The Indian had not been gone much over five minutes when the light became suddenly brighter, the flicker ceased.

"The darn fool!" groaned Red in a whisper. "He made some noise; they heard him an' got up. They lit the lamp."

A moment later the cabin door opened. In the oblong of light stood the figure of Swift Eagle. He raised one arm and called something. Bob's heart sank.

"Nobody there — they left!"

The two ran forward. In a moment they were rushing into a little adobe room; that one room seemed to be the whole house.

"Ask him —"

Bob stopped suddenly. Stella, white-faced, bound, was staring at him from a narrow bunk built against the wall. There were two other bunks against the same wall, and in each was a figure. The figures lay as though asleep, still covered by their blankets. But Bob shuddered; he had seen something drip from one of the bunks to the floor, something that splashed; he thought of that long, wicked knife with the homemade handle.

"Bob! How did you get here!"

He rushed across to Stella and cut her bonds. She looked very white, disheveled, her clothing and hair rumpled.

"Stell, did — did they hurt you?"

"No — outside of dragging me around. But — what —" She was gazing at him bewildered. "I woke up, and he was lighting the lamp —"

178

She glanced to where Swift Eagle, a pot of cold beans in one hand and a spoon in the other, was eating expressionlessly.

"Bob — where — where are they?" She shivered.

For the first time Bob noticed that from where she was she could not see clearly into the other two bunks. He gave Red a quick, meaning look.

"They may be back; let's get out of here. Hurry!"

He took one arm, Red the other, and they hustled her unceremoniously out of the house. When they got through the door, Bob heaved a sigh of relief. They had not given her time to glance around, to look back; she did not know. He called:

"Come on, Eagle."

The Indian padded softly from the door and after them, the pot of beans still in his hand. He was not going to relinquish that; he was hungry; he probably knew of no earthly reason for not being hungry.

On the way back to the horses, she told them what had happened. She had little to tell, at that. She was returning to the ranch, just as it was getting dark, when four handkerchief-masked men had suddenly leaped their horses from the cedars and surrounded her. She had struggled, but it did her no good; she was gagged, tied on her horse, and taken here. No, she had not recognized any of them; they had kept the masks on all the time, even the two in the cabin.

"Was one of them," asked Bob, "big enough to be Al Boyd?"

She hesitated.

"N-no — I don't know. It was getting dark, and I was so scared."

"You poor kid!" Bob, his hand on her arm, helped her pick her way among the stones.

Back at the horses, they held a brief debate. Should they build a fire and camp there until daylight, or should they begin the long ride back to the ranch?

"How about it, Stella?" asked Bob. "It's up to you."

She shivered.

"Ugh! We must hurry off. What if they come back and find I'm gone? They'd look for me."

"That's right," agreed Bob; she did not notice that his voice sounded queer as though he shuddered. "But we could make a fire up some other canyon, out of sight."

"I can stand the ride. I want to go home."

There was something childlike about how she said it; "want to go home". Bob patted her arm.

"All right. You'll have to ride double with one of us; the rest of us are kind of heavy for double ridin'. Say, the Indian's light; you can ride with him part of the way, if you don't mind."

"Of course I don't mind!"

"Ask him about it, Red."

Red explained at length. The Navajo answered briefly. "He — he says he swore some sort of oath not to let a woman ride his horse. They're funny that way — sort of religion with 'em, oaths like that."

Bob nodded. He would not interfere with any man's oaths or religion. She mounted behind Bob to begin the long journey, and they filed slowly off in the darkness.

180

Bob was trying not to remember what he had seen in the two bunks back there. In spite of it, he felt very nearly happy. Stella was behind him on his horse, safe, her hands on his shoulders to balance herself. Yes, things had turned out pretty well after all.

He might not have felt so contented if Red had dared to translate Swift Eagle's uncivil words correctly:

"The white squaw can walk; no white squaw rides with me."

CHAPTER
THIRTEEN

The Veiled Woman

They got home in the small hours of the morning. Bob had not been in bed more than two hours when a cowboy came rushing into his room and woke him up.

"Say! That Injun's gone, an' he took that long-legged buckskin I was to ride today, an' Lew's saddle."

"He did!" Bob stared blankly, sleepily. "Oh, well, we can stand the loss of one horse, an' the outfit'll buy Lew another saddle."

Of course he didn't like this thing, but he could hardly have the Navajo arrested for it, after his helping them so much.

Red came running in, in his shirt tail, rubbing his eyes and blinking; he, too, had been awakened by the excitement.

"How about that fifty dollars' fine you guaranteed for him?"

"I'll have to pay it, I reckon; they'd never find him if he gets back into his own country." Presently he added, with a trace of a grin, "Don't know that I want 'em to, anyway; I've seen too much of Swift Eagle already."

Red nodded sagely.

"Don't worry, you'll never see him again. Bob, would you believe that I was a smart, sensible kid once, an' could learn the multiplication table an' spellin'? It was dealin' with Navvies made me like I am." He emitted a long, quavering sigh, and stalked with bowed head from the room, staring fixedly at his two forefingers which he held pressed together in front of him.

Bob grinned, and called after him:

"One more day of the Eagle an' I'd be the same. It's worth all he took to get rid of him."

He swung back into his bed and pulled the covers over his head to keep the daylight out. He tried to tell himself that he despised the young Navajo for an insolent pup, but he had a sneaking feeling that he had stood a little in awe of him. How different was that young savage from the dirty, shuffling Indians of other tribes who hung around the towns!

True, he thought, young Swift Eagle took shamelessly all he could get from the whites. But when had whites felt shame in robbing Indians? Of all the unnumbered tribes that had once occupied the United States, the Navajos alone had been powerful and clever enough to get their whole ancient homeland declared their reservation; their children were of unmixed blood, spoke the old tongue, and lived as their great-grandfathers had lived in childhood, knowing nothing and caring less about the despised pale race that now surrounded their huge territory.

Bob grinned sleepily. He was not quite sure that he did not respect Navajos, although the less dealings he had with them the better he would like it — and the better, too, would those copper-skinned tribesmen like it.

Along toward noon Bob awoke. He tossed the covers back, and lay yawning a moment before getting up. He heard a tinkle of spurs and the hollow click of high-heeled boots come hurrying down the middle of the bunk house. His door opened, and a cowboy stuck his head in to speak quickly:

"Bob, there's a lady to see you."

"A — *a lady?*"

"Uh-huh."

"Who is she?"

"I dunno; she has a big veil on. She come horseback." The cowboy seemed excited about the event. "You can see her from the window."

Bob peeped out. He saw a small, graceful young woman or girl swing from a sorrel horse and stand beside it waiting. She was very well and neatly dressed, and, as the cowboy had said, a heavy black veil hid her face. One hand, covered by a beaded buckskin gauntlet, reached up to pat her horse's head. She was used to horses; the way she patted and rubbed between the eyes told Bob that.

"Who the heck —" he gasped.

He dressed hurriedly; a young lady caller away back here at this lonesome ranch was an event indeed. To make it more so, Bob could not begin to guess who she might be. Golden hair showing at the back of her head — certainly no woman from any of the neighboring ranches.

184

Anxious though Bob was to solve the mystery, he made a careful toilet. He wished that he had time to shave. He did take time to dig a clean shirt out of his war bag.

At last he walked from the bunk house — as casually as though he had not been rushing like mad to prepare. She evidently knew him by sight; she turned and stood waiting for him.

"Good morning, ma'am." Bob raised his Stetson in a very creditable manner indeed.

"Good morning. I'd like to speak to you alone, Mr. Edwards."

What the devil! Nice voice — very nice. She had not *quite* said "mawnin'", but she was undeniably Southern; that soft, gentle drawl suggested Georgia. Southerner who had lived some time in the West, thought Bob.

"Yes, ma'am — certainly. I reckon Miss Davis will let us use the living room."

They walked together toward the house. Bob's mind was racing, trying to guess who she was. Stella heard them crossing the porch and opened the door casually. She started at seeing Bob with a girl; her face seemed to freeze just a trifle.

"Stella, this lady wants to speak to me alone. Would you mind if we use the living room?"

"Not at all. Make yourself quite at home."

Bob thought that Stella sounded very sweet and gracious; it did not come to him that perhaps she was a trifle too much so. She turned and entered the kitchen without another word, closing the door behind her.

"Sit down, ma'am."

"Thank you." She had good manners.

She removed her gloves. Bob noticed that she had nice hands, white. Then the white hands raised, pushed up her veil, and caught it somehow on the brim of her hat. This was what Bob was waiting for; he stared all he could without appearing unmannerly. Pretty — she sure was! Must be twenty-five anyway. Yes, pretty.

"You don't recognize me, Mr. Edwards?"

"Why — why —"

He was vaguely conscious of having seen her somewhere before.

"I'm Mrs. Boyd."

Bob gasped. Now he remembered her face; he had seen it but that one time when her husband had threatened to shoot him, and then only dimly, through the open doorway. Anyway, he would not have recognized her in these clothes. Who'd have thought a nester would dress his wife so neatly, let her keep her hands so white?

"I — uh — excuse me, ma'am, for not remembering. The boy about twelve years old — I didn't think you were old enough to —" Bob stopped suddenly; this didn't seem to be the thing to say.

She smiled faintly. Bob's tone and words were flattering, although he had not meant them to be. And what woman does not like to be told that she looks young?

"He's my stepson."

"Well, what can I do for you, ma'am?"

186

She was silent just a moment; evidently she did not know how to begin. Finally she spoke:

"Mr. Edwards, you had my husband sent to jail."

"No, ma'am!" said Bob. "I didn't have a thing to do with that. The sheriff thought he'd be safer —"

He stopped, reddened; one couldn't very well inform a charming young woman that everyone in the countryside wanted to lynch her husband.

"I came here to tell you that he had nothing whatever to do with taking Stella; if he had known of it, he'd have been the first to try to stop it."

"But — his spur —"

"The sheriff showed it to us. It wasn't his. There must be a good many other men with the initials *AAB*."

"Who, for instance, around here?"

Bob was going to be polite, but he was not going to let Mrs. Boyd make a fool of him.

"I don't know. I do know that Al got home that evening about four o'clock, and wasn't out of sight of the house again until next morning — not until the sheriff came and got him."

Bob tried not to look dubious. She leaned forward and placed a hand on his knee; she looked very eager now, very serious:

"Mr. Edwards, if you'll bring me the Bible, I'll swear to it."

Bob absently rubbed the back of his neck with his fingertips. She had all the appearance of a person telling the truth. What the deuce sort of mix-up was this anyway?

"I'm sure sorry, ma'am, but I didn't have anything to do with getting him locked up."

"But you can get him out. Miss Davis is back again, and not hurt; the hard feeling will die down. It isn't as if he had anything to do with it."

Bob thought of other charges he meant to bring against Al. He hated to refuse her request, but his helping Al was clearly out of the question.

"I'm sorry, ma'am." His tone was politely final.

"But, Mr. Edwards" — again she was leaning forward eagerly — "you *have* to get him out; he's innocent!"

"I'm sure sorry, ma'am." He shook his head firmly.

She was silent a moment. Evidently she had something else to say and did not know how to put it. At last she turned her head and glanced at the door through which Stella had gone. She lowered her voice:

"Mr. Edwards, what if I could make it worth your while to get him out?"

"Pay me, you mean?" A hard look came into Bob's eyes.

"Yes — well."

"Thanks, ma'am, but I'm not that sort. That all you wanted to see me about?"

He made a motion as though to stand up. She signed to him to remain seated.

"What if I paid you in advance?"

"I happen to be honest, ma'am." Bob's tone was sarcastic now, in spite of her good looks. He stood up with finality.

Again she glanced at the door. She almost whispered:

"In advance — mailed to you — tied with a leather string."

Bob slumped back into his chair.

"So — so it was you —"

"Mr. Edwards. I'm not admitting anything that might get Al into further trouble. I'll only say that he never stole a penny in his life. Oh," she blurted suddenly, "I wish you *knew* Al Boyd! A finer man never lived."

Here *was* a mess! It was she who had returned the money that meant so much — returned every cent of it. Why? And where had she got it if Al hadn't taken it? But the fact remained that Bob owed this woman a very great debt indeed; she had probably saved him at least five years of labor and scrimping trying to get another stake to start his own brand.

Bob was not one to forget obligations, and he was about convinced that Al had nothing to do with the abduction of Stella, after all. As to the robbery — well, Al had probably told this woman some cock-and-bull story to account for his having the money. She would not stand for anything of that sort. The point was, of course, that she had returned it, every cent.

"Very well, ma'am," Bob spoke suddenly, "I'll get him out if I can."

"Oh, thank you!" Her hand reached out impulsively and seized his. Now that the strain of the interview was over, her lips began to tremble, her eyelashes to quiver. She hastily reached up and pulled down her veil.

"Fine little woman!" thought Bob as he escorted her back to her horse. "Too darn bad she's wasted on that kind of brute." He felt almost happy over what he was going to do.

He had left his hat in the living room. He went back and got it after she had left. As he was leaving the doorway again, a cowboy lounging near by asked curiously:

"Who was she, Bob?"

Bob absently heard Stella enter the room behind him. He answered the cowboy stiffly, conclusively:

"It was a lady that wanted to see me private."

He turned back to say something to Stella, but she spoke first:

"Bob, when are you going to pay the men off?"

"Not going to," he answered.

"What! What do you mean?" Her voice was cold.

"I mean I have a plan to whip the sheepmen without fighting."

"Oh! Let's hear it." Sarcastically.

"Simple. I thought pingüe was coming up, and all we'd have to do was sit tight until the sheepmen went broke. Well, it wasn't."

"Well?"

She almost sniffed at him.

"Well, finally it got into my thick head that I didn't have to depend on pingüe. The cattlemen are all gathering money to help us; it's their fight as well as ours. That will let us hire a little army, and keep it as long as we want it."

"I told you I'd have no shooting."

"Uh-huh — glad you did, or I wouldn't have thought of this plan. I'm not wild about getting shot, either, or having any of the boys shot."

"Well, what's the plan?" She sounded skeptical.

"Why, don't you see? Keep Butch hiring high-priced gunmen till he goes broke. Make out like we're going to start fireworks any minute. Have 'em rushing to hire more men every day, before we come down on 'em like a thousand of brick. It'll soon bust 'em. How's that?" he finished triumphantly.

"Simply crazy."

"Huh?"

"Nothing short of idiotic. The sheepmen would force a battle on us. Please pay the men off."

She turned and walked from the room leaving Bob gasping. He knew the plan would work — could see no logical reason why it would not. What ailed Stella anyway? He had never seen her act that way toward him before. Acted as if she hated him!

He walked glumly from the house. So he had to lick not only the sheepmen but Stella — and she might prove the harder of the two. Shot — his plan shot! Would he have to quit after all? Or could he think of the last little detail he needed, a means of circumventing Stella?

He caught a horse and struck out toward town. Arriving there, he went straight to the sheriff's office. Wilson, his heels cocked carelessly up on his battered desk, informed Bob that he had had a "sorter hectic time", but the crowd around the jail had withdrawn as soon as word came that Stella was safe. The town looked quiet enough now.

After a brief consultation, they went together to see Judge Cox, a fat, pleasant-looking little gray-haired man who had become an institution in Danvers. Here there was another consultation. Bob wanted to get Al out, but he also wanted to be able to have him locked up again immediately if that became necessary. The judge solved it; he lowered the bail from five thousand dollars to ten dollars — quite a drop! Bob signed some papers, and followed Wilson to the jail. Here the sheriff unlocked a heavy door and, leaving Bob to open it, withdrew down the corridor.

Bob pushed the door open. Al was seated on an iron bunk, staring gloomily at the window. He turned, saw Bob, and stood up slowly; his bulk seemed to almost fill the little cell.

"Comin' to see the show, Bob — to have some fun?" he asked.

He did not display temper this time; he was clever enough to know that doing so would only make things all the worse for him; his tone was almost genially sarcastic. Bob stepped into the room.

"No, Al. I saw your wife, an' she swears you had nothing to do with what happened. She says you were at home all that evening and night."

"I was," he said simply. He added: "Bob, I reckon I should be sore at you for gettin' me locked up, but if you really think I done anything *that* dirty — well, I don't see how I can blame you."

Nothing could seem more honest than Al's words. In spite of his cool attitude toward Bob now, he seemed straightforward, likable. Bob had learned from the sheriff that no word about finding Stella had been brought to Al. He watched the bearded face closely as he spoke again:

"Well, we got Stella back all right — not hurt, outside of losin' a little sleep."

"You did!"

There was no mistaking the joy on the man's face; but then of course it might be relief for personal reasons that caused it.

"Uh-huh. The two fellers that had her got knifed — killed."

"Too good for 'em! Bob, if I could have got a shot at 'em myself, I might have saved somebody the trouble of knifin' 'em."

Bob casually asked a sudden question:

"Al, how often have you taken shots at people?"

The nester grinned.

"You're the only man I ever pointed a gun at. You're the first — an' you're shore the last! Do you know how near I come to pullin' the trigger?"

Bob nodded.

"Well, Bob, like most fellers I don't like to talk about it, but I'm sorter religious; I don't want any man's blood on my hands. Besides, gettin' hung ain't a nice way o' cashin' in."

Bob studied his face. It was hard to see any expression through the heavy beard. Pretty good acting, though: Bob could almost believe him if he tried hard enough. This man was a lot more clever than anyone gave him credit for being.

"Well, Al, I've just signed bail for you. Let's go."

"You signed bail for me!"

"Uh-huh."

The nester stared at him a moment. Then he threw back his great, shaggy head and roared with laughter; his huge, booming voice seemed to shake the walls of the little cell.

"*You* signed bail for me! What's goin' to happen next?"

"That," said Bob coolly, "is what I've been tryin' to figure out ever since this row first came up — and I never could."

"Well, Bob" — the nester's great paw came down on Bob's shoulder — "let's go out an' I'll buy you a drink; this is so funny that we have to celebrate it somehow!" He roared again.

"No, thanks."

Bob turned abruptly on his heel and walked away. He was beginning to have a vague suspicion that Mrs. Boyd and her big husband had succeeded in making a thorough fool of him. Anyway he was in no social mood; he was not yet over the blow of Stella's last order. All the way in he had been thinking; there seemed no way of getting around it.

CHAPTER
FOURTEEN

Predicate Adjectives

As he left the jail building, Bob found a man waiting for him on the sidewalk — a medium-sized man, gray-haired, kindly-looking. In spite of his staid business suit, his bronzed face and wiry actions showed him a man of the outdoors rather than of the towns.

"Hello, Bob. I was waitin' for you. I heard you went in here."

"Why, hello, Jerry."

Bob's tone was friendly; he and everybody else liked Jerry Mallett; they could not help liking him.

"Come in the Spreadeagle, Bob. I want to talk to you."

They went down the street together and entered the saloon. Mallett ordered a small glass of beer; Bob, to be polite, took the same. They carried their drinks to a small round table and sat down.

"Bob" — there was a mild, quizzical look on Mallett's face — "I hear you're goin' around cussin' sheepmen from hell to breakfast. Sorry you feel that way about me; I can't remember ever doing anything to you."

Bob reddened.

"Heck, Jerry, you know very well I don't count you in on that cussin'. There are honest sheepmen."

The other took a sip of his beer, wiped his lips, and smiled gently.

"You sound like you're admittin' that maybe some rattlesnakes ain't as bad as others. Bob" — he leaned across the table earnestly — "I wish you'd get it into your head that you're not fightin' sheepmen; you're fightin' crooks. If you were my age, maybe you wouldn't be so ready to cuss a whole class of men without hearin' their side of things."

"Jerry" — Bob sounded as anxious to be believed as the other had a moment before — "you know I'm not cussin' you. I — I suppose sheepmen have some excuse for tearing up the range, if I knew what it was."

"They haven't — not a bit."

"Huh?"

"I mean no sheepman does that — it's would-be sheepmen. I've run sheep twenty years now on one range. Will you come out some time an' spend two or three days lookin' it over with me? You'll find more grass right now than on your own range, an' more water."

"Well," admitted Bob ruefully, "if you know how to have grass an' water in this drought, I'll take my hat off to you as a stockman. Yes, sir, I'll sure go out just to see what grass an' water look like; I forget."

"You'll see both, Bob, an' I guarantee that you'll be well treated; some of us sheepmen are doin' our dangdest to stop the crazy hard feelin' between us an'

196

the cattlemen. But that's not what I wanted to see you about — not all of it. Here."

He tossed something across the table. Bob stared at a fairly thick roll of bills.

"What — what's that for?"

"The story leaked out that the other cowmen are helpin' the Bar Diamond fight Butch Johnson an' his crowd. Ab Hennicker was by my place this mornin' an' told me about it. Here's somethin' we're throwin' in to help you, an' we're goin' to see what the other sheep outfits around us will do. I think I can promise you they'll do more than you expect."

"But — but it's sheepmen we're fighting!" gasped Bob.

Mallett shook his gray head stubbornly.

"I'm tryin' to get it into your skull that it's not. That Butch Johnson crowd would just as soon pick on us as on you. Us honest stockmen, no matter if we're raisin' spotted jack rabbits for the hides, will have to stick together. See it now?"

Bob sat thoughtful a moment. Then his hand shot suddenly across the table.

"Jerry, I do see it; thanks for makin' me see it. There's plenty of room for both of us in Arizona."

"That's it! — an' we're both needed. You're wearin' woolen pants, an' I'm wearin' cowhide shoes; we sorter need each other."

"Just the same," Bob spoke regretfully, "I can't take the money."

He shoved it back across the table. He was thinking, of course, that he would have to call the war off as soon

197

as he got home. Of course Mallett knew nothing of that. A dull red mounted to the sheepman's cheeks.

"Bob, I thought you shook hands with me just now. Then why slap my face like this?"

"I didn't mean it that way," Bob said quickly. "It — it was something you don't understand."

"Then shove that in your pocket."

There was nothing else for it; Bob did. He could mail it back after the news of the crash got out.

"Thanks, Jerry."

He pressed the other's hand again, warmly, and hurried away. A man turned and stared at him as he went down the sidewalk; he had groaned aloud. Here sheepmen, as well as the cattlemen, were offering to help finance his war — and war was forbidden him; he had to quit.

If that blamed pingüe had only appeared in sufficient quantities on the sheep range, all he'd have to do now would be to sit tight and wait for Butch to go broke. That would be —

He stopped as though he had run into a brick wall. The missing detail of his plan had come to him.

Presently he heard a voice not far off, a casual voice:

"That's the first time I ever saw Bob Edwards drunk."

He suddenly realized that he was standing in the middle of the sidewalk, that two or three people had had to circle around him, that he was staring into the air with his mouth half open. He hurried away, but he even did that absently.

198

Fifteen minutes later he was again closeted with Judge Cox, a notedly clever lawyer in spite of his innocent appearance. Ten minutes after that, he was at the telegraph office. He did not know the operator on duty this time. He carefully wrote a message; he handed it to the man only after a second reading.

MRS NEWTON DAVIS

SANTA ELENA HOSPITAL

SAN FRANCISCO

SLIGHT TROUBLE WITH SHEEPMEN STOP DON'T WORRY AND DON'T TELL NEWT STOP POWER OF ATTORNEY FOR ME PERSONALLY NECESSARY TO HOLD RANGE STOP GET FROM NEWT ON SOME EXCUSE

BOB EDWARDS

He nodded cheerfully at the operator.

"I'm gettin' to be a regular customer here."

"That's good; we need the business."

"Get it out right away or sooner."

"You bet!"

The man had a clear wire and, with the message before him, began tapping steadily. He did not have the dizzy speed of the night operator, but even at that Bob knew that his message would be in San Francisco before he could roll and smoke a cigarette. This telegraph was sure some invention.

Within an hour the answer came:

POWER OF ATTORNEY FOLLOWING BY FIRST
MAIL STOP USE THIS AS AUTHORITY TO ACT FOR
ME MEANWHILE

NEWTON C DAVIS

Bob was whistling cheerfully as he swung out of
the waiting room. The deep line that for many days
had been drawn between his eyebrows had vanished.
He called a cheery "Hello, *muchachos!*" to two little
Mexican boys playing with a puppy in the dust, and
tossed them a quarter to buy *dulces*. He even went as
far as to wish that his young Navajo friend, Swift Eagle,
were there, so that he could give him a few sacks of
tobacco. No further could geniality go.

He took his horse to the livery stable and went to
the shabby little frame hotel for the night. In spite of
his having spent almost half the day in bed after his ride
of the night before, he slept like a log. He had a very
pleasant dream of Bar Diamond cattle grazing
contentedly through a herd of sheep, calmly taking a
sheep or two with every mouthful of grass until not one
of the woolly beasts was left.

He got up early, and was back at the ranch before
noon. Word awaited him, as he expected, that Stella
wanted to see him on important business. He
unsaddled his horse and walked to the house. In the
living room, they sat down opposite each other. Stella
had an expression on her face that he had never seen
there before; she looked at him unemotionally, as
though he were a stranger. She opened the conversation.

"Bob, I gave you orders to pay off all the extra men. Why didn't you do it?"

Bob sat up stiff and stared at her; she had never talked this way to him before. This was the owner's daughter speaking to the hired foreman. Bob could not see it quite that way; he wanted to start his own outfit; he had only offered as an accommodation to take charge of things during her father's absence.

"What's the matter, Stell?" he inquired; he was not angry.

"I want to know why you didn't do as you were told."

"Oh, for goodness' sake, come out of it, Stell!"

He grinned at her. They had had tiffs before, when she was a long-legged tomboy and he a "kid cowboy".

She sat silently waiting for an answer.

"Well," he said good-naturedly, "you gave me a day to find a plan, and I took it. Then I came to you with the plan — and I gave you another day to think it over."

"Don't you think you were taking quite an unwarranted liberty in letting the thing go another day?"

"Six-bit words — I'll have to remember 'em," mused Bob, just loudly enough for her to hear.

She was flushed now, undeniably angry.

"Bob, I must warn you that you're going entirely too far!"

"Ugh!" He shivered. "You remind me of a cranky old school-ma'am I had when I was a kid. She'd look at me just that way an' say, 'Robert, what is a predicate adjective?' I never did figure it out."

201

She said nothing, just glared at him. He dropped his bantering tone, spoke pleadingly:

"Listen, Stell! Let me tell you all over about that plan. Why, it can't help working!"

"I heard it once; that's enough. Will you be so kind as to pay the men off immediately?"

"You mean it?"

"I certainly do. If you don't pay them off, I'll do it myself."

Bob sighed. He didn't want to use that last detail of his plan.

"Stell, let me ask you for the last time to climb off your high horse — unsaddle him an' turn him loose. Will you do it, Stell?"

"I don't know what you mean" — coldly.

Bob sighed again. "I hate to do it, Stell. Here."

He handed her a yellow slip. She glanced at it, her eyes widened. "What — what does this mean?"

"It means that I'm running this outfit legally. You have no more say about it than the man in the moon."

She stared at him; her face went a trifle white with rage. But she was a good loser. She turned toward the door. "You win."

"Wait a minute. I want to talk to you."

He almost forced her back into her chair.

"You saw that woman come to see me yesterday morning — the woman in the big veil?"

"Bob, I'm not interested in your private affairs."

"It was Mrs. Boyd — Al's wife."

"A married woman!"

"Sure. She wanted me to get Al out of jail. I did it."

202

"Very accommodating, weren't you!"

"What the heck does ail you, Stell?" he asked.

"Nothing. But why should I be interested in your friend Mrs. Boyd?"

"Oh, dang it!" Bob scratched the back of his neck violently. "Well, I didn't tell you that that time I got shot in the head coming home from town I was robbed of a big roll of money. That's what came in that package the other day — the day you gave me the glasses. She'd sent it back to me."

"It *is* useful to have friends like that," said Stella sweetly.

Again Bob stared at her; girls were a deeper mystery to him than predicate adjectives, and those had been the bugbear of his younger life.

"That's the trouble! We weren't friends. In fact I'd never seen her before only once, an' then I wasn't close enough to speak to her. Why did she do it?"

"Oh!" The word was long-drawn.

Stella sat considering. She raised her eyes to take in Bob's tall, clean-cut figure with the very wide shoulders, the tanned, ruggedly handsome face. She nodded, as though the whole thing were perfectly clear.

"Bob, you're like most cowboys; you know nothing about women. You think they're all angels. Well" — her lips tightened an instant — "they're not. I've known you a good many years, so I feel that I should give you a little friendly advice: that Boyd woman doesn't mean you any good; the less you see of her the better."

Bob nodded sadly.

"I know it, I'd figured that out for myself. She only wants to make a fool of me."

Stella brightened.

"You can see that! Oh, Bob, I'm so glad! I hate to see anyone I've known all my life made a fool of."

He stood up to go.

"Well, chuck should be about ready at the cook shack. I'm hungry as a bear."

"Bob" — she laid her hand on his arm — "don't you get tired of Beans Bailey's cooking? Won't you have dinner with me and Mrs. Doheney? We have layer cake today."

"Huh?" He stared. "I thought you were — aren't you mad at me for getting that power of attorney?"

"*Me* angry with you! Why, the *idea!* I know you did it for the good of the outfit."

"Good heavens! I wish I knew something about girls!" Bob sighed and shook his head.

"Don't *I!*" she exclaimed with what to Bob seemed wholly unwarranted feeling. "Well, are you going to have dinner with us?"

"Layer cake? Well, you bet I am!"

She looked at him a moment in silence, sniffed, and turned to hurry from the room. Bob shook his head in awe. She was mad at him again! Women — why, predicate adjectives were a joke compared to them, clear as *A. B. C.* With wrinkled forehead he left the room; he would go to the bunk house and clean up before that dinner.

He turned the corner of the house. Stella was looking out through her bedroom window, both elbows on the

204

sill — probably kneeling on the floor. She gave him a sweet smile. "Bob, if you happen to see a high horse wandering around the corral, would you shove it through the gate and let it go to the wild bunch; I won't need it any more."

Huh! She was in good humor again!

"Stell, I'd come pretty near doin' anything you asked me to."

"*Thank* you, Bob."

Bob shook his head as he walked away. Predicate adjectives weren't a patch on girls. It would take a bug-hunter in horn-rimmed glasses to figure out what one would do or say two seconds ahead — and then he'd be wrong every blamed time!

Bob had been pushing himself mercilessly since his coming to the Bar Diamond. When he looked in the mirror, he could notice that his face was getting thin — a result of combined hard work and worry. He decided to take things easy a day or two. Anyway, his new plans called for nothing but taking things easy, sitting down and waiting for the sheepmen to go broke.

Of course he had a strong suspicion that his plans might not work out very well, that the sheep outfits would make a last desperate effort before going under. That effort might take the form of a mass attack on the Bar Diamond. No, it would be something unexpected; Butch was too clever to do the obvious. Anyway, thought Bob, he could pretend to Stella that he was sure of this peaceful solution. If the sheepmen started something, and he had to fight in self-defense — well, she could not blame him for that.

He spent most of next morning resetting the shoes on Flight. His care of Flight's hoofs had become a matter of amusement to the other cowboys — but nothing was too good for Flight. Then he saddled him, taking pains to see that there was not the slightest wrinkle in the blanket, that the saddle fitted up just so close to his withers and no more. He swung on his back, and trotted up the draw; he was not going anywhere in particular; just riding around, noting the condition of the cattle, of the feed — what little feed there was left.

His new binoculars, which he always carried now, proved a great help. Through them he could carefully examine a bunch of cattle at a distance, see their condition, read their brands, and all without running his horse or chasing the cattle — a good cowboy disturbs cattle as little as possible.

He was passing a sharp little butte a couple of miles from the ranch when he saw some loose horses grazing near the top. He considered a moment. He could climb the other side and examine them from the peak without their seeing him. Yes, glasses sure were handy; he'd like to furnish them to all the cowboys but that he knew the last pair would be smashed within a month; they wouldn't take care of them.

It took him more than twenty minutes to reach the top; he had to leave Flight and climb afoot the last fifty yards. He squatted on the flat rock which formed the summit, elbows on knees to steady the glasses.

Mares and colts — and a very bossy, fussy stallion. Some of the colts were pretty big; he'd have to get the boys to run them in and brand them while they were so near the ranch.

He laid the glasses down and rolled a cigarette. He always liked, when he had time, to sit on a high place like this and look off at the view. In the clear Arizona air, mountains a hundred miles off stood out so sharply that he could see every gulch running into them. Cattle dotted all the country below — too many cattle, for the feed there was.

He noticed a little streak of dust on a ridge. Must be one of the cowboys trying to rope a calf. Bob reached for the glasses and focused them on the spot. He caught a glimpse of the horseman disappearing into some cedars. He waited, watching the place where he would reappear.

Why, it was Boyd! Even with the strong glasses he could barely recognize him at that distance. What the deuce was he chasing? Bob could not see any calf ahead. Al's big horse seemed to be laboring heavily, as though it had run a long way. Queer! What was he up to *now?*

He saw Al stop the horse suddenly, leap to the ground, and pull his carbine from the scabbard. Al was running afoot now. There he was, throwing himself flat behind a boulder at the top of a little bluff overlooking a narrow draw below. Hunting deer? — he'd seen some headed that way and had cut in before them for a good shot?

Bob swung the glasses to watch the draw; he was anxious to see the result of Al's hunting. That cow trail beside the wash — that was where they'd come; he'd see them as soon as they came out of the cedars into the little opening below Al. Well, he was glad to see that Boyd ate venison instead of Bar Diamond beef; that was more than could be said for some other nesters.

Suddenly Bob gasped in horror; his eyes widened as he stared through the glasses. From the cedars came Clay Bozart, trotting slowly, absently. He was coming to visit the Bar Diamond; that trail would be a short cut for him.

Bob, without knowing it, shouted a hoarse warning. His muscles tensed until they almost pained; his breath came in gasps. His premonition had been true; Clay was marked for the next victim!

It was all like some strange dream. Bob could not hear a sound; he had the feeling of being a thousand miles off. He saw Clay double suddenly, convulsively, in his saddle. He saw him clutch in agony at his waistline, tumble to the ground, lie there squirming faintly. He saw the horse whirl off. Then only he heard a faint, distant crack.

Bob was almost paralyzed. With difficulty he moved the glasses a trifle. He saw Boyd rise to his knees, eject the empty shell, and stand up. He saw him walk unhurriedly to his horse, mount, and ride away in a slow walk.

And this was the man he had been fool enough to get out of jail! This was the man who had looked him in the eye and told him that he had never killed anybody, never would! He himself had signed Al's bail. Would he be held responsible for what Al did?

At least he held himself responsible, he would always blame himself for the death of his friend Clay Bozart.

Bob's face flamed. The red drained away slowly, leaving it white, white with rage. He quickly thrust the glasses back into their case and went leaping down among the rocks to his horse. Riding madly down the hill, he loosened his gun in its holster. Al was traveling slowly, on an exhausted horse; he could easily intercept him before he got home.

No, he would not shoot from ambush as Al had done; he would meet him face to face. They would shoot it out; he'd give Al an even break. But break or not, this giant nester had killed his last cattleman.

CHAPTER
FIFTEEN

Who?

Bob was riding wildly, dangerously for such broken ground, but he did not think of that. Tearing down the side of the butte at such speed would have meant a bad fall on almost any other horse; even Flight stumbled more than once, but somehow managed to keep his feet.

He had to come before Boyd in a wide circle and wait for him; if the nester heard him coming, he would lie in ambush and shoot him down as he had Clay; he probably wanted to shoot him, anyway. And to think that he had signed the man's bail only two days before! There was gratitude! But what does a nester know of gratitude?

Bob picked his best route mentally; he knew every inch of the Bar Diamond range so thoroughly that he had not needed to stop to look it over from the butte. The shortest way would be to cut across the ridges immediately, but that would be very hard on his horse. Better keep on up one of the draws to near the divide, where the ridges were lower, and then swing north.

Flight stumbled, and for fifty yards went plunging down with bent knees, trying to regain his balance. He succeeded; for a moment it had looked like a bad spill, broken bones. But Bob did not slack his pace in the least. He had to intercept Al before he got home. They were going to settle things.

Which draw should he follow? The first would save his horse, but by crossing to the next he would pass where Clay Bozart lay. Yes, he should do that. Clay might live a few minutes; he might have something to say before he died.

Bob took the ridge at a long angle; it gave him a quarter mile of gradual climb to where he reached the summit. That saved his horse, and it brought him to the head of a good cow trail going down the other side. Down he went, Flight covering the ground with his usual long, smooth stride, Bob ducking from side to side, leaning down beside the horse's neck to avoid the overhanging branches.

There was a good trail up the draw; he loosed his rein a trifle and let Flight take a faster gait. He'd have to stop and dismount to see if Clay still lived; that would give the bay a moment to catch his breath. He saw ahead of him the bluff from which Al had fired the shot, and a moment later he was racing out into the little opening.

There Clay Bozart lay. He was still alive; he seemed to be struggling, convulsed with pain. Poor devil! Never much of a man, as men went in Arizona, but always good-natured, friendly, anxious to be accommodating. Always his own worst enemy. Poor devil!

Bob slid his horse abruptly in a way he seldom did. He leaped from the saddle almost before Flight had

211

broken his run. There was a little cloud of dust from sliding hoofs and running boots. Bob knelt beside the struggling figure. "Clay! Did he get you, old man? Hurt bad?"

A moan. Clay was ghastly white, his eyes closed. His knees were doubled up nearly to his chin, and both hands clutched his waistline. His hands were red; the sand under him was red.

"Clay! It's Bob — Bob Edwards."

The eyes opened.

"Bob — Bob —"

"Hurt bad, ol' feller?"

"He — he got me, Bob! It was — it was —"

"I know — Al Boyd; I saw him through the glasses. Don't talk. Let's see how bad you're shot."

"Lemme alone — I — Oh, my stomach!" A moan.

"Here, let's see it; we have to."

Bob spoke firmly. Clay had never been able to withstand firmness; he straightened his knees and rolled almost on his back so that Bob could examine his wound; Bob helped him move to the new position.

"Now, let's take a look at it."

Bob's hands moved quickly to open the wide, heavy buckle of Clay's trousers; it was covered with blood.

"What the —"

The buckle was twisted and crumpled. Had it turned the bullet to any great extent? Bob's hands were flying; a sudden hope had come to him. In this haste he was rougher than he had meant to be. Clay groaned:

"E-easy, Bob!"

212

Bob pulled the trousers down, jerked up the shirt tail, tore the underwear open. He pulled the kerchief from his neck and wiped the blood away, holding his breath, fearing what he might see.

"Hurraw!" he shouted joyously. "Clay, you got an ugly piece gouged out of you, but the bullet didn't go through. Hit your belt buckle an' glanced."

A quavering groan, full of terror:

"No — no use kiddin' me, Bob. He got me."

Bob grinned, but it was a sympathetic grin.

"Reckon you feel that way; a heavy bullet whamming into your belt buckle like that must have hurt about as much as if it went through. When you get your wind back, you'll be nearly all right."

"No, it busted somethin' inside of me. I'm done for."

Bob unexpectedly shot a harsh order:

"Here! Sit up!"

Clay did, quickly. His face looked almost green, and he trembled violently. He seemed to be suffering more from fear than from the wound.

"Look at that!"

Clay bent his head and looked at his wound. He took Bob's bloodstained neckerchief and wiped gently.

"Queer," said Bob. "I saw a man get shot in the back once in Tombstone when he wasn't looking for it. He whirled around and yelled, 'Quit throwin' rocks, you fools!' Then he turned back an' grinned at me like it was all a joke — and fell over on his face. He died an hour later. Seems like you can't go by the feel when you're shot."

"Well, I know I feel —"

Clay stopped. He began suddenly to retch violently. Bob kept a hand on his shoulder sympathetically.

"You're sick all right, Clay; that wham would make anyone sick. But you'll be all right pretty soon. Take deep breaths."

In a few moments Clay felt better. He groaned and mopped his sweating forehead.

"Where — where did Boyd go?" He seemed to fear that he might return to finish his work.

"He was heading toward home. I was going to cut in before he got there an' make him shoot it out with me."

Clay straightened up.

"Go ahead! Shoot him, before he kills any more of us!"

"Any more?"

"He — he shot old Newt — he killed Jack Daly — he tried to kill you. If he wasn't such a bad shot, we'd all be dead."

"Who told you all that?" asked Bob.

"I — ouch! — one of my men has a brother workin' for Butch Johnson; all Johnson's men know it. Bob, me an' Al always was pretty good friends; I wouldn't believe what I heard about him. I was easy; wonder he didn't get me sooner."

"Well, I told you to look out for him. I wish you'd listened to me."

"He — he seemed so friendly." The breach of friendship seemed to hurt Clay more than his wound.

"Don't I know it! I was jackass enough to bail him out of jail the other day; let his wife talk me into it."

"Her!" Clay shuddered. "She's worse than he is. They're not human; they'd kill a man for a nickel! Go after him, Bob, an' get him before he gets home."

"That'll have to wait. I have to get you in to the ranch and get a doctor for you. If blood poisoning set in, you'd be done for. Can you ride, do you think? We'd never get a wagon in here."

"I dunno."

"Let's try it. I'll bandage you up a bit first."

It was crude bandaging with torn strips of Clay's shirt, but the best Bob could do. Clay stood up, and Bob lifted him across his shoulder and set him in the saddle; luckily Clay's horse was gentle or he could not have done it.

"All right. We'll take it in a slow walk, not to jar you."

"I can make it, Bob. You go after Boyd."

"Seem to have changed your opinion of your pal Boyd!"

"Bob, that man told me that Al has swore to get you next, an' soon. I didn't believe it, but I do now. Better beat him to it, before he does any more damage."

"So *that's* his plan!"

Bob's lips tightened. The scene in the jail, when he had gone to bail Al out, came back to him. Al had roared with laughter until he almost shook the ceiling; he seemed to know of some huge joke or other. Laughed in Bob's face; laughed at him for being such an easy mark for Mrs. Boyd's clever tricks.

"I'll get him all right!" muttered Bob grimly. "But I'm going to take you to the ranch first."

Clay reached the Bar Diamond very ill and almost exhausted. The blow in the belt line, from a bullet traveling downward, had been very severe, and besides he had lost a considerable amount of blood. Bob could not find Stella immediately, so took the liberty of carrying him into old Newt's room at the ranch house. He redressed the wound, using antiseptic liberally; this would prevent infection until the doctor arrived.

Then he considered what to do next. He wanted to go straight to Boyd's, call Al to the door, and demand that they shoot it out on the spot. That might be dangerous business. But then Al would not think that his bushwhacking of Clay was known; he might come out to talk instead of shooting from a window.

Bob would have risked it, but another thing held him back: he could not shoot a man down before his wife, no matter how well the man deserved it. It was more Bob's range-bred chivalry that stopped him than any respect for Mrs. Boyd. She was no better than her husband. She deserved just the same thing herself — hot lead — but that of course was entirely out of the question.

He stood outside the bunk house, gazing broodingly at the ground. He had heard of people so cold-blooded that they had no human feelings, that they were no better than beasts of prey, but he had never met any of that sort before — at least not a woman. He had not believed there really were women that way — as bad as the worst men. He heard his name called, and turned. It was Stella. As he went toward her, she sat down on the top step of the porch and motioned him to a place beside her. Her face looked hard.

"Bob, have you ever figured out why Mrs. Boyd sent that money back, or where she got it?"

Bob started.

"Huh? No." That was something that had been troubling him all the time, the one white spot on the black Boyd record.

"I think I can tell you something about it. Here's the wrapper off the package it came in; you left it on the living-room table."

He glanced at it and nodded. He wondered what Stella was leading up to.

"Well, I wanted to get hold of some of her writing. I asked the sheriff about it, and he gave me a letter of hers that Al had left in the jail. Here it is."

Bob took the letter and read it:

DEAREST AL: Keep your head up, hubby dear. I know you had nothing to do with it, and everyone will find that out very soon. I have a plan to get you out. I know it will work.

Love from wifie and Danny,

EMILY.

"Sounds," muttered Bob uneasily, "as though she really believed he had nothing to do with it."

"Does it?" Stella asked dryly. "She knew the sheriff would read this before giving it to him, afraid it might be about a jail break. Al, to make sure of it being read,

217

left it behind — which was stupid of him. I think she's the brains of whatever's going on."

"Oh, heck, no!" Bob could not believe this. "But what did you want with her writing, anyway?"

Stella gave a hard little laugh.

"Compare it with that on the wrapper."

He did not need to. He suddenly remembered the graceful, forward-sloping lines on the package. This was backhand, smaller letters, thicker strokes; it did not bear the faintest resemblance to the other.

"Stung!" he groaned. "She just made a monkey out of me."

"She did, Bob." Stella placed her hand consolingly on his arm. "I knew what she was from the moment I saw her; any woman would. A big, honest cowboy like you can never get it into his head that there are women just as bad as men, if not worse."

"Well," said Bob dejectedly, "I learn a lot as I grow older."

They were silent a moment. Suddenly Bob turned.

"But where did she find out that the money was sent back? And who the heck did send it back, anyway? Some woman that writes a hand like she's educated."

"I've a notion she found out from Butch. I may be wrong, but it wouldn't surprise me to hear that she knew a whole lot about Butch's business."

No! That couldn't be! All Bob's chivalry fought to disbelieve it. He sighed. The world was beginning to look like a pretty rotten place — not at all what young cowboys thought it to be.

218

"But," he exclaimed, "*who* sent it back? That only gets the whole business more mixed up than ever." He waved helplessly toward the letter.

Stella shook her head. There was a line drawn between her eyes; she looked worried.

"That's it! This poor unfortunate ranch is getting more twisted up in mysteries every day. Could it be" — her color heightened — "some of the girls in the dance hall? They might have taken it from somebody while he was drunk."

Bob reddened a trifle, too.

"They're not likely to be very educated. Besides, I don't know any of them — never spoke to 'em."

"Then that's out!" Bob could not help noticing a lilt in Stella's voice.

"But — *who* sent it?" he repeated.

He shook his puzzled head, stood up, and walked unseeingly toward the corrals. This business, he thought, was getting far too deep for a cowpuncher.

CHAPTER
SIXTEEN

The Unpardonable Crime

That evening something happened that was of such importance as to make them forget the war with the sheepmen, forget Al Boyd, forget even the mysterious debt that threatened to ruin the outfit. On the far south-western horizon a bank of clouds appeared. It came up in an even line, blue-black, looking as solid as the mountains under it. Inch by inch it stole up.

Bob and Stella watched it in the gathering darkness, watched anxiously. All the cowboys were outside, too, gathered in little groups. No matter what their conversations, their heads kept turning often to the southwest.

Clouds! It had been months since they had seen any before, months of that clear blue brilliance of northern Arizona. Red Selby came by. He turned a broad, cheery grin to Bob and Stella.

"Look at them cowboys — draggin' their beds into the barn an' saddle house. Ain't seen that in a long time!"

Stella smiled back at him cheerfully. That darkening sky had brought a new light to her eyes.

"Better be getting your own in, Red. Pull it up on the porch."

"Mine's in the bunk house. I'm jest goin' there now to get it outside."

"What for?" she asked, puzzled.

"So's it'll get a good soakin', ma'am, to see what it feels like. My poor ol' soogans have forgot, old as they are."

And he did. They saw him come staggering out under the tarp-covered roll, to spread it in the most exposed place he could find. Stella laughed.

"Why does Red always have to do the opposite of what everyone else is doing?"

"Just to be comical." Bob grinned. "But don't you think for a minute he's as foolish as he acts. Good night!" he gasped. "What's he doing now?"

Red was calmly stripping the tarp from his bed and carrying it back into the bunk house; it seemed that he wanted to be sure of getting his blankets thoroughly soaked. Stella gave a little chuckle.

"Bob, if it does give him the wetting he wants, raise his wages ten a month, and — Oh!" She caught herself. "I forgot! You're the big boss around here now, with power of attorney and everything. I apologize." She looked at him quizzically.

Bob nodded solemnly.

"But you're head adviser. Ten a month it is."

She pointed suddenly across the brown range. "Look!"

A lurid flame had lighted up the southwest, trembling above the mountains. Lightning! Bob rubbed his hands gleefully and turned to her.

"Stell, do you know what a good rain means?"

"Uh-huh!" She nodded cheerfully. "Feed — water — fat cattle."

"That all?"

"What else?"

"The bank lending us that fifty thousand — they'd be begging stockmen to take their money. I didn't bother to ask 'em about it before, with the cattle so weak that it looked like we'd have to start shippin' out within a month."

"Bo-ob!"

Her clasped hands raised to her chin; her eyes danced, shone.

"Uh-huh." Bob nodded cheerfully. "It looks like the ol' Bar Diamond mightn't to *pfhs-s-st!*, after all." He made a noise like a cheap firecracker fizzling out; they were both in a mood for nonsense.

"But, would they lend it, with the sheepmen —"

"Sheep! *Sheep! S-s-sphut!*" He grinned; this firecracker barely sputtered like a damp match head.

Mrs. Doheney's plump, cheery figure appeared at the kitchen door.

"Chuck, Stella! Come an' git it or, by gosh, out it goes!" She tried to sound like the terrible "Beans" Bailey. Everyone on the ranch was happy this evening.

Stella linked her arm in Bob's.

"Race you to the house! You're eating with us this evening, cowboy!"

Off they went. She could have won — Bob's chaps and very high heels were too much handicap — but she did not let go of his arm.

Everyone on the ranch went to bed an hour late. Those in the houses tried to move their beds so that they could see through the windows or open doors. Not that they could see much; the sky was as black as ink. Many of the cowboys had remained outside; their tarps, unless very old or slightly torn, were waterproof.

About two in the morning a terrific crash of thunder woke them up. As though it were waiting for the signal, a sheet of water struck the roofs. From out in the roaring darkness a faint shout came:

"Boys, think it'll be damp tonight — or not?" That was Red.

Very soon the downpour settled to a steady drizzle. Bob rolled over luxuriantly and fell asleep. Rain, at last!

The brilliant sunshine in his face woke him up; his window faced the east. For a second he did not realize the significance of it; then he went leaping out of bed, flinging himself into his clothes. He hurried outside, kicking the earth with the toe of his boot. Two or three inches on top were damp; below that was dust. And the brilliant sun was rapidly drying this damp surface.

His eyes swept the horizon. Glaring blue, with not a trace of a cloud as big as a saddle blanket. Never since he had been a small child had he felt such a desire to cry. His head hung; the corners of his mouth drooped. Gradually burning out was bad enough, but fooling them this way . . .

With dragging steps, he walked to where he saw Stella on the edge of the porch, her favorite seat. Her chin was in her hands, and she was staring miserably out across the yellowish-brown, burned range. There was a pathetic twist to the corners of her mouth, but she was struggling hard to keep them from trembling. There was a shiny, glassy look to her eyes; no, she would not cry!

"Blowed up, Bob!" She did not look at him.

"Poor kid!"

He patted her shoulder. Bad as he felt, she must feel a thousand times worse.

"What'll we do, Bob? Quit?"

He shook his head slowly. His voice was low:

"We'll fight — an' fight — an' fight. We're licked, Stell, but only a dirty coward quits just because he's licked."

"Bob, can anyone that looks at it that way be licked? What on earth would I — I mean the outfit — do without you?"

She took one of his hands in both hers. With his free hand he patted her shoulder again.

"Why, sure, Stell; you can bank on me to do my dangdest. That's what I'm here for; that's what any range boss is for. If I wasn't that way, you'd have your father fire me and get someone that was."

"Oh, Bob, Bob!" She shook her head, sighed, and stood up to enter the house.

Something in her voice made Bob feel that she was not far from angry with him again, that she would have been angry only that she was too dispirited this morning to feel anger. He wondered what he had done; probably the poor kid was just angry with everyone and everything after this blow; he didn't blame her.

It never occurred to him that she stood inside the living-room window, watching his broad back when he turned away. The boss's daughter was a great girl — a great girl. If he wasn't just a poverty-stricken cowpuncher, he — Bob sighed. Yes, the world was a pretty rotten place; everything was wrong in it.

There was almost total silence during breakfast. The cowboys hung over their tin plates, gulped big cups of hot coffee. Even Red had nothing to say. No one thought of joking him about leaving his bed out the night before; if anyone had, he'd have had a fight on his hands. Red seemed to feel the blow no less than Bob himself.

Everything was an hour late. The wranglers could not find the horses for a long time; the men seemed slow and pottering as they roped and saddled. When they asked Bob what to do that day, he shrugged indifferently and told them that they likely knew of something that needed looking after.

As the cowboys trailed over the ridge with their horses in a slow walk, Bob, watching them go, thought bitterly that it reminded him of a funeral. Didn't come far from being one, at that — the funeral of the Bar Diamond, one of the oldest brands in northern Arizona.

He turned and went slowly to the house; he had to see how Clay Bozart was getting along. Doctor Varney, who had recently returned from San Francisco, had paid a hurried visit the evening before; he was very busy. He had taken a few stitches, plastered on some strips of adhesive tape to keep the stitches from tearing, and rushed off again. This case was not serious, but Clay had to stay in bed two or three days. Riding was of course out of the question until he was practically well.

Bob entered the room to find Clay propped up in bed with a cigarette in his mouth. Old Newt's clothes still hung on nails on the wall, a pair of boots stood in the corner; like most wealthy Arizona cattlemen, Newt had never owned more than two pairs of boots at a time, and one of those worn almost to shreds before he got the next. The old safe stood back in its place, the twisted and bent door half ajar. Newt liked the old relic; they would not throw it out until he got back.

"Well, Clay, how're you feeling?"

Bob sat down on the foot of the bed.

"Pretty good. Wisht I could get up, but Varney said not to."

"Better do what he tells you, he's sure a good doctor — see how he got Newt to San Francisco alive."

"Is he out of danger yet?"

"Well, you know how cautious doctors are about promising anything — but we hope he is."

Clay shook his head.

"You never can tell what might set in in a case like that. Me, I ain't got much hope for him."

"Just our luck," brooded Bob, "if he did die, with the outfit in this bad shape. How could we settle things up? Everybody the ranch owes a cent to would come jumping on us at once."

"That note he owes me? Stella was settin' with me a long time yesterday, an' a while this mornin' again. I — uh — I told her I wouldn't crowd her for the money if there was any way out of it."

"Heck, don't I know that, Clay? I've heard you called lots of things, but never a skinflint. You've sure been white about letting that run."

"Bob, I couldn't bear down if I wanted to, after all this outfit has done for me now — not even if I was losin' my own place."

Bob sighed; it seemed that he was finding a great deal to sigh about lately.

"You know danged well this outfit wouldn't see that happen to you, Clay; the Davises aren't that way. If it gets to looking too bad for you, they'll turn this place over to you an' let you sell it for enough to put your own on its feet."

"Gosh, Bob, I'd hate to ask 'em to do that!"

"You won't have to ask 'em; they'd just do it. I know the Davises."

Bob rolled a cigarette. They were silent a moment.

"Clay, what do you reckon Boyd shot at you for yesterday? Just sort of on general principles — because you're a cattleman?"

"Worse than that. What do you suppose I caught him at?"

"Might be pretty near anything. I'd about believe it if someone told me he'd shot down a baby."

"Something pretty near as bad — how they look at it in this country. I happened to see him potterin' around in a little draw, an' after he left, I rode down to see what he'd been doin'. What you reckon I found?"

"What?"

"Why, a cow lyin' dead in the wash, with part of the bank caved in on her. I climbed down an' examined her. She'd just been shot with a .22."

"Wha-at!"

In spite of what Bob had said, he stared unbelievingly. This was a crime that put one beyond the pale even more than would killing a man under ordinary circumstances.

"Jest what I found, Bob. She was a Bar Diamond, too. The calf was bawlin' around in the cedars. He was foxy enough not to brand it till it quit bawlin'; he'll get it in a day or two. Pretty safe way to steal calves, if someone didn't happen to see you carryin' the .22 rifle an' get suspicious."

"Rifle, nothin'! I heard of that trick down South; the man doing it died sort of sudden when he was caught at it. He used a .22 pistol; he could carry it in his pocket out of sight. Reckon Al killed any more, or is he just beginning it?"

"Well, about a mile farther back I come on another dead cow lyin' in some thick algeritas, under a big cedar. I wondered what had happened to her, but I didn't pay much attention — jest figured she lay down an' died."

"Where was she?"

Clay described the place minutely, and also the location of the dry wash where the first lay — near the head of the draw in which he had been shot. Bob thought a moment.

"He must have seen you ride down there to look at her; that's how he knew where to get ahead of you."

"That's what I figured. He knew I'd head straight for here to report the thing to you."

"Looks to me," said Bob, "like you came pretty near getting yourself killed trying to do a good turn for the Bar Diamond."

"Aw, forget it, Bob! How did I know the cow wasn't mine till I looked?"

"You had a pretty good idea; you have no stock to amount to anything on that part of the range."

"Well, wouldn't you have done as much for me?"

"Why, sure."

Of course Bob could not say so, but what surprised him was to find that Clay had shown so much manliness; he would have expected him to ride home through the cedars and forget what he had seen, and so keep out of trouble. Friendly though he had always been with Clay, it seemed that he had underestimated his courage, his sense of honor.

"Well," Bob stood up, "I reckon I'll ride over there and take a look at both of them. From how you say the one under the cedar was lying, she must have died natural."

"Wish I could go with you to show you the place. Say, Bob, could you have a wagon hitched up to take me home? Stella won't do it; she wants me to stay here till I can ride again."

"Well, I sure could, Clay — but I won't. What would you do lying over there all alone all day?"

"We-ell, I could take along some books or magazines or something. Bob, I shore feel that I'm imposin' here."

Clay's usual diffidence and meekness. Bob wished that he had more confidence in himself.

"Uh-huh — you're an awful lot of bother!" He grinned. "But don't worry too much about it. We'll kick you out as soon as we get tired of you."

He waved good-bye and left the room, to go to the corral and saddle Conejo. As he mounted, he thought of what had happened to him the last time he rode this horse; that was the time he had got shot in the head and robbed. Lucky, he thought, that cowboys weren't superstitious, or he might be worrying about something happening to him this time.

Bob found the dead cow in the wash. Everything was just as Clay had said; the bank had been caved in until she was almost covered; it was only by the merest chance that Clay had found her. Indeed, if anyone had run across her after two or three days, he'd have thought that she had fallen in and broken her neck. The cattle were getting pretty weak from the drought, and such a thing might easily happen.

Bob climbed down and examined the brand. Bar Diamond she was. If this wasn't low-down dirty! Stealing an occasional calf might be overlooked, but this came pretty near being a lynching matter.

All this time he had heard the frequent bawling of a calf in the cedars; it seemed to be circling around him. He rode out, and found it easily. He roped and branded it; Al's dirty work was going to do him no good in this case at least.

Liberating the calf, he continued on up the draw to its head, and then up over the divide. He found the patch of tall algeritas that Clay had described, found the dead cow. Dismounting, he examined her carefully.

No, Clay was wrong in his guess about this one; she had died naturally. There was no bullet hole, and no sign of a struggle. In fact the very place she lay proved natural death; she was under low cedar limbs and concealed by the algeritas — just where an animal would hide itself to die. Anyway, nobody could very well have rolled her under those low limbs.

Back beside his horse, he stood thinking. What had she died of? She was a three-year-old in better condition than the average. Probably larkspur poisoning; that acted quickly, not with the slow effect of loco. He hadn't noticed any larkspur around here, but then there was a little of it all over; one lost a few head from it every year.

Bob tightened his cinch. Somehow, he felt reluctant to mount. He rolled a cigarette. At last he went slowly back to the dead cow. He crawled back under the limbs, seized a hind leg, and with a good deal of difficulty turned her over.

He stood up so quickly that he bumped his head on a limb and knocked his hat off. He did not know that he had knocked it off; he did not know that he put it back on again. His face was white with fury. For under the cow lay a tiny pool of dried blood, barely to be seen.

He examined her side, and with difficulty found a hole less than a quarter of an inch across, hidden by the hair. So that was it! The cleverest, most sneaking trick of the most unscrupulous rustlers — and the most brutal!

Shoot a cow in the body with a .22 pistol — one had to be close so that the light bullet would penetrate. She would bleed outwardly little or none. Not one time in a thousand would she die in the open like that one back in the wash; the bullet must accidentally have hit a main artery. No, she'd be able to walk, to find a hidden spot like this; any dying animal, from a house cat to a bear, hides itself when it is reaching the last stages of weakness.

The worst of it was that she might be any time from a day to a week or more in dying. Just crawl into some bushes and lie moaning there day and night until the end came slowly, painfully.

Bob thought of what would happen then. This cedar country was alive with coyotes, skunks, gray foxes, and many other animals of the kind. When one of them found a carcass, it always began to eat where there was blood or a wound. If the bullet hole happened to be on top, the animals would soon tear the flesh around it so that shooting would never be suspected. If it was at the bottom, as in this case, it would be out of sight anyway.

Clever — devilishly clever, whoever had first thought this up. Hidden thus, the dead cow would rarely be found; if she were, nobody would do more than look at her once and ride away, perhaps remembering to report her to the boss, perhaps not. And, if she were reported, the boss would do no more than curse the drought, larkspur, perhaps rattlesnakes.

How many head had Boyd killed in this way? Could be almost any number; he might have been doing it for years. Knowing exactly where the long-eared calf was, and when it had had its last milk, he could judge from its age about when it would stop bawling around. Then it would be a maverick, safe for any finder to brand. Knowing where to look for it, and when, there was hardly a chance in five hundred that anybody else would run across it before him.

Bob groaned with rage. There were rustlers and rustlers, but he, at least, had never before seen anything so completely low-down as this.

He searched around for the calf but could not find it there, so he went to the nearest water hole, less than half a mile off. There he found a six-month-old heifer whose markings very much resembled those of the dead cow. He sat his horse, staring at her. A strictly first-class cowboy can identify a calf as belonging to a certain cow and be right nineteen times out of twenty. Yes, this was the calf of that cow back there.

His face was hard with anger. The calf was already branded, branded with Al Boyd's AB. Not a single thing to do about it legally, no means of actually proving that this heifer belonged to the dead cow. If there had been — a scar of some sort, for instance, that one of the cowboys remembered and could swear to — Al could still laugh in their faces, could insist that he had found a maverick and knew nothing of the mother.

No, there was nothing to be done legally. That was why cattlemen sometimes had to take the law into their own hands.

Bob spent two or three hours riding around, searching for more dead cattle. He found only one, which had obviously been killed by a grizzly bear. At least it seemed obvious; but bears, in spite of their reputation, seldom kill stock; they prefer to find a carcass. More likely this one had been shot with the .22 and the bear had found it dead. In that case, the shooting was now impossible to prove; the carcass was too badly torn.

At any rate, Bob did not believe for an instant that he had found all the cattle that had been shot. He couldn't hope to find them; they'd hide themselves so well that it was useless to look for them. All that he could do now was to send two or three good cowboys over here to scour the range steadily for long-ears.

As to Al Boyd: was there ever before anyone so completely lowdown? Bob deliberately turned over toward the Boyd homestead. No, he wasn't going to the house. He wouldn't have the thing come up before Al's wife; after all, a woman was a woman. Still, Al did a good deal of riding for a nester; if he kept dropping over that way, sooner or later he'd meet him.

And when he did! Well, what Al really deserved was the same thing that he did to the cows — to be shot in the stomach with his own .22 and left lying there on the range to die. Of course, Bob couldn't do that — but he could put a thorough and abrupt stop to Al's devilishness. He took his gun from the holster, examined it carefully, spun the cylinder. Before he put it back, he pressed the edges of the holster together, worked the leather with his hands. He wanted to be sure that the gun would not hang, that he could make a quick draw. Mightn't meet Al this time, but it could not be long.

CHAPTER
SEVENTEEN

Shorty's End

Bob did not meet Al. Furthermore, it came to him that he was doing a very foolish thing in riding around openly in that place. If Al should chance to see him first it would mean a bullet in the back. Then there was the boy, Danny — he would probably shoot just as quickly as his father; he would think killing a cowpuncher a meritorious act. Bob would be handicapped there; he could not shoot at a boy. Less than a quarter mile from the Boyd place, he turned and went home. But he'd be back — regularly. He couldn't let Boyd go much longer.

It almost surprised him to find the Bar Diamond quiet and peaceful — things had reached the stage where nothing but peace and quietness could surprise Bob. He dropped in for a short visit with Clay Bozart, to report what he had found. He was about to leave when Clay called him back.

"Bob — uh — some of the boys come in to see me today. They tell me there's a story gettin' around."

"About what?"

Clay watched Bob narrowly. "Why, they're beginnin' to say that old Newt died over in San Francisco, but the

236

outfit is keepin' it quiet because it's in such bad shape an' don't want to settle up the affairs."

"Why, that's —"

Bob stopped suddenly. Why not let the yarn spread? It might bring things out into the open a little more. Mightn't do any good, of course, but it could do no harm. He'd like to tell Clay the truth, but Clay was hardly the one to trust with anything resembling a secret.

Clay spoke again:

"I — I didn't want to ask Stella about it; it would make her feel bad."

"Well, I'd as soon you didn't ask me about it either, Clay; I wouldn't lie to you, you know."

"You mean it's so?" Clay sat up suddenly in the bed.

"I didn't say that — but this outfit *is* in bad shape."

Clay shook his head. "Pore ol' Newt!" He added: "I reckon Mrs. Davis is stayin' a while with Newt's sister in San Francisco — that woman that come over here to visit one time."

"That wasn't Newt's sister, it was her own."

"Oh." Clay stared at the bedspread. "Somehow, I had a feelin' all the time that there was somethin' queer about him bein' over there. Gosh, ain't that too bad?"

Bob did not like to deceive him thus. He opened his mouth to speak — but instead he turned on his heel and left the room. He'd have to remember when anyone inquired about the old man, to answer "All right" very shortly, and let it go at that; that would confirm their suspicions. Then, even the most tactless would say no more to Stella.

As he went out, he saw some letters on the living-room table. He paused to glance at them; his mail was generally left here, although that for the other men was sent to the bunk house. Yes, he had one letter.

Bad writing, in pencil — likely some cowboy asking for a job. No return address. He opened it and glanced first at the signature. Why, it was from Slim Blake, the man he had sent to the sheep camp as a spy. Standing on the porch, he read it quickly:

DEAR BOB: They is something fishy gone on but Butch dont have confidence enough in me to let me in. Im pretty sure theyr fixin to make a raid on the ranch thursday nite. I think Butch is worryin about how hes gone to pay all the men and has to do somethin.

Sincerely yours

THOMAS P BLAKE slim.

He might have known it! Things had looked too peaceful to be natural. Now, what?

He stood on the porch with his forehead wrinkled. Butch must really be getting into bad shape financially, to think of anything as desperate as that.

Here was the crucial point of all Bob's plans: He had to find a way now of making Butch change his mind about that raid. If it went through, it would be the beginning of a series of killings that might not stop for years.

But then Slim wasn't certain about it. That made matters all the worse. It might be something else, something unexpected. He had to find out.

He walked around until he saw the man he wanted — Whitey Wheeler. It was Whitey who had demanded weekly payment. He had been grumbling about the food, grumbling about everything; he seemed to be deliberately trying to keep the other men dissatisfied. Bob called to him:

"Whitey, I want to talk to you."

Whitey turned and waited with eyes half closed sleepily, a limp brown cigarette dangling from one extreme corner of his thin mouth. He waited for Bob to come to him.

"Yeah?"

Bob strode abruptly up to him and shot a question:

"Whitey, what's Butch payin' you to act as a spy here?"

Whitey grinned dryly with the corner of his mouth not holding the cigarette.

"Crazy, Bob?" he drawled.

"Well, you can keep what I'm paying you now, an' what Butch is paying you. I'll give you another seventy-five a month to tell me all you know about Butch an' his plans."

This was suggesting a very involved form of double-crossing — triple-crossing, in fact — but Whitey did not seem angry. He grinned again, and shook his head.

"Smokin' hop, Bob?"

"All right — you're fired. By the time you get your bed rolled, I'll have your pay ready for you."

"The devil with you!"

Whitey's dry voice was not raised, but he gave Bob a venomous glance. He made no motion toward his gun; Bob had too much reputation for that — and, anyway, shooting it out face to face was not Whitey's strong point.

Bob watched him walk off, moving perhaps a trifle faster than his customary limp slouch; his movements always reminded Bob of a rattlesnake on a cold morning. So he had been wrong — Whitey had honestly hired out to him as gunman. Should he apologize to him when he came for his pay? Should he tell him to go back to "work"? He didn't want his kind on the place, but, being in the wrong —

Suddenly Whitey turned; he started back rapidly. Bob twitched erect; he caught his breath. So Whitey was going to shoot it out with him, after all — he had made him angry enough for that. There would be a killing right here in front of the house, with Stella perhaps watching from the window.

"Bob," spat Whitey, "I'm goin' to call you on that."

"I — uh —" Bob's breath came quickly; he did not know what to do, what to say.

"Maybe you're only trickin' me, Bob, but as I'm fired, anyway, I don't stand to lose anything. I can go back to the sheep camp."

Bob took a long breath; he almost groaned with relief. Whitey spoke again:

"Well, what you want to know?"

240

Bob thought quickly. Whitey was perfectly capable of carrying his duplicity still another step — of reselling his services to Butch for a few dollars more. But if he thought that Bob already knew —

"All right, I'll begin by asking you about something that I know already: What's Butch figuring on doing tonight?"

"Comin' over with all his men an' cleanin' up on you."

"How many men has he?"

"Nearly twice as many as you have — he's payin' more."

"Not," growled Bob, "more than you're getting!"

"I'm doin' pretty well, thanks," answered Whitey insolently.

Bob turned and walked quickly away. He could not trust himself to speak further to this rat; he might lose his temper. He called Red from where he was working colts in the corrals, and together they sat under a cedar to talk it over.

For the first time he told Red, told anybody besides Stella, of his plan for a bloodless war. He looked for the hot-headed, clowning Red to sniff at the whole idea, to want to fight; but Red, like so many who like to play the fool, had plenty of sound common sense; he approved the plan heartily, thought it a true stroke of genius.

"But," he said gloomily, "it don't look like it's goin' to work out — Butch ain't waitin' for that."

"Well, I have a scheme. It's a crazy one; but I can't think of any other."

"What is it?"

241

"I thought of taking you and some more of the boys that I could depend on not to shoot anybody, and going over there after dark. We could wait till they were nearly ready to start, and then tear through the sheep, shooting in the air and yelling."

"What good would that do?"

"It would upset them so bad, between scattering the sheep and letting 'em see we know what they're up to, that they wouldn't go through with it."

Red thought this over. He shook his head.

"*Might* work — the trouble would be to get away without a big free-for-all fight."

"If we work it right, we can get away."

"If I worked it right, I could play the fiddle — think I'll try it some day."

"Well, I see nothing else. Let's start picking out some of the most reliable men. We'll whisper to 'em to saddle their horses and wander over to that little water hole near Coyote Butte. It'll be nearly dark before they all get there — time to start."

"All right. Bob, times bein' so hard, don't you think it might be a good plan if I'd run over an' tell Beans Bailey not to cook breakfast till he sees how many of us are left? No use in wastin' good chuck." He walked off shaking his head; he did not seem to think much of Bob's plan.

The two strolled quietly around, sometimes stopping to speak as if casually with a man. It was early, so most of them had their horses still saddled; they had only to mount and ride off unnoticed, in twos and threes or

242

singly. The few who had to resaddle caused no comment.

Most of them were at the little water hole when Bob got there, and the last came within a few minutes. Bob looked them over. They were mostly his old hands, with a few of the cowboys who had come from neighboring outfits. Fifteen altogether, counting himself and Red.

He'd have liked to have a few more along, but he did not want to take chances on any man he did not know thoroughly.

He had told all who could to rake up a second gun and belt. Less than half of them had been able to — shabby, discarded belts and holsters, and battered revolvers that didn't match their others. With one exception the holsters on the left had been made for the right, so one gun butt pointed forward and the other back. No difference, of course — the thing was to make as much noise as possible, to sound like a little army.

It was getting pretty dark now. Bob gave the men their last orders:

"When I toss this rag onto Butch's tent — if I get that close — that'll be the signal. Tear through the sheep like mad, yelling your heads off. Just go through them once and *keep going*. Pull the old Indian trick — every man turn a different way once you're out of the camp again, and we'll meet here."

"*Viva la vaca!*" shouted somebody; Bob's war cry had become a popular, catchy yell among the cowboys.

Shorty Jones spoke disgustedly: "*An'* no shootin' at anybody. Great sheep war I call this!"

Bob turned on him.

"Wait till you see one or two of your pals lyin' dead, and then we'll see how you feel about it. As it is, it'll be only luck if we're all alive tomorrow."

That sobered them; their faces took on a more serious look. Still, they had not begun to realize how dangerous their night's work was. Bob jerked his head.

"Let's go!"

He struck out, his men around him. He had, of course, found out the exact location of the camp; it moved a short distance every day or two, following the band of sheep.

Midnight came, passed. Bob, watching from a hill, saw a slight increase of the activity in the sheep camp below. A man came hurrying out of the darkness.

"Bob, they're drivin' in the horses."

"All right, let's get down there before they can get saddled; I don't want 'em making a quick start after us."

Those who were afoot swung into their saddles. In a slow, quiet walk, they rode down the hill, keeping to a close band. Very near the camp, they stopped. The white canvas of Johnson's tent loomed plainly from a light within. Bob whispered:

"Wait here."

He rode off, rolling a cigarette. Behind a thick cedar, he lighted it — as he was almost in the camp, this would cause no suspicion, but he did not want the flame of the match to show his face. Then, his horse at a walk, he rode straight toward Butch's tent.

Presently he saw two shadowy figures of men just ahead; probably waiting for the horses. He rode by calmly, puffing his cigarette; the little spot of fire showed plainly. He would likely be mistaken for one of the wranglers. Anyway, who would suspect a man riding calmly through camp thus, smoking a cigarette? Probably some of the men had their horses already.

He had expected one of the two men to speak to him, but neither did; they were chatting together and did not pay any attention to him. Before him in his saddle rested an old coffee can; he pulled something from it and threw the empty can into a bush where it would make little noise.

Now he was almost to the tent. This was the dangerous part; he would be outlined plainly against the glowing white canvas. He loosened his rein and let the horse take a leisurely running walk. Now he stopped puffing his cigarette; the glow died away quickly as it does from a cigarette rolled in the cowboy's brown paper.

He was within eight feet of the tent; he could hear Butch's voice within. He struck a match on the rough hammer of his six-shooter; anyone seeing it would think he was about to relight his cigarette. He held the flame under the thing in his left hand — a large rag soaked in coal oil.

The rag flared up more quickly than he had expected. He tossed it hastily on the tent roof. The flame had lighted up his face for an instant. A voice rang out:

"Bob Edwards! Get him!"

He whirled his horse. He threw back his head.

"*Viva la vaca!*"

The yell echoed through the camp. Now he was flying away, stooped over his saddle horn. A bullet

245

whistled past his head. There were shouts of consternation.

From the cedars came the answer to Bob's yell:

"Viva la vaca!"

It came from all the cowboys at once; it sounded like ten times their number. Into the camp they came, tearing straight through the sheep. Bob dashed to join them.

Something behind him was lighting up the scene with a weird, reddish flame. He glanced back to see a tongue of fire leaping madly skyward; the roof of Butch's tent had been soaked with some waterproofing compound that made it as inflammable as the rag Bob had thrown. He had a glimpse of Butch plunging from the tent hatless, to sprawl in the dust outside. Another man dashed out to fall over him.

Yells, shots, running horses, wild confusion!

Out on the edge of the reddish light one could just see bechapped cowboys riding furiously, their horses stumbling over sheep, leaping them. Not light enough to see how many there were — might have been a hundred from the noise they made. And always that wild, crackling yell:

"Viva la vaca!"

Now Bob was leading his men. He looked back at those spurts of flame behind him. His men were not firing into the air as he had ordered; they were shooting sheep right and left, shooting them with both hands. But at least they were not firing at the other men.

From around the burning tent, men were coming, running afoot. As if they had any chance of catching the riders! In this excitement, not one of the sheepmen knew just what he was doing. They were shooting, of course, but most of them were shooting as they ran — a futile thing. One or two had sense enough to drop to a squatting position, but those could not fire because of the mob of their comrades running before them.

Bullets were whistling past the cowboys, but now they were in darkness again. There was a chance that this wild shooting might hit somebody, but only a chance. Now they were almost through the sheep. Bob shouted at the top of his voice:

"Separate, boys! Scatter!"

From near Bob came the long-drawn Texas cowboy's yell, to echo back mockingly to the sheepmen. A last volley, then silence but for the clatter of hoofs. That scattered, died away, and Bob found himself flying through the cedars alone. His careful planning had been to good purpose; everything had gone far better than he had expected.

He stopped to listen. He could hear a horseman off to the right; one of his own men. No sound from behind; the sheepmen knew the futility of pursuit, the likelihood of falling into a trap. There would be no raid on the Bar Diamond that night.

But one thing remained: Had any of the boys been hit in that hail of random bullets that had been sent after them? Bob struck a hurried lope to the meeting place; he felt that he could not take a full breath until he had found out if all the boys were safe.

One by one they came riding in. They were in high spirits. Cheers and cries of "*Viva la vaca!*" greeted every new arrival. They were slapping each other on the back, laughing boisterously. It just went to show what happened when cowboys got after sheepmen! Why, they hadn't had so much fun since Hector was a pup!

Bob did not join in the merriment. He sat his horse with a worried look on his face that the others could not see in the darkness; he was not going to say anything to dampen their spirits. Mentally, he checked every man who rode in with those who had left with him earlier in the night.

Nearly an hour passed. For half that time there had been no new arrival — and still three men were missing; Shorty Jones, Paul Crosby, and Tom Richardson. The first two were old hands on the Bar Diamond; Richardson was a young man who had worked for Brad Simpson three or four years but had come to this outfit lately — a good hand, and a good fellow. If something had happened to them —

A cowboy spoke:

"Everybody here? Might as well be goin' home."

"Three not in yet," said Bob shortly. He told them who was missing.

There was a pause, a slight dampening of the enthusiasm. Somebody shrugged it off.

"They'll be here soon."

Another half hour went. Now there were no more yells. A nervous silence was beginning to replace the hilarity. When still another half hour passed and no sign of the missing men, Bob raised his voice:

"Well, we can't keep hoping any longer that something has delayed them. What do we do about it?"

No answer for a time, and then a gloomy question: "What *is* there to do?"

"We can't leave 'em without finding out what happened — and I don't want to get you boys into any trouble. Go on to the ranch; I'll ride back an' take a look."

"Fine! What sort of yaller curs do you think we are, Bob, to go back on you that way?"

"I know — but — Well, we'll wait a while more."

It was now breaking day; dawn crept up the east slowly until they could faintly see each other's faces — pale faces, worried. Three of the best-liked men on the outfit were missing.

A dozen times Bob opened his mouth to speak. He could not wait any longer — and he could not lead these eleven men back to the sheep camp to be shot down. Nor would he gather all those at the ranch and make an attack; it would do no good, if those boys were dead. A voice spoke quickly:

"Listen! What's that?"

A slow click of hoofs came from the cedars. Peering through the grayness, Bob saw three horses approach. They were crowded together, the men on those outside were holding the third in his saddle. On they came, in a slow, slow walk.

Shorty! He was as gray as cold ashes. He would have tumbled down from his saddle but for the arms around him. He raised his head with difficulty, spoke:

"Well, Bob — you'll be shy — a — a cowpuncher —"

He could not finish, but he tried to grin. A little trickle of blood came from one corner of his mouth.

249

His head sank again. Shot through the lungs — that queer sound when he breathed told that. There was no hope for him.

Gentle hands lifted him from the saddle, laid him under a cedar.

Bob spoke quietly to one of the men: "Get back to the ranch an' bring a wagon — mattresses. Quick as you can!" To another, "Run for the doctor!"

Again that ghastly attempt at a brave grin.

"Bob — I wanted — wanted a fight and —"

Bob knelt beside him.

"Don't try to talk, Shorty; it'll weaken you."

"No — diff — difference. Listen, Bob —"

Bob bent close; poor Shorty's voice was rapidly growing weaker.

"Never — religious, Bob. Danged — heathen. You —"

He stopped. Somebody gently wiped the blood from his lips.

"— know ol' cowboy way of — of buryin'. Horse —"

"I know, Shorty. If things go wrong with you, I'll see that you're buried that way. But you should make it yet. I sent for a doctor."

"Give — Red — my saddle. I — I want —"

He closed his eyes. His breath came more and more weakly. And still Shorty tried to grin, although he must have known that he could not live until the wagon came. Bob looked up at the silent group that pressed close around. He spoke; his voice trembled:

"Anyone else want a real sheep war?"

250

CHAPTER
EIGHTEEN

Cowboy Burial

That morning Stella sent for Bob.

"Bob" — her voice was low — "I thought you said that there would be nobody killed."

"I couldn't help it; it was a wild shot that got him."

"Does that help him?"

Bob shook his head.

"Stell, look things square in the face — try to look at it as a man would. Would a man — anyone worth calling a man — quit and let somebody take his ranch?"

"But getting the boys killed — is it worth it?"

"It is. It's one of the things a man has to do, like going to war. I took more chances than the rest; I went up to Johnson's tent."

"I can't see it, Bob. The way things stand here, we'll lose the outfit, anyway. Hadn't you better give up?"

"What would your father do? — and he's one of the most peaceable men I ever saw."

"He'd fight."

She had to admit it; she knew her father.

"And as to being no use, Stell — we have a pretty good chance yet; if we can hang onto the outfit till it rains, the banks will lend us money to pull us through."

"The sheepmen?"

"They'll likely be broke by that time. If not — well, we'll know what we're fighting for then. Can't you see it?"

She sat looking at the floor a while. At last she nodded.

"Yes, I see it. It's what my father would want us to do. I'm afraid it's useless —"

Her voice trailed off, and again she was silent for a while. Then:

"But, Bob, what good did it do — going over there? Won't they come tonight and raid us?"

"No. They likely mean to, but I have a plan to stop them."

She caught her breath sharply; her voice raised a trifle:

"By getting more men killed?"

"No — a trick."

She did not ask what the trick was; this thing had got out of her control. Presently she spoke again, hesitantly:

"Bob, about burying Shorty the old cowboy way — I've heard my father talk of it often. Don't you think it would really be better to send for a preacher and have the usual services? That other way sounds too much like reservation Indians."

Bob stood up. His jaw tightened.

"Stell, what Shorty wanted, he gets. I'm seeing to that."

From his set tone she knew that there would be no budging him.

252

She followed him to the door. She spoke sorrowfully, pleadingly:

"Bob, will you at least promise me that you won't get any more men killed if there's any way out of it?"

He turned on her almost savagely. He threw out both hands.

"Do you have to ask me that? Do you suppose I want to see any of them shot? What do you think I am?"

"I — I'm sorry, Bob, but — I suppose a girl can't see this sort of thing as a man sees it."

Bob turned away. Now for his plan to avert a future raid. He walked around among his men till he found the one he wanted, Whitey Wheeler. He sauntered up to him with a casual, friendly nod, and offered tobacco and papers.

"Smoke, Whitey?"

Whitey grinned crookedly, pleased by this friendliness; he regarded Bob as now perhaps the leading "hard hombre" of Arizona. They squatted on their heels, talking casually of different things. Whitey congratulated himself that they were out in the open where everyone could see what close pals he and Big Bob Edwards were.

Bob, for his part, found this sneaking gunman as repulsive to him as a snake, but he hid his feelings; he told himself that the whole future of the ranch depended on his good acting, on his pretending that he was taking Whitey unreservedly into his confidence as the most trusted man on the place. He negligently flicked the ash from his cigarette and brought up a new subject, very casually:

"Wonder if Butch'll try that raid again?"

"I'll find out for you, Bob. Reckon he will."

Bob puffed a moment. He nodded.

"Hope he does, now!"

"How come?" Whitey kept to his dry drawl, as though not particularly interested.

"Why, you saw old Brad Simpson ride up here a while ago. I had him seeing all the other cattlemen about a plan. We got it fixed so that if Butch and his crowd do come over, every outfit in the country is going to send all its men to help us."

"That would fix him!"

"Uh-huh. I tried to get the cattlemen to help us in a raid on his camp, but they won't do it — afraid of getting into trouble with the law. But they'll be only too glad to jump on him if he starts any fight at the ranch here."

"They'd clean up on him if they got together."

"Clean up! Well, what I want is for you to try somehow to get him to raid this place — tell him we're weak, and it would be easy. Besides you can tell him that us raidin' him last night gives him an excuse. Will you do that?"

"Shore!"

"Fine! I got a certain plan to send signals to the others if he comes on us unexpectedly; we could stand him off till the crowd got here, the houses being 'dobe."

"All right, Bob; I'll get word to him. He has lots of confidence in me."

Bob would have liked to remark that he had his own opinion of anyone who had confidence in Whitey.

Instead, he stood up, yawned, asked a casual question before turning away:

"Anybody been over to Badger Dam lately, that you know of?"

"I don't think so; it's an all-day ride from here."

"I think I'll drop over an' see about it; it must be near dry. I'll have to hurry to get back in time for the burying of Shorty this evening."

He walked to his horse, swung into the saddle, and struck out up the hill in the steady trot of a man beginning a long ride.

Once out of sight, he put the spurs to his horse and made a quick half circle around the ranch. He was riding Jimcrow, a big, strong black not particularly fast or active but very long-winded; he had picked him for this ride because of his wind. Still, the black was in a lather of sweat when Bob stopped him near the top of a high hill with a good command of the country around.

Bob stretched himself on the summit, elbows propped on the ground, peering through his glasses at the head of a trail leading up from the Bar Diamond ranch houses. He kept telling himself that his judgment of Whitey must be correct — telling himself over and over again, fearing that he might have erred.

He expected a long wait, but he had hardly lain there more than ten minutes when Whitey appeared, riding slowly, carelessly. Bob knew the cattle trail he was following, so he easily picked him up with the glasses as he crossed little openings in the cedars.

He came jogging along until he was almost under the hill on which Bob lay. Bob hastily shoved the glasses back in their case, ran to his horse, and went plunging down the back of the hill. A mile and a half away, he threw himself panting on the top of a second; he had been forced to climb afoot nearly two hundred yards because of a bluff on that side.

At first he thought he had lost Whitey, but at last he picked him up. He was still jogging steadily, apparently absently, paying little attention to the cattle he saw. Bob let him pass his hill this time; he was afraid of losing him.

And suddenly another man rode into the circle of the lenses. Bob almost yelled in his relief — so he had been right! It was Al Boyd.

The two stopped and began to talk. Presently Whitey threw one leg over his saddle horn and rolled a cigarette. They did not remain long together, soon each continued on as he had been going. To anyone watching, it would appear the most casual of chance meetings; it was cleverly done.

Bob lay watching Al until presently the nester circled around toward home. Bob crawled back from the skyline, returned the binoculars to their case, mounted Jimcrow, and struck a trot back to the Bar Diamond. His plan had worked; his neatly concocted yarn was on its way to Butch. There would be no raid on the Bar Diamond.

He had hardly been at the ranch more than half an hour when Whitey came riding casually in. Bob was waiting for him; he strode up to him.

"Where have you been, Whitey?"

"Huh? Just ridin' around, lookin' at the cattle."

"Meet anybody?"

"Heck, no. Who'd I meet?"

"Sure of that?"

"Think I'd lie to you, Bob?" Whitey looked almost hurt.

Bob sniffed. He had never wanted a man of this sort around, and now that he had been given further evidence of Whitey's duplicity — even if that duplicity was just what he had counted on — he wanted him still less. This fellow could be of no more use to him, and the next message sent to Butch by Al Boyd might do damage.

"Whitey, I've decided I can't use you any longer. Get your bed rolled and come up to the house for your pay."

"You — you mean you're firin' me?"

"Something like that. I saw you meet Al Boyd and send a message to Butch warning him of our plan. You've ruined everything for me. I should do more than fire you for it!"

"But —"

Whitey stopped, probably concluding that Bob would not believe anything he said, which came close to being the truth. He faced Bob with a snarl. For an instant the thought came to Bob that perhaps Whitey had sent the message that he had told him to — that he was playing square. But no — his arranging meetings with Al Boyd showed that he had been keeping in close contact with Butch all the time. Whitey could not be square if he tried.

257

A pause, the men facing each other. Bob certainly did not mean to be the first to turn his back. At last, with an oath, Whitey turned and started hurriedly toward the corral to rope his horses.

"Dirty rat!" growled Bob to himself. The ranch would seem several degrees cleaner with Whitey off the place.

Now for poor Shorty's funeral. Bob spent an hour or more consulting various men on the outfit. To him, the old cowboy's burial rites were but hearsay, tradition; his men knew no more of them; some of them had barely heard of such a thing, some of the younger ones.

Then he thought of Brad Simpson — old Brad was, of course, there for the funeral. Yes, Brad knew all about it; his harsh face softened and his eyes took on a distant look, as though he could see gaping holes in the brown hillsides of long ago, see companions of the night herd and the Chisholm Trail lowered into them, wrapped in their tarps.

Yes, Brad could tell Bob about it; he'd a notion to leave it in his will that he'd be buried the same way himself. Still, nowadays — His low voice droned on, telling of how Zack Pierce had been buried, and Jed Cooper, and other cowboys who had been young when he was young, but never grew old. And as he talked, from the barn came the repeated crescendo of hammer blows as nail after nail was driven in rough pine. Shorty would not be buried in his tarp.

The sun was low, already taking on a reddish tint, as the wagon crept slowly up the draw from the ranch. Behind it came Bob, leading a saddled horse —

Moreno, Shorty's favorite, his "top horse". Next rode Brad and Stella, Stella dabbing at her eyes with a small handkerchief — those old hands were like brothers to her.

Then came all the other cowboys, all on their top horses. Even the cook rode, short though the distance was; to walk beyond the limits of the ranch buildings always carries a faint trace of ignominy to a cowboy, and they were trying to honor Shorty.

Up a steep hillside the little procession crept, to a spot that gave a broad view of the range and of distant mountains. Here it stopped. Everyone dismounted and gathered around the gaping hole already dug. All were in full riding clothes, with chaps and spurs; now they removed their wide-brimmed, battered sombreros.

With their reatas, four of Shorty's closest friends gently lowered the rough coffin. The four stepped back, and others came with shovels. The falling earth made a hollow sound on the pine at first, but gradually the sound became duller. Soon there was a mound over the spot.

Bob, as range boss, came forward; until this he had taken no part. He stood a moment at the head of the grave. He had not meant to say anything, but overcome by feeling, he spoke very briefly:

"Boys, we don't claim to know much about heaven, but I leave it to you who'd go there — a man like Shorty Jones that always did the right thing, or a man that went to church oftener and wasn't as square? He wasn't religious, but he'd have given the shirt off his back to anybody he thought needed it worse than he did. He was *white* all through — what better could I say of him?"

Bob might have said more but for a lump that rose suddenly to his throat. His simple words fitted his audience, fitted the man they were leaving there; his was not the only throat that held a lump when he stopped speaking.

Red Selby came up; he was leading Moreno. Bob took the reins and went to the off side of the horse. He drew his knife, cut the cinch, and pulled saddle and blankets off from the wrong side — it signified that nobody but Shorty could even unsaddle a horse properly; it was the last tribute to his horsemanship. Now Bob removed the bridle, and through a lane of cowboys the brown trotted in a direction away from the ranch — he, Shorty's pet, was never to be saddled again, he could never be abused or overridden.

One more thing: the wagon was still beside the grave; all waited until a cowboy climbed to the seat and drove slowly back to the ranch. In the order they had come, they followed it away. They must not seem too anxious to leave a partner's grave; they must not seem to hurry.

Thus ended the little ceremony, plain and rough, but touching to those men who knew not which of them might be the next to go. Now they knew what a true sheep war brought.

Back at the ranch, old Brad and Stella went to the living room and sat down. They said little at first. Stella was in no mood for talk, and Brad was thinking sadly of other days, of other such burials. At last he spoke:

"Bob Edwards shore went through with it fine. He made it sound so — I dunno what to call it."

He nodded silently.

"Yes, sir, he shore did. Reminds me of his dad — he was a preacher. You didn't know him, did you, Stell? No, you're too young, you was only a kid when he died."

Silence again. Stella sat looking into the cold fireplace. Brad nodded slowly.

"Uh-huh. He come from the Big Bend of Texas, like yore dad. Used to have the Episcopalian church in Prescott. Fine man, Robert Edwards — fine."

She spoke at last:

"What was he like? Of course I've heard Dad speak of him often, but what did you think of him?"

"Big man, fine-lookin' — like Bob. *Real* preacher — I 'member one time I saw a bad man in Prescott stop a dance-hall girl on the street an' begin cussin' her. Some fellers think they have a right to cuss that kind of girl. I was gettin' sore about it myself, especially when he took hold of her arm an' began shakin' her."

Brad had been absently rolling a brown cigarette; he paused to light it, and went on:

"Uh-huh. I was gettin' sore, but before I figgered out what to do, Preacher Edwards came up with that long walk of his. He whipped the man's gun out of the holster an' threw it into the middle of the street. Then he knocked him down. He turned to the girl real kind an' told her she'd better go home."

Brad stopped to wag his head.

261

"They say she quit her job soon after that. Then she disappeared. Preacher Edwards wouldn't say anything when we asked about her, but from how he'd grin when we asked questions, we figured she'd gone somewhere an' straightened up. *That's* a real preacher for you! I've heard him say often that he didn't care what church a man belonged to, he'd go to heaven if he lived square."

The story touched Stella almost as much as had the funeral. There seemed to be so much left unsaid — the story of a noble life. She spoke:

"Died of smallpox, didn't he?"

"Uh-huh — got it nursin' Mexicans. Bob was twelve then. The pore kid had a tough time knockin' around for about a year, doin' any odd jobs he could find. Then yore dad took him out here an' made a cowboy of him. He was pretty useful even from the start — big kid for his age — but jest the same I'll never forget it for old Newt."

"Too bad Bob's father couldn't have lived; then Bob would have gone to college," mused Stella.

Brad sniffed.

"College! That would have ruined him — by the time he could have got out he'd be too old to learn cowboyin'."

"Well — he might have been something else." She sounded doubtful.

"*Pfhut!*" A contemptuous snort. "Bob anything but a cowboy! Don't worry about him; he's young — he'll be a big man yet."

"Maybe you're right." She spoke abstractedly. "College — Clay Bozart went to college —"

"Huh! Two year — till he got kicked out — an' four year wasted in high school before that. An' he don't act half as eddicated as Bob. If Clay's dad had made him work like heck on the outfit, he'd have been better off — at least he'd know what work was when he saw it." Another snort.

"Ye-es, but if Bob —"

"Listen here, young lady!" Brad got up suddenly and wagged a finger under her nose. "I don't want you to say nothin' again' Bob Edwards; he's a good kid, an' a friend of mine."

Stella smiled faintly.

"Brad, you old sinner, don't blow up at me that way. I hadn't the slightest idea of saying anything against Bob."

"Well, I'm warnin' you you'd better not — not while I'm around to hear it. *Phfut!*" And he stamped off.

Now he had to hunt Bob up and give him a darned good cussing, and tell him how completely worthless he was — that was the only way he could think of to even things up after having let himself talk that way. Had to see him, anyway, dang the luck! Nice message he had for him!

Behind him, Stella smiled wistfully at the floor. It seemed really funny that anybody should tell her about Bob's good points.

Bob saw Brad come stumping toward him, and his heart sank. He could see that the thing he had been expecting for days was at hand. The old man kept full speed until he was within four feet of Bob, and came to a sudden stop. He shook a finger under Bob's nose.

263

"Young man, I want to talk to you — an' right now!"

"Uh — what about, Brad?"

"What about! *What about!* You know danged well what about!" fumed Brad.

Bob did know, but he shook his head meekly; he had to keep on good terms with Brad no matter what came up — the fight against the sheepmen could hardly go on without Brad. Then, one didn't have to take offense from an old man as one would have to from a younger one — there would be no question of one's courage here.

"Bob, I want to know what the devil kind of mess you're makin' of runnin' this row for us cattlemen — us jest shovelin' hard-earned money into it, with beef as low as it is, an' here you set down doin' nothin' outside o' paintin' the sheep camp red without takin' no chances o' settlin' anything!"

The whole thing had come out on one irate breath; now old Brad had to stop to puff. He shook a finger again.

"What sorter danged picnic you think you're runnin', anyway?"

He waved to the little groups of men loafing everywhere. Bob nodded sadly; he didn't like the looks of it either.

"Brad, I — uh — I'm sure anxious to go over an' clean up on 'em, but they have twice as many men as we have. They'd do the cleanin' up."

"Cleanin' up! Cleanin' *up!* You've pretty near cleaned every cattleman in the country out of money. What you mean by it, you young whippersnapper? Uh

264

— I don't want you to take this personal, Bob — I'm jest talkin' business in a cool way."

Bob wondered how he'd act if he weren't cool — and what he'd call him. Inspiration came; he knew Brad's main weakness.

"I'll tell you how it is, Brad," he spoke soberly. "Butch has got more men than we have because he's paying 'em nearly twice as much on the average. Look at 'em." He waved a hand. "Look at the wages we're giving 'em — an' not a lick of work out of 'em. Think how much more it would be if I had to pay 'em double!"

Brad groaned.

"Well, it's a gosh-awful waste."

"And feeding 'em!" said Bob. His inspiration seemed to be working out; Brad was turning from angry to sad.

"Uh-huh — feedin' 'em!"

Suddenly Brad's finger came up to shake again.

"*Feedin'* 'em! I saw 'em eatin' dinner today. What did I see?"

"Uh — what?"

"*Canned peaches!* Feedin' canned peaches to that gang, at what they cost now. Who ever heard of cowpunchers gettin' canned peaches, anyway?"

Bob shuffled his feet uncomfortably; he wanted to groan but did not dare. But Brad did; he seemed almost ready to weep. Then came the bombshell — Brad had been trying to work himself up to say it:

"Bob, I brought you no more money; there'll be no more."

"Huh? What?"

"If you don't do something about cleanin' 'em up, there'll be no more from us. I mean — we'll have to put someone else in charge of this thing — somebody that'll go over an' mop up on 'em. You're jest lettin' it drag along an' doin' nothin'."

He did not say that at a meeting of the cattlemen he had argued himself hoarse against this. No. Brad would not admit to that; by some curious twist of his cranky nature, he could not let himself appear any man's friend to his face, whatever he might be to his back. The very fact that he liked Bob made him all the more abrupt with him.

"But," gasped Bob, "that leaves the whole thing blowed up! Why, it's pretty near the first of the month — pay day. And I'll have to get a lot more supplies from town; you don't know how much it takes to feed all of them."

"No? Well, I know that *my* money ain't buyin' 'em any more canned peaches."

"But — Brad —"

"But nothin'! Call yore men an' go over an' raise Cain with them sheepmen. Then I can get you more money. Loafin'! Jest plain loafin'!"

With a last snort, he turned away — mentally cursing the cattlemen who had made him bear such a message.

Bob stood there, staring blankly at the ground. He knew that a lot of that talk was merely Brad Simpson; but the decision to oust him was the decision of all the cattlemen who were backing the fight. Now, what was he to do? Perhaps some bluff that would satisfy the

266

cattlemen. But what was it to be? He decided to talk the matter over with Stella.

He turned, to see Mrs. Doheney sitting on the edge of the porch, with old Brad standing opposite her wagging a finger severely. Bob quickened his pace. Brad might scold him, but he'd better be careful how he spoke to women on this ranch. Bob came quietly up from behind. He paused to roll a cigarette that he might hear the monologue:

"Yes, sir, ma'am. I don't believe in chousin' cattle an' runnin' the fat offin 'em; I'd fire a man in a minute for it. But when you come to startin' a bunch o' newly-weaned calves off to the railroad — run 'em! Run the heck out of 'em a mile or so, so's they won't git to lookin' back an' bawlin'. If they do that, you're sunk — they'll scatter all over the place, an' you'll kill yore horse chasin' 'em single. Run 'em, I say — *run 'em!*"

Cattle again — could Brad never get his thoughts off them for two consecutive minutes? Bob felt sorry for Mrs. Doheney, forced to listen to this lecture, but he did not feel called upon to interfere. He hurried past and entered the house, leaving Brad still excitedly talking. As if this plump little widow would ever be in charge of cowboys driving a herd!

Seated in the living room, Bob told Stella his troubles. She could offer no suggestion, but she was suddenly wildly anxious that the leadership should not get into other hands than Bob's; the cattlemen would undoubtedly choose some hard-boiled gunman who

267

would have the countryside plunged in bloodshed. Bob, to her, had all at once become the angel of peace.

They sat by the fireside long into the night. The talk drifted from the sheep war to more personal things — to what Bob would do if the outfit went broke, to what the Davis family would do — they soon left that gloomy subject.

There was a long discussion as to where Bob should start his own brand, and how much of his little capital should go into cattle and how much into a shack and corrals. Bob, his eyes on Stella, held out for a fairly good house and fewer cattle; he said he wanted some comfort. But Stella was firm; it should be the cheapest kind of cabin, rough boards and only two rooms. Cattle were the thing — get all the stock he could and wait a few years for the luxuries.

That was the whole gist of the conversation, but now that everything seemed pretty sure to be lost, a gentle, almost pleasant gravity crept into their words. They nodded at each other, agreed and disagreed — and, strangest of all, seemed to enjoy that fireside chat.

When Bob left, Stella went with him to the door, and smiled a little and turned a trifle pink. And Bob said good night very gently and politely and went to the bunk house.

But this time Stella smiled after him as he left, and hummed a little air as she went to her room to go to bed. Too bad if they lost the Bar Diamond, of course, but they'd get along some way. Later on she'd be wealthy again, and have good clothes again. And those neighbors were just the meanest things to even think they could find anybody better than Bob!

In spite of the late hour Bob was tactless enough to go through the bunk house to his little room, instead of going to the outside door. He seemed absent-minded — so much so that he whistled very softly as he picked his way among the tarps on the floor. A thrown boot bounced against his shins, and some very hot language, came to stop this. He was sorry for his thoughtlessness.

But five minutes later the butt of a six-shooter thumped heavily against the thin partition, and an irate, sarcastic voice came:

"Bob, pass out the bottle if you ain't emptied it, an' fer Pete's sake go to bed an' shet up!"

"Huh-uh —"

"Anyway, Bob, be so dog-gone kind as to tell us whether we should send for a singin' teacher or a doctor — you shore need either one danged bad."

Bob only grinned as he crawled into bed — it was less than a week since he had been kept awake all night by something that sounded like a cross between a pillow fight and a Mexican revolution.

And then he suddenly remembered Shorty. He caught his breath as he pulled the covers over him. Poor Shorty; his bed wasn't in the bunk house that night!

It is curious that one waking up in the middle of the night can sometimes make a pretty accurate guess at how long he has been asleep. Bob figured it was around two o'clock when he suddenly found himself awake. Why had he awakened — just because there was so much worry on his mind? His eyes went to the pale square of his little window.

And then he heard a faint, shuffling sound. He tensed. There was somebody in his room! His hand stole up to where his gun hung in its belt near his head; he hushed his breathing.

Then a thought came to him — was it one of the boys trying to repay him for waking them up? It might be, and it might not. Cautiously, he reached out and found a match on the chair beside his bed. With a leap he sat up, the match flaring at the same time; he was ready to grin and throw a boot.

There came a sudden whiplash sound. Something just burned across his side under his left arm. He closed his hand on the flaring sulphur match head and leaped in the darkness for his gun. The flare had been too brief to show anything, but he knew that sound — a .22 pistol.

His sweeping hand found his gun, jerked it quickly from the holster. Again came that deadly, spatting little crack; he could hear the bullet strike the wall near his head.

Now, in the dark little bedroom came a pause that was harder on Bob's nerves than any action could have been. He crouched, gun in hand, near the head of the bed, under the window. He strained his eyes to see the man in his room, but could not. Neither could the other see him, or he would have fired again.

Bob had a sick feeling in the pit of his stomach. Anyone who had come really to shoot it out would have carried a heavier weapon. A man with a .22 pistol could only figure on one thing — he had meant to creep to Bob's bedside and put a bullet through his brains while he slept. Bob would never have known of it. The cowboys would have found him there in the morning. Lucky that he woke up easily!

He hardly dared to breathe; one could hear the slightest sound in the stillness. Sometimes he thought he heard the breathing of the other man; he would swing his gun muzzle, but he never was sure enough to fire. One leg became cramped under him from his awkward position, but he could not risk moving it.

He heard the rustle of a tarp on the other side of the partition. He had been hoping that some of the cowboys in the main room would have heard the little spatting shot and would come to investigate. There came a sleepy voice:

"What was that?"

A still more sleepy answer:

"Boards in the house crackin'. Go to sleep an' shet up."

Was that something over near the far corner of the room? He turned his gun that way. Or over there by the door? He was certain now that he heard hushed breathing, but it came so faintly that he could not locate it.

All the time a thought was running through his head like a refrain: .22 — Al Boyd; Al Boyd — .22. That was just the size pistol Al had been using to shoot Bar Diamond cattle, and it was doubtful if there was another within a hundred miles. Bob thought of how those cows had died — slow, lingering deaths. If one of those deadly little pellets caught him in the body, he'd go the same way. Ugh! He had to do something!

A plan came to him at last — a simple plan, as are most good ones. He groped cautiously on the floor. The first thing his hand came to was an old magazine that he had been reading a night or two before. Careful not to let it rustle in his hand, he picked it up gently and tossed it down toward the foot of the bed.

It evidently struck his boot and slid off; it made very little noise. All the better; even that noise was loud in the stillness.

The little gun spat again. Bob saw the tiny spurt of red fire. He shot on the instant. In the stillness and the small space, his .45 roared like dynamite exploding; the flare of his revolver seemed almost blinding in that darkness.

An instant's pause. A yell from the main room; sound of bare feet on the floor there. It was the other's turn to shoot; Bob would not empty his gun by firing blindly. The boys would come rushing in soon now; things had to happen fast.

CHAPTER
NINETEEN

A Walk in the Cedars

Suddenly there came a crash against the outside door. For a moment Bob thought that he had hit the man, that he was at last falling. He lowered his gun. Then the door whipped open, slammed again. He took a hasty shot at a dim figure that showed for an instant against the starlight — again that great roar of his six-shooter.

He leaped to his door and shoved — it opened outward. Something, perhaps a board, had been pushed under the knob; the man had prepared carefully for his flight in case of things going wrong in this way. Bob dashed back to the window, flung it open. Of course he could see nothing. He yelled and emptied his gun in the air in signal to the men who were sleeping outside.

By this time the place was pandemonium. Cowboys seemed to be tumbling all over each other in the main room of the bunk house. Bob shouted at the top of his voice:

"Out after him! Tried to kill me!"

But he knew it was useless. He stopped to jerk on his trousers and boots before scrambling through the window. He bumped into Red, who had come running

— he was still sleeping outside. Other men were pouring from the bunk house; everyone was shouting questions. Somebody fired a shot.

Panic came to Bob. In all this excitement, one of these suddenly awakened men might shoot another; they were running excitedly around yelling challenges at each other. He shouted:

"Hold on there! No shooting!"

There was now a light in the bunk house, another in the ranch house. The light in the ranch house moved from a bedroom to the living room, and he saw Stella appear outside the open door, some sort of wrapper hastily thrown around her. She called:

"What happened?"

Bob answered on the instant:

"Some of these fools playin' jokes. I'm telling them what I think of them."

"Oh!" She paused a moment and went back into the room.

In the bunk house, Bob turned to the men:

"You heard what I told her? Well, stick to it; no use in getting her more scared than she is now of what'll happen."

"But," demanded Red, "what did happen?"

He told them.

"A .22 pistol!" Red scratched his head. "Who'd have a .22 pistol around here?"

Bob remembered that he had said nothing yet to them about the cattle killing. Suddenly he decided not to; there was a possibility that they would make a raid on Boyd's place and drag the nester out before his wife

274

and son. The cattle killing alone might be called a lynching matter; if further excuse were needed, this cowardly attempt to murder a man in his sleep would furnish it.

Bob shook his head as though puzzled as they. That was the best plan. They didn't realize how dangerous Al was; some of them would be likely to get killed. Anyway, he himself wanted to attend to Boyd. Too bad that he hadn't hit him there in the room; he didn't like to shoot it out in cold blood with any man, no matter what the justification.

He lighted the lamp in his room, after having first hung a heavy blanket over the window. Every cowboy on the place tried to crowd in there all at once, to examine the bullet holes. There were two in the wall behind Bob's bed. The other he did not find until next day, when he discovered little holes in his blankets where it had passed through into the frame of his bunk.

Of his own bullets, one had cut the strap of his binoculars case — he was thankful that it had not crashed into the glasses and destroyed them; he valued them more than highly. The other had bit a piece out of the door jamb about six feet above the floor; it could hardly have missed the assailant's head by more than a few inches. Again he thought "too bad!" — if that shot had been a foot to the left, it would have saved him a disagreeable duty.

With some trouble he got the crowd out of the room. He warned the cowboys that too much excitement down here would let Stella know that it was not a joke after all. That of course did the trick. Stella, as the only

275

girl within miles, was regarded with a solicitude that a young empress might have envied.

Back in bed — his door and window securely fastened this time — Bob lay thinking. Fine homecoming he'd had to the ranch that he had always regarded as the most peaceful spot in the world! Men killed, cattle killed, attempts at midnight murder. A sheep war. Robbery — with that mysterious return of the money by an unknown woman.

Still greater mystery — why had old Newt had to borrow fifty thousand dollars, and so bankrupt the outfit he had been a lifetime building up? What had Newt done? What was the old man hiding?

Peaceful! Why, that big, wild, "company" ranch where he had been foreman was a sanitarium for nervous young ladies compared to this!

Queer, he thought, that he could make up a little joke about it like that; showed how quickly one got used to things — even to being shot at in one's room at night. Well, nervous young ladies had better stay away from the Bar Diamond!

Stella? She wasn't a nervous young lady — but she would be if this business kept up much longer — she was beginning to look thin and worried already. Bob found himself thinking of this as one of the most serious matters of all. He'd have to figure up something to do about it. He rolled over and fell asleep.

Two or three days passed without the slightest occurrence of importance. Bob could hardly understand it — until he heard that Al Boyd had gone to Prescott for a few days on some business. Business? — thought

Bob — business of avoiding him until he had cooled off. Well, he wasn't going to cool off — or, rather, he was going to be ice-cold about it.

Then came the first of the month — that brought pay day for all the men, and necessitated sending a four-mule wagon to town for supplies. There was no office at the ranch; Bob sat on the porch steps with his books, and paid the men as they came up in little groups.

The last given his wages to date, he stood up to carry the book in to the old desk in the living room. Stella was waiting there for him; she had an almost grim look on her face that he did not like — he knew what was coming.

"Sit down, Bob."

"Uh — Stell, I'm sure in a hurry."

"Sit down, please: I want to talk to you."

He did, reluctantly, prepared to give battle.

"Bob, what happened at the bunk house the other night?"

"Why, I told you it was some of the cowboys raising a rumpus."

"Did you think I was simple enough to believe that?"

"Well, then, ask some of the boys for another story."

She saw that she could get no more out of him on that subject; she took up another.

"Bob, where did you get the money to pay the men off, and for the supplies?" she demanded.

"Why, there was some left in the bank; I used it with what was left of the last Brad gave me."

"Not outfit money — I transferred all that to San Francisco to pay Dad's expenses there."

"You're forgetting that the sheepmen gave me some."

"Where did you get the rest?"

There was no getting out of it; she seemed to know already. Bob cleared his throat.

"Well, I had a little of my own I thought I'd sort of lend to the outfit. Newt'll be coming home soon now and he'll pay me back."

"Where'll he get it to pay back?" she asked relentlessly.

Bob could not answer that. She spoke again:

"How much of yours is gone now, Bob?"

"Not much yet."

"But you mean to spend all of it?"

"I sure do."

"And how about that little outfit of your own you were to start if this one goes broke?"

"That's shot."

That was the easiest question to answer that she had asked yet.

"Bob, we expect a cowboy to be loyal to the outfit; but don't you think you've gone entirely too far with it?"

She seemed very badly upset. Bob wondered if he could guess why — their talk of the other night — he had hinted —

"Bob" — coldly — "I'd like to hear some explanation."

He faced her suddenly, squaring his shoulders; he was tired of the defensive attitude.

"All right, Stell! Do I have to go back to when I was a kid and tell you all old Newt did for me?"

"Don't tell me anything sentimental about Dad having made you what you are. A boy of thirteen is what he's going to be — why, you even speak better English than most cowboys."

"Maybe so. That doesn't change the fact that this outfit gave me the finest home a kid ever had. Your dad and this outfit stuck by me when I was out of luck. Now that your dad and the outfit is in trouble, what do you expect me to do — pull out like a dirty cur and save my own hide?"

In spite of herself her anger was leaving her, being replaced by even greater respect for Bob than she had ever felt before. Bob was all man — almost too much man. She sighed, shook her head.

"Bob, you should be back among the early Romans — Horatius Cocles at the bridge."

He grinned — it was never hard to bring Bob's ready grin.

"Well, my education didn't get to Latin, so I don't know about him. Besides, this country's too dry to need a bridge — make it Bob Edwards at the water hole, and don't make the water hole too big or it won't look natural now."

There was a faint answering twinkle in her eyes.

"I don't read Latin either — only translations. But he was just like you; didn't know when to quit. Wish I had him for straw boss."

He pretended to bridle.

"I'm givin' you notice that no danged Latin-talkin' cowpokes work under me!"

In spite of herself, she smiled.

"Bob, you're — I hate to use such a long word — you're incorrigible!"

"So're you!"

He grinned down on her. For a moment it looked as though he were going to take a step toward her. No — he turned, reached for his hat, and left the room.

She heard a bantering voice behind her:

"I caught you!"

She turned to find Mrs. Doheney in the kitchen doorway, wagging a roguish finger.

"What do you mean, Jennie?" Stella looked surprised.

"You and Bob. I don't blame you — any girl that wouldn't fall for Bob Edwards would be crazy."

Stella's eyes opened. She laughed suddenly — a rather high-pitched laugh for her.

"Why, Jennie, what a funny idea! Bob and I are just like brother and sister — reared together, almost."

"Oh!" Mrs. Doheney's face fell. "That — that's too bad. He's the nicest — Well, I'm sorry about it."

She shook her head — she implied by the headshake that Stella had very little sense or judgment. With a sigh of regret for a beautiful romance that wasn't going to pan out, she turned and re-entered the kitchen.

Stella had a set look on her face as she stared after her. She had always been to a certain extent the belle of the whole countryside. Here she had humiliated herself by leaving openings for Bob time and time again — he must have seen them! — and he, the range boss, took little more notice of her than if she had been a piece of furniture; he would pay more attention to an old work mule. That in itself was bad enough without having everyone in the county know that her father's foreman had "turned her down".

She heard Clay Bozart come down the passage slowly; he was permitted to walk now, but not to ride. He entered the room. She noticed the change that had come over him in a week or so; he was freshly shaved, neatly dressed, trim — not at all a bad figure of a young man in his light, high-heeled boots of fine leather.

"Hello, Stella."

"Why, howdy, invalid! How about a walk with me? As your nurse, I have to see that you get fresh air."

"Gosh, Stella — Well, you bet your life, I will!"

He flushed with pleasure; anyone might feel honored by a public walk with Stella. She set a hat gaily on her head, and they left the house, she supporting him by one arm. He was not really in need of help, but far be it from him to object! Going toward the cedars, she chanced to look back. Bob, down by the corrals, was sidewise to them; she wondered if he saw them.

He did. From the corner of his eye he watched the wealthy young cattleman and the heiress — the most natural companions in the world. A fine thing for the outfit, Bob told himself, if they should get married — yes, fine!

But his horse shifted slightly as he threw the saddle on. He dropped the saddle, placed both hands on his hips, and stood there cursing the horse monotonously and feelingly. Any horse that didn't know enough to stand perfectly still!

Red came hurrying toward Bob.

"Bob, gentleman at the bunk house to see you. Hurry up!"

"Gentleman?"

"Uh-huh — looks like some punkins." Red looked deeply impressed by the visitor's importance.

Bob hurried to the bunk house and entered expectantly, curiously. If he hadn't been so angry — with his horse — he might have turned and taken a playful but none too gentle punch at Red. In the middle of the floor squatted an ancient, withered Indian wrapped in his blanket.

"What does he want?" snapped Bob.

Red spoke deferentially — he was evidently going to get all the fun he could out of this affair.

"Friendly visit, I reckon; he's an uncle o' yore pal Swift Eagle."

"Ask him what he wants."

Red spoke in his broken Navajo. The old man stood up slowly and began a formal oration. When he finished, Red translated briefly:

"An Injun won't talk business to start out, Bob. He wants to know how your health is, an' the health of your wife an' family. I reckon he never saw a man of your age without a hogan full of kids."

"Tell him I feel just fine, an' that I've got a lot more sense than to get married to any girl ever lived."

Red looked at Bob, shook his head, and turned. Imitating the Navajo's tone, he began a long, grave speech; he looked so solemn and dignified that Bob almost had to laugh in spite of how he felt. At last Red turned back.

"Bob, I done the right thing by you — whether you wanted it or not. I told him that you belong to a little tribe o' Bulgarian sun-worshippers that's not like the rest of us whites. I told that you have six wives an' nineteen kids, fifteen of 'em boys."

"You — you did!"

"Uh-huh. Look at his face — how respectfully he looks now. I told him that you were takin' another wife in eleven days — Stella. He saw her an' thinks she's heap pretty squaw. He says to tell you he hopes you two have many papooses."

"Listen, Red —"

Bob flushed angrily, but he bit his words off. If he had finished what he started to say, it would have meant a row with the hotheaded Red. Red was a fool!

"Find out what he wants, an' quick! I can't waste all day on an Indian."

The Navajo drew a bundle from under his blanket. There came another oration, far longer than the first. Bob seated himself wearily, disgustedly on the edge of a bunk and rolled a cigarette. He would have walked out but that he got a suspicion that Swift Eagle wanted to return the horse and saddle that he had stolen; that was ranch business and something that Bob had to look after.

At last the old man finished. He handed the bundle to Red, who passed it on to Bob.

"He says you an' Swift Eagle are all-same brothers. He says you paid Eagle's fine and got him out of jail, and Eagle owes you fifty dollars for it. But accordin' to his figgerin' he don't owe you anything for the horse an' saddle, because he stole 'em honest."

"What kind of figgering is that?" snorted Bob.

"Injun figgerin'," sighed Red. "I've seen a lot worse than that back at the tradin' post. Swift Eagle didn't have any money, but he sent you this."

Bob untied the buckskin thong and unwrapped the bundle, itself done in soft-tanned doeskin of fine texture. There were two blankets of Navajo make, and an immense belt of silver plaques set with turquoise.

"We-outch!" gasped Red.

"What'll I do with this junk?" asked Bob indifferently.

"Junk! Man, man! Sell 'em to a museum — I know Navvy stuff; I didn't think any of 'em could make that kind any more. Look at them blankets — real vegetable dye, an' a lot finer weave than you can get now. An' that turquoise — feller, that's turquoise! Bob, you got somethin' good here, but you're too dumb to know it."

"Tell him thanks." Bob was beginning to be impressed.

Red did; this time he probably took his own oration seriously, although Bob could not be sure. The old Indian grunted, slipped quietly through the door, and started to his horse.

"Watch him," ordered Bob, "till he gets off the place. I don't want any more good horses run off with — honestly or not."

284

"Huh!" Red sniffed. "Him or any other Navvy of the tribe would get killed now trying to keep someone from stealin' a match from you. If you get tired of workin', you can just go up there an' live offn 'em free the rest o' yore life."

Bob shook his head.

"I don't understand Indians."

"That's funny! I had to be raised among 'em not to understand 'em, an' here you caught on right away. An Eastern dude generally takes twelve years not to understand 'em — at first he knows all about what he calls the simple, innocent children o' Nature."

"Queer people!" Bob was thinking of Swift Eagle.

"Uh-huh — dudes shore is — got Navvies skinned a mile at it. Well, I gave you eleven days to marry Stella — better be gettin' busy or somebody will cut in on you."

"Red," growled Bob, "you're even crazier than I thought you were. Stella! Why, I never even thought of her that way!"

"No?" Red looked knowingly down his nose at him.

"No. And if you had brains the size of a peanut . . ."

Without finishing, Bob turned and hurried away. He saddled quickly, mounted and struck up the ridge in a fast lope, taking good care to go in the opposite direction to that taken by Clay and Stella. The ridge was high where he went up, but he followed a cow trail that took it at a long, easy angle.

His horse seemed restless on the way up; it humped its back several times as though ready to buck. What ailed the fool animal, anyway? Then he guessed the reason; he had in his hasty saddling left a wrinkle in the blankets.

Ashamed of such carelessness, he stopped on the summit of the ridge and unsaddled again. Yes, a wrinkle there was. This time he spread the blanket carefully and swung the heavy saddle so that it would flop straight down. He tightened his cinch. Then he paused to roll a cigarette.

He had one foot in the stirrup to mount again when he chanced to look back toward the ranch through a light screen of branches. He started. Had he seen somebody just disappearing through a window on the side of the ranch house next the cedars?

He hastily untied his binoculars from behind his saddle, and focused them. So many things had happened lately that he was perpetually uneasy. Nobody there, of course, except Mrs. Doheney — but he certainly did not want anyone murdering that plump, pleasant little woman.

He swept the glass quickly around. He sighed with relief — there she was, down by the corrals, talking to a little group of cowboys. Mrs. Doheney had here, to her surprise, found herself quite a belle, attentions being paid to her by handsome young cowboys little more than half her age.

Bob turned the glasses on the house again. He wondered if he would have time to dash down before whoever it was could get away. Not likely, he decided; the fellow would hear or see him and slip back into the cedars. Better try to recognize whoever it was when he came out.

Suddenly a head bobbed out through a bedroom window, jerked right and left in a hasty, cautious glance. Then came a boot, a leg. Now a man was running quickly and furtively from the window toward the cedars, taking care to keep the house between him and the corrals so that he could not be seen.

Bob lowered his glasses and gulped unbelievingly. Why, it was Red Selby! What had Red been doing sneaking in through a window of an empty house?

The answer came immediately — the only possible answer. Of course Red was up to some of his eternal jokes. Who was the victim this time? Probably Clay; Red would hardly play tricks on Stella or on the plump little widow.

Well, possibly on the widow. He might do something to her kitchen — steal a pie, perhaps, to share with the other boys. Bob, as range boss, could not of course countenance such goings-on, but he decided with a grin that he could forget what he had seen. Red was "top hand" on the place; the most trusted and efficient cowboy. One had to overlook a few little things in such a valuable man as that.

CHAPTER
TWENTY

Bob Faces Al Boyd

Bob rambled several miles through the cedars. He had hardly meant to work when he rode out, but he was too good a cowboy to overlook anything; had someone asked him at the end of a ride, he could have described the condition of every cow he had seen, just the state of the feed on every inch of range he had ridden over. He had been so accustomed all his life to seeing those things that he did not know he looked for them.

One thing he noticed was pingüe. The shower of the other night had been just enough to give it a slight start without helping the grass. There were a good many tiny patches of it. It looked small, stunted; no doubt it would grow no more now. Well, he didn't care whether it did or not now; he had laid his plans without counting on it. At the best, it could but hurry matters a very few days.

He was passing through a patch of cedars thicker than the rest when he heard voices — a woman's and a boy's. It surprised him at first, but he knew instantly who it must be — Mrs. Boyd and the boy Danny. His chance! Like a flash he was off his horse, holding its muzzle so that it could not whinny. He saw the two ride by, passing within a hundred yards of him.

He waited until they were well out of hearing, and then he mounted quickly. His face was grim, flushed; here was just what he had been waiting for. It was hope of some such luck as this that had kept him coming back toward the Boyd place. Now he could confront Al!

A sudden panic came to him. Was Al back yet from Prescott? He put his horse to a run straight toward the Boyd homestead. From a ridge nearly a mile off, he saw it first. Smoke came thickly from the chimney — yes, Al was at home. Bob saw that his gun worked smoothly, came easily from the holster, then he swung down toward the house. At last he and Boyd could settle things!

He rode quietly up. This time he did not shout in the usual manner before approaching; he went softly to the door and knocked. Almost instantly it opened.

"Why, howdy, Bob!"

The huge nester's bearded face grinned at him in a manner that showed friendliness mixed with surprise at the visit. Al held out his hand. Bob coldly ignored it.

"What's the matter, Bob?"

Boyd seemed amazed at Bob's refusing to shake hands.

"Boyd, I've had enough of your two-faced tricks. I came here to shoot it out with you; one of us is going to be dead inside of five minutes."

The nester changed color. He gulped.

"Bob, I thought we — I ain't got my gun on."

"Get it on. I don't do my killings your way."

289

Boyd gasped. He turned, walked to the far wall of the room, and took his gun belt from a wooden peg. Bob watched him like a hawk; he was prepared for tricks. But Boyd only buckled the gun on slowly, turned slowly, and came back.

"Ready?" asked Bob. He felt that his face was white; he did not like this thing.

Al nodded. He did not show the least fear, but there was something else on his face — regret. He looked baffled. He spoke: "Yes, Bob, I'm ready. But first I'd like you to tell me what this shootin' is to be about."

"You know danged well!" Bob spoke savagely.

"Bob, if I did, I wouldn't ask you."

Boyd's voice sounded sincere — he was the most accomplished actor, thought Bob, that he had ever met.

"Well, I'm going to pay you back for the .22 bullets you fired at me the other night, for one thing. With good interest — mine are .45s."

"*I* fired at you! What night?"

"Wednesday — in case you have a bad memory."

Bob's voice was cold, bleak; this farce was going too far. He made a significant motion toward his gun.

"Hold on a minnit! Let me show you somethin' first."

Al turned and went to a cupboard. After rummaging a few seconds, he returned with a handful of flimsy little slips of various colors. He handed them to Bob.

Bob feared it was a trick to get his attention off the nester. He took the papers with his left hand, held them up so that he could glance at them and still keep Boyd in view. Yes, it was a trick — they were nothing but receipted bills for small purchases at Prescott stores. Al had got a rope, two shirts, some saddle strings, and such — but what of it?

"Well?" asked Bob.

"Look at the dates."

He did. They were the dates of the preceding Tuesday, Wednesday, and Thursday.

"Wha-at!" Bob gasped.

"If you don't believe that, I'll lay off my gun an' ride to town with you an' we can telegraph. I can get fifty witnesses that I wasn't within a day's ride of here that night."

"But your .22 pistol?"

"Bob, I never owned a .22 pistol in my life. My kid has a .22 rifle he uses on rabbits an' prairie dogs."

Bob stood gulping. Could it be that there was some mistake after all? Could it be that he had nearly shot an innocent man? Suddenly he turned back to Boyd.

"But Clay saw you down there by the dead cow — pottering around, he said."

"Dead cow? Oh, I know where you mean. I found that calf runnin' around by itself, an' I was lookin' about to see if I could find its mother. Nacherally, I thought of brandin' it for myself, but from how it was bawlin' I figgered the mammy might be somewhere; I'd a notion she was dead, maybe killed by a bear or something. I didn't find her, but I decided to come back in a day or two an' see if the calf was still alone."

It was the most reasonable explanation in the world — just what Bob himself would have done. But Bob's grim air did not relax. This fellow was tricky.

"Well, that may be. But you can't say you didn't shoot at Clay Bozart — or did you shoot at him?"

That last came as an inspiration — a trap for Boyd. Boyd flushed and bared his teeth.

"You bet I shot at him! And I hope I make a better shot next time."

"Why?"

"To teach him to stop botherin' respectable married women like my wife. Come around here while I was locked up, tryin' to get funny with her, an' beggin' her to run away with him."

Bob suddenly felt as though he were about to collapse like a rubber balloon. That this charge was true he did not doubt; he himself had angrily advised Clay to leave Mrs. Boyd alone and not play the fool. But Clay, the ass, had not listened.

"But — the night Newt was shot? The killing of Jack Daly?"

"Bob, I only got my wife an' kid to prove that I was at home both times — an' I reckon their words ain't worth a whoop, no more than mine."

"There may be another way. Mind taking off your gun a while?"

The nester silently pulled off his gun belt and tossed it on the table. He deliberately walked away from it. Bob went to a corner and picked up a carbine that stood there. He thrust the muzzle from a window and pulled the trigger. Then he threw the breech open and extracted the empty shell.

He scanned it carefully. It was smooth and shiny — no sign of the two little scratches that had marred those he had found at the scenes of the shootings. This gun had not fired those shots.

The cartridge dropped from Bob's fingers. He was breathing rapidly, his face white. He turned, held out a shaking hand.

"Al, I refused to shake hands with you a few minutes ago. Will you shake hands with me, and let me apologize? I was wrong, and I nearly got one of us killed over it."

He knew which one — that was why he was so pale. He had nearly killed an innocent man. He probably would have killed him had the bunkhouse attack been made on a night when Al was home — the attacker had not known of his absence, and so had planned to blame the affair on him.

The nester gave a huge sigh of relief.

"Dang glad to, Bob! While I ain't as scared o' bein' killed as some people, I don't reckon it would be a lot of fun."

They sat down at the table — Bob was only too glad to sit down; he had a shaky feeling. His head whirled at the thought of what might have happened, of what Mrs. Boyd and the boy might have found on the floor when they got home from their ride. He began at the beginning, told the whole story so far as he knew it. The return of the money Al explained:

"Bob, I didn't leave town right away after I saw you that day; I went up to see old Billy Green first. From his place I cut over the ridge to strike the road in the gulch. I saw a man below there actin' mighty suspicious — an' I thought I'd watch him a while."

"Who was he?" asked Bob.

Boyd hesitated.

"I don't like to turn anyone in — but it was Butch Johnson."

"All by himself?"

"Uh-huh. Too foxy to whack up with anyone else, or to have any witnesses. Well, he had one — me. I didn't see you comin' till jest before he shot. All I could do then was to lay beside his horse an' stick a gun in his ribs when he come back. I took the money away from him."

"Didn't seem very neighborly to leave me lyin' there," remarked Bob.

Boyd flushed.

"I know it. But everyone knew we'd had a row an' come near shootin'. I thought you were dead. What would happen if you were an' I'd been found down there, or my tracks?"

"You're right, Al!"

"Well, I got home with the money and —"

He stopped suddenly, began again:

"See here, Bob; I'm not goin' to lie to you. I was half drunk that day, an' was more or less figgerin' if I should keep the money to get even with the Bar Diamond; I hadn't made up my mind. Well" — he grinned broadly — "my wife made it up for me, an' mighty quick. Course," he added hurriedly, "I'd have sent it back anyway soon as I got sober."

"I know you would." Bob meant it.

Al looked up, a twinkle in his eyes.

"Changin' yore opinion o' nesters, Bob?"

294

"Some of 'em." Bob grinned. His first instinctive liking for this bearded, rough-and-ready giant was coming back to him.

"Bob, it's mighty plain. Some of yore own men is doin' it. One of 'em has sold out to the sheepmen, likely gettin' a fortune for it."

"Looks like it." Bob hated to make the admission, but it seemed only too clear that it was true.

"Well, I seen one o' yore old hands ridin' over toward the sheep camp more than — Sh-h-h! Here comes Emily — don't let her know we come near shootin' each other."

She had seen the horse at the door, and she came hurrying in apprehensively — she had heard too much about the murderous ways of cowboys to have confidence in any of them. She found the two men seated at the table and looking up at her innocently. Boyd spoke — his booming voice was jocular, tender; evidently he worshiped this blonde little woman:

"Emily, here a friend o' mine comes over for dinner an' you gallivantin' around an' nothin' fixed for him to eat."

She hesitated. Suddenly her eyes filled with tears, and she rushed across to Bob with both hands out.

"Oh, I'm so glad you're friends! I — I was afraid something might happen."

The roaring laugh of the nester filled the little room.

"Me an' Bob row about anything! We're the best o' pals — always were. That right, Bob?"

Bob grinned.

"Well, I wouldn't say that but we are now."

Bob had to stay for dinner. Al built a fire while his wife hurriedly peeled potatoes. She loved to cook, she said. She mentioned lonesome years of "batching" while teaching a backwoods school before her marriage. She loved the ranch here, although times were not so good.

Now that she was not under a strain, as on her visit to the ranch, Bob found her inclined to chatter a trifle more than he thought becoming — but it was cheerful chatter, amusing. She was just the type that would appeal to the impressionable and weak-headed Clay. Once when Al stepped outside for a moment, Bob asked her a hurried question:

"That writing on the package you sent me — who addressed it?"

She giggled.

"Don't you think an old school-ma'am knows enough to change her writing? Sh-h-h! Here's Al." Her blue eyes were twinkling confidentially into Bob's. Yes, he could readily see why Clay had misunderstood her.

It was almost dark when Bob left. Al walked with him to the gate, and so they found time for a few more hurried words.

"Got any idea who'd have done it?" asked Bob.

"No. Pretty slick, whoever he is. Was any of the men outside the night Newt was shot?"

"I — I never thought to ask. Didn't suspect any of 'em then."

"Who got to the house first?"

"Red Selby. I must ask him if he saw anybody loafing around before that."

Boyd opened his mouth to say something but stopped himself. The look on his face said plainly that he did not like Red. Bob spoke hastily: "Red's the best man on the place. We've been friends a good many years now."

Still Al said nothing. Bob swung into his saddle.

"Well, you an' the family drop over for dinner any time."

"Shore will, Bob — 'bout time us an' the cowboys learned something about each other."

Bob rode home in the gathering darkness. He had not even bothered to ask Al about some things, such as the spur found where Stella had been waylaid. Anybody could cut AAB on a spur and then drop it there. The other minor things could be explained just as easily.

And — jumping jack rabbits! — he had seen Whitey's accidental meeting with Boyd and jumped to the conclusion that the nester was carrying messages to Butch. Of course it was Whitey himself who had carried the false message, after he had been fired. If it hadn't got there, what might have happened!

Big, hearty Al; lively, talkative Mrs. Boyd with her golden curls — each seemed to think the other the world's greatest achievement. Bob grinned; he liked both of them. What a ghastly thing it would have been if he had shot Al!

But the farther he rode the more a new, disconcerting fact grew in his mind: Suspicion removed from Al, everything that had happened was all the more mysterious. Who was behind all of it? Butch, of course

— behind it. But who was Butch's clever and deadly tool?

The truth had to be faced — it did look as though it must be one of Bob's own men. But which of them? At least now Bob would be wary, he decided; he would not start off on a false trail again.

There was one thing in his favor — the culprit would not know that Al had been exonerated. All that now remained was to think up some clever trap for him. Red could help him with that; Red was full of tricks. The main thing was not to let it be known that he was watching his own men.

That night he signaled Red to slip quietly to his little bedroom. He had not long to wait until Red entered from the outside door. They sat side by side on the bunk and rolled cigarettes from Bob's tobacco.

"Somethin' new?" asked Red. "Or is this jest a social call?"

"New is right!" Bob paused to light his cigarette, and finished: "Red, I was over to see Al —"

"You got him!" It was an exclamation of joy from Red.

"No. I found that he had nothing to do with it."

"Wha-at!" Red stared at him. "You're crazy!"

"Oh, no! Let me tell you about it."

Red sat puffing his cigarette, listening attentively to every word. When Bob finished, he sniffed.

"So you believe that! Well, what did Al say about me? I know he holds a grudge against me."

"Grudge! What for?"

298

"Uh — I thought he'd have told you. I — I had a little row with him in a saloon once. He" — Red flushed — "he knocked me down. I pulled my gun, but some fellers grabbed me an' took it away from me."

Bob would have liked to know what the row was about, but the cardinal point of cowboy etiquette is never to ask personal questions. He wondered if Red, too, could have been paying attentions to the pretty Mrs. Boyd — Red was about as impressionable as Clay where women were concerned; he might even be fool enough to fall in love with a married woman.

"Red, he never said a thing about it to me."

"No? Well, he's no good, that feller. The sooner you put him out of the way the better."

"Looks to me," remarked Bob, "as though you're the one that's holding a grudge."

"Grudge, nothin' — it's common sense! If you believe that wild yarn he gave you, you're crazier than I thought you were."

Bob stood up half angrily; he did not like to hear Red talk thus, influenced by something personal.

"Well, if that's how you feel about it —"

"That's jest how I feel about it! If you got any remarks to make about how I feel —"

"Oh, forget it!" This fool hothead was almost ready to fight now. "I have to see Stella about something."

Bob was almost to the door when he heard Red's voice:

"She's busy — playin' the piano an' Clay singin'."

Bob darted through the door. If he hadn't, he might not have been able to overcome the temptation to strike

299

Red. Something about that last remark had stung — Red had meant it to sting.

Hearing no music, he started toward the house. But just as he was about to step onto the porch, he chanced to glance through an open window. Stella sat at the piano, with Clay leaning over her; both were laughing softly. Bob had promised to see her at that hour about some business matters, but he turned away quickly and strode in the darkness toward the corrals.

He swung to the top rail of the round corral and sat there staring down on the backs of the old wrangle horses. A strange, miserable feeling crept over him. For the first time, he fully, thoroughly understood how he felt about Stella.

He might have known how it would work out! The two of them together every day and all day — the heiress and the wealthy young cattleman. Yes, Clay must be wealthy, in spite of a few debts; his range was at least as large as the Bar Diamond. Good-looking, too, now that he had spruced up and was shaving every day. Bob had noticed the change in him.

Yes, and another change, too — Clay had gradually been taking a new attitude toward him; the cattle owner and the neighbor's foreman. Probably Clay himself hadn't noticed it coming on, it was growing so gradually.

Bob sighed. Just a few days ago he and Stella — Well, she had probably liked him before Clay came along. All very fine, but he was not the kind of whom it would be said that he lived off his rich old father-in-law. And Stella had always had things; it would be out of the question to ask her to share the miserable shack of a cowboy just starting his own brand. So, Clay or no Clay, it was and always had been out of the question. This was really all for the best.

Clay? With the right kind of wife he'd soon forget his slightly wild tricks; he had never been really bad, just reckless. Both outfits in poor shape — but by selling half of one, there would be a great combined range still left, and left in the best financial condition. That would keep soft-hearted Clay from seizing a neighbor's outfit, and keep the neighbor from losing his brand.

And old Newt and his wife would have a home. Clay had little sentiment about land or cattle; he would sell part of his own outfit and keep the Bar Diamond intact. It was all very simple, and logical, and desirable. And Bob wished he were one of the stove-up old wrangle horses down below him.

Now he realized that all the time he was down South he had been lonesome, without knowing it, for a scrawny, long-legged little pal of his. He had come back to find her another girl — but he wondered if he wouldn't miss this one even more. What luck! Why were some fellows born rich and others poor?

Oh, well — he could drift over into New Mexico, or up to Nevada, and get a job. With his experience, he could work up to a foremanship again. He'd lost interest in that outfit of his own, and besides most of his money threatened to be gone if this trouble with the sheepmen lasted a little longer. No, danged if he'd ask anybody to pay it back! He owed that to the Bar Diamond. And he didn't need it anyway.

301

Outfit of his own! Sit around some dirty little shack in the evening, too tired to clean it up — a new outfit was *work*. Patch his own torn clothes, do his own washing, cook — and ride eighteen hours a day.

Of course if this outfit did pay him back what he'd spent, he could work along four or five years more and then have a better stake to go in business — if he felt like it then. How about wiring that outfit down south? They had told him that he could come back whenever there was an opening. And — Oh, to the devil with everything!

He got down and strode quickly to his room: he entered by the outside door. To his surprise he found Red still there, still seated on the bunk.

"Bob, will you do me a big favor?" — earnestly.

"I sure will, Red!" Bob did not know what the word *grudge* meant.

Red stood up, turned his back, bent over with his hands on his knees. He looked lugubriously around his shoulder. "Now kick — hard!"

Miserable though he felt, Bob could not help grinning.

"Heck, Red, I didn't mind; it wasn't our first little row."

"Don't go back on me, Bob; I'm askin' it as a special favor from a pal."

"Get out!"

Bob took him by the seat of the trousers and the collar and heaved him through the door into the main bunk house. Red picked himself up, dusted his clothes, and spoke, solemnly, respectfully:

"Thanks, Bob. Good night."

"Good *night!*"

Bob slammed his door and threw himself on his bunk. What would he do without Red, lovable in spite of his faults?

CHAPTER
TWENTY-ONE

Strychnine

Next morning Bob met Clay Bozart down by the barn; it almost seemed that Clay was lying in wait to catch him alone. He spoke:

"Bob, what did I say to you about that note the day you come over to see me about it? I can't remember how much I told you."

"Why, nothing much, Clay. What's the trouble?"

Clay hesitated.

"Why — uh — I don't want it gettin' out why old Newt had to borrow fifty thousand; there's no use in disgracin' the family."

"Well, I know nothing about it, and I don't want to. Newt sure was white to me, and that's what I'll always remember."

Casually though Bob spoke, his head was whirling. So his suspicions were justified — but he had not thought it would be anything so terrible as Clay's gloomy tone hinted. Another thing — so Clay was beginning to worry about the reputation of the Davis family. One could guess why.

"Bob — uh — remember not to say a single word to the boys."

"Heck, no! I'd be the last one to."

"Well, don't."

Clay hurried off. Bob's eyes kindled a trifle as he looked after him. That last remark was not as friend to friend; it was as boss to working man. Bob did not like that.

He talk! It was his own tongue that Clay had better watch. From the bottom of his heart Bob hoped that Clay would keep the secret, whatever it was. But of course he would as a matter of family pride; he seemed very badly upset about the thing.

Had Stella told Clay that old Newt was still alive, and now expected to be returning before long? The yarn of Newt's death had spread among all the cowboys, and Bob had not contradicted it. He had not even told Red, afraid Red would in strict confidence tell a pal or two, who would have other pals — within a week the truth would be all over the place.

What if they did find out? Bob asked himself. It seemed only a fool notion on his part to have let the rumor go. Still, something kept him from refuting it, some hazy mixture of hunch and half-formed plan.

About dark that evening Bob was surprised to see Slim Blake come riding in openly — a spy who did that sort of thing could not long be of use. Slim rode straight to where Bob stood with two or three men.

"Howdy, Bob."

"Hello, Slim." There was something in how Slim met his eye that kept Bob from saying more.

"How's the chances for a job here?"

"Wait a minute and we'll see about it."

Bob casually sent the men around him to do some work, and so found himself alone with Slim Blake. He feared that Slim had some message that could not wait.

"What's the matter?" he asked anxiously.

Slim grinned.

"Nothing much — only Butch sent me over here as a spy, to replace a man of his you canned."

"Well, what'll we do about it?"

Slim rubbed his nose.

"Why, you can kick me off the place mad — you'd heard that I'd been workin' for Butch. Or you can let me spy an' send him messages — genuwine hand-rolled messages." He grinned again.

Bob considered.

"How's Butch fixed now?"

"Pretty near to the end of his rope, Bob, to judge by his face. You'd think he was a sheep that had put in a hard winter, he looks so worried."

"That right?" exclaimed Bob eagerly.

"Uh-huh. He's been turnin' down the last men to come to him for jobs; reckon he don't know how he can pay 'em. There's a yarn in the camp that he'll have to let some of the others go any day now."

"Fine!"

Bob was beaming. He thought a moment, and spoke again:

"Well, let's help him out — of business. You start in here and do a real good job of spyin'. Get word to him that the cattlemen around here have got over being so cautious — that they're all fixing to meet and go over and raise more Cain than Arizona ever saw before "

"Turrible, Bob! I'll have to make a good yarn of it."

"Double wages, Slim, as you hired out to me twice."

"Double nothin', Bob! You don't have to pay me extra for not double-crossin' you. If you want to do somethin' for me, just give me a steady job here after the row is over; I shore would like that."

"Why, we'll see about it, Slim."

Bob hurried off. His elation over the prospect of Butch's quitting had been damped as though with a bucket of ice water; it had come to him that if Slim stayed with the Bar Diamond, he'd only be back working for Clay, whom he had left once.

Still, it was good news to know that Johnson was about through — Bob would have the sheepmen off the range before old Newt got back. All the other things that were to be solved — well, Newt himself could see to that.

Or perhaps he wouldn't want them solved.

Bob saw the remuda come streaming down the trail and into the corrals. He hurried down and gave orders to each man to rope his best horse and turn it into the small wrangle trap, so that they could get an early start for the next day's work; he had decided to make a long ride on a distant part of the range that he had been neglecting.

Clay came down with orders to catch his horse and turn it in there too, and Stella's pet, Rabbit, a well-bred roan. Yes, they were orders. Bob did not relish Clay's commanding tone; he was about to tell him to rope them himself and turn them in there when he remembered that, after all, Clay was recovering from a wound, and so could be regarded as more or less of an invalid. Not that he looked it, or walked like one.

Still, Bob did not trouble to be polite enough to answer Clay; he asked one of the men to catch the two horses and put them through the gate. Then he himself turned to rope Flight — the blood bay was getting almost fat; he needed a pretty stiff ride to keep him hard.

At last the horses were all through, and Bob closed the gate. This tiny wrangle trap with its own watering trough was a plan of old Newt's, and one that Bob had found very convenient. It was just a few acres that could be wrangled in fifteen minutes of a morning — and there would be no unwanted horses to bother with. Barely grass enough for a few head once a week or so, but that was enough.

Bob turned to see Clay walking back to where Stella was swaying gently in the porch swing. Yes, Clay sat down beside her in it. And their two horses kept up; that meant that Clay was going to take his first ride in the morning — in company with Stella.

Yes, everything was working out fine for the outfit, thought Bob — but one might have wondered why, as he walked to his dark little room, his face was as long as one of his boot legs.

That night he surprised the rest of the boys by joining in a game of dominoes in the main bunk house — he did not want to be alone. In spite of what is often heard to the contrary, cards have always been strictly forbidden on a large majority of cow outfits, liquor on all. This is not from Puritanism. The work is dangerous enough for sober men; it would be suicidal for anyone even slightly befogged by whisky. As to cards — they, at the best, would keep the men up so late that they would not be very wide-awake next day; at the worst — and an extremely likely worst — they would lead to quarrels among a crowd of pretty reckless young fellows nearly all of whom carried guns. Therefore, dominoes it was.

But Bob was so absent-minded, so apparently stupid, that he was soon indignantly ordered out of the game. He went to his room and tried to read a magazine — like all cowboys, he read mostly cowboy stories if he could get them, perhaps because that was the only life he could fully understand.

But tonight his mind kept turning to affairs at the Bar Diamond, and he soon put the magazine down. He kicked off his clothes and crawled under the blankets.

Through a crack in the wall, he could see when the light in the main room was blown out, the last man in bed. Still he lay there awake. So Butch was about whipped — looked like a very few days more would do it. And every day eating into Bob's own savings — there was nothing else now to pay and feed all the men. Well, he owed that much to Newt. Al Boyd — pretty darned good fellow —

He was just dozing off when a sudden wild yell outside brought him leaping to his feet.

"*He-e-elp!* Quick!"

He flung himself into his trousers and boots — that was the second time in a week that he had had to run out thus! If this wasn't a heck of a ranch! A man or two from the rear of the bunk house came dashing through his room, falling over things — that was a shorter way out for them than going to the door at the other end of the main room. Again the voice:

"This way! Spread out an' ketch him!"

The voice had come from down by the corrals.

"Scatter out, boys!" yelled Bob.

He himself ran straight to the corrals; he had to find out what it was all about. There were two or three others there before him, some of the men who had been sleeping outside. A match flared. He saw on the ground a dusty, disheveled figure with torn shirt — Clay Bozart!

"What happened?" Bob exclaimed, running up.

Clay turned to him as the match went out; Clay looked very excited, a trifle white.

"Why — why, Stella an' me were settin' on the porch in the dark, an' I thought I saw someone sneakin' down this way. I stole after him to see what was goin' on. He was creepin' up to the horse trough of the small wrangle trap when I jumped on him. I'd have held him, too, only that he hit me, or kicked, or somethin', right where I'd been shot in the stomach — he knew about it."

Clay had got this out between puffs; he seemed to be badly winded, panting. He was standing up now but with two men holding his arms to steady him.

"Horse trough!" gasped Bob. "What would anyone want to sneak up to a horse trough for? He couldn't steal it."

Nobody could even guess what the reason might have been. Bob sent a man to the house for a lantern;

310

soon it came glimmering back. They searched the ground; there was a crowd there now, all talking at once, all making different guesses as to what the fellow had been trying to do. Suddenly came an exclamation:

"What's this?"

Bob turned over with the lantern. A man was standing beside the horse trough with something in his hand; a squat bottle holding about two ounces of some white powder that showed through the glass.

"Medicine of some sort — no label on it," someone offered.

Bob reached out his hand; his face was almost as white as the powder in the bottle.

"Strychnine! It's a bottle of it that has been kicking around the house; someone got it to poison coyotes and never used it."

He took the bottle, shook it. The cork had been half withdrawn but not removed; as well as he could judge, none of the deadly stuff was gone.

"Strychnine!" This from Clay, who was still gasping — he gasped particularly on the word, seemed unable to believe what Bob had said. "What was that feller doin' with strychnine?"

"Looks pretty plain!" Bob spoke harshly through thin lips. "Going to poison the water — poison all our top horses — Flight, Stella's roan, yours."

"Gosh!" Clay gasped.

"Uh-huh. Clay, you sure did a good turn for the Bar Diamond tonight — and for me, in saving Flight. Let me help you back to the house."

"Aw, heck, Bob, it was nothin' — I mean it was only an accident got me into it. I can walk fine."

He went shuffling off, still bent over and weak. Same old Clay — would not take credit for what he had done. With all his faults, Clay was rapidly proving himself pretty much a man, and Bob felt a great sense of thankfulness for it. He wanted Clay to be a man for Stella's sake.

What to Bob had been a suspicion was now a ghastly certainty — these things were being done by one of his own men; nobody else could have known about the best horses being there tonight, for Bob had only given the instructions on a sudden impulse.

That strychnine, too — only one of the men could have got it from the living-room desk. One of the old hands; none of the others would have felt sufficiently at home to walk up to the house and enter when there was nobody there. And the man had known just where to strike Clay, at the risk of seriously injuring him. A traitor among them — the thought came to Bob like a blow.

And trying to poison horses! Butch must be desperate indeed to order such a thing in his attempt to weaken the Bar Diamond. Poison horses!

Bob had thought he had discovered the lowest depths of human depravity with the mysterious shooting of the cattle in such a brutal manner. He hadn't. He wondered now if there could be something even worse than what had been attempted tonight. Would it be below the traitor to poison the food the

312

cowboys ate? Bob shivered; he was beginning to fear even that.

Traitor! That was a thousand times too good a name for whoever had attempted this! And to think that it was one of his own men — a man with whom he ate every day, with whom he swapped cigarettes. Bob groaned with bitterness. What a fool somebody was making of him!

CHAPTER
TWENTY-TWO

Setting a Trap

Next morning Bob decided that he and Red should stay at home to see if they couldn't investigate the affair of the night before — he was pretty hazy as to what form the investigation could take. He saw the men ride off; they were all old hands who would do just as well without a boss; they had indeed been going ahead with the ranch work pretty much ignoring not only the new men who loafed around but even Bob himself, who had been busy with other things.

Stella had sent word that she wanted to see Bob when he had time. That was almost a daily message; things were always coming up regarding which they had to consult — things regarding the management of the ranch. He was starting toward the house when Clay approached.

"Bob," he spoke good-naturedly, "catch my horse an' Stella's, an' saddle 'em an' bring 'em up to the house."

Bob stopped dead in his tracks; his face went very red. This was entirely too much, in spite of the friendly tone.

"Clay, what do you think I am — a servant?"

Clay looked astonished, hurt.

"Why, Bob — I didn't mean — Good gosh, Bob, ain't you workin' here?"

"I'm the boss, if you want to know. I'm going to be the boss while I hold power of attorney — and then I'm through here. Got that?"

Clay's face, too, was slightly flushed now, but he had not quite got over his thunderstruck air.

"Bob, I didn't mean no harm, an' you know it."

"Clay, you haven't got brains enough to know what you mean. Next time you come around trying to give me orders, you're going to get knocked on your ear so quick you won't know what happened."

Clay looked for an instant as though he might be going to apologize. But suddenly he turned on his heel and started toward the corral. He was muttering under his breath; Bob could only catch the words, "swell-head cowpuncher", but that was enough. A quick stride or two and he had Clay by the shoulder, whirling him around.

"Clay" — Bob's tone was ominously quiet — "would you repeat that? I'm not sure I got it right."

Clay looked up belligerently, but Bob towered above him too much.

"I didn't say nothin'," he growled.

"That's good. Don't, if you know what's good for you."

Bob turned again and strode toward the house. Before he was halfway there, he was sorry for what he had said and done. After all, Clay might have meant to ask as an invalid, not as a boss. Bob looked back and saw him enter the corral with his rope on his arm.

Now what if Clay got himself jammed by a horse somehow, and tore his wound open? Bob could never forgive himself if that happened. He tried to force a sneaking, unwelcome thought out of his mind; if there were no Stella, he would not have got angry with Clay as he had. He was in the wrong again.

As he went toward the house, he saw a man ride up to the porch, hand something to Stella without dismounting, and turn away. She entered the living room and a moment later he followed her. She was standing with a yellow slip of paper in her hand, and her eyes were dancing.

"Bob! Guess what I just got! A wire to say that Dad and Mother are coming home tomorrow on the afternoon train!"

"Great!" He almost whooped it.

"Isn't it? Goodness, look at the mess the house is in! We'll *never* get it straight before they get here. What'll Mother think of my housekeeping?"

"I see nothing wrong with it." He glanced around.

"You wouldn't — but there is. I'll have to stay at home and straighten things up instead of meeting them."

"I'll meet them with the buckboard." He spoke eagerly.

"Very well, Bob, if you want to. I wanted to see you about some business matters, but we can let it go now that Dad's coming home."

"Yes, I'd rather we did. I can't take any more responsibility now that he's coming back."

Their little burst of enthusiasm was gone, they were talking with cool friendliness, but with none of their old familiarity. She spoke to Bob as to a trusted and valuable range manager about to relinquish his position. Bob was courteous, giving her all the respect due her sex. He was about to leave when she called him back:

"Bob, did you have some row with Clay, down by the corrals? I saw you from the porch."

"Yes." He flushed. "Clay started giving me orders."

Now she, too, flushed slightly.

"Clay has no business to do that!" It came from her quickly. "But," she added, "you might try to keep your temper with him, Bob; he's an influential neighbor and a close friend of ours."

"I know — I should be kicked for it." There was gloomy apology in Bob's tone.

She shook her head regretfully.

"I can't tell you how sorry I am that it happened; I do want you and Clay to be friends. You should have remembered that he's an invalid now, and also what he went through last night — I think it was very brave of him."

"And so do I!" exclaimed Bob heartily. "I always did say that Clay was all right. Uh — I'm going down to apologize to him."

"Wait, Bob! You don't have to do that — not if he started ordering you around. The best way is just to forget the whole thing and I'll ask Clay to do the same."

"Well, whatever you say."

Bob grabbed his hat from the table and got away as fast as he could; the interview had been pretty embarrassing to him.

Red was waiting for him near the house. He came rushing up, joy written all over his face.

"Bob, you had a row with Clay! I saw it."

"Did I?"

"Say, that's great! I never liked that feller. If I was you, I'd watch him."

"Would you? Well, I wouldn't — I don't hold grudges like some people."

"Meanin' me?"

"Maybe." Bob's lips bit hard on the word.

Red opened his mouth to speak hastily. He closed it again, and stared at Bob.

"Bob, do you know what ails you?"

"Nothing ails *me*."

"No? Well, I'll tell you. You've had such a hectic time lately, with all the worry and responsibility, and everythin' goin' wrong, that you're gettin' nervous an' short-tempered. Why, look at yore face! You must have lost twenty pounds since you come here."

"Huh?"

"Uh-huh. So we'll have to reverse things. You always had to keep yore temper with my fool hot head; now I'll do the same for you. Gosh knows it'll be a strain on me — like sleepin' with a porcupine. Oh, well, turn about is fair play. Come on with the next dirty crack — I'm listenin' — I won't mind."

Bob answered slowly:

"You're right. Only that I'm worse than a porcupine."

318

Yes, Red was right — that accounted for his short temper with Clay. He spoke again, relief in his voice:

"I'll be danged glad when the Old Man gets back tomorrow so that I can get a thousand miles away from this crazy ranch."

"When — when — *What!*"

Red was staring as though his eyes would fall from his head; his mouth hung partly open.

"We just got word."

"But — but ain't he *dead?*"

"Good for many a year yet. I let that yarn stand because I thought it would bring something out in the open."

"Of all — So he's alive!"

Suddenly Red whirled and started toward the empty bunk house; evidently he did not want Bob to see his feelings. Bob cursed himself for his useless plan. Why had he upset the men thus for nothing?

He went to the corral and saddled Flight. He disappeared into the horse pasture and presently returned with the remuda, from which he roped out a pair of fine, long-legged sorrels — Newt's high-stepping buggy team. Newt had left in a wagon, behind a team of sleepy old browns noted for their slow gait; he was going to come home in style.

Bob began vigorously to curry the sorrels; they might have been prize racehorses from his care to get a high gloss on them. Presently Red came from the bunk house and toward him.

"Bob — uh — that shore was a surprise to me, about Newt bein' alive. I — I can't tell you how glad I am."

"You don't have to — I know."

Bob dropped the currycomb, wiped the horse's shoulder with a rag barely dampened with olive oil, and began to apply a stiff bristle brush with all his might. He stood back to view his work from a little distance. He could almost see his face in the sorrel coat.

"Shinin' 'em up to bring him back?" asked Red.

"Uh-huh."

"That other one has a witch lock startin' in his tail. Want me to comb it out?"

Bob paused and ran his shirt sleeve across his perspiring forehead.

"Why, if you want to, you can let that tangle go, an' I'll get it when I come to him. But you might be shining the buckboard up a little."

"Shore!"

Red hurried off for a bucket and cloths. A few minutes later Bob saw him, shirt sleeves rolled up, attacking the buckboard with vigor. Bob nodded with satisfaction — whatever Red did, he did thoroughly; one could always depend on him.

They finished their tasks almost at the same time; Red had to wait but a moment while Bob blacked a last hoof — he was overlooking nothing to have a stylish turnout.

"There!" He dropped the hoof. "Now for the harness. Where's the brass polish?"

Red found it — somewhat hardened and dried. Together they sat in the saddle-house doorway, Red remixing the polish with a little water, Bob carefully stirring a black powder into a small pail of neat's-foot oil. Red looked disgustedly at Bob's mixture.

"Bob, I can't use that — it'll ruin my mannercure!"

Bob grinned, as he always did at Red's solemn-faced comedy. Probably Red had half meant it — like any other self-respecting cowboy he prided himself on having hands as soft and white as a woman's. How else could one tell a cowboy from a common working man? Certainly not by his leathery, sun-wrinkled face!

"All right; I'll use the stuff myself."

"Heck, I'm only kiddin'! Jest the same, there's only two things would make me ruin my lily-whites with that junk."

"What's that?"

"Bringin' the Old Man home — an' yore funeral."

Bob had dipped a rag in the black oil and was rubbing it vigorously on the leather.

"Well, I come near giving you a chance for that more than once lately. Here, dang you! — *shine* that ring and don't be afraid it'll bite you."

It was late afternoon when they were putting the finishing touches on the harness. They had been working silently for a long time. Bob had been rolling a certain matter over in his mind. He glanced up at Red.

"You know, I got a hunch — I'm pretty sure of it — that the shooting at Newt wasn't entirely about the sheep war."

"What else could it be?"

"That's what I don't know. But I'll bet my saddle whoever did it will want to take another crack at him, to finish him."

"Bob, I told you several times to lay off'n the loco salad."

"I don't care what you think — I *know* I'm right about it."

"Oh, well — never was any use in arguin' with you, Bob. What are you goin' to do about it?"

"I'm going to set a trap for the fellow, and I want you to help me."

"Shore I'll help you — even if you are crazy. What you want me to do?"

"Well, either one of us will have to keep an eye on Newt all day, without letting him know it. Then, we'll have to watch outside his window at night; we'll take turns."

"Suits me fine. I was thinkin' o' movin' my bed from down near the corrals anyway; the horses keep me awake sneezin'."

"Say, that reminds me," interjected Bob, "I meant to ask you if you were down there when we found Clay. I didn't notice you."

"I took a look an' went back to bed," answered Red very shortly.

"Well, what I wanted to know: Clay got his shirt torn, and got sort of mussed up in general — likely the other fellow must have showed some signs; his shirt might have been torn, too. Did you notice anything wrong?"

"No."

"Well, they weren't all there — if one of 'em *was* mussed up, he'd take care to keep out of sight. Wish I'd thought to rush 'em into the bunk house before any of 'em had time to change his shirt."

"Uh-huh. Why didn't we think of that?"

Red did not even take his eyes from the throat latch he was oiling. Bob thought he noticed something odd about his voice, but judged that it was only due to his absorption in his work. He changed the subject:

"But to get back to our trap for that fellow. As I said, one of us will have to keep watch outside his window every night, and not be seen."

"Let's see. Did I notice a gopher hole out there, or not?"

"What do you mean?"

"Why, to crawl into and hide — it's a patch of bare sand out there."

"I've thought of a way of fixing that. When we come driving up, some of the boys will rush to get the team and unhitch it. I want you to beat the others to it; you can make it look natural. Stand the buckboard about ten feet out from Newt's window, and leave it there."

"Won't that look queer, leavin' it in such a place as that?"

"Nobody will notice it in the excitement of him getting back home."

"N-no, you're right. Who watches the first night — or does one of us watch?"

"You bet one of us watches! I figger that it'll happen the first night if it's going to happen at all."

"Well, I'll watch till bedtime anyway — the boys'll all be waitin' to ask you what Newt had to say on the way home. It'll be late when he gets here, an' bein' sick like he is, he'll go right to bed."

Bob nodded.

"Good plan. Then when the boys go to bed, I'll slip out my door and relieve you. Have your bed not too far off, so that you can take a spell of it again toward morning — that way, we'll both get some sleep."

"Bed! Why can't I sleep near the window? I wake up easy."

"Don't be crazy. Do you reckon whoever comes along would make noise enough to wake a mouse up?"

Red looked up interestedly.

"Do mice wake up easy?"

Bob grinned and walked off. He was so accustomed to laughing at Red's jokes that he did not stop to think this was a pretty flat one.

CHAPTER
TWENTY-THREE

Butch's Dilemma

Bob went to his room and carefully oiled his six-shooter. Before loading it, he buckled it on and practiced for a few minutes at drawing and snapping it. He alone knew his weak point in handling a gun — he was noted as an extremely good shot; in fact he was often called one of the best revolver shots in northern Arizona.

So he was — if he had a reasonable amount of time to aim. He was no more than fair at a quick draw or a strictly offhand shot; there were probably half a dozen men on the place who could beat him. But nobody thought of that; they had seen his good shooting at marks and called him an expert.

Red, for instance — as one might have suspected from his temperamental nature — was just the opposite; like lightning on the draw, deadly up to ten feet or so, but beyond that erratic, if not positively a bad marksman. Still, Red had no reputation whatever; he could not, like Bob, stand and coolly punch holes in distant cans one after another.

That shooting at empty cans was one of the most popular games on the ranch. The steady banging

325

outside told that it was going on even now. Bob went to his window and looked out; there were half a dozen men at it, taking their practice very seriously. Another little group had got up some sort of rope-spinning contest.

Bob shook his head. If this wasn't a fine thing, for men drawing the wages he was paying — killing time in any way they could think of. Still, there was little they could do; the old hands might even have resented their interference in the work. But just the same it hurt him to see so much money going to waste. His money — he had worked hard for it.

Perhaps it was seeing so many men loafing that made him anxious to be doing something. He mounted Flight and turned up the ridge. He took the same long trail from the head of which he had seen Red steal through the window of the empty house. He thought now that he should have asked Red about that. Jokes were jokes, but he had to see to it that Red did not go too far.

He was again almost to the head of the trail, riding casually, when there came a sudden whacking sound and Flight skittered sidewise. Bob wondered what it was — probably a dead stick that the horse had stepped on. He continued as he was going.

And then something like a swallow *whooshed* by his cheek — he could hear it, and feel the wind of it, but he saw nothing. But he knew what it was this time. He whirled Flight and leaped into the cedars, bent over in his saddle. Keeping to the thickest of the trees, he raced to put the summit of the ridge between him and the ranch. Whether any more shots came or not he did not know; the clatter of Flight's hoofs would have smothered the sound.

He stopped and swung from the saddle. Even as he did so, he noticed a queer bulge in the front of the cantle. He looked at the back of it. There was a large round hole, with fresh leather showing around the edges. He glanced at Flight's croup; the skin had barely been broken in a tiny furrow.

He took a deep breath. If that bullet had come through the cantle and struck his backbone, he would have been paralyzed for life, if not dead. No — it was not wild shots from the men practicing; someone had used their practice to cover his rifle shots. Someone had deliberately tried to kill him, and whoever it was had shot from the ranch, probably from a window.

He dared not ride back to investigate — he would not reach the foot of the ridge alive. Nice state of affairs, he thought, when a cowboy had to wait for dark to sneak down to the home ranch, but that was just what he would have to do.

Suddenly he thought of his glasses. As he carried them well down on the left side of his rear saddle skirts, they were undamaged. He stole back with them in his hand and examined the ranch carefully from a place of concealment.

Nothing could have looked more peaceful. The shooters had stopped their practice; the riders had just come in and were unsaddling down by the corrals, laughing and joking among themselves. On the edge of the porch sat Stella and Clay, Clay lounged back against the wall smoking a cigarette. Bob turned his glasses hastily from that view and toward the bunk house. Nobody in sight there except Red lounging lazily out, he, too, smoking a cigarette.

Bob did all there was for him to do — kept well out of sight of the ranch until after dark, then rode quietly to the corrals, unsaddled, and went to his room. But before coming down, he had made sure that his gun was loose in the holster. There was one of his own men there that wanted to kill him, but he could not even guess which one.

Next morning he was up early. He hitched the sorrels to the buckboard and went spinning jauntily up to the house. He gasped when he saw the living-room. The evening before it had looked neat and clean, as far as his masculine eyes could see. Now it looked as though a bad cyclone had struck it — furniture upside down, piled on tables; Navajo rugs on top of the upset chairs. Stella and Mrs. Doheney, towels around their heads, were tearing around in a manner that looked to Bob as though they had gone slightly crazy. Why hadn't they left things alone? Too bad to have the Old Man come back and find his home a wreck.

"Want anything from town, Stella?" he asked.

She whirled and pointed a feather duster.

"There's the list on the table. Tell Brenner not to send me out any more green potatoes like he did last time."

She took a whack at the old upright piano and turned again.

"Oh, say, Bob! Clay told me there was a yarn going around that Dad was dead. How about it?"

"Uh-huh — I heard it."

He did not say that he had tacitly encouraged it, and she was too busy to question him. Bob, with a last stare at the wreckage, turned and left.

He wanted to save the horses, to have them lively when old Newt saw them first, so he drove so slowly that it was almost noon when he reached town.

At the very edge of Danvers, he noticed something in the air. People stared at him, pointed. Surely his smart-looking turnout could not be causing all that sensation — many of the cattlemen had teams almost as good as these sorrels.

He turned a corner and struck down the main business street. Instantly he jerked erect. There were men all over the streets, men with guns — little groups of them loafing everywhere. He recognized some of them — Butch Johnson's gunmen. Butch had heard that Newt was coming home; there was going to be trouble.

Bob cursed weakly. Why had he not brought a few of his men with him? What was he to do now? And then he thought of quiet, silent, Sheriff Ben Wilson. Ben would help him out; he would gather every deputy he had and escort the Old Man home. Bob drove up to the sheriff's office to be met by Ben himself coming running out — Wilson had seen him from a window.

"Congratulations, Bob!" he shouted.

"Huh! What for?"

"You — you mean you don't know?" Wilson stared at him.

"Know what?"

"*Whew-w-w!*" The sheriff whistled. "Do you see all the men?"

"Sure — that's what I came to see you about."

"Why, Bob, Butch has gone broke — paid all his men off early this mornin'. Sold all his sheep to Jerry Mallett for a song."

Bob had been standing up, ready to step from the buckboard. He sat down again, suddenly. So, after all, Butch had quit flat without the last expected struggle. Bob remembered the yarn he had had Slim send over — of a coming raid on the sheep camp by all the cattlemen around. That story had probably kept Butch from doing anything — and also had proved the last straw on his back. And it had undoubtedly saved at least a score of lives.

"He'd have quit sooner," continued Wilson, "but that the shower the other day started so much pingüe up on his range that he daren't move 'em back — they'd all have died. He was in a pretty fix — couldn't move back on his own range, an' scared to stay on yores. Nothing left but to sell the sheep, quick."

"But — why should there be more pingüe on his range than on ours? I was looking for it, and didn't see much."

"Always more on sheep range — they say the sheep carry the seed in their wool and scatter it all over the place."

"Like grama grass." Bob nodded. "That's the most valuable grass in Arizona now, and there wasn't a blade of it till sheep brought the seed in from California in their wool."

"I reckon. Anyway, you shore handled the thing like no sheep war I ever heard of before. Why, but for yore clever headwork this county would be runnin' in blood like a slaughterhouse."

"I — I suppose it looked like that was goin' to happen. But I didn't do a thing only use a little common sense."

"Well, if that's common sense, what the devil's cleverness?"

"Oh, heck!" Bob grunted uneasily; he did not like praise.

He flipped the lines and went spinning down the street before the sheriff could say more. A man on the sidewalk waved to him to stop — Butch Johnson! Well, if there was to be a row, he might as well have it over. Bob pulled in beside the board sidewalk. The sheepman's face startled him. Butch looked lined and haggard; his eyes looked as though he had not slept for nights.

"Howdy, Bob."

"Howdy," answered Bob shortly.

"Bob, I reckon you know I've quit. I ain't sayin' anything about how you fought me — I don't hold hard feelin's."

Bob laughed coldly in his face; that was his only comment.

"Bob, now that you've licked me, how about you askin' old Newt to buy my place? I don't want to stay neighbors to an outfit I'm havin' trouble with."

"You mean, Butch, the pingüe took your range, so you couldn't move back on it, and you were scared to stay on ours. You were sort of caught between the devil an' the deep sea. That right?"

"We-ell, mebbe. But it's safe for cattle — they don't eat it much. Newt could use the range, an' I'd sure give him a good buy on it. I might take as low as twenty-five thousand dollars."

"Sure — because nobody else would want a range fighting the Bar Diamond and everyone else. Butch, you have nothing to sell anyway but a few dry water holes and some corrals too low for cattle. Besides, Newt *might* be sore about how you did Stella."

"Why, Bob." Butch looked almost shocked. "I didn't have a thing to do with that. I'd fired them two men the day before."

Bob glanced at him with contempt and turned away. That story was a little too thin. Bob, driving down the street, felt almost sorry for the man. How he had changed in a few days! Swaggering, bold when he had the upper hand; but broken now, unable to stand up under a blow — utterly crushed.

It did not occur to Bob to compare Butch's actions with his own when he had seemed the underdog, had seemed utterly and hopelessly beaten into the ground. No, Bob never would see that he had done anything out of the ordinary, could never see it.

In the doorway of a store, he ran into Jerry Mallett. Jerry pulled a thick roll of bills from his pocket.

"Collected this from the honest sheepmen for you, Bob — but I reckon I'll have the bother of givin' it back to 'em again."

"You will, Jerry. But don't you think I'll ever forget it for you, and for the others. I'm sure sorry to hear that pingüe is likely to ruin some of you."

Jerry grinned calmly.

"Ain't botherin' me. Sheep won't eat it while they have grass, an' mine have enough grass to get along nicely."

"Fine! I was wondering why you bought Johnson's sheep."

"Sellin' the same number of mine — mine are fat and I'm gettin' a good price for 'em. Nearly got Butch's for a present. Morehouse is broke, too — he's been after me all day to buy him out, but I can't risk even the little he asks in this drought. Sure would be a buy, if the country wasn't burned up for rain."

"Sure dry!" Bob shook his head and entered the store.

He did his shopping and then took the team to the livery. He gave a loafer a dollar to groom them some more, to rid them of the dust they had acquired on the way in. He had some time to wait until Newt's train arrived; he spent most of it at the livery stable because he found it too embarrassing to stay on the streets — everybody was congratulating him and making a fuss over him. Why, for goodness sake? — he wondered.

At last it came time to drive to the station. He found the whole town there to greet old Newt; the owner of the Bar Diamond had suddenly become a man of even greater importance than before. The train came puffing in. People began to crowd off it. Before long Bob saw a stumpy hand wave to him above the heads of those in a coach doorway. Now Newt came clambering off. Bob rushed to help him.

"Welcome home, old-timer!"

"Howdy, Bob."

They were pumping each other's hands. Bob was trying hard not to gasp publicly — the diminutive cattleman was dressed in a suit of extraordinary heavy material that was two sizes too big for his scant figure. It was of an unearthly dull green mixed with black, with brownish-red dots thickly bestrewing it. The old man saw Bob's amazed eyes on his clothes. He turned slowly around, showing the suit off, and nodded proudly.

"Latest style from New York — the man said so. Like it?"

Bob gulped.

"Uh — uh — I never saw anything like it before!"

He glanced at Mrs. Davis; she was beaming proudly on her well-dressed husband. The thing drew Bob's eyes again, but he forced them away.

"Ready to go home?" he asked.

Mrs. Davis answered: "He must see Doctor Varney first — that's the orders."

"All right; let me help you in, and we'll go up there."

On the way, Bob asked casually:

"Well, what's going on in San Francisco?"

"Nothin' perticular. Only it's been cloudin' up every mornin' for a week; it's goin' to bust loose in a sho'-nuff rain over there any day now."

"Wish we'd get some here!" exclaimed Bob fervently.

"Uh-huh; I wasn't right shore when I got out of the Mojave Desert — if I am out of it. Well, it won't be long now."

334

"It — What?" Bob glanced at the cloudless sky. Had Newt got childish from his wound?

"No, sir, Bob. It never comes up a real good rain on the coast without it workin' inland here; never saw it fail yet. Where else could we get rain from?"

"Say — that sounds — Well, you've lived here long enough to know something about it."

Bob suddenly seemed to fall into a fit of abstraction. Once the old man asked him what had happened since his leaving. Bob started.

"How? Oh — some sheep got on the range, but they got off again."

Reaching Varney's, he helped the old couple out. The doctor and his wife were there to greet them. Varney was trying hard to keep from strutting and puffing out his chest; Newt was his Exhibit A in life-saving.

"Hey, sawbones!" greeted Newt irreverently.

"How are you feeling, Mr. Davis?"

"Don't know about him, but old Newt's all right — thanks to somebody." Newt winked at Varney. "That specialist said there ain't a doctor in five thousand could have got me halfway over there alive — an' jest look at me now!"

Varney flushed with pleasure — such praise from Doctor Barnes meant something. His wife tried to look unconcerned — *she* had always known what a wonder he was. She spoke:

"Come in; I have lunch all ready for you, and you'll want to rest an hour before going home. You, too, Bob — come in."

Bob was too abstracted to notice that she was already becoming Westernized — she'd got down to first names for younger people.

"Uh — sorry, ma'am, but I have some business to look after downtown. Don't keep dinner waiting for me if I'm not back."

He drove away. To get matters straight in his head, he took a turn out to the edge of town, around a block, and back.

Rain — Newt thought it was going to rain, and those old-timers knew something. If it did, the Johnson sheep range would double in value overnight. Furthermore, the banks would be begging stockmen to borrow money — now, they might as well be closed for all they'd lend on cattle or range security. Bob knew cow-town banks, tied up with range conditions as they were.

Did he dare gamble? Would Butch gamble that much? Suddenly he headed the horses straight for the business section. What had he to lose compared to what he might win? And who wanted to start a two-by-four outfit anyway, a hundred miles from a road?

He chanced to see Jerry Mallett climbing into his buggy to go home. He stopped, and for a few minutes the two engaged in earnest whispers. Then Bob went on. He looked back to see Mallett retying his team and starting hurriedly down the sidewalk afoot. Now, what if he'd got his friend Mallett into trouble, talking him into plunging that way, into buying the Morehouse sheep outfit? Wouldn't that be a fine way to repay Jerry's friendship!

336

Bob drew the sorrels in to the curb — as though by accident he had stopped nearly opposite Butch, who was standing gloomily on the sidewalk. Bob tied the team to a hitch rack; only as he stepped up on the sidewalk did he seem to notice Butch. He spoke, half coldly, half jocularly:

"Sold that sand pile yet, Butch?"

Butch shook his head.

"No. Did you ask the Old Man about it?"

"He don't buy dry water holes."

"They control a heap o' range, Bob."

Bob laughed; he was casually rolling a cigarette.

"They would — if there was any water in 'em. Say, how about selling it to me? I'm just fool enough to buy something that way."

Butch looked up quickly.

"Why, I didn't think you had money enough to swing a deal like that."

"I got two thousand cash. I'll give you that now, and a thirty-day note for ten thousand more — full payment."

"That's only twelve thousand."

"I know it — but if I fail to borrow ten thousand inside of a month, you'd have the range an' the two thousand as well."

Bob saw a cunning look come into Butch's eyes; Butch thought he saw a chance to get even with Bob for everything. Still, he was cautious.

"Somebody promisin' to back you, Bob?"

"Heck, no — I haven't asked anybody."

A pause. Bob started to turn away. Butch spoke hurriedly; this cowboy was too "green" to have anything up his sleeve.

"Hold on, Bob! I'll take you up on it; let's go sign papers."

All at once Butch seemed in a great hurry to get the deal closed. He insisted on a certified check, and he almost rushed Bob into Judge Cox's office. Presently the contract was drawn up, witnessed, and signed. Butch put Bob's certified check in his pocket and hurried away. The fat, shrewd little judge looked up at Bob.

"Bob, there's something wrong. Why was he in such a hurry to get your money?"

"Broke and needs it." Bob grinned, folding his contract.

The judge started to say more, but stopped. Why throw a wet blanket on Bob's enthusiasm? He wished Bob had delayed a day or two about handing over his money. What did Bob know of the thousand and one crooked tricks of law and business? And what was there about them that Butch did not know?

Judge Cox shook his head after Bob had left; he liked Bob. And he was ready to bet his law books that Butch had worked some clever game that was as crooked as it was clever.

CHAPTER
TWENTY-FOUR

Home-Coming

Bob drove to Varney's and picked up the old couple — Newt was more than anxious to get back home. They were hardly out of town when Bob told Newt of his purchase, asked him what he thought of it; he had great respect for Newt's business judgment. The old man was jubilant.

"Great, Bob! I'll lend you the rest o' the money."

Bob thought of that mysterious fifty-thousand-dollar note. Wasn't old Newt worrying about it?

"Why, Newt, I wouldn't want to borrow from you; that's a lot of money, ten thousand dollars."

Newt nodded in a self-satisfied manner.

"Uh-huh — for a young feller like you. I got quite a bit salted down besides the ranch — railroad stock, a few bonds an' things. I wouldn't even miss it."

Bob gasped. And here he had thought the outfit broke!

"Well, I wouldn't take it from you, Newt. If it don't rain, you'd lose the money; if it does, I can borrow it easy from the bank, and enough more to get me a few head of cattle."

"Not too many, Bob — not too many! Graze it mighty light for five or six years, an' you'll have a better range than mine, an' jest as big. Let the grass go to seed a bit; it needs it."

Bob grinned.

"It'll be grazed light, all right; I won't be able to raise enough to stock it heavy."

"Good thing — you won't be tempted. Bob, 'member what I said about yore business head the day you come back to the outfit? Was I right or not? You'll have as good an outfit as mine inside o' ten years — an' think how long I was buildin' mine up!"

"Heck!" Bob grinned sheepishly. "We're talking as if it was raining bucketfuls. I haven't even got the outfit yet, and I stand a good show to only lose my two thousand."

"Jest like a young feller — settin' talkin' an' thinkin' an' starin' at a horse's tail! Look at them mountains over there."

Bob looked. He started, and his mouth opened. A few faint, fleecy white clouds hung above the horizon.

"Gosh — I wonder!" he gasped.

A sudden wave of something like awe came over him — the thing had not seemed real before. Clouds? Were they going to fool him as had the last to appear? If not — Again he seemed to be looking at the sorrel tail before him, but he was seeing himself master of a huge but poorly stocked range.

The clouds mounted. Patches at first, they grew thicker until they formed a solid bank. Bob was driving very slowly on account of the old man's weak

340

condition. Night came while he was still a long way from the Bar Diamond — a dark, gloomy night, with not a star in sight. A little wind moaned through the cedars. Still darker it grew. From beyond the old man on the wide seat came the worried voice of Mrs. Davis:

"Hadn't you better whip 'em up, Bob? I'm afraid Newt will get wet, an' that would be bad for him."

A chuckle from between Bob and her.

"Hope I do, hon! Hope it washes the danged buckboard away! I used to be able to swim when I was a kid, an' they say a feller don't forget. Shore like to find out, right down this gulch!"

It was about nine o'clock when they drove around the curve and came in sight of the ranch. In sight it was, in spite of the darkness of the night — two huge bonfires blazed before the house; others, smaller, were scattered all over the place; they could see every building as though it were daylight.

Nor was this the crowning achievement. Some cowboy of British parentage had remembered being told of the "wisp" — the peasant's torch. He and others had whittled pitchy pine into slivers and bound these into long, slender bundles. Now these flaring torches stood along both sides of the road, producing an effect spectacular in the extreme.

Bob felt the old man fairly jumping on the seat beside him; he felt an elbow prod him in the ribs. An excited whisper:

"Let 'em out, Bob; let 'em out!"

Bob grinned in the darkness. He chirruped to the sorrels. They needed no more; they swung into their long-legged stride, down between the wisps, snorting and prancing. Immediately they appeared in sight, a great yell came from the crowd assembled before the ranch house.

The crowd separated to leave a lane. Through it dashed the spirited team, heads and tails high, nostrils dilated — the fires and the yelling excited them. Bob glanced around quickly. On the steps, waiting, were Stella, Mrs. Doheney, and old Brad. And — good gosh! — if that wasn't Mrs. Boyd; she and Stella had an arm each around the other! And there was Al, heaving an immense cedar log on a fire as though it were a pencil.

How old Newt must like this! Bob swept the team to a showy halt before the door — did it with a flourish. The sorrels were now rearing, pawing; two cowboys dashed out and seized their heads before they could break the tongue.

"Well, here we are!" The little man was almost too excited to talk; this was the proudest moment of his life.

Boyd was the first to shake his hand — his mere bulk and weight assured that.

"Welcome home, you danged cattle-rustlin' horse thief!"

Boyd could have been heard almost to his homestead five miles away.

"Howdy, nester! Shore glad to have a neighbor like you here to welcome me."

Newt was grinning almost straight up at the bristling yellow beard — Al made him look like a pigmy. Boyd grinned down and made room for others. It looked as though Newt's arm were to be pumped off him.

Old Brad, from the top of the steps took control:

"Hey, you fellers!"

Partial silence. He shouted again:

"Let him git in an' git to bed — he's a sick man."

"I'm all right — I'm all right!"

Newt seemed unable to get enough of it. Still, he was undoubtedly a trifle shaky as he went up the steps, Bob holding one arm and Stella the other. Bob could see Stella's amazed glance out of the corner of her eye at the new suit — he shivered for what might happen to it. Now the little man was standing grinning in the living room; he seemed totally unable to get that grin off his face.

"Well, sir, if this ain't what I call comin' home right! I didn't know anybody thought that much of a little dried-up remains of a cowpuncher like me!"

His wife spoke, gently but firmly:

"Newt, you have to go right to bed; you're all tired out."

"I won't do it! I got a lot to talk about."

"It can wait till morning, hon. Come on now, Newt!"

She, backed by Stella and Bob, almost pushed him into his room. He turned for a last happy grin.

"Well, sir, if this ain't comin' home!"

The scene had touched Bob. There was a queer little smile on his face as he left the house. He paused for an astonished glance at the living-room on his way out. Why, the place was as neat as a pin! — showed no sign of the wreckage of the morning. Bob had been worrying about that all day. Queer what women can do!

Two men were leading the sorrels away, the harness still on them; they had become so excited that nobody dared risk driving them.

Some men were just preparing to push the buckboard out of the way. Bob noticed that Red had taken the tongue, and so would be the one to guide it wherever it went. Red shouted:

"All right, boys!"

A dozen hands sent the vehicle off to a flying start. Red whirled it around the corner of the house — he had to run or be run over. Bob looked a shade worried — they had started as though they meant to race the thing clear into the cedars; every one was full of hilarity.

By the side of the house the buckboard flew; Red or no other one man could stop it, thought Bob. But he had not counted sufficiently on Red's quick wits. Red suddenly dropped the tongue and threw his weight on it. It buried deep in the ground.

"*Outch!*"

The men behind had dashed into the buckboard, bumping grunts out of themselves. They turned on Red.

"Let's get him for that! Let's duck him in the horse trough!"

They rushed upon him, yelling.

"Boys!"

Red was standing with one hand held up warningly; he looked as sedate as a minister during services. They paused an instant. What was he going to do now?

"Boys," he spoke in a deep, solemn voice, slowly, "this is a tremenjus night on this here cow outfit — a night long to be remembered in the annuals of northern Arizona. Let us not disturb the peaceful scene with unseemly levity."

A pause. Someone yelled, "Let's get him!" But by now more of the cowboys were running up. One of them raised his voice:

"Lay off'n him, you fellers, or we'll all pile onto you! Anyone can use six-bit words like that should be let get away."

"Gentlemen, I thank you."

Red turned gravely off and went toward the bunk house. A roar of laughter followed him. Bob chuckled. Anyway, Red had got the buckboard stopped exactly in the right place. Trust Red!

The next thing was to get everyone to bed — they seemed due to stay up yelling around the fires all night. But the matter solved itself. Bob was helping Mrs. Boyd into her open buggy, and joking with her husband, when a sudden crash drowned his words. A green flare showed even above the light of the huge fires.

"Thunder!" gasped Al.

"Oh," exclaimed Mrs. Boyd. "We'll get wet going home!"

"Wait a minute," said Bob.

He rushed to the bunk house and returned with three borrowed slickers; on the way back, drops of rain began to patter gently against his hat. The Boyds donned the slickers and drove off.

345

Bob turned and hunted up Brad. He had noticed that the old man was dressed up in a new suit — one in considerably better taste than Newt's, it must be admitted.

"You look like you're going to a wedding, Brad!"

"Well, Newt comin' home is somethin' to celebrate, ain't it?" snorted Brad.

"Sure is! Not riding home in the rain tonight, are you?"

"Didn't ride — come in the rig. I meant to stay; I got some important business here in the mornin'."

"Fine! Come on down to the bunk house, and I'll find a bed for you." He wondered what Brad's important business was.

There always is room for guests on a cow ranch — simply a case of asking two of the cowboys to double up and leave a bed for the visitor. A younger man, of course, would have crawled into the first bed that happened to be convenient when he became sleepy, indignantly ordering the owner to move over and not be a hog, taking all the room.

Bob and Brad had to run the last few yards — the rain had begun to pour steadily down. Brad chuckled and wiped his face. Bob was beyond the chuckling stage; he wanted to dance a jig, at the very least. Of course he was besieged with questions about Newt, but he put the cowboys off by saying that the Old Man had been too weak to talk.

CHAPTER
TWENTY-FIVE

Trapped

He hurried to his room and lighted the lamp. He stood in the middle of the floor, delightedly listening to the steady patter on the shake roof above him, on the panes of the little window. Might have a big window some day, if this kept up!

A crash of distant thunder, another, closer. The little square of his window flickered greenish. Sure looked like the drought was broken at last! He sat on the edge of his bunk, listening happily. Why, it might just as well be pouring silver dollars down on him!

It was almost eleven when the telltale crack in the wall showed him that the light had at last been blown out in the main room — he had put his own out long before. He waited until he thought the last of the men asleep.

Now to relieve Red. He wondered if their carefully planned trap was going to catch anybody. He was stealing to his door when, with startling suddenness, a loud but hardly musical voice crashed suddenly into the stillness beyond the partition:

"Oh-h, it's cloudy in the west, an' it looks like rain,
An' my damned ol' slicker's in the wagon again.
Come a ki yi yippey yippey yi yippey yay,
Come a ki yi yippey yippey ya-a-ay."

Bob grinned. There was a rustle beyond the wall. Ordinarily the disturbance would have got its creator almost slaughtered in indignation. Now only merry yells answered him.

Somebody struck up the rest of "The Chisholm Trail", beginning at the first stanza — a thing of somewhat ribald implications, but such as only a cowboy would understand. In a moment every man in the house had joined in; Bob even heard a weird croaking that he judged to be Brad's contribution to the unholy discord.

He gasped — they were singing the original version; it certainly bore no resemblance whatever to a Sunday-school hymn. They roared the part about the "cowpuncher's daughter", and her hardly ladylike remark when asked to do something that she "hadn't oughter". The next line or two would be — gosh-awful! He had to stop it!

He pounded on the partition with the butt of his gun; he yelled to them. He got partial silence. He shouted:

"Cut it out, fellers! The women can hear you up at the house."

A gasp of horror:

"Gosh, we forgot that!"

The voices died away suddenly. Bob could imagine flaming faces in there in the darkness — a cow ranch, rough as it is, has always been a place of the utmost chivalry and respect for the gentler sex. The theory was that a male person must have reached the lowest stages of emasculation before he'd bring a decent woman into contact with dirt — or permit her to touch it of her own accord. All of which suited the ranch women perfectly — they got their own way about most things, through respect, and always found strong male hands ready to lift the slightest burden from their shoulders as a matter of course. So the Romans had found it with those cowboys' savage ancestors in the forests of northern Europe, and so it seems to be wherever men of their lineage are still virile — a racial characteristic, bred in the bone.

Silence in the bunk house. Now was the time!

Bob crept to his door on tiptoes, opened it quietly, and stood peering into the dripping darkness — the huge bonfires had been drowned out long ago. He dared not wear his long slicker; it was light yellow and easily seen, and it rustled loudly when he walked.

A glare of lightning. Could he get up there before the next? He ducked his head, jerked his hat brim down to keep the rain out of his eyes, and ran, sloshing through the mud. Mud — how good it felt to be slipping in mud!

Before he reached the house, his eyes were becoming accustomed to the darkness — a true inky darkness seems unknown in Arizona. He saw the buckboard looming before him, and a moment later his hand touched it. A whisper came:

"That you, Bob?"

"Uh-huh. Seen anything?"

"No."

"Get out quick and let me in there before I get soaked. Where's your bed?"

"On the front porch."

Red was climbing down quickly but silently. He whispered once more:

"Pull the lap robe over you — I did."

Then he had vanished in the darkness. Bob climbed in hastily and found the robe; it was already wet through in spite of the slight shelter afforded by the buckboard top. He crouched between the seats, completely covered by the robe. If the sides were down, the buckboard would be as dry as a room, but he dared not roll them down — that would look suspicious.

He wondered how long he'd have to wait, if there would be many other nights of waiting, all useless. The rain began to soak through between his shoulders. This was going to be a pretty miserable night, crouching here.

And then, before he had been there twenty minutes, a flare of lightning showed the figure of a man crouched under the wall of the house. He was coming this way! Bob had not been able to recognize the man, to judge his size, even, in the sudden dazzling glare.

For an instant he was blinded. Then the outlines of the roof appeared; he was beginning to see again. He stared at Newt's window. Then he looked beside it; having ridden much at night, of course he knew the trick of not looking directly at a thing in darkness — the sides of one's eyes seemed to see better in dim light.

350

There — directly opposite the window, creeping in toward it! Quietly, Bob slipped the lap robe off. He partly raised, placed one foot on the side of the buckboard, ready for a leap.

Another quick flare of lightning. Instantly Bob launched himself out and downward. A startled grunt. A crash as Bob and the other fell against the wall under the window. A yell from Bob:

"Red! Come on!"

They were rolling silently in the mud. The other was far smaller than Bob, but that .22 — he must not let the man get it pointed toward him! Faintly he saw the lighter color of the man's face. His fist whipped toward it with all his strength behind it.

For an instant the man went limp. Only for an instant, but that was enough; Bob had him spread-eagled on the ground, sitting on the small of his back. He had both his arms held down, out from his sides, pinning them into the mud. But he dared not change his hold to try to get the gun away. Again he shouted:

"Red! Hurry up!"

Sloshing footsteps came tearing along beside the house. An exclamation in Red's voice:

"You — you got somebody!"

"Quick — take the gun away from him; it's in one of his hands."

Red was groping in the darkness.

"I got it!"

The window suddenly flew open. Old Newt's astonished voice came:

"What the heck's goin' on?"

Bob turned to him.

"Get someone to make a light in the living room, quick. I got the fellow that shot you — he came back to finish you."

A swallowing, gulping sound from Newt. His faint white blur disappeared; he left the window open in his haste, letting the rain beat in.

"All right — march!"

"I'll help you," said Red.

"I got him — hammer lock. If he tries anything, I'll break his arm for him."

From Bob's tone, there could be little doubt that he would not hesitate to do it. He shoved the man ahead of him, around the house, up the steps. He could see a light in the living room already.

"Open the door, Red."

Red did. Bob saw old Newt standing in the middle of the room, holding a coal-oil lamp high above his head. He was dressed only in a very long white nightgown far too big for him. Stella was coming, and Mrs. Doheney, both with some sort of wrappers thrown hastily over them. And Mrs. Davis.

"Get in there!"

Bob shoved the man roughly through the door. He released one arm and suddenly whirled him around to face him.

"Clay!"

Bob's eyes opened; his jaw dropped — if it had been Stella he held, he could hardly have been more surprised.

352

Clay Bozart stood there with hanging head, muddy, disheveled, an ugly bruise on his jaw where Bob had struck him. His wet hair straggled across his eyes, and his lower lip hung down showing his mouth half open. He was the picture of terror and dejection.

In his surprise, Bob had released his hold of Clay. Suddenly he reached out, picked him up, and flung him backward into a chair.

"Sit down there!"

Bob could see it all now — most of it, anyway.

"So, you dirty little rat, you're the fellow shot the cattle! Branded our calves in Al's iron an' his in ours — an' tried to get him shot for it! Wanted Al killed, wanted his wife."

No answer. Clay's head hung; he seemed to think himself already as good as dead.

"But why did you want to kill Newt?"

No answer.

"Something about that note for fifty thousand you held on this outfit?"

Still no answer. But Newt spoke, staring at Bob:

"What note? I have no notes out."

Suddenly it came to Bob.

"I see it now — I should have guessed. A forged note — you're the fellow that pretended to rob this house, so as to leave that note with the papers from the safe. Killed Jack Daly to do it. And so's he couldn't recognize you next time he saw you as the fellow that sent him out here with the fake message."

Clay's head went lower. Bob glared at him.

"Reckon you might have let bad enough alone if you could have said you knew nothing about the note. Couldn't, after I'd let you think Newt was dead — make cracks about knowing all about it — got big-headed all at once, thinking you were safe. Uh-huh — had to go back to finish him tonight before it all came out."

Still Clay sat silent with lowered head. Misery was written all over him, misery and pity for himself. Bob knew how to handle him — Clay could never withstand firmness. Bob leaped forward suddenly, seized Clay's shoulder, and dashed him against the back of his chair.

"Come out with it! Why did you do it?"

A preliminary gulp — Clay could hardly speak for fright.

"Ugh-ugh — I — my outfit was broke. Butch — I owed him money. He said he'd cancel the notes — an' give me a little extra — if I'd help him get hold of this outfit."

"And you figured out that you might as well get something for yourself out of this outfit, while you were at it?"

No answer. Bob shook him until his teeth rattled — they were not far from it anyway.

"How about Al's tracks out here — how did you work that?"

"I — ugh — ugh — I found his horse loose on the range on my way here. I — I got an idea — I roped him an' changed my saddle to him; left my own there till I got back."

"And the big boots? But that's easy — had a pair wrapped in a coat on the back of your saddle."

Bob paused, thinking what to ask next.

"Why, sure. How about running off with Stella?"

For the first time Clay looked up.

"Bob, I didn't have nothin' to do with that; it was Butch — honest! I wouldn't do a thing like that!"

"Oh, no! Your delicate conscience might hurt! I don't know whether to believe you or not, but it makes no difference."

He turned to the others.

"Well, what else?"

Red spoke, a curious note in his voice:

"The strychnine."

"Oh, yes! How about it? Who was your pal?"

No answer. Bob threw him back in his chair again, seized his hair, and jerked his head up.

"*Who?*"

"N-nobody, I — I —"

"If you don't tell me —"

Red took hold of Bob's arm.

"Hold on, Bob! He's tellin' the truth — it's what I thought all the time; there was nobody. He pretended he was going to poison 'em was all — why, his own horse was in there. Jest wanted to be a big hero — an' keep us scared up some more, too."

"What!" Bob stared unbelievingly.

"Uh-huh. I suspected it that night. I was the first one down there, but I had such a hunch about what happened that I got disgusted an' went back to bed. I figgered that was just about the size of a man he was."

Again Bob turned to the others.

"What do we do with the dirty little rat?"

Nobody else answering, he himself decided it.

"Well, we can figure that out in the morning. We can lock him in his room for the night."

He turned to Red.

"Go down to the bunk house and get some of the boys to stand guard over him, so's he won't get away."

Red went running off. In a few moments the room was jammed with hastily-dressed men. Bob suspected that many of them wore slickers and boots and nothing else over their underwear. There were more men on the porch, standing on tiptoe to see over each other's heads, pushing, crowding.

There was something grim, threatening, about how those men all kept their eyes fixed on the prisoner. Clay saw their look. He shivered as though with a deadly chill; he turned a ghastly face up to Bob.

"Bob — Bob! Don't leave 'em to watch me — they'll take me out an' — Bob — *Bob!*"

"Get in there!"

Bob flung him through the door. Clay struggled to his knees, threw out his arms.

"Bob — send me to jail! Don't leave me here — they'll — they'll —"

Bob slammed the door and turned the key in the lock. "Boys, I know you wouldn't try anything like that — with women in the house."

Someone answered, quietly:

"Heck, no! But I shore wish there wasn't any women around."

356

Mrs. Doheney was almost hysterical, Mrs. Davis in tears; Stella, herself as white as paper, was trying to calm both of them. She got them back to their rooms. Bob turned to old Newt.

"You'd better get back to bed, too — you have to rest."

Newt nodded, shook his head sadly, and left the room; he had not said a single word in all the time. Red and two or three others took seats from which they could watch Clay's door. As Bob left the house, he saw a dozen others, in slickers, standing outside Clay's window. One of them spoke, loudly — it was meant to penetrate the glass.

"Gosh, but I shore do hope he tries to get out this way! I'd give a hundred dollars for a shot at him!"

Bob went back to his room and to bed. He did not expect to sleep; he wondered if anyone in the place would sleep that night. But he was tired from weeks of overwork, he had had a more than exciting day to wear him out. Soon his eyes closed.

He was awakened by a crash against his door. He leaped up in bed, groping quickly for his gun — anything might happen on this ranch! His door was flung open, letting in a gust of wind and rain. He heard Red's excited shout:

"Light the lamp! Oh, gosh. The lamp, Bob!"

Quickly, Bob lighted it. As the yellow flames mounted, he looked up. Red, white-faced, shaking, was staring at him; he seemed almost to have lost his power of speech:

"What happened, man?"

357

"He — we — he — Bob, I heard somethin' fall in Clay's room, an' opened the door to find out. He — he'd shot himself through the head with the .22. He's dead on the floor."

Bob gulped.

"But — how did he get hold of it?"

"Why, when we brought him in, I laid it on the table — I dunno."

Bob shook his head.

"Same old Clay — couldn't face it; never could face anything. Couldn't face the debts he ran up — that's what got him into it."

Suddenly he took Red by the shoulders.

"The women — do they know about it?"

"No. I jest locked the door an' rushed down here."

"Then let's hurry up an' get a team hitched up. We can stop the wagon a ways from the house an' carry him to it; we'll haul him to town. Don't let 'em know."

"But they'll find out."

"Sure — in a day or two. We'll say we took him to jail like he wanted. When they'll get word that he killed himself, they'll think he did it in the jail. By the time they know the truth, it'll have come to 'em sort of gradual — not like the blow of hearing all at once that a man killed himself in the house."

He reached for his clothes. Red saw the look on his face.

"Bob," he spoke hesitantly, "you an' him was friends. I never liked him — in fact I sneaked into his room an' searched it one day when there was nobody in the

358

house. I had a hunch, sort of, but when I tried to say something to you about it, you got mad."

Bob nodded dismally.

"I remember. I thought he was a friend of mine. He told Butch I was carrying that money — tried to get me shot. Then he tried twice to shoot me himself."

"Tell you what, Bob," said Red gently. "I'll take care of this thing for you. You go back to bed."

"You don't mind?" Bob looked up eagerly.

"Heck, no!"

Red turned and left the room. Good old Red, he was always saving the day in some manner or other.

CHAPTER
TWENTY-SIX

Cattlemen All

It was long after daylight when Bob woke up next morning. Like all cowboys, accustomed to sleeping outdoors on the ground in a country of many crawling insects, of prowling animals, of occasional rattlesnakes, he always slept with the covers over his head — the habit was so strong that although he left his head uncovered in a house, he generally pulled the blankets over it in his sleep.

He lay there an instant. Suddenly a thought came to him with panic: Not long ago he had woken up thus to find the rain disappeared, the sun bright. With one sweeping motion he flung the covers back and sat up. His head jerked toward the window.

A gray, dismal, dripping window. Still there came that steady little roar against the roof. A gust of wind moaned miserably, lonesomely, around a corner of the bunk house.

It was the brightest day of Bob's life. He leaped out of bed with a joyous little yell.

If it didn't rain another drop, he had won — in a week green grass would make a heavy carpet on every hillside in the country; already the water holes must be nearly full. And Jerry Mallett — Jerry now owned the Jeff Morehouse sheep outfit, beyond Bob's new range. Good old Jerry! Finest neighbor in the world.

Bob remembered Clay and tried to feel gloomy. He could not; nothing could make him gloomy today. Dinky new outfit be danged! He had one of the biggest ranges in this part of Arizona. Such as it was, of course — but wait and see it in five years more!

He dressed, shaved, and went swishing in his long slicker to the house. Newt was in a rocking-chair on the porch. He managed to take his eyes off the rain long enough to wave cheerily at Bob.

"Mornin', Cattleman Edwards!"

"Mornin', Neighbor Davis! If you're short of water, run some of your cattle over to my water holes."

"Water!" The old man ducked his head out beyond the eaves, looked upward, and drew it back, blinking rain out of his eyes. He grinned at Bob. "Water, did you say!"

Bob glanced curiously at Mrs. Doheney, who was standing beside Newt. She was all dressed up in her Sunday best. She looked flushed, excited.

"Not leaving us so soon?" asked Bob, glancing at her clothes and hat.

She giggled like a girl of sixteen, but did not otherwise answer. Newt chuckled. Just then there came a crash against the door, and Brad Simpson bustled out carrying a small trunk. Brad in his best clothes — Mrs. Doheney in hers. Mrs. Doheney simpering; Brad grinning like a Cheshire cat.

"Huh! What!" gasped Bob.

361

Brad dropped the trunk with a grunt.

"Well, what of it?" he demanded. "Jest because I batched this much o' my life don't mean I'm goin' to batch the rest of it. Ain't that feller got my rig up here yet?"

So this was his "important business"! Bob hurried to shake his hand and congratulate him — Mrs. Doheney, too. But Brad wasted little time on such foolishness. He turned to Newt.

"Like I was sayin', Newt, the Bozart outfit can be bought for a song — wisht I could swing the whole deal myself. Will you promise to take half of it — so's no cranky neighbors will git in between us to steal calves?"

"We-ell, I might — if it was a real good buy."

"Good buy!" Brad looked grim. "It'll *be* a good buy after I git through bargainin'. Don't you know me yet?"

"Well," drawled Newt gently, "I wisht you'd wait here till the rain is over anyway. You can get married tomorrow."

"Tomorrow! An' here I been mixin' up in sheep wars an' gosh knows what, an' comin' chasin' over here to see — I mean, dang it, I been lettin' my outfit go to rack an' ruin! I gotta git back to work — my cattle will be gone wild an' maverick. Ain't that right, Jennie?"

"Yes, dear." She actually blushed.

Bob could hardly keep a straight face; it would make anyone blush to call that hard-boiled sinner "dear"! Brad was grumbling half to himself:

"Think I can spend *my* time loafin'? She had one loafer — George Doheney. Only thing he ever did for

362

her was to fall off'n a roof an' break his neck. She ain't no young rattle-head; she knows what a good husband should do." Suddenly he raised his voice: "Ain't that right, Jennie?"

"Yes, Brad, dear."

"Here's the rig. All right — all right — somebuddy help me git this trunk in! All right, Jennie. My gosh, look at the time it is! 'Member, Newt — I'm holdin' you to buyin' half. Giddap! I wonder if them cows over in —"

His rig, behind two ungainly horses, went sloshing quickly off through the mud and the rain. Everyone on the porch was talking excitedly, half laughing. It was the sensation of the year. But they should have suspected! Brad had been a far more regular visitor lately than business warranted. So *that*, thought Bob, was why he had howled "The Chisholm Trail" so energetically last night.

Why the old devil! He had been "up the trail" himself, long before Bob was born. Only the year before, he and Newt had discovered that they had met each other in Abilene in those wild days — at least each had met a man that might have been the other, and after a month or two of talking it over, the other it was admitted to be, without further evidence. In fact each was by this time firmly convinced that he now remembered exactly what the other had looked like at the meeting, and what he had worn.

Bob heard running footsteps behind him. A cry: "Oh, Dad!"

It was a wail from Stella, who had come dashing from the house holding something before her. Newt turned. He gasped with horror.

"Ruined! My new suit!"

"Ruined!" Stella gazed at it sadly. "You left it on a chair last night, and left the window open. I hung it over the stove to dry, and it fell down."

Newt gulped; his eyes were wistfully fixed on the remains. His pride and joy burned almost to a cinder.

"Gosh, Stell — gosh; I'll never get another like it!"

"Never!"

Bob happened to catch Stella's eye; it held grim determination. She spoke consolingly:

"But I'll go to town with you myself and help you pick out another just as nice."

She went back into the house. Newt sighed.

"Reckon she was all excited about Jennie gettin' married — that's how she let it happen."

He shook his head. After a while of silence, he turned to Bob.

"Bob, I shore want to thank you for the full account o' things you gave me on the way home."

"How's that, Newt?" asked Bob unsuspectingly.

"Tellin' me all about the sheep war. You said some sheep had come on the range, but they went off again. My, my!"

Bob reddened. This gentle little man could, when he chose, employ sarcasm that would make a fence post redden.

"Well, Bob, I heard jest a little more about it from Brad an' Stell. If I'd known what was goin' on, I'd have

364

give up an' died over there — they say I wasn't far from it anyway. Or I'd have come rushin' back half dead to run things myself. An' then what would have happened?"

"Why, you'd have straightened it out in half the time."

"Straightened a lot o' cowboys out — in holes in the ground. An' likely got whipped an' lost my place. An' they tell me that you did it without you or one o' yore men firin' a shot, or even p'intin' a gun at anybody!"

"Why — I shore did have luck." Bob shifted uncomfortably.

"Shore did — luck enough to be born with a couple o' sperrit levels in yore head, to keep it level. A doctor over there told me that the more wrinkles a feller has in his brain the cleverer he is — I'll bet yores looks like an ol' dried-up cowhide a-layin' out in the sun. Wisht I could see it."

To Bob's great relief an interruption came; he heard the sloshing of a horse behind him and turned to see the sheriff ride up. He had been expecting him, of course, to investigate the Clay Bozart affair. Just then Stella returned to the porch.

Wilson answered their greetings, meanwhile pulling off his dripping slicker and hanging it on a nail against the wall of the house. He turned to Bob.

"Well, Bob, I had to ride all the way out here in the rain to serve a paper on you."

"Paper!" gasped Bob. He knew that the kind of papers a sheriff served always brought trouble to somebody. "What is it about?"

"Injunction. About Butch sellin' you the place."

Bob felt as though his knees were going to let him crash to the floor. He should have known! Butch's actions had been suspicious; he had been entirely too anxious to get hold of Bob's money. Anyway, why had he sold the outfit for so little?

Bob took the long paper, unfolded it. The printed form swam before his eyes, the filled-in writing became a blur; he could not have read it if it had been in plain English instead of this involved legal language. To him as from a great distance the sheriff's voice came:

"Newt, I had to come out anyway to see about that Bozart business. You shouldn't have sent him in till we —"

Bob, the paper clutched in his hand, interrupted hurriedly — Stella must not know!

"Say, Ben! Come down here to the end of the porch. I want to see you about this paper."

The sheriff looked at him curiously, and went. Out of hearing of the others, Bob whispered to him. Wilson shook his head; Bob had had no business to send Clay in before the coroner saw him. Still, he didn't know of anything he could do about it. Clear case anyway — didn't make so much difference. Sure, he'd say nothing to the women.

"Now, this." Bob held out the injunction as though it were red hot. "Nobody can read this kind of thing without all day to do it. What is it?"

"Nothin' much — jest a court order for you not to pay any more money to Butch. The rest goes to old Dave Newman of Prescott — it came out that Butch was runnin' mostly on his money and lost all of it."

"You — you mean I don't lose the place?"

The sheriff grinned quietly.

"Heck, no! Butch sold it to you before he got the injunction to stop him, so that's legal — that's why he was in such a hurry. Didn't do him no good — he rushed over to the bank to find an attachment all set for him like a bear trap. They jest locked yore check in the safe."

"You mean — Didn't he get any money?"

"Not a cent — an' won't. Old Newman has attached everything but the shirt on Butch's back. He's wailin' all over town about Butch sellin' the place before he grabbed it, but he's too foxy to waste any money tryin' to get it back."

"But —" Bob stared at the ground. He spoke slowly: "I — uh — if he has the place coming, for debts —"

Wilson sniffed disgustedly.

"Newman, that miserable little skunk! If you'd had to serve his foreclosure papers on ol' men an' widders like I had to, you wouldn't worry about him. Anyway, it's none of yore funeral."

"Oh, if he's that kind!"

Bob grinned cheerfully — so *that* had come out all right; his somewhat freakish business deal was an entire success.

"How about Butch?" asked Wilson. "Want him locked up?"

Bob did not want anybody locked up this morning — indeed, such was his mood that if Butch had been there he would have cheerfully lent him a few dollars.

"Well, we haven't got any whole lot against him — only holding me up, and I'm none the worse for that. We can't prove that he ran off with Stella, after the Indian knifing both of his men."

"That's right. So what'll we do?"

"Heck, as far as I'm concerned, give him twenty-four hours to get out of the county, an' let it go at that."

"Whatever you say." The sheriff nodded and went back to where Newt and Stella were.

Later, Bob found Red in the bunk house, shoving his extra shirts into his war bag.

"Looking everywhere for you, Red."

"Wanted to see you, too. You said the other day that you're leavin' here as soon as the Old Man got back. Well, I'm trailin' along with you, if you can stand me."

"Better stick around here — good outfit."

"Shore is! But I'm goin' with you, Bob; I'm never goin' to get far away from you again."

"How come?"

Red placed an affectionate hand on Bob's shoulder, his voice shook brokenly:

"Ol' pardner, I want to be so's I can see yore face every day; you don't know how consolin' it is to me. I mean, no matter what's goin' wrong, I can always think how much worse off I'd be if I'd fell on my head when I was a kid an' acted an' looked like you."

This time Bob did not laugh at Red's humor. He shook his head firmly. "Sorry, Red — I can't take you."

He waited for Red to blow up. Red didn't. Instead, he looked hurt; his eyes were fixed queerly on Bob's face, and he caught his breath. Then Bob knew what he had always suspected — all Red's clowning was but a mask to hide what he considered the disgrace of a sensitive disposition. Bob had seen it show through before, when he had told that Newt still lived. He spoke very quickly, pretending to misread the look:

"Now don't blow up! I'm not going far. Besides, you're the big range boss here now — I was just fixing it with Newt."

"I'm — *What?*"

"Uh-huh. You'll be surprised at the salary I held out for him to give you — it's too big to be called wages. Go up and see him; he wants you to ride over an' talk to Al Boyd about buying some cattle on time — he wants him to have enough to make a good living."

"Ohmigosh!" A pause. Red spoke dubiously: "Al — I dunno — he don't like me much. I sneaked over a couple of times to spy around the sheep camp, but I gave it up because Al was trailin' me around watchin' me."

Bob grinned.

"I know about that — he thought you were in with Butch, and you thought he was. That's your chance to get friendly with him; make out like it's a big joke on both of you — whale him on the back. If he doesn't give you the feed of your life, I miss my guess — Al wouldn't know what a grudge is if he met one."

Red wrinkled his nose.

"*Me* whale him on the back! Nothin' doing! He might whale back, an' I'd come ridin' back here hammered down to about three foot seven. But it's my

369

duty as range boss to make myself eat some of that good pie of his wife's you've been bragging about." Red tried to look martyred at the thought, but forgot himself and licked his lips in the middle of a lugubrious look.

Bob grinned at him.

"I'll bet my best water hole you an' Al are bosom pals inside a week — you're just the kind to get along with each other."

"Best — huh? Where did *you* get even a mud puddle?"

Bob told him. Red was so astonished that for once he could not think of anything allegedly funny to say. Bob watched him hurrying toward the house; he looked as though he might stop to turn a handspring or two on the way. For a young fellow of his age, this was more than an opportunity.

Bob went slowly to the corral and saddled Flight. He was going over to his own outfit; there were shacks there that would do until he got time to build a better house — next year, maybe. Somehow, he did not feel so happy as he should have felt, now that leaving time had come. Why, he was trying to hide from himself the fact that he felt sort of blue.

He rode up to the house, dismounted, and dropped his reins. He wanted to talk to Newt, but the old man was in earnest conversation with his new range boss. Bob hesitated. Well, he could be saying good-bye to the others while he was waiting.

He crossed the porch, removed his slicker, and entered the living room. Stella was there alone. She was sitting staring absently into the fire that the damp weather made necessary. From her expression, one might have said that she was moping. Bob could guess why — it must have been a terrible blow to her. He walked in, retaining his hat.

"Stella, I can't tell you how bad I feel about Clay being caught at all that."

She looked up at him, tried to smile, spoke absently: "Yes, wasn't it?"

"I know you an' him were friends and —"

"I don't know, Bob; I never did like Clay. I just couldn't help it, but he always made me feel creepy."

"Huh! But — walking around —"

"I know; it was hard on me. But of course I had to try to be friendly with him, since he owned the outfit next to us — and there was that note he held."

She, of course, didn't mention her main reason for flaunting Clay in public — anyway, it had produced the opposite effect to what she had counted on.

"For goodness —"

Bob sat down suddenly. He hesitated an instant, and tossed his hat into a corner. Suddenly he remembered something else — Stella's foolish jealousy of Mrs. Boyd. Oh, yes, he had seen it! He wasn't entirely blind.

"Stell" — he'd got back to the old nickname — "I want to tell you about a dam site I saw on my new range."

"What!"

"I'm not cussin', Stell — I mean a site for a dam. There's a big flat that drains out through a small crack in a bluff — two or three men with four-horse fresnoes can scrape enough dirt in there in a few days to dam it up. It'll make a lake nearly a mile long."

"How interesting!" He did not notice the faint irony in her voice.

"Uh-huh. There's a flat below that I can pipe water to, for the house, an' for a garden."

"Oh — you're talking about building a house."

"Uh-huh. An' the dam'll have a natural spillway — it won't have to be riprapped."

In spite of his businesslike conversation, Bob's face was gradually getting redder and redder.

"That's fine, Bob!" She spoke encouragingly.

"And — uh — it's right on the edge of my range — hardly more than five miles from here."

"Well?" She was wiggling excitedly in her chair.

"Well — Oh, gosh!"

"Bob, are — are you trying to propose to me, or what?"

"I am — uh — I never did before. I mean —"

Stella spoke softly, her eyes bright:

"I think I know what you mean, Bob."

She stood up and started gently toward him. He plunged from his chair and met her halfway. A little laugh, smothered giggles.

"Bob, Bob! Easy! You're not bulldogging calves!"

More than an hour later, Bob, his hat at a jaunty angle, walked from the door. He congratulated himself on looking the picture of easy indifference — he did not notice old Newt jab an elbow into his wife's ribs as they sat side by side on the swing.

"It's a nice day, isn't it?" Bob remarked.

"Shore is!" Newt glanced approvingly at the dripping grayness.

"Rainin'."

"I'd sorter noticed it."

"Uh — think it'll keep up?"

Newt shook his head.

"Bob, if you got somethin' to say, say it, for gosh sake!"

"I — uh — I —"

Stella, pink-faced, came from the door to his rescue.

"You see, Dad —"

"Ain't blind."

"I mean — Bob was asking —"

"For a raise?"

"Oh, *Dad!*"

"All right, Stell — all right! Shore you can marry him. Me an' Ma was talkin' it over all the time we was in San Francisco, figgerin' how fine a match it would be."

"But" — Bob spoke desperately — "it'll be hard on her. A new outfit — just starting up."

"Jest what she needs — she's sp'iled, Bob."

Stella tossed her head indignantly.

"I'll show you! I'm sick and tired of hearing Mother talk of what she went through when you first got married and started a ranch. Oh, it's just what I want — to build up a ranch with Bob, like you and Mother did!"

She turned to Bob.

"Do you think we'll have to live on brown beans and biscuits?"

"Well, not exactly." He smiled fondly down on her. "But," he added reluctantly, "there'll be hardship enough, and lots of things we'll have to go without."

373

Her eyes were shining.

"Isn't that grand! I'll show Mother! And if you think I won't like it —"

A chuckle from the old man.

"She will! She has enough Davis in her — 'scuse me, hon — enough Brewster, too. Only trouble is that Bob'll be a rich man in no time — look at the head for things he has!"

He sat nodding a moment contentedly. Then he turned to Stella.

"Shore has! He got Butch not knowin' whether he was settin' in the fryin' pan or the fire — either way he jumped he'd git his pants burned off. Funny about that pingüe; it only made Butch harder to get out, an' made more fight for Bob. But it was the cause o' Bob bein' able to buy the place — pingüe will make him a rich man."

Mrs. Davis had been thinking of matters more important to a woman. She looked up suddenly.

"Too bad we didn't know about it before we came back from California — we could have brought some orange blossoms. They might have kept in water."

Newt sniffed.

"Hon, *them* wouldn't be right! I'll pick her the right flowers to wear, seein' as they fixed her up with a husband an' a cow outfit — pingüe blossoms!"

He sat chuckling a moment at his own humor, then turned to whisper to his wife — unfortunately the whisper carried clearly to the embarrassed Bob and Stella:

"Hon, let's git in outa here! Young folks the way they are shore like to set in a swing. 'Member?"

374

ISIS publish a wide range of books in large print, from fiction to biography. Any suggestions for books you would like to see in large print or audio are always welcome. Please send to the Editorial Department at:

ISIS Publishing Limited
7 Centremead
Osney Mead
Oxford OX2 0ES

A full list of titles is available free of charge from:

Ulverscroft Large Print Books Limited

(UK)
The Green
Bradgate Road, Anstey
Leicester LE7 7FU
Tel: (0116) 236 4325

(Australia)
P.O. Box 314
St Leonards
NSW 1590
Tel: (02) 9436 2622

(USA)
P.O. Box 1230
West Seneca
N.Y. 14224-1230
Tel: (716) 674 4270

(Canada)
P.O. Box 80038
Burlington
Ontario L7L 6B1
Tel: (905) 637 8734

(New Zealand)
P.O. Box 456
Feilding
Tel: (06) 323 6828

Details of **ISIS** complete and unabridged audio books are also available from these offices. Alternatively, contact your local library for details of their collection of **ISIS** large print and unabridged audio books.